For my daughters, Danielle and Gabrielle

FINDING ROUND

ALEX SHERIDAN

Published by Treasure Life Press

By Alex Sheridan

Dance of Spies
Treasure Life
Finding Round
Chasing Free (coming winter 2012)
Buried Life (coming spring 2013)

Acknowledgements

This book is dedicated to my mother whose enthusiasm
and collaboration were invaluable in making it come to life.

And to all the authors who have blazed the path ahead of me,
who generously shared their time and advice through
interviews, conferences and books of their own.
Special thanks to James Rollins, Stephen King
and Dean Koontz.

CHAPTER 1

He hesitated as pebbles skittered over the edge. They fell silently into the abyss while the corners of his jacket flapped in the wind and his frustration grew. Broken off at a jagged angle, the road looked like a puzzle piece sitting on top of a hole. The scent of newly exposed earth climbed toward him.

He stood on the remaining section of highway and aimed at the empty cavity, leaning out to snap a better shot of the erosion. The damage was incredible, it would take months to repair. His cell started buzzing in his pocket and he walked inland a few feet, turned to look at the waves, answered, "Craig Noble."

"Dad?"

"Hey, Ethan."

"I figured out what to write my essay on. There are these weird little spheres—"

"This is kind of a bad time, Son." Craig raised a hand in greeting at his co-worker walking toward him. "The meeting with the City ran over this afternoon, and I'm still at the job site. I should be home by seven. Can we talk about it then?"

"It can wait. See you later."

The phone clicked in his ear as his co-worker stepped up.

"Hey, Craig. Hell of a mess out here, huh?"

He didn't respond for a moment, frowning as he slipped the phone in a pocket, thinking about his family and the drive ahead. Thunder rumbled from storm clouds building in the east. It looked like it was going to pour soon. Ron shifted a foot, snapping Craig's attention back to the job site.

"It's a hell of a mess all right. I can't believe the City and County couldn't come to an agreement today."

"As if that's ever been easy."

"No kidding. But this situation can't wait. We could lose the entire bluff, maybe the pipeline too. And there's nothing we can do about it." Craig shrugged his frustration off, said, "Looks like we're on hold for now. We might as well go home and enjoy the weekend. Nothing more we can do until they give us the go-ahead. Chances are we'll be back here on Tuesday. At least I hope so. I'll give you a call and let you know as soon as I get word we can move forward."

They walked fifty yards down the road together, slipped past the barricades and climbed into their cars as fat rain drops began to fall.

Craig waited until he got past the heavy city traffic and onto Interstate 280 to call his wife. The interstate would take him a little out of the way but it would save him from the inevitable delays on Highway 101. At least until he got down to San Jose. Chelsea picked up on the third ring.

"Hi, Babe. I'm headed home now. I should be there by seven."

A beat of silence stretched from the phone then she said two words and hung up.

His marriage scraped the rocks when the second word left her beautiful mouth. The dial tone buzzed in his ear. He tapped the end button and tossed the phone in a cup-holder. It would do no good to call her back.

He did his best to focus on the rain-soaked road instead of the boulder that rolled in his gut beneath the seatbelt. The clouds continued to darken and lightening flashed frequently as he drove toward the storm.

Being in between destinations while trouble brewed caused a curl of desperation to creep in and sit down beside him. The Lexus was a superb highway car, but one short call had turned it into a steel cage. The drive went by in a rainy blur as his thoughts roamed over the situation.

He'd been crazy in love with Chelsea Carrington since his senior year at Santa Barbara High and she still made his blood pound. They'd made it eighteen years so far, in spite of the odds and parenting two kids.

The problem was he also loved the career he had chosen. As a geologist he had to do a lot of traveling, but there wasn't much choice at this point. His salary was twice what Chelsea made at BioGen and it was expensive living in California. If he refused to travel it could mean the end of his job, possibly the end of his career. For sure it would be the end of being able to enjoy what he did for a living. Who wanted to be stuck behind a desk all day when a guy could be out exploring the world? He sure as hell didn't.

But, when a man hears his wife say *"Why bother?"* after telling her he's on his way home, it's time to take serious stock of the situation.

He had ridden the past week out at the Holiday Inn. San Francisco was only a hundred miles away from Hollister, but between traffic congestion and meetings running from breakfast through dinner each day it hadn't been feasible to commute.

The rain increased to a roar. He flipped the wipers on high and reduced speed, knowing the deluge would only cause more trouble. The conditions at San Francisco's Ocean Beach had reached a critical point. Multiple agencies had gathered to discuss solutions to the extreme erosion issues being caused from rough surf generated by El Niño conditions.

Craig figured taming the ocean was almost as impossible as controlling fog but Ocean Beach was now a top priority because of what it protected; the Great Highway, a multi-million dollar wastewater plant and a huge underground sewage pipe. The local government was facing hundreds of millions of dollars to remediate the situation with no guarantee it would work over the long term. They were all under a lot of pressure and a solid action plan was needed as soon as possible. The weather was not going to wait.

A sheet of muddy rain shot up from beneath a semi as the Lexus passed it. His hands tightened on the wheel as visibility dropped to zero and he resisted the urge to hit the brake. He cleared the truck and forced his hands to loosen. The onslaught of water took his thoughts back to the job site. It was a very popular beach with locals as well as tourists and people were curious to see the damage. The city was struggling to keep onlookers away from the area. A man had lost his life when the bluff collapsed under him.

Being a geological engineer was a bit like being a superhero sometimes. Working with a team on resolving problems like the one at Ocean Beach had a huge impact on thousands of lives, not to mention the tax payers' pockets. It got his adrenaline pumping and constantly challenged his mind. Even if the meetings did run to the boring side sometimes.

The rain eased up when he reached the sleepy outskirts of Hollister. It was a short drive across town to home. He pulled in the drive of their almost new beige and white two-story and glanced at his watch. It was just past seven and he looked forward to spending time with his family. But first he had to talk Chelsea out of her mad. Again. He grabbed his briefcase and tweeted the alarm.

"Daddy, Daddy, Daddy!" Lily plowed into his legs as he shut the kitchen door. His smile brightened and he struggled to set the briefcase down without being knocked over.

"Hello, Sweetheart." He scooped his daughter up, hugging her close. "How's my favorite girl doing?"

Lily planted a kiss on his cheek and wrapped her arms tighter around his neck. It felt good. He gave her another squeeze then set her down.

"I really misthed you Daddy. Do you want sthome pizza? There's loths left." Lily's lisp made him grin and her words were the best welcome a dad could ask for.

"I'd love some. Did you save me a slice of cheese?" Lily nodded and scampered back to the table. Craig followed and stopped beside Ethan. "You been taking good care of our women while I've been gone?" He ruffled the boy's spiky brown hair, gave his shoulder a rub. His son was almost a man. It was hard to believe how fast time was flying by.

"Hey Dad, welcome back. How'd it go in San Francisco?"

Craig's eyes shot to his wife who had her back to them as she loaded the dishwasher. Knowing better than to attempt giving her a hug at that point, he slid out a chair and sat down.

"Lots of meetings and I brought home a briefcase full of reports. Now all we have to do is wait for the City to approve the work." He reached into the pizza box and dropped a slice on a paper plate, grabbed a Pepsi from the six pack beside it.

"That reminds me, I want to talk with you later about my idea. There are these strange metal spheres—"

"Daddy, will you take usth to the mall tomorrow? I want to get a new pair of shoesth like Becky." His son scowled at Lily's interruption. She wiggled around in the chair and sat on her knees to make herself taller. Her smile was missing two front teeth and made Craig grin every time he saw it. He nodded at Ethan, acknowledging his request, then addressed Lily's question.

"You bet, Princess. What kind of shoes are we talking about here? Cowboy boots? Air Jordans?" He bit into his pizza and swiped at a glob of sauce as Lily squealed.

"Daddy, you're sthilly. We have to go to the Penney sthore. That's where Becky got hersth. They're neon pink with sthparkles and light up when you walk."

He looked at Ethan who rolled his eyes and stuffed more pizza in his mouth.

"How about you, Sport? The mall sound good for tomorrow?"

"Sure, as long as we're back by two. I'm playing B-ball with Mike and Tony and they're counting on me."

"Now that sounds like fun. You guys playing over at Tony's?"

"Yeah. His mom said we can have the driveway until four."

"Okay, sounds like a plan. We'll head out to the mall after breakfast and get Lilybit her sparkle gear. Who knows, maybe they come in your size too?"

They laughed until Chelsea turned from the dishwasher and stepped toward the table. He snuck a quick glance at her lithe frame and curly mop of blond hair. Lips tight with tension, her eyes had an edge that told him he would not be enjoying his marital rights later that evening.

He held back a sigh and waded in, "Hi Hon. How was your week?"

"It was stressful as usual. Doing double duty all week didn't help. But tomorrow's Saturday, so things are looking up."

"Yep, tomorrow's Saturday." Silence ticked away a moment. "How about you? Want to go to the mall and get some sparkly shoes, too?"

"No, I'll let you have some time with the kids. I should go back into work and take a look at the results of the tests we ran today. That way I can hit the ground running on Monday. Orlon's been on a tear all week. The sooner we get through this stage the better my life will be."

He looked closer at his wife—she looked tired. "Are you sure? Maybe you should go with us and get a pedicure or something instead? It sounds like you've earned it."

Chelsea glanced at him but shook her head. "I wish. I haven't been able to work late all week so I'm behind. We've got an investors meeting at the end of April. I have to push myself until we've completed this last batch of tests and I've got the reports written."

"Okay, I understand."

A pool of silence slid over the table.

"How about I grill steaks tomorrow night? I'll stop at the store on the way home." Weekend meals were Craig's job.

"That will work."

"We'll meet you back here around one."

"Maybe." She avoided his eyes and bit into a slice of pizza.

CHAPTER 2

"Hey, Dad, have you got a minute?" Ethan stood in the study doorway with an anxious look on his face. Craig set the detailed Ocean Beach impact report down and smiled at his son.

"Sure, come on in, what's up?"

"You know how I've got to figure out what controversial geological issue I'm going to base my scholarship essay on for Berkley?"

"Right..."

"I've been surfing the net all week, trying to come up with something that I'm hoping the other kids aren't focusing on. I came across a couple articles about these weird metal spheres that no one can explain. So I was wondering if you'd take a look and tell me if you think it's a good idea."

Craig took the papers from him. "I'll read the articles, but first tell me what made you pick this topic? That's a big part of what the college will be looking at when they review the essays. They want to see how the candidates interpret the issues."

Ethan's eyes lit up, "Okay, what's got me really wondering about these spheres is they were found embedded in pyrophyllite deposits that are three billion years old."

"Really?" Craig swung his feet off the desk and sat up. "That right there makes it interesting. Chances are your competitors won't focus on issues that go that far back. Most of them will probably use global warming."

He glanced down at the photo that accompanied the article and saw a small dark metal orb with three grooves around its equator. "So how do these little spheres relate to a controversial issue?"

"Well, they were found in a South African mine in a place called Ottosdal, back in the late seventies. Geologists have been debating ever since then whether these spheres are naturally occurring concretions or manufactured by ancient intelligent beings."

"I think I remember hearing something about those. Are they also known as the Klerksdorp spheres?"

"Yeah, but that's a misnomer—it's just the name of a museum they were displayed in."

"So what's the deal—are there any scientific studies available?"

"From what I've read on the net, there hasn't been much testing done on them, just the basic stuff, and nothing since 2008. They range in size from an inch up to two inches in diameter. Some have uniform grooves around their equator, some don't."

Ethan took a seat on the sofa as he explained, "There are two types of spheres; one kind is bluish grey and solid throughout. The other kind is made of hematite and wallastonite, about a fourth of an inch thick on the outer shell, and those have a white spongy substance in the center."

"Huh. So what do you think? Are they naturally occurring or out-of-place artifacts?"

"I haven't decided yet. From the articles, I'm leaning toward concretions, but there are things about them that really make me wonder." Ethan grinned and scooted forward on his seat.

"I'd love to go to that mine and see some of the spheres in person and the pyrophyllite they came out of. It might help me make up my mind."

Craig studied his son's face a moment, completely understanding his curiosity and desire to go direct to the source and check it out.

"That's what being a geologist is all about, Son—getting out there and seeing things in person. It never pays to take someone's opinion or a photograph as fact on an issue. Scientific tests can be wrong occasionally, especially if they're based on a biased opinion at the outset." He shuffled the papers in his hand and grinned at his son.

"When's your spring break?"

Ethan's eyes widened. "It's in ten days, April ninth through the thirteenth. Why?"

"How about you and I take a trip to Africa and check that mine out?"

"Dad, are you serious? That would be beyond awesome!"

Then his son's face sobered as he asked, "What about Mom? I know she's not happy with the traveling you have to do for work…"

He paused as the words hit home and his own grin began to dim. Backtracking around the foot in his mouth he said, "I tell you what, I'll speak with your mom and if she's okay with it, we're going. I'll talk to her when she gets back. Besides, I've never been to Africa, and neither has your mom. Maybe she'll want to go too. Cross your fingers."

* * *

Chelsea shoved the chair under the desk and turned back to him. "I can't believe we're having this conversation. All you do is travel. As it is, the kids and I only see you ten days out of thirty, sometimes less, Craig. I don't think this trip is necessary. Not to mention the expense."

Resentment flared in her eyes. "How much does it cost to fly to South Africa? And what about your work? I sure as hell can't leave right now. Orlon would fire my ass faster than you can say unemployed if I left before the investors meeting, and I wouldn't blame him."

"Chelsea, we can handle the expense, you know that. I really want to do this for Ethan."

"Look, I've been feeling like a single mother for way too long and this African trip won't help." He watched her temper snap and words flew out of her mouth before he could respond. "Frankly, I don't think it's a good idea for Ethan to focus on geology already. He needs a chance to explore different fields of work, a chance to become well-rounded before he gets sucked into that world for the rest of his life."

"Isn't that Ethan's choice?"

"All that traveling and exploration sounds great when you're young, but it's not working for our family Craig, and you know it.

Is that what you want for Ethan? Always living out of a suitcase, coming home to a pissed off wife and kids that hardly recognize him?"

He studied the top of his shoe as her words sank in. He kept his voice to a whisper as he looked back up at her, "You knew I wanted to be a geologist since high school. Would you rather be married to a car salesman now?"

"Oh, give me a break. I was eighteen when we got married. I had no idea how much traveling you'd do once you got out of college. I'm sick of being a single parent all week. Right now it seems to me the only thing you're contributing to our family is your paycheck." Her green eyes stabbed along with the words then she turned and stalked out of the room.

He paused before following Chelsea out, working on keeping a lid on his temper. He stepped through the doorway and stopped short at seeing Ethan leaning up against the wall outside the den. One look at his son's face and he knew the boy had eavesdropped on their conversation.

"Hey, Ethan—"

"Forget it, Dad."

He watched his son rush up the stairs and decided to give him a few minutes alone while he got his own head together. With one foot on the steps, his thoughts swirled, none of them good. After a moment he realized they'd benefit more from getting out of the house for a while then from a heart-to-heart right then so he called his brother.

Jimmy was at home and didn't have any company. Craig jogged up the stairs, knocked on his son's door and pushed it open. Ethan stood staring out the window, hands clenched around the top of his desk chair.

"What do you say we go over to Uncle Jimmy's and hang out a little while?"

"That sounds great." Relief swam in his son's voice, "You want to go now?"

"Yeah, let's go. Jimmy said he's grilling some ribs. Your mom and Lily can handle a couple hours without us." He did his best to keep a negative tone from his voice. The phrase henpecked kept looping through his brain and that was the last thing he wanted to believe about his life. Maybe a couple cold beers and a dose of

Jimmy's special way of looking at the world would give him some needed perspective.

He grabbed his keys and hollered toward the kitchen, "We're going to Jimmy's to watch the game." He pulled the door shut and left, not knowing whether Chelsea had heard, not caring.

CHAPTER 3

They piled in the Lexus and drove the twelve blocks to Jimmy's house. Craig scanned the sprawling red brick structure as they walked up the drive. The lawn was immaculate and the white wood trim and large old fashioned porch swing made the entrance inviting. A brand-new black Lincoln Navigator sat sparkling in the sun with a puddle of soapy water pooled beneath it. There was no denying Jimmy had done amazingly well for himself over the years.

"I can smell those ribs already." Ethan rubbed his belly as they stepped on the porch.

"You know your Uncle Jimmy—the grill master of Hollister."

His brother had a lot of skills that had paid off over the years. He owned a huge auto repair business and had invested heavily in real estate. He could retire tomorrow if he wanted to. Who would have thought it possible after the crazy animal he'd been in high school? And the man was one of the happiest guys he knew. Maybe that had something to do with being single. He reached up to knock but Jimmy opened the door before his knuckles met the frame.

"Come on in. Game's on in the back, ribs are on the grill. Got a cooler full of beer and some snacks while we wait on the pig meat," Jimmy rattled off as he led the way through the house and out to the huge screened patio.

"You guys bring your swim trunks by any chance?" They looked down at Jimmy's bright yellow trunks dotted with barbeque sauce.

"No, but I'll bet you've got a couple spares." Craig grinned at his brother's attire; t-shirt with holes in it from last Fourth of July, barefoot with beer in hand. It was good to be back in the testosterone zone.

"Sure, you bet, as long as you're not too worried about your fashion." Jimmy chuckled and grabbed beers from the cooler, handed one to Craig, gave Ethan a Coke. They settled into deeply cushioned patio chairs.

A ceiling fan made of dried palm leaves whirred overhead, casting a light breeze over them. Sunlight winked off the heated pool. A perfect spring day in central California. He took a deep breath.

"Those ribs smell great, Jimmy. Yours always turn out so tender, I'm gonna have to sneak over here one of these days and learn your secret."

"No secret to it, just buy some quality pig and cook 'em slow. Now the sauce is another story, as you know." The men chuckled and tapped beers. Craig had been trying to talk Jimmy out of his recipe for years and he always got the same reply, "You'll get it in my will."

"Hey Uncle Jimmy, did you get a new pinball machine?"

"Yep, I just got that one the other day. Got sick of Spiderman, had it down pat, got boring. You ever played on a Ripley's Believe It or Not before? It's got great multi ball action and says the funniest stuff you've ever heard. The guy who designed it must think he's a philosopher or something." Jimmy waved a hand toward the game in the corner. "Go ahead, I can tell you want to try it out. Your dad and I'll just sit here and soak up the suds while you practice. Then after you're warmed up we'll have a little competition."

"Awesome. I'm all over it."

Craig sat grinning at his brother, took a pull of his beer, reached for a pretzel.

"What?"

"I'm just glad to be here. Something about your bachelor pad always makes me smile."

"Ha. I'll tell you what it is. It's the free beer." They laughed and tapped bottles again.

"So how's the big rock treating you these days, bro?"

It had been a few weeks since he'd seen Jimmy and he was glad they'd come over, even if the push out of the house had been ugly. It was crazy how fast time could slip by.

"Work's going okay, but it's also the reason why I needed a break today."

"I hear you there, bro. A man's got to relax once in a while or else what the hell is it all for, anyway?" Jimmy stood up to turn the ribs. "So, got the hard rock blues do ya? I can see it in those big brown eyes of yours, Craig-O."

He scrubbed a palm over his face, glanced at his son. Ethan was absorbed in the new game and he doubted the boy could hear much of their conversation between its beeping and the ballgame on the TV up in the corner.

"Work's not the issue per se. It's the constant traveling that's causing the problem."

"I gotcha. So we're talking Chelsea, right?"

"You got it. She's had it with my being gone so often and let me know exactly how she feels about it."

"Well, I'm sorry to hear she's upset." Jimmy sipped, eyes off in the distance, then he said, "I guess if you didn't love each other so much, you being gone a lot wouldn't matter. Hell, if she was like most wives she'd throw a party every time your sorry ass backed off the drive."

"I hadn't thought about it quite like that before."

"Look, you and I might not be blessed with movie star faces, but you're one of the smartest people I know. I'm sure you can resolve this traveling thing if you put your mind to it."

"What, you don't think we're lucky to have this pond brown hair and eyes to match?" He couldn't debate the insult—they both looked just like their dad—average. Not ugly, not handsome. Tall, big shouldered.

Craig shook his head, "I'm glad you think I'm so smart, but I sure don't see a way to resolve the traveling problem. Not right now, anyway."

He watched as his brother tossed a cashew up in the air, tipped his head back and caught it in his mouth then crunched away. In the brief silence the pinball game's voice parsed out a dollop of wisdom as it informed his son, *"Everywhere you go…there you are."*

"See what I mean?" Jimmy chuckled and swigged more beer. Then he looked at him, grin fading. "So, what's the verdict? Is that pretty lady of yours gonna divorce your ass 'cause she doesn't see it enough or what? I haven't seen you look this down since I skunked you out of that twenty on the golf course last year."

"I sure hope not, you know how I feel about her. But Chelsea wasn't kidding when she laid into me today. The thing is, there's no way to be a geologist without some traveling. It would mean passing up assignments and could hurt my career." He snapped the pretzel into pieces as he spoke, scooted them into a pile with his pinky.

"At the same time, I really do miss my family when I'm in some backwater for days, studying whatever problem needs to be solved. Sometimes I wonder if it's worth it. But I sure as hell don't know what else I'd do for a living. My job pays pretty damn good."

"I hear you. Ever since you were a kid you've been fascinated with rocks and dirt. I always did think you were kinda weird like that." Jimmy laughed at him and sipped more beer.

"Thanks, bro. I appreciate the kind words. What about your grease monkey ass? You've had your head under the hood of a car since you were old enough to see over the side of one. I always wondered why you liked cars so much until that day you fixed Dad's truck when no one was home. How old were you? Twelve?"

"I think so, yeah that seems about right. I'll never forget trying to talk Dad out of whipping me for thinking I was lying to him. Thank God Mrs. Swanson saw me out there working on that old truck or my ass would have been sore for a week."

Their father had been a great parent but a strong disciplinarian who considered lying to be one of the worst things a person could do, barring illegal activities. He had tolerated a swear word or two, a poor grade now and then with verbal admonishments, but if he caught one of his sons in a lie there was hell to pay.

"You know, it's funny we're sitting here talking about the careers we've chosen because that was a big part of the word smack Chelsea threw on me earlier." He looked over at his son who stood talking back to the game, engrossed with winning. "Ethan's decided he wants to become a geologist too. He's researched all the best colleges and wants to go to Berkley next year. He got online, downloaded the forms and found out they require an essay as part of the application process."

His agitated fingers toyed with the bottle cap as he spoke, "Ethan came to me this morning to discuss the idea he's been working on for his paper while I was away this week. I have to say, I find the idea fascinating myself. When he told me about those little metal spheres I got almost as excited about it as he is. I up and suggested we go to Africa during his spring break to check out the mine they came from."

"Hey, that's fantastic. So are you guys gonna go?"

"Well, the words were out of my mouth before I thought about Chelsea's already upset with my traveling. I told Ethan I'd talk to her about it when she got home from the lab today, and so I did." Another pretzel crumbled on the table. "No surprise, she was instantly ticked off at the idea. She can't get away from work and doesn't want Ethan following in my footsteps."

As he finished telling Jimmy what Chelsea had said, Ethan pushed away from the game and came back to join them. His son glanced from Jimmy to him.

"Dad, you know I love geology. I'm not going into it just because that's what you do. Sure, you're the one that got me interested in it, but I really love it."

He pulled out a chair, sat down. "I like learning all the cool stuff about our planet and the idea of helping solve problems from the weather and shifts in the earth. Like that project you worked on in Colorado last year, how awesome was that? You even won an award for it and got your picture in the paper." His son picked up Jimmy's bottle cap and gave it a frustrated spin.

"I guess I could try to figure out something else to focus on but I don't know what it would be. I've wanted to be a geologist forever, since I was like ten."

The men studied Ethan a moment. Jimmy spoke first, "Well hell Ethan, you don't want to end up being a duck on dirt do ya, boy?"

"What do you mean Uncle Jimmy?"

"You ever see a duck at the park?"

"Sure. Lotsa times. What about it?"

"Okay, so what are ducks best at?"

"I guess that would be swimming, right?"

"Right. They glide along over the water all graceful, their little feet are great for paddling. Got those waterproof feathers and that really cool way of bobbing under the water and popping right back up like a cork. It's fun to watch. But, you ever watch a duck on dirt?"

Ethan thought about it and laughed. "Yeah, they look kinda silly, waddling along."

"Exactly. God made 'em so they can go on land to lay their eggs and sleep but walking on land is not what their best at, not their higher calling you might say. So, if ya know you really want to be a geologist like your good-lookin' dad here, then that's exactly what you should do. Sure, you could spend some time checking out other possibilities, but chances are ya might end up looking like a duck on dirt. You become a geologist and next thing ya know, you're gonna be gliding boy." Jimmy beamed at Ethan then stood up to turn the ribs again.

Craig smiled at his son, loving the glow of confidence in his eyes that replaced the question marks his mother had planted there earlier. He knew Chelsea had meant well but was coming from the wrong place on the subject. Leave it to his crazy brother to nail it down. Nobody wanted to waddle if they didn't have to.

The three of them had a shoot-out on the Ripley's machine. Jimmy had been right about the multi ball action and they shared some good laughs at the crazy stuff the game said. They worked up an appetite and sat down to eat some of the tangy ribs and smoky baked beans.

Ethan came back out to the patio after a restroom break and asked, "Did you get a new revolver Uncle Jimmy? That silver one in the gun case looks pretty bad-ass."

"Yeah, I picked it up last week from a client of mine. It's a Smith & Wesson .44. I'll take you out to the shooting range in the fall when you turn eighteen and you can try it out."

"Sweet!"

Craig scooted his chair back. The clock was pushing five and he had kitchen duty that night. "I think we'd better head home, Son. Jimmy, it was good, as always." He reached out and gave his brother a one-armed hug, holding tight for a second. "Thanks for having us over."

"Any time, bro, anytime. You know you're always welcome.

They followed Ethan to the door as Jimmy said, "Look, Craig-O, you know I'm not one to get up in anybody's business, but I think you guys should go check out that mine in Africa. Not only will it help Ethan with his paper, it'll give you a chance for some solid one-on-one time before he flies the coop. Because that's what little ducks do, ya know."

Jimmy slapped him on the back, "Chelsea won't be able to say no if ya put it that way."

CHAPTER 4

"Catherine Elizabeth Noble! Get out of that mud right now." Chelsea caught movement from the corner of her eye as she leaned over the tomato plant and looked up just in time to watch her daughter stomp a bare foot in the freshly-watered soil between the corn rows.

"Okay, Mommy. Sthorry. Come on Sthevie, let's go on the sthwings." Lily ran to the back of the yard, giggles popping out of her like bubbles. Steve silently followed with a beatific smile on his face. Their Irish setter, Bell, jogged behind, limping from an arthritic hip.

"She reminds me of myself at seven. Puddles were magnets." Ann Mathers chuckled, kneeling on the grass alongside Chelsea's garden. She gently placed a ripe tomato in the basket between them. "Lily is so good with Steve. I'm really grateful for it."

"It's good to see them having fun, isn't it?" Chelsea smiled at her friend and neighbor and felt her garden-gloved finger leave a spot of dirt on her cheek as she swiped at a loose strand of hair. "So, is school going any better for him since you requested a switch in teachers?"

Ann let out a sigh, "No, just the opposite, and I know it's not the teacher's fault this time. She's wonderful. His autism is digressing in a lot of ways and I don't know why. He's eight now and getting more sensitive to the other kids' behavior toward him. Maybe that's part of it."

Chelsea's heart went out to her as Ann frowned and plucked at a weed.

"Mrs. Dobbs said his hand-flapping got so bad the other day she sent him to the nurse's office so the rest of her students could concentrate. I can't pinpoint anything that would be causing it. He wasn't doing the hand thing until a couple weeks ago. This past week he's even started rocking in his chair; at school and at home. It's so frustrating." She shook her head, long dark hair glinting in the sunlight, rosy lips pressed tight.

"What are the doctors saying?" Chelsea asked.

"They're stumped too. I've followed doctors' advice to the letter: we're careful about his diet, I try to keep our routines down pat, monitor his T.V. time, never miss his meds. It's hard to watch him suffer." She bent over and plucked another tomato, placed it in the basket. "Being a nurse makes it even tougher. There's so much stress at the hospital it's hard to come home with a calm mind."

"I'm sorry to hear that Ann. I know you're working your tail off, just like I am. It's got to be really hard on you."

"Some days are better than others, but lately it's been especially tough. Steve has only been sleeping three or four hours at night then he wakes up and starts thumping his headboard until I come in. He can't go back to sleep after that. It's like he's on overdrive or something." Guilt washed over Ann's face as she admitted how hard things had been for her. Chelsea thought the dark circles around her eyes looked like bruises from a fight.

"It's terrible, but I was so desperate for some good rest the other night, I put a sleeping pill in his bedtime snack. That little trick backfired on me—I felt so bad for drugging my own kid I lay awake for hours after he went to sleep. I finally nodded off at two and he was awake by six. Sometimes it feels like I can't win." She let out a breath, reached out for another tomato.

"Listen, don't beat yourself up. Being a single parent is really rough, especially with a child with special needs. I don't know how you do it." Chelsea stood up and moved around Ann to start on the green bean plants. She set the basket down between them again and glanced at Ann, unable to keep the anger out of her voice as she confessed to her own unhappiness.

"Being married isn't helping me much, I can tell you that. Most of the time it seems like I don't have a husband. Craig's home on weekends but after being the cook, maid, chauffer, home-work buddy, referee and a full-time employee all week I'm so drained I want to cry. He comes home all chipper, smiling from ear to ear after eating in restaurants all week, and acts like I should be glad to finally see him. Something's got to change and I told him so this afternoon." She blew bangs out of her eyes sat back on her heels and looked at Ann.

"So guess what he did? He took off with Ethan. They're over at Jimmy's right now. He's probably drinking beer and laughing, and here I am, picking vegetables. If it weren't for you and this garden I'd be completely crazy by now."

"Well, you know I feel the same way, Chelsea. I don't know what I'd do without you and Lily or my mom helping me. I'm sure that's the way it's been all through the millennia, women supporting each other while their men go off and do their own thing."

After a moment Ann said, "At least Craig is a good husband when he's home and a good provider. There's a lot to be said for both. Steve's dad couldn't handle the pressure, he left when Steve was only three. Maybe women are stronger than men when it comes to home life."

"I think you're right on all points." Chelsea's tone hardened, "But, I'm not kidding here, I see my lab partner a lot more than I see my husband. That's not what I signed on for. Craig loves his job and that's great, but it would be nice if he made me feel like our marriage was more important to him, you know?" She dipped her head down to the plant, swiped at a tear that sneaked out, leaving a wide streak of mud across her nose. Green beans snapped off the vine in a quick staccato and she dropped a handful in the basket.

"Sorry to unload on you."

"I understand, I really do. " Ann looked at her with tired brown eyes. "What does he say when you ask him to stop traveling so much?"

"He always comes back with the same thing—he has to travel or he'll lose his job. If he could keep it to only one or two days a week it wouldn't be so bad, but four or five is too much. It's not working, not at all." Melancholy replaced the anger as she spoke, "Brad had to pinch hit for me the other day so I could go to Lily's recital. She deserved to have at least one parent there. She was so excited and so cute."

"I'm glad your lab partner was able to cover for you. I know you said your boss is a real jerk. I'm surprised you were able to get away."

"Orlon is a complete ass and ugly to boot. On the other hand, Brad is wonderful, and easy on the eyes. If it weren't for him I would have quit or been fired by now. Between the stress at work and Craig being gone so much I've reached the breaking point. When I was younger it didn't seem so bad, but I guess after so many years of it, I've got a short fuse."

Chelsea forced a light laugh, trying to brighten the mood. "That's one of the reasons why I planted this garden. Getting my hands in the soil, yanking weeds and watching things grow keeps my temper in check. The plants at work are all about science, not gardening."

She also gardened because she knew it would help Ann without hurting her pride. The doctors had told Ann it was critical to Steve's health that he eat as much fresh produce as she could get down him. A lot of tests had been done on autism symptoms and the impact of vitamin deficiencies. Ann had jumped at the chance to share gardening chores with her in exchange for free vegetables.

Chelsea stood up and pulled the dirty gloves off. "It looks like we're finished for today." She turned toward the swings, "Lily, bring Steve and come inside now, okay?"

They slowly headed toward the house, Ann carrying the basket of vegetables, Chelsea carried a box of weeds and two small trowels.

As they reached the door she said, "I'll say a prayer for both of us tonight. Lord knows we need some help with the men in our lives. I've tried to talk to Craig until I'm blue in the face and you need some sleep."

She watched as Lily zipped through the door. Steve followed behind, silent as a mouse.

CHAPTER 5

"**D**ad, I've been thinking…."

Craig glanced at Ethan as he turned the corner onto their street and waited for him to elaborate. He clicked the turn signal off, tapped the radio volume down a notch.

"…let me talk to Mom tonight, okay? Uncle Jimmy was right. I'm not gonna waste time trying to be something I'm not just so I don't have to travel. Besides, I might not ever get married. Look at Uncle Jimmy. He seems pretty happy, right? So, since it's my choice what I do for a living, I should be the one to talk to her about it. And the trip. That pinball game told me four times today, *'You are going toooo… Africaaaa!'*. I'm taking it as a sign, Dad."

Craig looked back at his son, gave him a nod as he held his fist out for a bump.

"I'm proud of you for stepping up for yourself…and I'm glad you're taking her on instead of me. You know I'll back you up, whatever it takes, I promise."

"Just make sure she has a glass of wine with the steaks, okay?"

"Buddy, I'll do my best to get two down her." He winked at his son as they climbed out of the car. "Trust me, I've got my own reasons."

They walked into a quiet house. Ethan headed upstairs and Craig started on dinner. He was marinating the filets when he heard Lily and Chelsea come in through the front door. He stepped over to the sink to rinse his hands as he hollered, "In the kitchen!"

He heard pink sparkly sneakers thumping down the hall, a moment later, "Hi Daddy! What ya doin'?" She plopped her head against his hip, an arm around his legs.

"I'm getting the steaks ready for tonight." He watched her nose wrinkle. "Don't worry, I'll grill hotdogs for you."

"Good. I don't like stheak." She smiled up at him. "I'm gonna go watch TV, Daddy."

"Okay, Lilybit, see you in a bit. You want to play a game after your show?" He grinned as she nodded and skipped out of the room, long golden curls bouncing.

Tomatoes from the basket on the counter went under the water next. The lettuce was getting a bath when Chelsea walked in.

"Hi Hon, how's your garden growing?" He tried a grin. From her frown, his humor wasn't working for him. He rinsed faster then snagged the big salad bowl from its perch above the refrigerator, gave it a swipe and slid the vegetables in.

Chelsea made herself a glass of tea and sat down at the table.

"So, how's Jimmy doing?"

From her tone they were going to play truce, at least through dinner. Good, progress. He dried his hands then turned to the wine rack.

"Oh, you know my brother. He's always Jimmy. He got a new pinball machine. You should hear the crazy things that game says." He popped the cork out of the wine, pulled two glasses out of the cabinet and poured, set one down in front of her. "Enjoy, you earned it."

"Thanks." She sat in silence.

"I'm gonna put the steaks on after I get the potatoes going. Dinner should be ready in about forty-five, how's that sound?"

"Good." She picked up the wine and took a sip. More silence.

He took a sip, attempted conversation. "How did things go with the test results today?"

She let out a long breath. "Not as well as we'd hoped, unfortunately. Orlon is going to go crazy on Monday. I'm dreading it."

"What are you guys working on right now?" He slid out a chair and sat down with her.

"This recent round of investment funding is for development of a plant-derived vaccine against Alzheimer's. We immunized mice with transgenic tomato plants once a week for three weeks, and gave the mice a booster seven weeks after that, which is what we ran the tests on yesterday." She let out another long sigh. "Blood analyses showed a strong immune response after the booster, with the production of antibodies to the human foreign protein."

"Well, that sounds like progress, right?"

"Yes and no. Mostly no. We were hoping to show a reduction in beta-amyloids in the brains of the mice that were given the vaccine, but that didn't happen. If we can't achieve that milestone, we'll likely lose our funding for this project."

She sipped more wine then said, "Orlon's got us looking at strategies to increase the potency of the tomato-based vaccine, but I think that's chasing the wrong end of the rainbow. Fresh tomatoes contain less than one percent protein and the levels of foreign protein are even lower. I'm pulling for finding another plant to work with but Orlon insists we have to stay with the tomato for now. Frustrating."

"Huh. Sounds like you're the one that should be in charge of the project."

"I wish. Brad and I can both run circles around Orlon in the lab, trust me. But he's really good at bringing in the bucks so he gets to be in charge. That's how things go in my world."

"I think that's how things go in most worlds these days, unfortunately." They sat in silence a minute then he stood up. "I'm going to put the potatoes on now, be right back."

An hour later, the family sat around the kitchen table, enjoying the meal.

"These steaks are great Dad, thanks."

"They did turn out well if I do say so myself." He reached over and poured the rest of the wine into Chelsea's glass, winked at Ethan across the table.

"Everything's good. Thanks for cooking. It's nice to get a break." Chelsea gave him a half-smile as she lifted her glass and sipped.

Lily took a last bite of her hot dog and pushed her plate back. He watched as she chewed and made sure to swallow before she spoke. Chelsea was a stickler for table manners.

"Daddy, are we sthill gonna play Trouble?"

"Let me get the dishes cleaned up and then we'll play.?"

"Kay. I'm gonna watch T.V." She headed out to the sofa.

"Hey, Mom. You wanna go for a walk while Dad does the dishes?" Ethan asked.

"Sure. That sounds great. We haven't gone for a walk together in a long time. Let me get a jacket and I'm ready."

Craig fist-bumped Ethan as his wife disappeared down the hall. "Good luck, young man. I'll be thinking of you while I load the dishwasher."

* * *

Ethan looked up and smiled at the sky as they stepped outside. The sun cast an amber glow over the neighborhood. Its gold and pink glory licked the clouds into a fiery show as they set out under the arch of palm trees lining the street.

"This is such a beautiful evening and a great idea, Ethan. Skinny girls need exercise, too, and I'm way behind." She chuckled and rubbed his shoulder.

"Yeah, the sunset's great, huh?"

They walked in silence a couple minutes then took turns pointing out things that caught their eye. The Myerson's dog ran out to greet them as Mr. Myerson waved from the porch. They waved back and gave the dog a pat. Ethan worked up the courage to jump in with both feet as they looped around the small neighborhood playground.

"So…you know I want to be a geologist, right?"

She gave him the mom look. "Yes, but we really need to talk about that. I think you should consider other avenues before you make up your mind. You're so young, only seventeen."

"That's why I wanted to go for a walk with you. So we can talk about it."

He waded in deeper, "Did you know the geology job market is supposed to grow twenty-two percent in the next five years?"

"Really?" She seemed genuinely curious. "Where'd you hear that?"

"I read it on the internet, on three different sites. Really." He smiled at her and continued, "See, the thing is, even though I'm still a teenager, I've wanted to be a geologist for years. I'm good at science and math, so the engineering stuff comes naturally to me. I guess that's because of you and dad."

"Yeah, I guess so."

"Right, so it's like Uncle Jimmy said today. I gotta be able to glide, Mom."

"I think I need the full picture on that one..."

Ethan did his best to relate the duck-on-dirt story as well as his uncle had. "...I don't want to waste time waddling, Mom. Not if I don't have to."

She stopped in the street and looked him in the eye. He saw the corner of her mouth jerk a little. He wasn't sure if that was a good sign or a bad one. He held his breath and waited.

A choked laugh escaped her as she shook her head. "Now there's a classic Jimmy-ism. It makes the top three for sure."

His breath came out in a whoosh of relief. "So, you understand where I'm coming from, right?" *Maybe this was going to be okay.*

"Yes, I do. But do you understand what kind of life you're looking at? Have you noticed how much your dad is gone?" She gave him a questioning look but didn't seem mad.

"Yeah, and I'm okay with that. I really haven't seen much of the world at all. I want to travel, Mom. Maybe not forever, but I'm really young. I could travel for ten years and still be only twenty-seven."

"I guess I can't argue with that. It's your choice. I just want to make sure you are making it with your eyes open. You know I've been upset about your dad being gone so much. Don't you miss him, too?"

He gulped. "Yeah, you know how much I love Dad. I really miss him when he's gone. But I understand why he travels. It's for his job. It's not like he's off having fun without us."

"True, but he's still gone."

"What if I talk to him about it for you?"

"What do you mean?"

"Well, you know that Dad said he'd take me to Africa to see the spheres?"

"Yeah..." His mom's eyes narrowed as she looked at him.

"What if Dad agrees to stay home between now and when we go to South Africa, and for a week when we get back? Then would you be okay with us going?"

His mom scanned his face with her green eyes, reached out and rubbed his cheek with her thumb.

"You know how much I love you, right?"

"Sure. I love you too, Mom."

"Good."

She started walking again and he stepped to keep stride with her long legs.

"Okay, I'll leave it in your hands Ethan. If you can get your dad to agree to what you just said, you guys can go to Africa."

"Yes!" He bounced on the sidewalk and fist pumped the air. "Mom, you are so awesome! Don't worry, I'll talk to him. He said he'd do whatever it takes to help me get to Africa."

He turned and grinned at her. His smile slid a bit at seeing the quick frown in her eyes.

CHAPTER 6

"Frankly, I'm astonished you haven't asked before, Craig." Douglas Belmont leaned back in his chair and steepled his fingers as he quietly looked back at him over the highly polished cherrywood desk.

Doug was the president of their Pacific division and had been his supervisor for the past four years at Global Systems. He was a good man but also a very hard worker and a tough manager. There was no favoritism and no slacking in the Pacific division.

Craig tried to keep the surprise from his voice. "I realize this is bad timing with the project we have going at Ocean Beach, but there isn't much I can do about it." He was still waiting for Doug to give him the formal okay for the next three weeks, one of which would be a vacation week. As senior project manager for their division, he knew his absence would be an issue. Someone would have to step in and supervise the site work in San Francisco and Nevada while he stayed in the Hollister office and went to Africa.

"I appreciate your concern, but we're a highly successful company because of people like you, Craig. We've always got a big project going. We have a strong team, with a lot of good men who need the experience of temporarily stepping up to fill your shoes for a spell."

Doug shot him a quick smile. "I've met your family and they're delightful, I don't blame you a bit for wanting to spend more time with them. So, Ethan's gearing up for a degree in geology, is he?"

"Yep, a chip off the ol' block." He couldn't help the grin, it felt good.

"That's great, I'm happy to hear it. You know we're always looking for new talent. If he's anything like his father we'll be lucky to have him." Doug stood up, a signal he needed to move on with his day. "I'll speak with Barbara about coordinating the week you'll be in Africa. Otherwise, it should largely be business as usual around here. You might get a few paper cuts, but it'll be good to have you in the office a little more." Doug chuckled as he walked him to the doorway. "Say hello to your pretty wife for me. I'm sure she'll be glad to see more of you, too."

"Thanks, Doug. I appreciate your understanding." They shook hands and he headed down the hall, listening to Doug answer the phone that had been steadily ignored through their ten minute meeting.

He felt great knowing he would be keeping his promise to Chelsea and going to Africa with Ethan. But he couldn't shake off the sense of doubt that sifted into his mind at hearing Doug talk about the good men who could fill his shoes. He had worked his ass off to make senior project manager four years ago. Admittedly, he'd turned Doug down when his boss had mentioned making him a division Vice President last year. That had been a tricky conversation, but Craig knew the job title came with a ball and chain attached to a fancy cherrywood desk and a string of conference tables. Nothing but perusing written reports, managing managers, meetings and traveling for more meetings. He mentally shuddered at the thought as he stepped into his office. He picked up his cell phone, hit speed dial and listened to it ring.

"Hello?" Kids shouting, traffic noise. Ethan was on the bus headed home from school.

"Good news...looks like we're going to Africa." Craig felt his grin spread as he listened to his son shout out to his friends.

"Hey you guys—I'm going to Africa with my dad!"

* * *

It was after midnight and the candle had burned low in its glass cage. There was enough glow for him to clearly see his wife's beautiful face and forest green eyes. Bangs damp, lips a little swollen. Her skin glowed in the flickering light.

"Do you know how much I love you Chelsea?" His voice came out gruffer than he'd intended. He reached out and stroked the curve of her ribs as he rested his head in his palm, enjoying the view. He watched her breath catch and her lips part. She smiled at him. The same smile he remembered from the night he'd asked her to be his wife.

She reached out and rubbed a hand down his bare chest. "I'm really looking forward to sleeping with you for the next seven nights in a row."

She giggled and he thought how much she sounded like Lily right then. It had been a long time since he'd heard her sound so happy. Her laugh was one of his favorite things. He felt his heart skitter and he reached out to scoop his warm willing wife back into his arms. She laughed again as he slid on top of her and leaned over to blow out the candle.

Maybe he would have to rethink the travel thing.

CHAPTER 7

It had been an insanely long plane ride but worth it. Ethan couldn't stop grinning as they walked along a corridor of three billion-year old pyrophyllite. "This is so awesome, Dad. I'm never going to forget being here. It's way cool to be walking in the crater of an extinct volcano."

His dad returned the grin, "I agree."

The Wonderstone mine was a lot bigger than he had anticipated. It was the length of five football fields and almost as wide from what he could see. Several gravel roads wound through the variegated grey terraces where excavation had taken place. Men driving bulldozers and dump trucks moved in and out of sight among the terraces. It was a very busy place.

"I'm amazed to see what an incredible enterprise you've created here," his dad said to their guide. "I've never seen anything quite like this before, I'm impressed."

"Thank you." Jeff Connor, manager of the Wonderstone mine, gave his dad a quick nod. "We've tried to maximize the innovative uses for the pyrophyllite found here. It's used for many things; ceramics, as the base for many pesticides and heat deflection in space craft. It's even used for testing diamonds. We now produce many market-ready items. Some on-site, others within a few miles of the mine.

"Come, let me show you where the spheres were found." He motioned with his hand and led the way farther into an older area of the mine. "A little over two hundred of the spheres have been found so far. All came from this section." Connor motioned up at the eight-meter high dark grey slab in front of them. He stood aside, patiently waiting as they closely examined the pyrophillite.

"What do you think, Dad? See these round impressions?"

"Yep, I see them. It's interesting to imagine the spheres being formed through a concretion process." His dad brought out a magnifying glass from a jacket pocket and looked at Connor. "May I take a closer look?"

"Of course." Connor stood off to the side, hands loosely clasped in front of him, a quiet smile on his face. Ethan liked the man's neatly trimmed grey hair and beard. With his gold wire-rimmed glasses he looked more like a professor than a construction manager.

His dad took his time, examining the surface of several depressions then handed the magnifying glass to him. "Take a look."

He accepted the silver handle, warm from his dad's touch. He wasn't sure why he felt so nervous. All he was doing was looking through a magnifying glass. He shrugged and bent closer, slowly scanning the grey slab as his father had. It reminded him of the moon's surface.

After a moment, he handed the glass back then asked the manager, "Did the spheres fall right out of the stone when you cut it open?"

"It is a matter of our process here and how the pyrophyllite is cut. This stone flakes off in large sheets when it is heated. But when cool and wet it can be worked almost like clay. Much of our sales are in the form of large blocks of the stone, intended for artistic sculpting and other shaped objects.

"When we cut the block out from this wall, some of the unusual round objects were in the path of the blade. But upon closer examination we realized there were many more embedded within the cut block."

Connor reached out, smoothed a hand across the surface, "You see how this stone feels slick, almost greasy? It is very easily worked, even though it can stand up to extremely high temperatures. When we realized there were these round objects within, our craftsmen carefully worked to remove the spheres. To answer your question, once the proper amount of pyrophyllite was removed, we were able to lift the spheres out. They were not enmeshed with the stone, only embedded."

"As a geologist, I can see why a professional would report them as naturally occurring concretions rather than admit they are unexplainable formations." His dad raised a brow at him as he stroked a finger around one of the indentions. Ethan grinned back at the challenge.

"We'd really appreciate it if you would allow us to examine some of the spheres. Ethan has to come to his own conclusion in his essay. It would help him a lot if he could take a closer look at them before he makes that call."

"Certainly. I knew from our conversation on the phone that you wanted to examine them. It's been some time since we've had anyone come all the way here. We still get phone calls with long distance requests to buy the spheres, but not many visitors." He continued speaking as he led the way back to the main office building located on the rim of the defunct volcano crater, "We of course refuse to sell any, or ship any out from our facility, other than to museums or for scientific tests. We may find more of the spheres later, but for now, we have a limited amount to work with, so they aren't for sale."

They went in through a steel and glass door and followed Jeff down the grey tiled hall. The walls were painted a utilitarian white and the air smelled of rock dust and cleaning fluids. Florescent lights glowed overhead as they passed doors on the way to Jeff's office.

"Have a seat. I'll tell Emily to set up the viewing room for you, it'll just be a minute." He headed back out the door and down the hall.

Ethan looked at his dad, "This place is huge. It's totally different than I imagined. There aren't any pictures on the internet of the mine itself, just the spheres."

"Mining operations aren't considered glamorous by most people. Pictures of mines aren't what companies post on their websites or in their annual reports. Not unless they're full of gold or diamonds."

Connor walked back in. "Okay, we're ready. It's just down the hall to the left."

They stepped through a wooden swinging door and entered a second hall, turned in at the first room on the right. Large windows along the top of the west wall let in good light. Two drafting tables sat in the middle of the room, black cone lights hung above them. Wooden bar stools surrounded the tables and metal file cabinets lined the walls. The room smelled a bit like the library at his school.

The tables held small lamps, magnifying glasses and large grey cloths spread out at each end. Connor gestured with a palm, indicating they should take a seat at the first table.

Ethan sat down across from them and looked up as a young woman entered through the door they had just come in. She carried a large metal box and set it in the center of the table. She took a step back and waited quietly, glancing at Connor as he stood up and took the lid off the box.

"That will be all for now Emily, thank you. If you would please come back in fifteen minutes, we should be through and you can put the box away."

"Yes, sir." Ethan watched the girl's face as she spoke. She was really pretty. Maybe the prettiest girl he had ever seen; shiny mink brown hair fell like a waterfall over her shoulders. Copper eyes with long dark lashes. She glanced at him and his eyes widened, realizing he'd been caught staring. He felt himself blush as she smiled at him then turned and quietly left the room. His breath came out in a whoosh as the door swung shut behind her. Then he heard a chuckle and looked at the men sitting across from him.

"Let's get down to business, shall we?" His dad grinned at him as he fought down a second blush. They watched as Connor slid the box in front of him and selected six of the spheres. He set each one out on the grey cloth.

"These spheres are good examples of the various shapes we've found. You will see that some of them have one, two or three lines around their equator. Some have no lines at all. The grooves seem to be the big issue behind the controversy over whether these things are naturally occurring or were created by intelligent beings billions of years ago."

Connor smiled then said, "You may examine the spheres for the next fifteen minutes. Feel free to take notes and pictures. I'm afraid I can't give you any more time than that because we've got a lot going on today."

"Thanks." Ethan smiled at the manager, excited to get his hands on the spheres. Connor sat quietly as they switched on the desk lamp, held the magnifying glasses over the spheres and used rulers to measure various aspects of the round objects. Ethan made a few notations in a small notebook he had brought along, flipped a page and reviewed the questions he'd written down on the plane.

"Mr. Connor, I was wondering if you could tell me whether or not certain tests have been done on the spheres?"

"Certainly. What do you wish to know?"

"Has anyone tested the spongy white substance that's in the middle of them?"

"Cross-sections have been cut and we've been told by geologists that they exhibited an extremely well defined radial structure, terminating on the center of the sphere."

"Okay, that's good to know. Did anyone test the material from the center of the spheres to confirm what it consists of?"

Connor smiled at him, "I'm surprised by your detailed questions. Most people focus on the exterior of the spheres. We were told in 2008 that the center is a pseudomorph of the original crystalline structure of the original carbonite or pyrite."

Ethan felt himself blinking back like an idiot. He tried to sound like he'd just followed that explanation perfectly. "Hmm, interesting. Thanks for clearing that up for me."

"You are welcome."

The door opened and Emily leaned her head in, "Mr. Connor, there is an urgent call for you." Ethan watched stress play across her face as she spoke.

"Please excuse me, I'll be back in a moment." Connor nodded to them and left the room, quickly following Emily out as she began whispering to him and the door cut off their words.

"I guess we don't have much more time with the spheres. What do you think, Dad? Are these things concretions?"

"Well, I'm really not sure. That last spiel about what the center of the spheres is comprised of seemed a little vague, didn't it?"

"To be honest, I'm not sure I followed much of what he said. The best I could make out is the centers are made up from the crystals of whatever these spheres originated from."

"Yep, that's what I got, too." His dad grinned at him then stood up to look in the box in the middle of the table. He pulled one of the reddish-brown balls out and sat down to examine it under the light while Ethan snapped several digital photos.

"This one's a perfect sphere, it's got a single line around its equator, and a funny little indention on one side of it." His dad sat with eyebrows drawn, staring at the mini globe. "It reminds me of something but I can't put my finger on it. What's it remind you of?"

Ethan reached out and took it, rolled the reddish brown orb slowly around on his palm under the light until the indention was face up. He thought a moment then smiled. "It looks just like the Death Star planet from Star Wars."

He laughed as he held the magnifier over the sphere. "This is crazy. I've never seen anything like it. I know Mr. Connor said the six were good representatives of all the rest, but none of them look exactly the same." His excitement grew as he stood up and leaned over the box, pulled three more out and set them on the cloth.

He studied the objects as he held each one under the light. They were all different. Just as he picked up the death star sphere again the door swung open and Emily came back in. Ethan instantly knew something was wrong. She looked panicked; eyes wide, her skin the same grey color as the pyrophyllite outside the office building.

"I'm afraid you'll have to leave now. I'm really sorry but there's been an emergency."

His dad stood up and walked over to her, "What's wrong?"

"One of our workers has been injured. Please come with me, I'll show you out."

Ethan gave a last long look at the spheres on the table, picked up the camera and slipped his hands in his pockets then joined Emily and his dad. They looked at each other and shrugged in unison as they followed her hurrying figure.

"Thank you for letting us tour your company. I hope your worker is okay," Ethan said as he stepped out the front door and looked back at her. She gave him a quick nod, eyes dark with worry, then she scurried down the hall as the door shut behind her.

"That was kind of strange."

His dad shrugged, "I guess it's par for the course in a big enterprise like this."

They backed out of the lot then headed down the gravel road to the R505. An ambulance passed them a mile out, siren blaring.

CHAPTER 8

"Can he get any uglier?" Brad whispered to her as Orlon Millard droned on at the head of the table, forcing Chelsea to choke back a laugh.

"Now there's a scary thought." She glanced up at their boss, the board-appointed president of BioGen Technologies. Greasy grey hair hung in a long fringe around his prematurely balding head. It emphasized his flabby jowls and the stain on his collar.

"—and that takes us to the next item on the agenda today. Brad, please give us your report on the progress of the Alzheimer's transgenic vaccine." Orlon leaned back in his chair and scraped a puffy finger at the end of his double-bumped nose.

Brad glanced at her then replied, "We have mixed results following the seven-week immunizations testing. It's looking like we may need to find another plant source, if possible, in order to make real progress. That is our conclusive theory at this point."

Orlon's cheeks billowed with air as his ridiculous eyebrows drew together. Chelsea leaned back in her chair, forcing herself to project a relaxed serenity that she didn't feel as she braced for the storm.

Orlon was the world's definition of a human jackass and she would not allow him to see her upset or threatened by his bluster. He was a complete idiot in the labs. She had no doubt he'd secured his job on the hard-working backs of fellow scientists at every opportunity. That, and his ability to schmooze for money, on an expense account of course.

"What do you mean, conclusive theory? I have told you, Chelsea, twice already—the tomato is the answer. Why can't you seem to make this project work?" His bellicose voice rang out the open door and down the tiled corridor, ensuring every staff member was aware he was unhappy with her work.

She fought to keep a poker face as anger pulsed. It was always Brad he asked to speak on their team's behalf, but he never failed to loudly say her name in the course of expressing any unhappiness with their work. She had come close to giving her resignation several times and Brad had always managed to talk her out of it. It remained to be seen if he'd be able to pull it off again this week. She tossed her pen down on the legal pad and leaned forward.

"What part of *tomatoes don't have enough protein to generate the needed amount of antibodies* do you not understand, Orlon?" She forced herself to speak quietly but let her eyes gleam with malice. She felt everyone in the room staring at her as she gave the most-hated man in the company a taste of what they all wanted to feed him. She could almost hear the collective gasp of indrawn breaths as she watched Orlon flush brick red.

He jumped up, his extra-large ass shoving the conference chair into the wall behind him. His fat hands spread across the table under his weight.

"Don't be insubordinate with me, young lady!"

She rolled her eyes at the ridiculous statement—she was only six years younger than her boss.

"Our investors are counting on your project being a success. We must have positive results to plug into the status report for the meeting in two weeks. You know that, as well as I do. There isn't time to go around trying to identify another viable entity." He leaned his threatening girth halfway across the conference table and glowered at her. His attempt to intimidate gave her an unwanted close-up on the forest of skin tabs hanging from the bags under his eyes.

Her patience quickly reached its limit when Orlon crossed a line as he continued.

"Now quit making excuses and get back to work. And this time—pay attention!" The fat finger again. "No more mistakes. I want a satisfactory result and a revised report by the end of the week or we will need to review your performance, Ms. Noble."

It took all she had to hold in the spate of truth she wanted to pour on his head. She made herself pull in a breath and remember the huge mortgage on their house, the two car payments, private school fees and college to pay for next year. If she was going to quit, she wanted to do it with a calm mind and another job already lined up. The breath she had been holding slowly slipped out of her as she nodded and stood up.

"All right. Looks like I'd better get back to the lab." She picked up her legal pad and pen, chin held high. To hell with Orlon and his useless meeting. She couldn't care less if there were other items on the agenda.

As she walked down the hall, back ramrod straight, legal pad smacking against her side, she heard Orlon tell the group, "We're through here for today. Same time, next week, and I want progress from everyone. Let's make it happen folks. The investors' meeting is in sixteen days."

Chairs squeaked and low voices rumbled behind her as she reached the end of the corridor and headed into the lab she shared with Brad.

CHAPTER 9

South Africa looked a lot different than Ethan had imagined it, at
least the part they were in. They'd driven from Johannesburg to
Ottosdal on their first day, then after touring the Wonderstone mine,
they'd traveled north two hours on the R505 to the Madikwe Game
Reserve. Almost all the land he'd seen so far was brown and barren;
flat grassland and bushveld, a few rock outcroppings, a hill now and
then. Some tufts of green trees and bushes dotted the land between
the crop fields around Ottosdal and the huge grassland expanses as
they neared the reserve. In some ways it reminded him of Kansas.
Only the animals were more interesting.

Ethan spent part of their last evening in South Africa scouting
around the grounds of the Impodimo Game Lodge. He gathered a
small collection of rocks to take back as souvenirs, keeping only the
round ones. His dad sat on the patio, deep in conversation with a
couple of men they'd been out on the game trail with earlier that
day, and he walked over to join them.

The lodge had turned out to be much nicer than he'd thought it
would be. He had expected to be sleeping in a tent or a rough hut
but instead they were staying in a very modern and posh private
chalet built into the hillside. Their room had floor to ceiling
windows looking out on the reserve and the wild animals that ran
free. The drapes were opened first thing after waking that morning.
Within just a few minutes he'd seen a leopard chasing a small zebra
herd and managed to get several pictures of it from their covered
patio.

The outdoor shower was a trip. He'd smiled the whole time he soaped down, feeling like he was streaking even though he was hidden behind the rock wall of their private shower area. Being surrounded by nature and the sky while bathing had been fun. He'd enjoyed it until the distant roar of a lion made him realize he was nothing but a wet and naked piece of meat to the animals that roamed nearby.

After a quick early breakfast, they'd left in open Land Rovers on their game drive. They had seen all kinds of wild animals, most of what their ranger called the big five; lions, elephants, leopards, rhinos and the cape buffalo, plus several other animals. He was looking forward to posting the photos on Facebook when they got home.

A large water hole waited fifty yards from where they sat on the patio sipping cold drinks. A copse of trees grew on the far side of the water and otherwise it was flat grassland as far as he could see, with a small mountain range off in the distance.

"Did you find some good specimens?" His dad grinned up at him as Ethan settled into the chair and the sun dipped below the edge of the earth.

"Yeah, I found a few I liked. I put them in my bag." He looked at the glass in his dad's hand. A big pear slice sat on its lip. "What are you drinking?"

"It's called an Eldorado Sunset and it's delicious. As far as I can tell it's made of vodka, pear juice, maybe some ginger ale. Tasty. I think I'll have another one. You want a coke or something?"

He shrugged, wishing he could try what his dad was having but the legal drinking age in South Africa was eighteen, so he knew better than to ask. "Sure, a coke's fine."

"So, have you come to any conclusions yet on the spheres?" his dad asked.

Instead of answering, Ethan asked the men what he'd been pondering for days, "Let's assume for a minute that the spheres were created by ancient beings." He looked from the other men to his dad. "So, if that's the case, the question really is—what are the spheres for? Right?"

Just as he finished speaking a loud trumpet came from the direction of the water hole and the ground vibrated under his feet.

The men turned and watched as a large herd of elephants moved up to the water. Some stopped on the edge and immediately began drinking while others splashed in and showered themselves.

The dark-haired man sitting on his dad's right spoke up with a smile, "Water is extremely scarce in South Africa and animals sometimes go long periods in between water holes. The elephants will likely stay around for several hours before moving on. We are in for a show with our meal this evening, gentlemen."

"I've gotta get my camera."

Ethan raced back to their room and took pictures until a woman brought out a large tray and set plates on the table. The men spoke animatedly throughout the meal but he remained quiet. His dad noticed his silence as they forked up the last bites of the fantastic food.

"You're awfully quiet tonight. You feeling okay?"

"Yeah. I'm fine."

"Wishing we could stay longer?"

Ethan nodded as his nerves flared under his dad's continued scrutiny.

"I'm dreading the long flight home, too. But it was worth it, right?"

"Yeah, it's been great, Dad. Thanks." He did his best to smile back, hoping he'd found enough rocks and wondering whether it really had been worth it.

CHAPTER 10

Chelsea sat gripping a bottle of water like a grenade she contemplated tossing. Anger flared relentlessly and she forced herself to calm down. Brad walked through the lab door and over to the table. He raked a hand through coal black hair, pulled out a metal barstool.

"Hey, I'm really sorry about Orlon. Don't take it personally. He's under a lot of pressure right now. He's a total ass, but he's right—we've got to keep the investors motivated. We'll figure something out, don't worry." He swiveled around and gave her shoulder a gentle rub.

He had blue eyes so dark they were almost navy. A smile out of a toothpaste ad. Bangs that always seemed to fall in that superman look in spite of his constant hand-raking. She often found herself thinking he could be a model if he ever got tired of working in a lab.

"Brad, I know Orlon has to keep the investors happy. That's a given, I get that. But he doesn't have to be such a complete ass every minute of the damn day. And he sure as hell doesn't have to be a sexist pig. If it weren't for my mortgage I'd be sitting here writing my resignation. The paycheck's almost not worth it. I think today was the last straw. I really do."

His eyes flew to hers, "Don't say that. Come on, we're a team, remember?" He reached out and rubbed her shoulder again. "Listen, what do you say we bug out of here and go have a nice long lunch somewhere? We won't talk about vegetables."

"You know, I think I'm going to let you talk me into that." She stood up and walked over to the cupboard, pulled her purse out. "Let's get the hell out of here before he comes in."

They piled into Brad's black Porsche and zipped out of the lot. She ignored his shoulder as it brushed hers on the curves in the road. As she sat pulling her thoughts together and absorbing Brad's calm support once again, she realized how much it helped to have had the long week with Craig. But a week did not a marriage make. The void created by her husband's constant absence and the needs of a healthy woman had coalesced and she was no longer able to be objective with her lab partner. His constant presence and emotional support had grown important to her. She had come to rely on it and that scared her. That's how affairs got started. That's how marriages ended.

It was a quick five minutes to a good Mexican restaurant and the car came to a stop with a low growl. The hostess seated them immediately, giving them a booth at a window overlooking the valley. A pitcher of margaritas and a plate of tacos were ordered. After small talk about the weather and a few sips of tequila, Chelsea decided to be honest with Brad. He deserved that much.

"Look, after that meeting today, I'm finished with working at BioGen. I really am. I'm going to get my resume updated tonight and get it posted." She drained her margarita and poured another from the pitcher.

"Come on Chelsea. Please don't do that. You know how much I love working with you. If you quit, I'll have to quit too. The only reason I've tolerated Orlon is because of you."

The Colgate smile and his flattering words were hard to resist, but this time she really meant it.

"Brad, you know I feel the same way. But seriously, I'm done. It's like he's convinced because I'm a woman I should be seen and not heard. I can't take it any more."

She flicked a blond curve of bangs off her eyelid. "What are we supposed to do about the Alzheimer's vaccine? Does he think we're going to falsify the reports just so he can look good to the investors?"

"I think that's exactly what he expects."

"Well he can go straight to hell, Brad. I'm not going to risk my professional reputation to make Orlon happy. If we lose the funding, we lose the funding."

"I hear you." He sipped his drink.

"And what about the other teams? From what I heard in the meeting today, most of what the company is working on is coming out with only so-so results right now. Maybe I should be looking for another job regardless of what I think of Orlon."

"Well, that's probably a little extreme. All companies go through extensive research and development periods in between coming up with blockbusters, you know that."

"Yeah, I do, but it's been quite a while since BioGen has rolled out a blockbuster. If you ask me, it's largely due to Orlon driving the train. I've only worked for the company three years, and Orlon has been in charge the whole time. I don't have anything to measure our performance against other than the competition. From where I sit, we've got trouble."

"You really think so?"

She shrugged, "I don't have my crystal ball with me today, but yeah, this is the fourth company I've worked for in the past twelve years. It looks to me like we're headed for trouble, no doubt about it. The first company I worked for did end up folding. For the same reasons we're talking about here—bad management and bad timing on the projects. The other two are going stronger than ever, but they have strong management."

"This is the second company I've worked at in California." Brad drained his drink, poured another. "The last company lost most of their investors. I had to move on."

She shook her head and gazed through the window at the valley below them as she said, "I ended up at BioGen because I want to focus my work on plants, so I made the switch, even though the money isn't great. Looks like I'm going to be making another change. The sooner the better." There were not enough margaritas in the world to make up for dealing with Orlon every day. Life should be easier. She was doing everything she was supposed to do—to the best of her ability—and nothing was going her way.

He reached out and rubbed the back of her free hand. "I hate to think about not seeing your beautiful face every day."

She looked quietly back at him, knowing she shouldn't encourage him but it was hard not to. Hard for a lot of reasons. After a long moment she poured herself another drink and said, "Maybe we'll get lucky and I'll find a company that's looking for two bioengineers."

CHAPTER 11

Ethan's stomach felt like an open wound and could tolerate only water. It had been a grueling sixteen hour flight from Johannesburg to Miami and although he couldn't wait to get off the plane and stretch his legs he was also dreading it.

"Are you sure you're okay? You look a little peaked to me." His dad glanced at him with concern. He had watched him turn away the lunch and dinner trays. Ethan could see from his dad's face he'd better get his act together quick. He had never been in any kind of real trouble with his parents before and he sure didn't want to start now. The trip to Africa had been expensive and he didn't want to ruin it on the tail end. He mentally kicked himself as he gulped more water, slid the magazine back into the pouch.

At long last the plane's door opened and passengers slowly shuffled forward. A thin film of sweat rose on his brow as he pulled his carry-on bag out of the overhead bin and set it on the floor. He watched as his dad did the same. They shuffled forward another foot, then another. His stomach began to rumble and he hoped he wouldn't need to use the bathroom before they got off the plane and through customs.

Their suitcase wheels made small popping noises as they walked through the retractable walkway and into the Miami airport. People spread out into separate lines for customs inspections up ahead of them. He cleared his throat and swiped a hand across his brow. He'd read that customs officials kept an eye out for signs of nervousness. Sweating was one of them.

"Are you sure you're okay?" His dad asked as they approached the customs station.

"Yeah, I'll be fine. I just got a little air sick I guess." A customs official waved his dad over and took his passport, examined it closely then handed it back as a second official waved Ethan over into his line. He extended his passport, accepted it back and watched as the man pushed his suitcase on down to the next official.

"Do you have anything to declare?" The redheaded woman asked him as she stared into his eyes then unzipped his bag as he stood in front of her.

"Only a handful of rocks I brought back as souvenirs." He stopped speaking and watched as her hands unzipped the bag.

She ran a finger along the edges of the case, lifted clothing and felt under it. She slid his toiletry bag out, removed each item then placed them back in the leather case. Rubber gloved hands lifted the small zip lock bag from the mesh pouch on the top of the suitcase. She held it up, examined the bag of rocks, turned it over, looked at the other side. She glanced at him once more then put the rocks back in the suitcase and motioned him to move on.

His breath came out in a whoosh as he zipped up the case and joined his dad.

"Ready, Sport? Let's catch the shuttle over to the hotel. I want to hit the gym as soon as we get checked in. I need to work the kinks out after that flight."

His dad had planned their trip, coming and going, so that they stayed overnight in Miami, close to the airport. They were facing another eight hours of traveling tomorrow to get back to California and taking an early flight out. Ethan's spirits lifted the moment they cleared customs.

CHAPTER 12

"Stop it Lily!" Ethan shoulder-bounced his little sister away. "Cut it out, that hurts!" He had had enough of her seven-year old fists and knew he'd be in serious trouble if he hit her back. "Mom! Tell Lily to stop hitting me or I swear I'm not responsible for what's gonna happen," he shouted toward the staircase as he continued to fend off his little sister's hands from the TV remote.

"You sthop it, Ethan! You have a TV in your room, I don't!" Lily jerked at his sleeve, trying to get his hand closer to her.

"Mom!" No answer.

It finally dawned on him that if he stood up his height would put her at an extreme disadvantage. He stalked off toward the kitchen with the remote in his hand.

"Ethan—that'sth not fair! Justh becausthe you're bigger doesn't mean you get to be in charge of the TV!" Lily stomped her foot then chased after him as he swung into the kitchen.

"Stop it, brat!" He swiped at her, not really trying to hit her, but he was done dealing with the pest. "You've had the TV for the last six days, Lily, it's my turn."

"You got to go to Africa, I didn't!"

"You can go on trips with Dad when you're older, so get over it, creep."

Ethan had had enough. He swung the fridge open, yanked out a soda then snagged a bag of chips and headed back out to the family room and the big-screen TV. He plopped on the sofa, pointed the remote at the TV and switched to a sci-fi movie.

"You're a great big JERK!" Lily hollered and stomped off.

* * *

Ten minutes later the master bedroom door opened and Craig stepped out with a grin on his face as he looked back over his shoulder.

"I'll put the lasagna in the oven and make a salad. Take your time."

Chelsea laughed and turned the shower on as he shut the door. A minute later he was in the kitchen wearing a smile and old blue jeans when his daughter came running in.

"Daddy, why isth Ethan sthuch a big jerk?"

He snagged the Stouffer's box from the freezer, looked at his daughter as he thought a moment.

"Well, he's a guy, plus he's your brother, so that automatically makes him a jerk to you." His grin widened as he watched her scowl.

"Can we put him up for adoption or sthomething?" She was serious.

"Uh, no, Sweetheart. But relax, you only have to put up with him for another year then he's going to college. We'll be lucky to see him after that."

"What are you talking about, Daddy?" Her blue eyes grew huge, rosebud mouth hanging open as she stared back at him.

He blinked at her, realizing she was only in second grade and the idea of college life had not entered her mind yet.

"Well, if he gets into Berkley he'll be staying there while he goes to school. That's a pretty long drive from here. We'll only see him on the weekends, maybe not even then if he gets a job." His words drifted off along with the thought of no longer being able to see his son whenever he chose to. It was hard to believe he'd grown up so fast.

Chelsea swung into the kitchen, grinning, "Let's have wine."

"Mommy, isth Ethan really going to be in college?" Lily's voice rang with skepticism.

"Yes, Honey. He'll be a senior in the fall. After that is college."

She stared back at them then with solemn eyes announced, "Well, he'sth sthill a jerk!"

Craig watched as his daughter stomped out of the kitchen. Chelsea's puzzled look turned into a smile when the wine cork popped.

* * *

Lily watched as her brother held the small brown ball under his desk lamp and examined it with the magnifying glass. The one he wouldn't let her use. She held back a giggle as his brows furrowed and he sniffed at the ball like a dog. Then he did something really weird – he took a smelly sneaker out of the closet and dropped the ball into it. It almost made her gag watching him. His basketball shoes were gross-stinky and she could smell them through the crack in the doorway. He put the sneaker back in the closet and shut the door. That ball must be important if her brother hid it.

He sat back down at the desk and stared at his laptop screen a minute then started typing. She watched a little longer but it looked like he was going to type for a while. Boring. She slipped from the doorway and tiptoed back down the hall to her bedroom, thinking about his bus leaving earlier than hers in the morning.

CHAPTER 13

Ann Mathers glanced at her watch as she hustled back to the nurses' station. She had two hours left on her shift and had not been able to take so much as a bathroom break yet. They were short-handed on the floor and the nurses were scrambling to keep up with the usual patient needs and doctors' demands.

She popped onto the rolling chair behind the desk and began writing notes on a patient's chart. Her cell phone rang two second after her butt hit the chair. She glanced at the caller ID and rubbed a hand over her eyes, frowning as tears formed.

"Oh God, please, just two more hours, that's all I ask," her quiet voice came out a helpless whine. Two hours to get through her shift and then she could pick Steve up from his after-school care program. From the caller ID it looked like it wasn't meant to be.

"Hello?" Ann spoke quietly, glancing down the hall.

"Ann? This is Judy. I'm afraid you'll need to pick Steve up early today. He's had a problem with his bowels again and unfortunately, it's bad enough that wet wipes and a change of clothes won't work."

Silence drifted out of the phone as she thought for a second. Maybe her mom could pick Steve up. She couldn't recall what her mother's schedule was that day but she would give her a quick call. Either way, Steve had to be picked up.

"I'm sorry Judy. My mom or I will be there in the next fifteen minutes."

She let out a heavy sigh as she thumbed her mom's speed dial button and listened to it ring. She winced when it went to voice mail, knowing she'd have no choice but to leave work early. Again. The beep came, "Hi, Mom, it's me. Steve's had another accident and I'm heading to the school to pick him up…unless you happen to be available and can call me back in the next five minutes." She looked at her watch, "It's four-o-five right now…thanks." Another heavy sigh escaped as she put the phone on top of her purse and her eyes zipped over the desk.

Notes for the chart in front of her had to be finished before she could leave and she hurriedly wrote in it until a woman stepped up to the desk.

"Excuse me. Could someone please come and check on my mother? She's having pain in her side and I'm not sure whether it's serious." The woman gave her an anxious look.

Ann's headache ratcheted up a notch as she looked back at the woman. "What room is your mother in?" The woman gave the number and Ann did her best to give a reassuring smile.

"Okay, we'll get someone in to take a look at her as soon as we can."

She let out a tense breath and looked down at the chart, scribbling faster, hoping the desk phone wouldn't ring.

The head nurse stepped into the station, a tired look on her face. "Has this been the day from hell or what?"

Ann winced at her words as Linda pulled a chair out and sat down beside her to make notes on a patient chart.

She swallowed then said, "Linda, I'm really sorry, but I have to leave in a few minutes. Steve has had another accident at school and I can't reach my mom. Judy said he's in too much of a mess to get by with changing clothes. I can't leave him there like that. I'm so sorry."

Her palms grew sweaty as Linda stared back at her. She could see her boss trying to hide her anger but there was no mistaking the upset underneath the kind words she spoke.

"I'm sorry to hear that Ann. I guess you don't have any choice." Linda was the floor coordinator as well as her supervisor. They would now be down to only two nurses for the next two hours. Ann knew what a mess she was leaving them in but had no choice.

"Okay, tell me where you're at with the charts and then you can get out of here." Linda frowned at the stack that remained to be completed. Two were Ann's and five would have been the responsibility of the nurses who'd called in sick.

Ann swiped a lock of hair behind her ear and explained what was needed to complete the patient care routines for that shift then told her about the woman's mother in room 310. The clock in her head ticked away as the guilt of making her son wait washed through her heart.

CHAPTER 14

Craig flipped through the last page of the fax his field man had sent over. It was a status report on the latest bluff erosion following the second storm that had hit while he was in Africa. From the report, it looked like they had no choice but to shut the Great Highway down.

He laid the stack of papers on the desk and glanced around the den. Working from home on a Monday seemed strange to him but at least it gave him a chance to really use the space. This room had sold him on the house. Big double windows looked out on the back yard. It was a bright sunny day and he was having a hard time concentrating on paperwork.

His mind reeled out to Ocean Beach as he envisioned standing at the top of the bluffs, looking down at the now-extreme erosion Mark had highlighted in the fax. He wished Mark had gone into more detail about the extent of the pipeline's additional exposure. He reached out for his cell to give him a call. It rang before he could hit speed dial. It appeared to be an international call. He looked at the time, three-thirty.

"Damn!" He jumped out of the chair, realizing he should have left ten minutes ago to pick Lily up. The call went to voice mail as he grabbed his keys and rushed out the door.

Five minutes later he pulled up in front of Lily's school. She waved from beneath the portico the kids were lined under for parent pickup. Lily could have ridden the bus home but she'd sweet-talked him into picking her up. He rarely got a chance to and couldn't resist her gap-toothed smile when she'd asked that morning.

"Hey Lilybit. How was school?" He took her back pack and she hopped in the car.

"Hi Daddy. Sthchool was okay. Chrissthy threw up all over her jeans and went home."

"She didn't get any on you, did she?" Her nose wrinkled as he watched her face.

"Grossth, Daddy! No. She only threw up on hersthelf. I knew she was gonna barf 'causthe she drank chocolate milk at lunch. I told her not to." She rolled her eyes in exasperation.

He pulled away from the curb. "You hungry? Want to stop and get something at McDonald's on the way home?"

"Yes! Can we?"

"You bet. That reminds me, what should we make for dinner tonight?"

"Sthpaghetti! You're good at that Daddy."

"Sounds like a plan, Princess. Spaghetti it is."

A small fry and a chocolate milkshake later, Craig was back in the den reading through his work emails. An update report had come in from the oceanographer. It didn't provide any better news than Mark's report had. If anything, it was worse. He pulled out his phone to give Ron a call and realized he'd forgotten to check his voice mail in the hurly burly of picking Lily up. He had two waiting. The first was from the international caller and nothing but static. The second was Ron, asking him to call about the report.

"Daddy, I'm going out on the swings." Lily popped her head in the den as his thumb hit the speed dial button.

"Try not to get muddy. We have to pick your brother up from basketball practice in an hour."

"Okay, Daddy."

Blond curls flew as she took off and the call was answered.

"This is Ron."

"Hey, Ron. Do you have a minute to go over the report you sent me today? Is it really as bad as it sounds?"

* * *

"Let's go outside Bell. We're going to plant this big seed." Pausing at the back door she lifted the sphere from her pocket and let the dog sniff at it a moment. Bell let out a whine and licked it. Giggles rang at the sensation from the dog's tongue on her hand. She slid the door open and raced outside.

The garden was big and she stood considering the best spot. Her mom was kinda fussy about it, maybe she shouldn't plant the seed there. She glanced to the back of the yard and eyed the fence next to her play fort.

"Come on Bell, we'll plant it over there." She ran to the back with the small spade in her hand and plopped down on her knees. The spade had a sharp point and the dry ground came out easily with a couple scoops.

"What do you think, Bell? Isth that deep enough?"

She laughed as the dog gave a short bark in reply.

"Okay, me too." She dropped the sphere in the hole, and scooped dirt over it.

"There, that isth perfect." She stood and brushed palms against the side of her dress, looked at the dog and said, "I'll be right back, I have to get sthome water."

She turned and flew back to the house as Bell squatted over the freshly planted sphere and gave it a sprinkle of her own.

CHAPTER 15

The men sat at a window table covered with expensive white linen and watched as the wine steward poured a dram of the Rutherford cabernet sauvignon into a crystal goblet. It was an exquisite red from the Beaulieu vineyard and he knew from his sources that it was William Wadsworth's favorite wine at the moment. Orlon smiled as he sniffed the sample then sipped. He nodded at the steward and watched him pour out two glasses.

"Thank you for having dinner with me this evening, William. I want you to have a personal update on our progress before the shareholders meeting." Orlon gave the elegant man a smile then launched into a quick and sunny thumbnail sketch of the status on two of their most promising projects. He spoke in a quiet stream until the waiter stepped up to take their order.

"We'll have the pâté de foie gras to start, followed with the French onion soup. Then the chateaubriand, prepared medium. And bring a side of asparagus with it. Thank you." He gave the waiter a dismissive nod then turned his attention back to his important guest.

Not only was Wadsworth a board member, he was BioGen's largest shareholder. The man was also his preferred person to curry favor with because they shared similar gastronomic pleasures. The difference was Wadsworth's restraint and regular exercise at his various exclusive clubs around the world. It wasn't easy finding someone who still enjoyed red meat without remorse. Not to mention the hollandaise sauce and the wine.

Wadsworth placed the napkin in his lap and smiled at Orlon. "I appreciate your taking the time to update me. I prefer not being blindsided in meetings, even with good news. I'm glad to hear that we're making progress on the malaria drug. How long do you think it will be before your scientists have been able to scale up the plant's production of the chemical needed?"

Orlon blinked back at him. Wadsworth was no scientist but he was a smart, well-educated shareholder. He should have known better than to assume the man would take his pep talk at face value. He forced a grin he didn't feel and told the billionaire what he wanted to hear.

"I expect we will reach viable levels within the next three months." It was crucial to achieve newsworthy results during the fiscal year. BioGen's stock value had slowly slipped over the past eighteen months and the company desperately needed a shot in its Wall Street arm to gain momentum. With the prolific competition it was not an easy thing to do. Shucking and jiving were a given part of managing a company that relied on market opinion and investor cash flow but, at the end of the day, he knew he had to bring new and important products to the table or he'd be out of a job come January.

Wadsworth took another sip of the wine then threw him a curve ball he hadn't seen coming. "What is the progress on the Alzheimer's vaccine? My wife and I were just discussing it with some of our friends last evening. Did you know they're now saying one out of eight baby boomers will begin suffering from Alzheimer's in the next five years? They're anticipating the number of people suffering from the disease will more than double by 2050."

The investor leaned forward slightly as his voice dropped, "My wife's father has recently shown early signs of the disease. He's going in for testing next week. Helen is a mess with worry and she's pushing all my buttons to get a cure out of BioGen."

Orlon took a sip of wine, stalling. He knew if he was going to fudge he should make it in a pan coated with facts. It would be more believable that way. Reading volumes of news reports from the medical and scientific fields each day paid off in a moment like this. Knowledge and confidence were needed for an executive to stay on top of shareholders like Wadsworth.

A grin spread on his face as the article he'd read that morning flashed through his mind and inspiration bloomed. "I have very good news. In fact, I've deliberately saved the best for last." He rapped out a statistical nugget of his own.

"Did you know a report came out today that shows autism cases in children have increased seventy-eight percent since 2002?"

He let the data hang in the air a moment then plunged in with both pom poms.

"Not only has our work with the tomato vaccine progressed better than we hoped, one of our top scientists has discovered just this week that the Alzheimer's vaccine may also affect autism."

"That's fantastic! Wadsworth beamed at him, "What's the scientist's name?"

"Brad Peterson. The man's a genius in the lab, I tell you. We're very lucky to have him."

He paused a beat then heaped cream on top of the mythical pie he was serving.

"You know, as happy as I am to see BioGen produce a prevention for Alzheimer's, I am beyond delighted to be part of the team who may very well bring an end to the suffering of so many children." His volume dropped a notch, "Society as a whole is much more eager to get behind cures for children than the elderly. New funding should be a breeze once we're able to make the announcement."

Orlon settled his girth against the seat and basked in the pleased glow of the happy shareholder while the waiter served their dinner.

CHAPTER 16

The tomato smashed against the side of the house. It hit the patio door first, splattering wide. The tender flesh broke into large ricocheting missiles. Juice and seeds raced down in bright red streaks against the glass, swirled and dripped down the beige stucco.

She turned and looked at Craig with fire in her eyes as he attempted to keep pace with her across the yard.

Craig reached up and swiped at a blob of seeds sliding down his cheek. "Chelsea, wait."

"That wasn't our agreement and you know it," she choked out.

"Chelsea, I'm really sorry, but *come on*. No one knew that second storm would blow in and wipe out most of the bluff at Ocean Beach overnight. We've got to get an emergency plan drawn up. It can't wait. I have to go, that's my job."

"Why can't someone else cover through the rest of the week like your office planned on? Are you saying you're the only engineer that can develop an emergency plan at your company? Somehow I doubt that, Craig. Global Systems is a world-wide company. I'm not stupid. You need to get real about the choices you're making. I'm tired of asking you."

She turned and yanked the slider open, stalked into the kitchen. The basket of vegetables hit the table with an unbalanced thud. The kitchen faucet protested with a squeak as she jerked it on to wash her hands. Hairs bristled on her neck as he walked up behind her.

"Don't! Just don't," she bit out as he reached for her. From the corner of her eye she saw him pull his hand back as she slapped the faucet off and turned to the paper towel rack. She forced herself to slow down and take a deep breath.

"Chelsea, please don't do this. I spent eight days straight at home before we left for Africa. I've been home two days since then. I only need to go up to San Francisco for the rest of this week. I should be home Friday evening."

"And that would put us where, Craig? Back to our usual schedule?" She didn't attempt to keep the ice out of her voice. "How many ways do I have to ask you to make our family a priority? When do I get the option of making my job a priority?" She could feel the last strands of her temper snapping, knowing he would leave tomorrow regardless of what she said.

"I'm going over to Ann's." She snatched up the basket on her way out the door, feeling the anger sweeping off her like a jet trail on fire.

A minute later she stood on her neighbor's doorstep, breathing in and out a couple times before she rang the bell. Ann opened the door with a tired smile.

"Hi Chelsea. We're in the kitchen, come on back." Ann led the way through the living room. It was furnished for comfort rather than style and neat as a pin.

"Hi Steve." She stepped over to the kitchen table and set the basket down. He didn't respond, just continued to slowly rock himself forward and back on the edge of the wooden chair, staring at the place mat in front of him.

"I'm sorry to interrupt your evening, Ann. I brought some cucumbers and corn for you."

"Thank you, and don't worry, you're not interrupting a thing. Please, sit. I've got dinner under control already because I had to pick Steve up early from school. We're waiting for the casserole to bake. I've been puttering around in the kitchen because it's where he seems to want to be this time of day. Would you like a drink?"

"I'd love a glass of wine or a beer if you've got any."

"Is chardonnay okay?" Ann turned to the fridge and slid a bottle out then plucked two juice glasses from the cupboard and joined her at the table.

"I wish I'd known you had to pick Steve up early today. I could have done it for you because I left work early myself."

"The kids aren't sick are they?"

"No. It's me. I'm sick of my job." Chelsea gave her a lopsided grin. "I don't mean to unload on you Ann. I know you have all you can handle keeping up with your own stuff. I just needed to get out of the house for a few minutes."

"Sounds like it was a tough day on both sides of our fence. Work was crazy for me and then I had to leave early. You know how that goes. I really need my job, but I wouldn't blame Linda if she fires me. This is the third time I've had to leave early this month." A sigh escaped her lips as she glanced at Steve. "That's why we never go on vacation—I don't dare use the time to have fun. I've got to save it for days like this because I punch a time clock."

"I'm sorry to hear that Ann. Call me first the next time, okay?" She scooted the glass around in a circle on the table then said, "Speaking of clocks, Craig just told me he's leaving for San Francisco again tomorrow morning."

"I thought you said he promised to stay home all this week?"

"He did. But, there's been an escalation up at Ocean Beach and he says they can't possibly implement an emergency plan without him." She didn't try to keep the scorn from her voice but she kept the volume down for Steve's sake. Loud voices upset him.

"I'm sorry to hear that Chelsea. I'm sure he's really good at his job."

"You're trying to give him the benefit of the doubt, just like I have for years. But enough is enough. Things are tense for me at work right now. If Craig is out of town I don't have the option of working late, so that makes even more pressure for me." She stared at her place mat without realizing it. "I'm afraid this might be the end of what started out as a really great marriage. I'm tired of asking myself, 'Why be married without the husband?' Plus I'm really tired of being angry at him for being gone all the time."

She mentally winced at realizing she'd just done what she'd told herself she wouldn't.

"Enough about me. Why did you pick Steve up early?"

"Bathroom problems again. I feel so bad for him. He must have been embarrassed. Judy said two of the boys told her Steve wouldn't come out of the restroom. She had to get the janitor to go in and get him. He had messed himself pretty badly and there were kids in the hallway when the janitor had to force him out and down to the nurse's office." Ann swiped at a tear as she looked across at her son.

Chelsea reached out and gripped Ann's hand, held it for a moment as she looked at her friend. "Listen, from now on, you call me first before you take off work early again, all right? I really want to be here for you and the only way I can do that is if you let me. Okay?"

Ann slowly nodded and smiled back, "Okay, thanks." The oven timer dinged.

Chelsea stood up. "Thanks again for the wine. Listen, why don't you and Steve come over for dinner tomorrow night? I'll do something simple, say around six-thirty?"

"That would be great. We'd love to."

"Okay, we'll see you then. I'd better get back." She gave Ann a quick hug. "Bye Steve."

He sat in silence, staring at the place mat as he rocked.

CHAPTER 17

Craig stood on the beach, surveying the small remaining section of the bluff. The second storm had caused record-breaking destruction at Ocean Beach. The damage was even worse than the reports had indicated in his opinion. Most of the pipeline was exposed. It would take only a large object riding one of the huge waves to compromise the entire sewage system. That would be a catastrophe.

His cell phone buzzed in his pocket, "This is Craig."

"Mr. Noble?" a male voice asked.

"Yes. How can I help you?"

"This is Jeff Connor, the manager of Wonderstone Mines."

"Well, hello. Thanks again for giving us the tour last week."

"Unfortunately, that is why I'm calling. One of our spheres has gone missing. We haven't been able to locate it since the day you and your son toured our facility." His reserved tone was quiet, grave even. "I hate to ask, but did you or your son remove one of our spheres?"

Craig's eyes widened and he pulled the phone away from his ear a moment, stared at it, placed it back against his head. The wind seemed to grow colder as he struggled for calm.

"No, Mr. Connor. We certainly did not take your sphere. You guys had some kind of an emergency that day and we had to leave in a hurry. Your secretary rushed us out of there. The box of spheres was still on the table when we left." He did his best to keep a helpful tone in his voice. The man had done them a favor allowing them to personally handle the spheres. If Craig were not a geologist with one of the largest engineering firms in the world they would never have had the opportunity.

"I don't want to offend you, but we're having difficulty finding the sphere. Would you please double check with your son and then give me a call back?"

"Of course. I'll speak with him tonight and give you a call tomorrow. But I'm sure he didn't take it. Maybe it rolled off the table or something?"

"I can assure you that did not happen, Mr. Noble. I will wait for your call tomorrow. Good day."

The phone clicked in his ear as his co-worker stepped up.

Ron looked pissed off. "Here we are again. Are the powers-that-be ever going to get their act together and let us go to work on this?"

Craig slid the phone in his pocket, thinking back on Ethan collecting rocks at the Impodimo Lodge. His pulse ratcheted up while he stood wondering where this was headed. A seagull flew past, forcing his mind back to the job site. He'd have to deal with the problems at home later.

Scanning the length of exposed pipeline in front of them, Craig said, "Somebody better step up quick, or there's going to be no turning back on this one, that's for damn sure."

CHAPTER 18

"Come on, Sthevie, we'll go on the sthwings." Lily slid the door open and he silently followed her out.

"I can't get over what a magic spell she casts over him." Ann smiled, watching her son follow Lily to the back yard. "I swear, I can take him anywhere without a problem as long as she's with us."

"I'm glad she has someone to play with right next door. You're welcome to borrow her anytime." Chelsea smiled then asked, "You want iced tea or wine?"

"Oh, wine, definitely wine." Ann laughed and leaned back on the chair while Chelsea poured two glasses. "What's for dinner? Do you need any help?"

"We're having baked chicken, homemade gluten-free mac and cheese, green beans and salad. It's all ready, we're just waiting on the chicken."

"That sounds perfect. Thank you for the invite. It's nice to get a break from cooking."

"I'm happy to have some grown-up company. We should do this more often."

Chelsea knew Ann didn't have the option of picking up fast food. She couldn't purchase much in the way of frozen foods either. Preservatives and additives were a problem for autistic children. She had to make everything from scratch. To top it off, she also had to keep his intake of flour products down due to his intestinal problems, so sandwiches were out also.

"So, did work go better for you today?" Chelsea asked.

"Yes, thank God. That reminds me, you should see the new patient we got today. He looks like a movie star. His face is so familiar to me, but I can't quite place him."

"Oh, really? What's he look like?"

"He's a cross between Bradley Cooper and Hugh Jackman, I swear! There's something about him that makes me tingle every time I see him. Nursing duties have never been such a pleasure." Ann's laugh was wonderful to hear.

"Is he single? Maybe you should slip him your number."

Ann's smile started to fade. "I wish. But what would be the point? No man wants to take on my life. From what the doctors tell me, Steve and I are going to be roommates forever."

"Oh, Ann. There are lots of really nice guys out there who I'm sure would be understanding. The cutie in room three-twenty might be one of them. Besides, Steve is easy to be around. He's so quiet. At least he's not hyperactive like most kids these days, running around shouting and breaking stuff." A second too late she realized her attempt to encourage her friend might be hurting her feelings instead of helping. She quickly steered the focus back to the maybe-movie star.

"So have you given Mr. Tall-Dark-and-Handsome a bath yet?"

Ann's smile came back in a hurry. "Not yet. We don't do baths until a patient has been with us for a couple days. But who knows? I might get lucky later this week."

* * *

"Ohhh, wow. Look at my plant Sthevie!" Lily squealed as they rounded the play fort attached to the swing set. A grin spread across her face as she approached the two-foot tall plant. Its spiky leaves were dark green, almost black.

She bent down to examine the florescent orange and yellow berries hanging from the stems.

Steve stood silently beside her as she plucked a berry and looked closely at it. She sniffed it and smelled oranges, gave it a lick and caught a bit of sweetness.

Shrugging her shoulders, she popped it in her mouth.

"These are really good Sthevie! Try one."

She broke off a small bunch of the berries and held one out to him.

Without looking at her, he slowly reached out, gently took the berry from her palm and placed it in his mouth. A smile began to form on his face as he chewed. He held out his hand for more.

Lily giggled, "I know! They tasthe justh like orange sherbert, don't they?"

She put the small bunch of berries in his hand and plucked another cluster for herself.

They stood nibbling for a minute, then she said, "Come on, let's sthwing. We can eat more of theesthe later."

* * *

"Hey, Mom. Hi Ann."

Ethan smiled at the women as he stepped over to the fridge and pulled a Coke out. "How's Steve doing?"

"Hi Ethan. Steve's doing okay, thanks for asking. How about you? How was Africa?"

"Africa was good. You wouldn't believe all the animals we saw. Our room at the lodge was really awesome. I'll show you some pictures later if you want."

"That's great, Ethan. You're really blessed to have gone. And I'd love to see the pictures after dinner. Did you get your essay finished yet? I'd like to read it if you're willing to let me see it."

"Not yet, but I started on it a couple days ago. I should be finished in a day or two, and sure, I'd love to have you read it, thanks." He glanced at his mom. "When's dinner?"

"In ten minutes. And no, I don't need any help, but thanks for asking." She gave him a tongue-in-cheek smile.

He laughed and said, "Don't worry, I'll do the dishes. I'm gonna go watch TV."

He swung through the kitchen door and headed for the family room. His cell phone buzzed as he picked up the TV remote.

"Hey, Dad. How's it going?"

"Things are pretty bad up here, unfortunately. Most of the remainder of the highway got washed out and a majority of the pipeline is exposed. The road and the beach are going to be shut down for quite a while." Silence spooled out of the phone. "Listen,

I need to ask you a question. I got a call today from Jeff Connor. You know, the manager from the mine."

Ethan's heart hammered, he said nothing, waiting for the question he knew was coming.

"Connor called because one of their spheres is missing."

Two beats of quiet leaked over him as he waited for his dad to continue.

"You wouldn't happen to know anything about that would you?"

A thick fog of trouble filled the room as his throat tightened and his mouth went dry.

"No," he croaked out. "What happened?"

Sweat formed under his arms and the Coke suddenly tasted way too sweet. He set it on the end table and held his breath.

"Connor said they've been missing a sphere since the day we were there. I said I'd ask you about it but I'm sure you didn't take it. I told him to check around, see if one rolled off the table, but he's sure that didn't happen."

A black hole circled Ethan as he hustled up the stairs, phone bobbling against his ear. He swung into his room and shut the door, locked the knob. Heavy silence dripped with his sweat as he moved to the closet. He couldn't think of a thing to say—he could only think of checking the shoe.

"Okay, I'll give Connor a call tomorrow and let him know I talked to you about it and we don't have the sphere."

Ethan couldn't tell from his dad's tone whether he believed him or not.

"How's your sister doing?"

"She's okay." His voice came out in a wheeze as he fought to control his breathing.

"How's your mom? I know she was upset when I left this morning. Sorry about that."

Like a window flung open to a breeze he responded, "You know Mom. She's rolling with it now. Ann and Steve are here for dinner." He tried his best to sound hurried, "Listen, Dad. I gotta go help in the kitchen, okay?"

"Okay. Give Lily a kiss for me. I love you. Good night."

He realized he was still holding the dead phone to his ear as he bent over and picked the sneaker up. He set it on the desk then tilted the sneaker so the sphere would roll out. Nothing. He gave it a small shake. Nothing. He tilted the sneaker up to the light and strained the shoe's tongue back to see to the bottom of the toe area. Nothing.

"Lily!" He growled out to the empty room.

His pulse raced even faster as he realized not only was the sphere gone, his little sister could expose his crime. Panic surged and he fought it down. Maybe he'd been absent-minded the last time he'd looked at the sphere and had stuck it in his desk or something?

Drawers yanked open, a frantic search through the contents of each one. Nothing. He paused again, thinking hard, sure he remembered putting it in the shoe.

Grimacing at realizing he had to figure out a way to ask Lily about the sphere without her ratting on him, he walked to the window and looked out at the back yard. His sister was flying as high as the swing would go. Steve sat beside her, his swing barely moving. For a moment he envied his little sister's innocence then he snapped out of it and ground his teeth on the way to her room. She probably hid the stupid thing in her dollhouse. He searched for ten minutes without luck on his side, fear creeping in, knowing he was screwed.

Back in his room he sat down on the edge of the bed, stomach rumbling as he thought about the situation. Did Connor have proof that he'd taken the sphere? Maybe Emily had seen him take it? Or maybe Connor had called his dad because they were the only ones that handled the spheres that day? The box had still been on the table when they left. He tried to tell himself to chill out. Maybe he just needed to maintain a calm front and it would blow over.

"Ethan, dinner!"

He jerked at the sound of Mom hollering up the stairs. He blew out the breath he'd been holding and stood up, appetite completely gone.

CHAPTER 19

Fandango's was as close to a five-star restaurant as he feasibly dared write off for dinner with an employee. It was his favorite place when on his own dime. He knew the menu like a bird knows its nest and that a businessman had to be careful when making reservations.

It was popular for its mixture of cozy rooms combined with larger, more open areas. He did not want his words overheard and requested a table at the back of the main dining room. The combined volume of the diners' voices would cover their conversation.

He'd told his guest to meet him at seven and Orlon arrived early to settle in and get a leg up on the bar tab. With two sips left in his glass, he spotted Brad Peterson heading toward him, led by the owner's beautiful wife. A grunt escaped his lips at witnessing what phenomenal good looks could do for a man. He'd been coming here for five years, spent a lot of money and tipped well but the owner's wife had yet to lead him to his table. He bit down on the thought as Brad reached him, smiling at the woman who reluctantly turned and went back to the front.

"Thank you for joining me tonight." Orlon gave him a small nod and watched to see how Brad would handle himself in the setting. In spite of the man's incredible good looks, Orlon had a sneaking suspicion he came from very humble roots.

"Thank you for the invitation. I've heard a lot about this place but it's my first time here." Brad flashed a grin as he opened his napkin and placed it in his lap. He leaned back in his chair, matching Orlon's posture—a relaxed slump.

"Take a quick look at the menu. I come here all the time so I already know what I'm having." He nodded at the black and gold board on Brad's plate.

Orlon was very curious to learn more about the man he was attempting to climb in bed with. Once the sheets were turned back, there would be no getting out of it. Not until the end game. His choices were limited and he was going with his instincts. It didn't hurt that the man was a walking candy store to look at.

Brad gestured with his palm toward the menu, "Please, if you're a regular, order for me. I'm sure whatever you recommend will be excellent."

Score one for Romeo. Orlon enjoyed ordering for his guests and preferred that everyone at the table eat the same thing through all courses. It made everything so much easier, especially at the end of the evening.

The waiter stepped up to take their order. "We'll start with the escargots, then the Caesar salad. For the entrée we'll have the double lamb chops. Please bring an extra caddy of sauce and a side of the curried vegetables if you would. Then we'll see if we have room left for dessert."

He looked across at Brad. "Do you enjoy wine? Good."

With a sniff he said, "Bring a bottle of the Carmel Road pino noir with dinner, please. We'll have a cocktail first. Brad, what would you like?"

"Is that a martini you're finishing?"

"Yes, a dirty Ketel One."

"I'll have the same, thanks. Keep things simple that way."

Orlon studied his guest—the man had a movie star grin and a congenial personality. A hard to resist combo. Brad was the perfect dinner companion so far, but the jury would be out until after the entree. A person could learn a lot about someone from his table manners. That was one of the things he enjoyed most about Fandango's—it had a deceptively homey ambience. The rustic charm of the rock and plaster walls and large mullioned picture windows put people in a relaxed mood. But the place settings and linens rivaled any five-star restaurant and the menu featured mostly European dishes. Breeding would tell.

"I invited you to dine this evening so we can talk privately about how best to approach the testing and reports that are needed for the board meeting. What are your thoughts on finding a parallel component between Alzheimer's and autism."

He watched Brad's forehead crease in response to the unexpected question. The server brought their drinks along with a basket of fresh bread as Orlon waited for an answer. Brad sipped at the martini a moment, stalling.

"I'll have to do some research on autism before I can give you any concrete data on possible parallels. We know from Dr. Alzheimer's work that the disease is caused by the accumulation of human beta-amyloid, a toxic fibrous protein in the brain. The protein fibers lead to the death of neurons." Brad took another sip of his icy drink. "That's the focus of our work with the transgenic tomato vaccine—we're trying to achieve a reduction of beta-amyloid through the immune system. We believe that will slow or even eliminate the degeneration of the nervous system."

"Yes, I'm aware of that."

Orlon shifted his weight to his other hip, unable to hide his irritation at the man assuming he was unaware of the basic premise of their project.

The waiter approached with their escargots as he reminded himself to tread carefully with this man. He had to have those reports, whether they were based on facts or not, and he had a limited amount of time to get them generated. It would buy them another six months of funding and guarantee Orlon's sizeable annual bonus. His goal tonight was to ensure Brad was firmly on board with generating the necessary reports.

He studied his guest a moment as they started on the garlicky snails. It was almost disappointing when Brad turned the underplate and plucked the tiny fork from its hiding spot. He'd been sure the man would use the salad fork instead.

Regardless of whether his dinner companion would be willing to cooperate, Orlon knew the real catch in his plan was Chelsea Noble. The woman was an obstinate Amazon. She was brilliant in the lab but useless in the board room because she refused to roll with the times. Everything was black and white with her.

To survive in the corporate jungle one needed the ability to see many shades of grey and an innate flexibility. He would have fired

Chelsea long ago for her lack of pliability but her lab skills would be hard to replace, especially at her present salary. She was also every bit as beautiful as her partner and popular with the other employees. Some of the board members had taken notice of her and would question her absence.

"What do you think of the wine?" Orlon asked.

"I like the toasty finish."

Orlon forced his brow to remain still at hearing Brad's spot-on critique. He'd guessed Candyface would know his wines—what self-respecting Romeo wouldn't, after all? He mentally grimaced as he sipped, realizing the situation was complicated further by the romance factor. From what he had observed, Brad had a big soft spot for Ms. Noble.

If he fired Chelsea, Brad might quit on him and he'd be left without any reports. On the other hand, there was no doubt in his mind that Chelsea would go ballistic and refuse to sign off on any reports that did not contain hard, verifiable data. She might even go so far as to call his bluff and report his fudging directly to a board member. That was unthinkable.

"Perhaps the best way for us to achieve the data as quickly as possible is for you and Chelsea to work together on finding a parallel to autism." He sopped up the garlicky butter in the bottom of the empty dish with a pinch of bread as he spoke, "Even if it's only a very minor one, include it. If you need her assistance on the front end for preparing the reports, by all means, use her."

Orlon paused as the waiter cleared plates then he yanked the bed linens open.

"Once you have a rough draft ready, I think it would be best if you and I meet again privately to review it. There may be things that I can add that will be of benefit. I'll have my secretary make any changes needed for the final report that will go to the board. No need for Chelsea to give it her blessing."

With a chilly grin Brad said, "Perhaps this is a good time to talk about my compensation package, Orlon. Surely there is some sort of achievement bonus available? After all, what we're talking about here will cause BioGen's stock value to skyrocket."

Orlon struggled to bite back the instant retort that sprang to his lips and looked closer at the man sitting across from him. Gorgeous and greedy. Street wise. He should have seen it coming. With a wave of his finger he motioned the steward over to refill their glasses.

"That can be arranged. Wadsworth is delighted with our progress and mentioned success bonuses for the team. I can secure five thousand for you."

"I was thinking more along the lines of ten. It would take at least that much to make it worth risking my reputation in the scientific community."

Brad forked up another bite and fell silent. It was an obvious ploy to let the counter offer spin on the air as he chewed. Orlon counted twenty small motions of the man's chiseled jaw.

As president of BioGen, he'd learned long ago the best way to handle an employee's request for more money was to not be the first to respond. His companion continued to nibble and Orlon noticed Brad used his cutlery in the continental style. A grudging admiration for the man's table skills began to take hold but the greedy bastard ruined the moment by continuing to talk money in response to Orlon's silence.

"If we actually do come up with concrete achievements, I'll expect a much bigger reward in a few months—when the executives' annual bonuses come out. I'll take half of yours."

Orlon's teeth ground together until he felt his molars strain, knowing his puffy cheeks hid the fact from his guest. Damn the man!

He reminded himself that his annual executive bonus would be huge if specific milestones were met before year-end. It would finally send his bank balance into seven digits, and Candyface wasn't going to lay a finger on it. He'd make sure of it.

"You're a tough negotiator, Brad. Ten thousand it is. You'll get your check after the board meeting." He didn't bother to address the man's larger demand.

They made small talk through the rest of the meal and the last of the wine. Orlon wiped his lips a final time and asked for the check.

"I appreciate your meeting with me tonight and I'm pleased we were able to come to an agreement on how to proceed with the project. I won't keep you here any longer. I'll take care of the check, you don't need to wait. I know you want to get an early start tomorrow at the lab." He stood up and watched as Brad followed suit.

"Orlon, I really enjoyed dinner. I look forward to working with you on the reports and to getting that check." Brad placed his napkin next to his plate and extended his hand.

"Good night. Drive safely." Orlon watched the diners watching Brad as he departed.

A moment later the waiter handed him a plastic bag with a to-go box containing the left-over food along with two servings of red velvet cake. He had no dog but that's what he told the wait staff so they would go along with scraping food from both plates into one box.

"Did you include the left-over bread and a container of the sauce?" The waiter nodded. "Excellent. Thank you for your service. Good night."

He slipped the credit card back in his wallet and lumbered up from the table. Normally he would stay and enjoy a cognac after his guests left but he should get to the office early tomorrow as well. No doubt Chelsea would need handling in the morning.

* * *

Fifteen minutes later, Orlon pulled in the driveway of his townhome on Villa Pacheo. He had convinced his mother to sell the large home she owned and purchase the new property in his name to protect her estate from future medical expenses she might incur. The unit backed to a golf course and there was a clubhouse along with tennis courts, heated pool and exercise room.

He shifted the bag of leftovers to the other hand and unlocked the front door. "It's me, Mother," he called out as he stepped inside and removed his shoes. His feet slid easily into the calfskin slippers waiting beneath the entry table.

"I'm in the study." His mother's reedy voice was barely audible over the symphony music playing on the radio. The volume dropped and she called out, "I'll meet you in the dining room. I'm famished. Please use the Royal Albert place setting and the Waterford goblet. That would be lovely."

Plastic bag rustling against his side, he headed down the hall to the kitchen. He popped the foam box in the microwave, pushed a couple buttons then stepped into the dining room. The drawer on the sideboard squeaked as he opened it and pulled out the requested place setting. With efficiency achieved through practice, he had the table set before the microwave dinged.

Back in the kitchen, he carefully arranged the food on the plate. He stepped back into the dining room, set the plate on the table, centered exactly on the place mat and placed the bread basket at ten o'clock next to the plate. The wine goblet went at two o'clock. He watched as his eighty-four year old mother felt along the back of the chair, then the edge of the table as she guided herself into her seat.

"It smells wonderful. What am I having?"

"Lamb with curried vegetables. And I brought you a slice of red velvet cake."

"That sounds delightful."

Fingers walked her hand to the wine glass and she held it aloft, taking a couple slow sips of the inexpensive merlot. She set the glass down carefully, wiped her lips with the napkin.

"Oswald is waiting for you in the study."

Orlon held back a groan. He loathed his brother. The man was seedy, and that was putting it nicely. Oswald's questionable business concerns kept him too busy to have their mother living with him full time. Her care had fallen to Orlon two years ago when her sight finally went. He was making the most of it and didn't need his nosy brother screwing it up.

Although the man never failed to set his teeth on edge, Oswald had his uses on occasion, and since he was family he could be trusted to a certain degree. He pushed himself up from the table, knowing he had no choice but to deal with their guest.

"Enjoy your dinner, Mother. Let me know if you want coffee and I'll make it for you."

He stepped silently through the short hall and into the study. His brother sat on the sofa, knees touching the edge of the coffee table, cell phone in hand, scrolling through a text message. Oswald had gotten the height in the family and Orlon had always resented him for it. As well as many other things along the way—this visit would likely be one of them.

"Good evening, Oswald." Orlon greeted his brother with a cordial tone. Manners were important whether one felt like it or not.

"Take the stick out of your ass, Oddball. The name's Ozzie and you know it. Where the hell ya been all night? I come over and Ma's sittin' here starving her ass off. She looks like she's losin' weight, too. What the hell have ya been feedin' her? Or is it not feedin' her?"

Orlon's teeth ground against the onslaught of jibes. He drew a breath and turned to the built-in wetbar.

"I'm having a brandy, would you like one?"

"What kinda sissy-ass drink is that? If ya got whiskey, I'll take that, otherwise forget it. No ice."

He let the breath out slowly as he prepared their drinks. His brother could get under his skin like no one else. It was a shame a person couldn't divorce unwanted family.

Their mother, Ophelia Millard, had come from quality people but had been born a less than handsome woman. She'd remained unmarried into her forties when she'd become desperate and had fallen for trash. She'd tried to make the most of it until the man took off when the boys were six and four. Orlon had been glad to see the violent alcoholic brute go. Oswald had been crushed. He was his father's favored child and had a completely different view of things.

"Here's your whiskey. Now what can I do for you?"

"You can answer my damn questions."

"Our mother is being fed very well. The problem is she's not eating. I can't force feed her. Why don't you try spending some time with her yourself? Then you'd know what she's eating." He snatched the empty glass from his brother's hand and turned back to the bar.

"I'm here now, aren't I? Ma says you leave her alone for hours with no food. You better start feeding her regular meals or I'll kick your fat ass. She looks like a damn bag of bones!"

"There's no need to be vulgar." Orlon sipped his brandy and fought back the urge to hurl insults. Breeding would tell. His brother would not draw him out.

"Christ, ya talk fancy." Oswald drained his second drink, swiped a sleeve across his mouth. "And ya sure as hell must be eatin' fancy. It looks like ya gained every pound Ma lost, ya fatso."

He bit back a retort and told himself to remember it wasn't Oswald's fault he was so uncouth. He had no doubt his brother would have turned out differently if their mother's family had not disowned her for marrying so far down. Perhaps he and Oswald may have even had a chance at strong kinship. But due to the pecuniary limits suffered in their father's absence, they had turned out to be as night and day as brothers could be.

Orlon's strongest memory from childhood was hunger; for food, for luxuries, for a better life. Six month's into their father's absence, Oswald had become such a terror his mother was forced to allow him to go live with their father and the boy's fate was sealed.

"Earth to Oddball—I'm talking to your fat ass—pay attention. I said when's the last time you took Ma outta the house? She's blind, not dead."

"As I said a moment ago, you'd know these things if you visited more often."

Oswald gave him a dirty look and shoved his glass across the table again.

"I might do just that, butterball. Ma said she hasn't left the house for two weeks. And that was only after she begged you to take her out."

"Mother loses track of time—and I work for a living, remember?"

He poured his hollow-legged brother a third drink, sipped his brandy and visualized his bank balance to steady himself.

"You gettin' the message here, or what? I'll be back next week and Ma had damn well better have some meat on her bones or you and I are gonna step outside and I ain't kiddin'. If ya can't handle taking care of her, I'll get a nurse for her."

He endured another dirty look then his brother slapped the empty crystal down on the delicate antique table and stood up.

"Thanks for the drinks."

Orlon let out a breath of relief. "I'll see you to the door."

He watched his brother's departing back as his tall frame disappeared down the sidewalk, then he clicked the door shut, snicked the lock home. Another brandy was called for, perhaps two, then a hot shower and bed. He sat on the sofa and sipped his drink, waiting to see if his mother would want coffee.

He stared into his brandy as he recalled watching the door close behind his brother with relief on that other day long ago. Oswald had been absolutely wretched to live with after their father left. He'd staunchly refused to adhere to the social graces their mother had striven so hard to teach them in between the menial labor jobs she was forced to work. When Oswald had thrown a precious porcelain cup and saucer filled with hot tea across the room one afternoon, it ended his mother's insisting he live with them. The daily lessons in manners continued in peace after that.

Orlon had thoroughly enjoyed learning the finer points of living a quality life. His mother had inspired hope with the constant encouragement one could live well in spite of one's circumstances. It was a matter of choice. His mother had assured him that as long as he possessed top notch manners and earned significant money once he was out of college, they would eventually be able to re-enter the level of society she had enjoyed in her former life.

Society had proven much more difficult to navigate than Orlon had ever dreamed as an innocent child at his mother's side. It was crushing to learn the upper echelon didn't want him. He was too ugly. But he'd come to realize as an adult that ugly was socially accepted if the word millionaire was included in the description of the man. He was working hard to achieve that status but it wasn't easy.

CHAPTER 20

Craig punched in the number and listened to a couple clicks as the international call went through.

"Jeff Connor please."

He'd had to get an early start on the day due to the time difference between the States and South Africa. A full minute passed as he waited for the receptionist to transfer the call.

"This is Jeff speaking."

"Hello Mr. Connor, this is Craig Noble."

"Good afternoon. Thank you for calling me back. I take it you spoke with your son?"

"Yes, I did. He said he did not take your missing sphere."

"I'm afraid I have to disagree with him, Mr. Noble."

"What do you mean?" His eyes narrowed as he stared out across the beach. It was littered with chunks of asphalt and large rocks that had tumbled down after the waves washed out over half of the remaining bluff last weekend. Sandpipers hopped in and out of the foam at the edge of the shore, oblivious to the wreckage around them.

"Perhaps you weren't aware of it but we have cameras throughout our facility. When we realized the sphere was missing I had my security team play back the video from your visit." Connor cleared his throat. "The footage clearly shows your son putting one of the spheres in his pocket. There is no mistaking it."

Craig stood with the chill of the early morning wind blowing around him, a block of ice forming in his chest. He was at a complete loss of words for a minute as he tried to quickly put his legal thinking cap on. This could turn into a real mess, he had to be careful.

"Mr. Connor, I can't disagree with what you're telling me because I haven't seen the video for myself. All I can tell you is Ethan states he did not take the sphere. I wish you had shared with me before that you had reason to believe he had taken it. Look, I'm in San Francisco on a job site right now. Ethan's a hundred miles from me. I won't see him until tomorrow evening. I think it would be best if I address this with him face to face when I get back. I'm sorry to make you wait but I don't have much choice."

"I understand. I'm a father too. It can't be easy having to hear me tell you this. Speak with him again tomorrow. If we can get the sphere back, I'm willing to drop it. I assume you will properly punish your son as you see fit. We just want the sphere back. Frankly, I was shocked to learn of this myself. He seemed like a nice young man. It was very disappointing. I'll speak with you tomorrow evening."

Craig stood staring out at the ocean, a headache forming behind his eyes. He wasn't sure which upset him more; the fact that Ethan had stolen the sphere and put them in legal jeopardy or that he'd blatantly lied to him about it on the phone last night.

He looked at his watch and realized he was running late for the breakfast meeting with the city council. He climbed in the car and headed into town, lost in thought about his family.

CHAPTER 21

Thursday morning arrived along with a black cloud of depression. Chelsea tried to fight it off but it clung to her like a swarm of gnats. She forced herself out of bed and through the usual morning routines. It was a tall order, but she did her best to put a cheerful face on for the kids during the ride to school.

The drive to work went way too quickly and she deliberately parked at the back of the BioGen lot, shut the ignition off and sat listening to the song on the radio. Christopher Cross was singing *Sailing*—it had always been one of her favorites. She needed a meditation moment before climbing out to face another day in hell, but it was impossible to shut off her anger. Between her boss and her husband, she was going to end up on medication if things didn't change soon. The song came to an end and she made herself snag the keys and get out.

"Good morning, George," she returned the security guard's greeting. Normally, she would take time to have a short conversation with him but she wasn't in the mood today. Her purse and keys went in a plastic tray and moved down a conveyor belt as she stepped through the scanner. The company had increased security measures due to avid protestors who were against genetically altered foods. The guards had run off more than one crazy over the past year.

A left out of the lobby and she was heading down a sterile hallway, heels clicking on the white ceramic tiles. Another turn, second door on the right and she was back in the lab.

"Morning," she called out as she put her purse away. Seeing the dark curve of Brad's head leaning over a microscope lifted her mood a little. He turned on the metal stool and faced her as she walked toward him. From the concerned look in his eye something was up already.

"What?"

"First, let me say good morning, it's nice to see you." He gave her a strained smile. "Now let me ruin the rest of your day as gently as I can—"

"No, Brad. No. It's too early. I haven't even had a second cup of coffee. Have mercy on me. And if it starts with "O", I'm warning you, I might turn right back around and leave."

He scraped a hand through his hair, leaving tufts sticking straight up, some poked out sideways, but it worked for him anyway.

"What time did you get here?" She curled a derisive lip at him. The clock on the wall read eight-ten.

"You know me, early to bed, early to rise. I got here around six this morning. You want a blueberry muffin? I stopped at the Whole Foods place on the way in."

He was the best-looking man she'd ever worked with. Maybe the best looking guy she'd ever been in the same room with. He was single, always had fresh breath and ate organic foods. He was not gay. Sometimes she really couldn't stand his perfection. Especially on the days that Orlon used Brad as a communication funnel between them. She had been at BioGen a year longer than her lab partner and was officially the lead on their team.

With a clinched fist, she walked to the other side of the room and poured a cup of coffee. She took her time walking back to the table as his blue eyes stroked up her legs, caressed her middle then swept across her neck and into her eyes. Her breath caught. She lost her train of thought for a moment. It worked every time he did that to her but she wasn't in the mood today.

"Cut it out, Brat." The nickname was her subtle way of reminding both of them to behave. She sipped her coffee then nailed him with her eyes.

"Okay, go ahead, ruin my day. Tell me what Fat Wad had to say this morning."

"You aren't going to like it."

He looked away, pushed a drawer in with a thud, snapped the light off under the microscope.

"You sure you want to hear this?"

"No, but hit me anyway. Let's see how high my blood pressure can go before nine."

He stood up so they'd be at eye-level. She was a tall woman and in low heels she was five-ten. Brad was only five-eleven but he had perfect posture, so he seemed much taller. He stood farther away from her then he normally did. Not a good sign.

"Chelsea, what can I say? Let me give you the news in a nutshell; not only are we expected to report successful results and a recommendation to move forward on the Alzheimer's tomato vaccine, we are now supposed to report that it may also cure autism."

Brad glanced away and looked out the window when she slammed the cup on the table. Coffee sloshed out and ran in a pool toward the edge as she stared at his profile.

"What the hell did you just say to me? Did I hear you right?" Her voice was just above a whisper but its force could have blown a car over as she glared at him. "What did you tell him?"

"Those were pretty much his exact words. I wish to hell I'd had a tape recorder going but he walked through the door and hit me with that crap before I could get out 'good morning'. What could I do? I was barely awake, it was only seven o'clock. I sure wasn't ready to get into a debate with him about it right then. I told him I'd talk to you and we'd get back to him on it."

"You've got to be kidding me, Brad!" She shifted her hip and swung away from him, too upset to keep it professional right then. "You know, suddenly I feel really sick to my stomach. Tell Orlon I went home." She stalked over to the cupboard, snagged her purse. Coffee dripped off the edge of the table as she swept back around and stung him with her eyes.

"Good luck with the project, Brad. I'm going to get some therapy."

She climbed back in the SUV and headed out of the lot, anger building inside her with the force of a pressure cooker.

Concentrating on deep breaths, she made herself keep a light foot on the gas pedal as she drove down the highway. Too upset to go home and sit, she decided to take her own advice and headed to the mall in San Jose. It was an hour's drive but she needed to calm down before she let herself out in public anyway. Thank God for satellite radio. Commercials might put her over the edge.

She flipped the dial to a good rock station and turned it up as Def Leppard's *Foolin* took over the car. She sang along in a husky alto. The day almost began looking up when the DJ announced he was spinning a triple-play. After belting out every word, her mood began to lighten. The drive to San Jose went by in a blur and before she knew it, she was at the mall. She parked in front of Macy's and climbed out.

Walking toward the entrance, she tried to remember the last time she'd taken a couple hours and gone shopping or out to lunch with a friend. Way too long. The perfumed department store smell swirled around her as she swept through Macy's on her way out to the main mall area. She needed to walk for a bit and drink a cup of coffee before she could focus on material things.

The line at the Starbucks counter was six people deep and she stood just outside the store entrance, waiting her turn. She gazed at the names of the shops around her. A lot of them had changed since she'd last been there. Her eyes landed on the fancy glass and brass of a new office front at the end of the short corridor. She read the name of the law firm and right that minute she realized it was up to her to make things change in her life. She had been a duck on dirt at home and at work for way too long. Gliding or flying, things were going to change.

The clerk handed over the coffee and turned to the next customer before Chelsea could thank her. Nice world. She stepped over to the condiment bar. The cream poured and the lid snapped back on almost without her noticing.

She headed toward the glass and gold office, thinking about her mother and how hard she'd worked her whole life. Growing up without a dad around throughout her childhood had been tough on both of them. That wasn't what she wanted for her family, but it looked like Craig wasn't giving her a choice.

CHAPTER 22

Ann looked at her watch as she hurried back to the nurses' station. Ten minutes to quitting time. She let out a sigh of relief at being able to make it through her shift. The chair slid away from her and she caught the back of it. She'd just grabbed a patient chart when Linda walked into the cubicle with one of the other nurses.

"Ann, can you give me a couple minutes? I'd like to speak with you before you go." Linda didn't mince words. "Beth will cover the desk."

Her boss turned and headed toward her office, clearly expecting Ann to follow her.

Ann glanced at Beth, who avoided her eyes. Her coworker slid into the chair Ann had just pulled over and snatched up the ringing phone.

Dread crept over her She desperately needed her paycheck. It was rare when she got any child support out of her ex-husband, much less on a regular basis. Never knowing whether the check would show up left her covering everything on her own. The infrequent support checks were used to catch up the credit cards racked up in between.

She snagged a bottle of water then headed down the hall, whispering a prayer.

Linda was seated behind the desk and motioned for Ann to shut the door.

"I won't keep you long, I know you need to finish up and get out of here."

She cleared a stack of paper work from the center of her desk and turned back to Ann, a tense expression on her face. "I want you to know what a great nurse I think you are. You add a lot to our team, when you're here. But, I'm sure it's no surprise to hear me say, your need to leave early on a frequent basis has become a problem for us. The other nurses are complaining."

Ann spoke up quietly, "I appreciate your understanding and I realize it's become a problem. I spoke with my neighbor last night and she's agreed to help me. Hopefully, between Chelsea and my mom, I won't have to leave early any more. I'm really sorry."

"I'm glad to hear you've found another source of support, and I hope that does the trick. We really want to keep you." Linda looked at her a moment then said, "I do have to go on record that I have warned you about the problem. You need to make sure you get here on time and don't have to leave early for the next thirty days or I'll have to place you on formal notice. The three strike rule. I'm sorry, but I have to play fair across the board."

"I understand, Linda. I'll make sure it doesn't happen."

"All right. Well, scoot on out of here, I know you need to get going."

Ann stood up and headed toward the doorway. "Have a good evening," she said over her shoulder as she left the office.

Eyes closed, she drew in a deep breath and walked back to the nurses' station.

Bless Chelsea's heart for offering to help, but Ann didn't see how another hard-working, almost-single mom could help her plug all the holes that Steve needed filled. She said goodnight to Beth and headed to the elevator, wondering how much longer she'd have her job.

CHAPTER 23

"**H**ey, Lily. How was school?" Ethan greeted his little sister as she stepped through the front door. He made it home an hour before she did on the days he didn't have basketball practice.

"Why are you sitting on the stairs like that?" she asked.

"What do you mean?"

"I've never seen you sit there before."

"Oh—I was just getting ready to go in the kitchen and I heard your bus, so I waited for you." He looked down at his Ipod, flipped through the song selection, trying to play off his odd behavior as coincidence. His mom would be home in an hour and he needed to get information out of Lily before then.

She hung the pink book bag on a peg next to the stairs, kicked her shoes off under the bench then whirled around and looked at him.

"I'm gonna make myself some ice cream, do you want any?" he asked.

"Why are you acting so weird?"

"Come on, I'm not being weird. I'm just trying to be nice."

Inspiration struck as he said, "Mom's been pretty upset lately. I'm just trying to get along with you better for her sake. Do you want ice cream or not?" He deliberately cranked out the last words in a huff as he swung through the kitchen door.

Lily followed, a sad look on her face. "Yeah, I want ice cream, thanks." She dogged his steps right up to the freezer and stood leaning against the counter as he set the ice cream down and pulled out two bowls.

Huge blue eyes stared up at him, "Ethan, do you think Mom and Dad are going to get divorced?" Her voice caught on the last word and tears pooled along her lashes.

Normally he would blow her off and tell her to mind her own business or something like that, but he had a game plan he needed to stick to. And he was worried about his parents, too. He fought down guilt at manipulating a second-grader and considered how to respond in a way that was appropriate to the discussion, yet aided his own goals.

"I know they've been having some arguments about Dad being gone too much."

"Yeah, I heard 'em, too."

"Well, you know…Mom and Dad have been together forever, almost twenty years. They'll probably work things out. They always have before, right?"

"How should I know, I'm only seven."

He looked down at her. "Yeah, I guess I didn't think about that." He finished scooping, put the lid back on the container as he said, "But we don't want them to get divorced, right?"

"Right." Another tear swam down her cheek.

"Hey, don't cry. It'll make your ice cream melt." He tried to cheer her up so she'd be more cooperative. "You want some chocolate sauce?"

She nodded and swiped at her eyes.

He put both bowls down on the kitchen table then squirted Hershey's over the vanilla mounds. "Grab two spoons."

She pulled the drawer out and joined him at the table.

"So, that's what I was thinking, see. You and I getting along better will help Mom out, and maybe she won't be as upset at Dad being gone for work." He was swinging things around in his direction. "What do you think, can we do it?"

"Do what?"

"Get along better. You know, stop fighting with each other and stuff."

"You're the jerk, you tell me." She stuffed ice cream in her mouth, a chocolate mustache forming above her lip.

"Ha, ha. Good one." He gritted his teeth. *What were his parents thinking when they stuck him with a little sister?* "Okay, you tell me. What can I do so we get along better?"

"Well, for sure you have to share the TV remote. Every day. We should take turns." More ice cream hit the tunnel.

"All right. I can do that. How about if we make a chart? You write down when your favorite shows are on, and I'll do the same. Then we'll see if we have any conflicts and work it out. How's that sound?"

"That would be great!" She beamed at him, chocolate mustache now encircling her mouth.

He stared at her a moment. "Hey, wait a second. Did you have teeth yesterday?"

"You're silly. Yes, I had teeth, duh!"

"No, I mean your front teeth. And what happened to your lisp? You're saying all your 'S's' right all of a sudden. Did I miss something?"

Her head came up from the ice cream bowl with a snap. The spoon clattered on the side of the stoneware as she shot out of her chair and into the hall, back to the foyer. Ethan followed behind without even realizing what he was doing. He watched as she cheesed a huge grin in front of the hall mirror. She reached up and scrubbed a hand at the chocolate around her mouth, then turned to him, giant smile on her face.

"Look, Ethan! The tooth fairy must have come last night. Aren't they pretty?"

He shook his head and watched as she jumped up and down with delight, thrilled at finally getting her front teeth in.

"That's kinda weird, Lil. I've never seen anyone's front teeth grow that fast before."

She stepped right up to him and spoke through a wide grin, "See, teeth!"

"Congratulations." He grinned back at her and shrugged. Stranger things had probably happened before. It was time to get back to business.

"Hey, you know what, that reminds me. You found two new teeth, but I lost something."

She stopped grinning and looked up at him with an innocent face. "What?"

"A little round ball. It's brown, about an inch wide. And now I can't find it." He stared down at her as she whipped her head around at the sound of a car in the driveway.

"Mommy's home early! I can't wait to show her my new teeth!" She bolted to the door.

"Hey, wait a minute. What about that brown ball I lost? Have you seen it?"

"Nope," she tossed back over her shoulder as she ran out to greet their mom and Bell raced out behind her.

CHAPTER 24

"**H**i Mommy! You're home early!" Lily and Bell flew toward her and Chelsea braced for impact. Chelsea laughed and hung on to the car door to keep her balance.

"Hi Sweetie." She gave her daughter a hug then stood back up. "Guess what? I bought you something today."

"You did? What?" Lily beamed up at her.

"I got you the cutest dress. You will love—"

Chelsea stopped talking and stared at her daughter. "When did your front teeth come in, Sweetheart? I don't remember noticing them last night at dinner."

Lily laughed and danced past her, diving for the packages on the passenger's seat.

"Show me the dress! Show me the dress!"

Bell began jumping and barking as Lily's excitement rubbed off. It was all Chelsea could do to get out from behind the car door and stand clear on the drive.

She whipped out a hand toward Bell as the dog turned and bounded at her, "Down, girl! What has gotten into you today?" She gently held Bell back with a palm pressed against her forehead until the frisky dog backed off.

"Sheesh, you guys are really glad to see me. Come on, let's go inside and have a cold drink and I'll show you what I bought today."

Plastic and paper bags rustled as she squeezed her way through the door with the bounty. It had been a roller coaster day but nothing improved her mood like a few hours of intense shopping at the mall. There was something about getting lost in the creative process of pulling outfits together that renewed her spirits. It was definitely a welcome change from the lab.

She put the bags beside the kitchen table and turned to her daughter, "I'm having iced tea, what would you like?"

"I'm not thirsty. Can I see my dress now?"

Chelsea laughed and chugged down half the tea then set her glass down. They spent the next ten minutes looking at Lily's dress and the other things Chelsea had purchased after meeting with the attorney. Hours of retail therapy had taken her mind off her worries and she wasn't quite ready to fully immerse herself back in reality yet. She dragged out the shopping pleasure with her daughter until Lily got restless.

"What's for dinner, Mommy?"

"You know, I think we're going to order Chinese tonight. How's that sound?"

"Yummy! I want sesame chicken, okay? And crab ragoo." Lily grinned up at her and Chelsea took another look at her new teeth.

"Honey, did you have teeth yesterday?"

"Mommy! That's the same thing Ethan asked me. Yes, I had teeth yesterday."

Chelsea laughed at her blue-eyed angel. "I guess I've been pretty distracted to not notice. Come here and give me a hug. I need one." She held Lily close, doing her best to focus on how she felt in her arms and the softness of her blond curls. Try as she might to shut it all out for a little while, being home brought back thoughts of the meeting with the attorney earlier that day. Her nerves jangled as the cold advice from the attorney came pouring back in. She needed a moment alone and a big glass of wine.

"Thanks for the hug. Do you want to go play for a little bit while I call in the food?"

"Okay, Mommy. Ask for chopsticks, okay?" Lily grinned at her and flew out the door.

Chelsea poured herself a glass of wine then sat down at the table, guilt rushing in as she thought about being so distracted by work and her marriage problems that she hadn't even noticed Lily's front teeth coming in. She needed to spend more quality time with her kids.

* * *

Lily ran straight to the play fort then looked back at the house to see if her mom was watching. The fort and swing set were built of wood and a yellow plastic slide spiraled down from the second floor of the fort. It was big. She ran around to the other side and stopped along the fence and stared at her plant. There weren't very many berries left. They tasted so good she'd eaten almost all of them over the past two days.

A small sprig popped off in her hand and petite fingers flew from mouth to berries, eating them one at a time. She liked to press the berries up against the roof of her mouth and savor the ice cream taste as it spread on her tongue. The juice even felt cold like ice cream. She made herself stop after finishing the small cluster. She loved to eat with chopsticks and didn't want to be too full.

Lily hopped on the swing, full of energy, a vibrant glow on her skin as her legs pumped the swing as high as it would go.

CHAPTER 25

He opened his eyes and saw only darkness. A hushed silence as deep as the ocean accompanied the faint scent of soap. Eyes blinking in the inky black, it took him a moment to recall where he was. Another moment to focus on what day it was. San Francisco. Holiday Inn. Friday. He lay still in the quiet womb and ran through the schedule he was facing that day. He groaned as the thought of back to back meetings wound through his brain.

"God save me from another day of nonsense and grand standing, please."

Bed covers were reluctantly flung back and Craig swung his feet to the floor, wondering what time it was. His internal clock said it was around six. It was a minor irritation that many hotels had stopped providing bedside clocks but it was annoying to deal with on a regular basis. He made a mental note to purchase a traveling clock over the weekend as he fumbled for the light switch.

A quick glance at his cell phone and he realized it was earlier than he'd thought. Good, he'd have time for a workout in the hotel gym before he showered and dressed for the hours of butt-numbing meetings. If he worked out hard enough, maybe being it wouldn't seem so torturous.

A quick scan of the newspaper and a cup of coffee later he was in the gym. He started on the treadmill. A stretch of aerobics and then he'd hit the weights. Sweat had begun to dampen his t-shirt when a stunning brunette swiped her room key and came through the glass door.

He watched her from the corner of his eye as she headed toward him. Skin tight black workout pants, a florescent green half-tank that would be considered a swim suit top if they weren't in a gym. Golden tan. Great abs. She stepped on the treadmill next to him and he caught a whiff of light perfume. Nice.

She turned to him as she gained her balance on the black rubber, "Good morning."

He returned her greeting with a smile and a quick head to toe glance. Shiny dark hair pulled into a high ponytail, bright white teeth, brown eyes. Expensive Nike sneakers. Buttons beeped as she adjusted the settings for her workout and began moving on the machine.

It always felt a little strange to be in a small hotel gym alone with someone he didn't know. There was a heightened sense of awareness that didn't happen if more people were present. He wasn't sure whether he hoped another guest came in. The woman looked like a model and she smelled good too.

They ran side by side for several minutes until the timer on his machine hit the twenty minute mark. He slowed his pace and got off the treadmill, walked over to the metal rack in the corner and snagged a towel to mop his face and neck. A water cooler held paper cups and he drained one then another, wiped his face a second time then headed for the weight machines.

Thighs and ass straining on the reverse leg lift until his muscles began to scream, he turned his head and saw the gorgeous woman staring at him. She smiled and ran her eyes along his prone frame, then she turned back to read the settings in front of her.

He grinned to himself as he rose and moved to the bench press. It was nice to have a good looking twenty-something notice him. As he considered the stranger's smile his libido kicked up. It made him think of Chelsea and how she had looked at him the last time they'd made love. Chelsea's smile was better. The problem was he rarely saw it any more. He shook the thought off and got on with his workout.

The bench press pad was cold against his back as he lay down and prepared to do a couple sets. A deep breath then he lifted the bar off the rack and slowly pressed the weights above his head as he blew air out and thought about his marriage. He was at a complete loss for how to make Chelsea happy. It seemed ridiculous to him that she was so upset about his traveling and it was starting to piss him off. He'd been traveling for years. Nothing had changed, so why was she going crazy about it all of a sudden?

If anything, it should be easier dealing with their household these days while he was away. The kids were older, not nearly as much work as they used to be. They were both in school all day. He was home on the weekends. He really didn't get where Chelsea was coming from on the double-duty thing. Sure, she had to make dinner, but she always had the option of going out to eat or phoning food in. How hard was that?

He pressed on, the weights straining his biceps and shoulders. After the twentieth rep he placed the bar back on its rack with a clang of metal on metal and rested on the bench, muscles tweaking. The woman was staring at him again, this time looking at his reflection in the mirror instead of straight at him. She must be really fit because she'd been on the machine close to thirty minutes and didn't seem winded. She wasn't even sweating. He admired her tight tush for a second then wrapped his hands around the bar again.

The weights forced his muscles to work while he thought about the woman's body, then flashed on his wife's. He didn't mean to compare the two but his mind seemed to do it without his consent. He checked off the mental list, and realized once again how beautiful his wife truly was. Even after two kids and thirty-six years of life. He'd pick her out of a harem any day. He grinned to himself and pumped out one last rep then dropped the bar onto its rack. He blew out a deep breath as florescent green flashed beside him.

"Wow, you're really getting in a great workout today. Are you here on business?" Her voice was disappointing—breathy and a little high—it made her sound like a kid.

He sat up on the bench, plucking his wet t-shirt away from his chest. "Yep. I've got a day full of meetings so I'm trying to wear myself out before I get stuck in a chair all day." He gave her a small grin as he stood up and moved to the towel rack again. They were still the only people in the gym.

She followed him as she asked, "Are you staying through the weekend or heading home tonight?" A flash of smile as she reached for a cup of water. She was close enough for him to realize she was wearing makeup. He considered that a loss of points. It was six-thirty in the morning, who needed eye shadow, mascara and lip gloss that time of day? It made her seem fake, even if she'd applied it lightly. And now that he had a closer look, a couple of her other assets seemed enhanced. Major loss of points for that

"I'm heading home to my family right after the meetings. How about you, staying here on business?" He watched her smile dim at hearing the word family. It worked almost every time. Some women could be pretty aggressive, and the words 'married' and 'children' didn't seem to phase their ardor. He usually left the room when that happened. Better safe than sorry.

The woman mumbled something about a convention and stepped over to a machine, clearly dismissing him from her radar. He smiled to himself as he pushed out the glass door and headed back to his room. It was pretty rare for him to make it more than three days in the same hotel without someone batting their eyelashes at him.

A light dawned as his finger hit the elevator button. Maybe that's why Chelsea was giving him such a hard time about traveling? Maybe she was worried he would stray? He knew men who handled things that way—their work lives were an excuse to have a second layer of romance and excitement in between being home with their families. Maybe her insecurities had surfaced? She had a birthday coming up next month. Relief washed over him as he stepped on the elevator. He'd do his best to reassure her when he got home.

* * *

At eight-twenty he was showered, shaved, buttoned down and sitting in a faux leather chair along with ten other people, most of them men. They were lined along both sides of the conference table and due to start in five minutes. He looked up as Doug Belmont walked through the door. He waved and pointed to the seat he'd saved.

"Good morning. It's good to see you, Craig."

"Morning Doug. I'm glad you could make it."

Global Systems had a large stake in the outcome of the meeting. They were potentially going to walk away with a construction management contract worth millions. Craig was there as the worker bee. His job was to dig into the meat of the reports provided by the various specialists and roll the data into a concrete action plan to present this morning for approval. It was critical the work begin immediately, before the sewage pipeline was breached.

Complicating the challenges of the project itself was the convoluted tangle of federal, state and local agencies that oversaw Ocean Beach. Each entity had different responsibilities and priorities as well as their own inner political issues. Following the meetings three weeks ago, the tangle had come to a stalemate. It all came down to which tax payer base should bear the largest burden and whether wildlife habitat and natural beauty should beat out infrastructure.

Meanwhile the three million people who visited the beach annually were hoping everyone would get their act together. Then the second storm had hit. Concerned citizens were crying foul and were outraged that the various government entities weren't doing something to resolve the problem. The beach was closed, along with a two-mile stretch of the highway, probably for several months. The powers-that-be who sat at the table that morning had come to the meeting knowing they could no longer afford to disagree. It was time to act.

Craig planned to capitalize on the public's clatter for action and hoped to wield the point with enough skill to get everyone on the same page by two o'clock. He needed to be home and wanted to be there before Chelsea got off work. For several reasons.

The meeting was called to order and they got down to work. Craig held the floor for the majority of the morning, detailing the efforts needed to refill the bluff beneath the highway and the revetment to protect the new fill on a long-term basis. They discussed the projected costs and completion timelines. Things got heated when approvals for the emergency budget were called for. Craig's patience with the posturing and political maneuvering reached an end and he jumped in. His soft baritone seemed to have a mesmerizing effect on the group. They all fell silent as he spoke.

"I think we can all agree we have no choice but to move forward with repair of the bluff and the highway itself. I propose that we vote on approving those two items. It will take some time to make those things happen. We can reconvene again at a later date to duke it out on how to address the long-term revetment. For now, we need to protect the pipeline and get the Great Highway re-opened as soon as possible, agreed?"

Heads nodded all around the table and within minutes the partial budget was approved and Global Systems formally awarded management of the project. Smiles came out as hands were shaken and business cards exchanged. The meeting had run just past one o'clock and luncheon plans were swiftly made. The group began shuffling out of the room and Craig was more than relieved they wouldn't have to reconvene again that afternoon.

Doug smiled and placed a hand on his shoulder as they made their way out the building.

"That was excellent work in there, Craig. I have a sneaking suspicion if you hadn't been here today I would be heading back in for another three hour session this afternoon." Doug rolled his eyes at the thought and stopped to face him. "There's something about the way you speak that seems to win people over every time. I love it."

"What do you mean?" Craig was curious.

"Well, I can't quite put my finger on it. In fact, I sat there today trying my best to nail it as I watched you in action. It's hard to describe—the best I could come up with is it's the way you round off your consonants." Doug chuckled again. "I don't mean to discount the brilliance of your words, but a great speaking voice is a real asset, Craig. It's part of the reason why I want to pull you onto our executive team. We're going to talk about that again, you know."

Craig scuffed a toe at the pavement and gave his head a shake as he looked back up at his boss. "Thanks, Doug. Round consonants, huh? Well, whatever I've got, I'm glad it worked. My butt didn't want to ride that chair a minute longer."

They laughed a moment then Doug gave him an apologetic look.

"I'm sorry you had to go back on the road earlier than you'd wanted to, but I guess a few days isn't a big a deal. At least I hope not. I appreciate your making the effort for us. We certainly needed you here today. Can I buy you lunch to make up for it?"

"Thanks, but I really need to get back. The weekend will go a lot smoother if I can make it home before Chelsea does."

"I understand. My wife and I are going down to San Diego for the weekend and I need to get back myself." They shook hands. "Have a great weekend, and say hello to Chelsea for me."

Craig turned and headed to his car. A glance at his watch told him it was one-thirty on the nose. Good, ahead of schedule. He'd stop at a drive-through then hit the road. Hopefully traffic would cooperate and he'd be home by four thirty at the latest. That would give him an hour with the kids before Chelsea got home.

He started the car and pulled out of the lot, thinking about the talk he had to have with Ethan. It seemed unlikely that Jeff Connor would lie about the security video. He knew he had no choice but to believe his son stole the missing sphere, and that opened up a huge can of worms for him, personally as well as legally. It really concerned him that his son had stolen something, but to have it happen during their first trip together really had his head spinning. He had yet to say anything to Chelsea about it because he wanted to speak with Ethan first. From what Connor had said, if they returned the sphere the issue would be dropped.

Although he knew he should tell Chelsea about the situation, he couldn't help but think it might be better to keep it to himself for now. She had tried to talk him out of going to Africa to start with. He would figure out how to properly punish Ethan under the radar, but first he had to get the sphere back to its owner. The sooner, the better.

CHAPTER 26

"Good morning."

Panic swept through Ann, jerking her out of a dream, heart clutching to a stop as she felt a hand stroke her cheek. Breath hitching in and out as if she'd run a hundred yards, her mind swam into focus and she realized her son stood beside the bed. It took her another moment to see he was dressed for school. He stood there patiently waiting for her to get with it.

"Good morning, Steve." Her voice came out a whispery croak as she stared at him. Her brain began to fully function and her heart beat picked up even faster. What in the world was going on? She looked at the clock on the nightstand, 7:10. She'd slept for nine hours solid.

"Honey, is somebody here?"

"You mean, besides us?"

"Yes." She held her breath as he scowled, considering her question.

"No, just you and me, Mom. Why?"

She tossed the covers back, her eyes never leaving her son's face as she watched him speak in full sentences. Tingles raced down her arms as she swung feet to the floor, a smile blossoming across her face.

"Did you get dressed yourself?"

He laughed at her. He actually, truly laughed at her. A feeling of disbelief stole over her as she slowly reached a hand out and hesitantly stroked his arm. Normally, he would have jerked away from her touch. He didn't like it when anyone touched him, not even her. It made him nervous, uncomfortable, and if the person didn't stop he would begin to groan, loudly, until the physical contact was broken.

Her fingers ran along the back of his arm and he smiled, "That tickles."

She decided she needed a hug and knew she risked rejection but wanted to find out what he'd do. She slowly wrapped her arms around him, holding him close. It felt so good.

"I love you, Steve."

Tears started down her face as her son replied, "I love you, too, Mommy."

It was all she could do to keep from sobbing as he squeezed her back. She had never heard her son speak those words. She would never ever forget this moment, right this very moment. It was the absolute best a mother could ask for.

"Mom? You're getting my head wet."

She choked back the need to shout out her joy and reluctantly released him from the embrace, her hands still holding his arms as she stepped back far enough to look at him.

"Why are you crying?" His mouth scrunched with worry as he looked at her.

She barked a quick laugh and swiped at the tears. Then she couldn't help herself, she pulled him back into her arms and gave him another hug. Finally, she got control of her emotions and let him go.

Beaming at him she said, "These are tears of joy. I'm just so happy you woke me up to tell me you love me. Thank you, Stevie. Thank you very much." She grabbed her robe and wrapped it around her as her mind began to broaden and she thought about what day it was.

It was Friday. Her day off. Her son had miraculously come out of the autistic bubble he'd been sinking deeper into each day. It was a day to celebrate, no question. She looked at him, grinning from ear to ear.

"How would you like to stay home from school today?"

"Really? That would be great!"

"You and I are going to do some celebrating today, all day long in fact." She beamed at him again as he gave her a puzzled look.

"What are we cel-brating?" It was a long word for an eight year old, so close enough to make her grin widen. He hadn't used more than two syllable words since he'd learned to talk.

She paused a moment, thinking about how to phrase they would be commemorating the fact he seemed normal all of a sudden.

"We're going to celebrate because…it's Joy Day. A day to be filled with joy and happiness, so we're going to spend it together, what do you say?"

"Can we have pancakes?"

"You bet we can have pancakes! With chocolate chips if you want them. Let me make some coffee and then we'll cook breakfast."

She stroked his head as she cleared the doorway, her son pulling her by the hand toward the kitchen.

CHAPTER 27

It had taken everything she had to make herself get up and go to work that morning. At least it was finally Friday. She consoled herself with the thought as she jerked the glass door open and headed through the security check point.

She used to enjoy being a scientist. Once she'd made the leap into the bioengineering field her natural curiosity and fascination with plants had kicked into high gear. She should love going to work each day. Just like her husband did. After bouncing around in various research fields, she'd hoped to be settled in at a strong company by now, one that shared her vision for finding ways to use plants to create a better future for humankind. But she worked at BioGen, home of the Giant Asshole who had managed to ruin the dreams she'd had.

Her heels clicked down the white hallway as she thought about her career. The field of plant bioengineering attracted her with the hope of being able to improve the world through nature and science. Whether it was increasing crop viability to help feed starving populations or discovering new cures for diseases, she wanted to help. It was important to her to know that the vast amount of hours she spent at work contributed something meaningful to humankind. Sure, a woman needed to be able to pay the bills but she figured a smart woman could find a way to combine earning a living with helping people.

The door swung shut behind her as she glanced across the lab. Mr. Perfect sat at the table, engrossed with work that he had no doubt started on before sunrise.

"Good morning, Chelsea. I'm really glad to see you." Relief sang through his words as he looked at her across the white tiles.

"Good morning." She didn't bother with a smile as she walked over to the coffee pot. Slim fingers poured cream in a biodegradable cup, plucked a wooden stir stick out of the box. Coffee swirled as she gathered her thoughts. As much as she liked working with Brad, she wasn't in the mood today. If he did the eye graze thing this morning she just might punch him. Turning on a slim black heel she'd picked up at the mall yesterday, she headed back to where he sat. It was almost disappointing when he only spared a quick smile at her then looked back at the pages in front of him. She came to a stop next to the table.

"So, what kind of nonsense are we working on today Early Bird?" Scorn dripped like a coat of grease through her quiet voice.

"Ha ha." Brad replied, ignoring her sarcasm. He dropped his pen on the papers and gave her his full attention. The silver bar stool slid out with a squeak as she sat down and faced him across the table. Navy eyes studied her a moment. He tried a smile, it didn't work and she could see that he knew it.

"Look, you and I both know Orlon is a complete idiot, but there is no denying he knows what he's doing when it comes to bringing funding in so we can keep fighting the good fight. You can't have a problem with that, Chelsea. We need him."

Lips flattened in a thin line, she kept quiet and waited to see how far he planned to wade in. She would make no effort to contribute—not a damn thing—for the remainder of her stay at BioGen. Coast mode was the only way she would survive it. She had already committed herself to spending the majority of the weekend surfing for job openings and sending her resume out. Real action was needed if she was going to make a change. The sooner, the better.

"What will it hurt if we spend some time looking at all the various aspects of Alzheimer's and autism to see if there is any connection? Orlon said even if it's only one similar symptom or other shared trait he wants us to put it in the report. I clarified things with him after you left in a huff yesterday." His tone had shifted to slightly insulted.

"He said he's not asking us to prove the two diseases are related, or that the tomato vaccine will impact autism to any degree.

He's just hoping we can pinpoint something to reference in the report as a possibility so he can use it to go after more funding. If nothing gels down the road, no harm, no foul. It will be just another failed possibility in the pursuit of new discoveries. But think of the impact if we can nail something down."

She studied his face. Although they had been lab partners for two years, she really didn't know much about him on a personal level. He had made noises in response to her expressing the desire to contribute to the world in a meaningful way but he hadn't actually stated any clear goals of his own along those lines. She had a suspicion he'd chosen his career path for the money and lack of manual labor more than anything else.

Bioengineering had been a groundbreaking field ten years ago and had grown significantly since then but it was still a controversial science in a lot of ways. Not as fraught as stem cell research, but still, there were people out there who thought it was wrong to change the way plants grew at the genetic level. A lot of people got really upset at the idea of man messing with what God had created.

A sigh escaped her as she picked up her cup and stared into it a moment. She took a sip then set it down again. A small twinge of guilt hit as she recalled leaving the dripping pool of coffee for him to clean up yesterday.

"Listen, at this point, I'm just here for my paycheck. Don't expect much out of me, okay?" She did her best to keep her tone neutral. Brad had been consistently kind and supportive, he didn't deserve her anger. "Tell me what you want me to do. I've been the lead on this project since October. You take the reins, I don't want them. Just keep my name off the report." She gave him a half-smile and took another sip.

A raccoon-in-the-road look of panic flashed in his eyes before he looked down and shuffled the papers in front him.

After a long beat he said, "Okay. I'm it. Let's get to work."

CHAPTER 28

Grey clouds loomed overhead as silence stretched out of the phone. He listened to the thrum of the tires on the highway until Jimmy responded to his question.

"You might want to rethink that one, Craig-O."

"What do you mean? That's all I've been doing."

He had called Jimmy from the road to get his advice on how to handle the situation with his wife. Things were coming to a head that seemed beyond his control. For the first time in eighteen years of marriage he felt like shouting "Man overboard!" and wasn't sure if he was the crewman doing the shouting or the guy drowning in the sea.

"Try to pretend you're Chelsea—see things through her eyes."

The Lexus was a quiet, smooth ride and the tan leather seats were as comfortable as a sofa but he squirmed at Jimmy's suggestion to think like a woman.

"That's exactly what I'm trying to do."

"Well…could be you're suffering from a blind spot, bro. It seems to me like you're missing something. But hey, I'm just a mechanic. You're the guy with two college degrees."

"Now how's that supposed to help me? Stop talking in circles and say what you mean."

"I'm gonna let you dwell on it. Maybe you need to meditate or something. From my experience, someone suffering from a blind spot can't be cured by a person telling him how to open his eyes.

You need to see things for yourself and I'm pretty sure you can, if you try."

Jimmy's tone and lack of willingness to help brainstorm the problem grated his already frayed nerves.

"Come on, give me a break. What in the hell do you mean—I have a blind spot? My eyes are wide open, thank you very much. I've got a wonderful wife, whom I've been completely faithful to, and all of a sudden she wants me to change what I do for a living after eighteen years. How does that make me blind?"

"Look, I gotta go. I've got a date with Rachel tonight and I don't wanna be late. We're going to listen to some jazz at the Brasserie and it gets crowded early. I need to get in the shower. Give me a call in a day or two. Talk to ya later, bro. Safe travels."

Craig scowled at the phone and dropped it on the seat beside him with a grunt of disgust. So much for his older brother's advice on this one.

As far as he could see, nothing had changed between him and Chelsea except her increased concern about him traveling. He was doing everything good husbands were supposed to: most of his paycheck went toward the family budget, he never forgot special occasions, spent the majority of his time at the house and rarely went anywhere without the kids on the weekends. He handled all the kitchen chores when he was home, listened to his wife whenever she had something to say and made passionate love to her whenever she'd let him. What else was he supposed to be doing?

He shook his head again as he drove down the highway, thinking about how his perfect life seemed to be going to hell in a hurry. Not only was his wife pissed off at him, his son was now an international thief. What next?

A feeling of doom settled on his shoulders. He tried to shrug it off as he gave himself a pep talk.

"I can handle this. It's Friday. I'll talk to Ethan, get the sphere back. I'll talk to Chelsea and we'll get things ironed out and have a great weekend. No reason to panic. We'll be back to normal on Monday."

Acid poured into his stomach as he steered the car around a curve. What in the hell was a blind spot supposed to be after eighteen years of marriage, and why in the hell did Ethan steal that sphere?

CHAPTER 29

Ethan dropped the remote back on the coffee table and stood up. Watching TV wasn't going to work, he was way too restless. The kitchen door swung shut behind him as he pulled the fridge open and stood staring into its chilly belly. Nothing sounded good and his stomach was irritated.

Knowing his dad was coming home had been the only thing he could think about all day. He was pretty sure his dad would ask about the sphere again when he got back. Lying to him on the phone Wednesday had been hard enough. Throat constricting, he gulped down panic and snagged a bottle of water, shut the door and wandered over to the kitchen table.

He stood staring out at the backyard, thinking of the best way to ask Lily about the sphere again. A search through every corner of his room last night had turned up zip. He wasn't sure whether to believe his sister's quick 'nope' from yesterday. She wasn't looking at him when she'd denied taking the sphere and had been concentrating on showing off her new teeth.

The front door opened and he heard Lily come in. He headed back down the hallway.

"Hey Lily. How was school?"

"Don't talk to me." She dragged the backpack off, kicked her shoes under the bench.

"What's wrong?" He scowled as she headed for the stairs.

"I don't feel good. Leave me alone."

Her little bare toes continued to climb as she spoke. Panic rose as he watched her disappear up the stairs. He really needed to talk to her before his dad got home.

"Hey, Lily, wait a second."

"No. I feel like I'm gonna puke. Leave me alone, I'm going to bed."

He stood at the bottom of the stairs, thinking a moment. Maybe she didn't take the sphere anyway. If she was sick, he didn't want anything to do with her—that was his mom's problem. He yanked a hand through his hair as he wandered back to the family room sofa.

*   *   *

Lily made it to her pink room and flopped down on the bed. Her head really hurt and she wanted her mom. Maybe if she took her jeans off her tummy would feel better. It took all she had to stand back up. Her arms and legs ached, maybe worse than her head.

A tear rolled down her cheek as she unbuttoned her jeans and sat down to kick them off. She was dizzy and her stomach rumbled while she tugged open a dresser drawer, grabbed her favorite PJs. She hurried to pull them on as a chill coursed down her bare skin. Bed sounded good. She would take a nap until her mom got home. She crawled under the covers and settled in with a sigh, aching all over.

*   *   *

He picked up the remote and clicked the TV on again, surfing through the channels without tuning in to anything. His stomach cramped and he swigged more water. A glance at the cable box told him it was three-fifty. He only had a couple hours before his dad got home.

Queasiness set in as he thought about having to admit to his dad that he'd taken the sphere. He had never stolen anything in his life and still wasn't sure what had come over him that day at the mine. He was so caught up in wanting to write a really great essay and winning a scholarship to make his dad proud of him, he hadn't thought any further than the driving need to run some tests on the contents of the spheres.

He screwed the lid back on the water and sat absently tumbling the bottle in his hands. The idea of a more detailed analysis kept poking at him and made him think it was the key to answering the mystery of the spheres. His mom worked in a lab and could probably do it for him. That was the train of thought he'd been following when Emily had suddenly come in and told them to leave. He'd stood there holding the death star sphere—looking at the metal box full of the little orbs—and instantly decided they probably wouldn't miss one. He'd stuck it in his pocket, not letting himself think any more about it.

Once they were home and he'd had a chance to think it through a little more, he'd realized he couldn't give the sphere to his mom to test because she'd probably talk with his dad about the test results. At that point, he wished he'd never taken the stupid thing but it was too late to unwind it and all he could do was hope the manager never noticed. That plan had fallen apart real quick. Stupid.

It had all gone backwards on him in a hurry. Sweat broke out on his forehead as he paced down the hallway then back to the family room sofa again. He fell onto it with a dejected flop. What would his dad say when he found out the truth? He hung his head and rubbed at his eyes, shame sliding over him like a bucket of ice water.

"Ethan, I don't feel good."

Lily's voice came out a panicked whine and he whipped his head up.

He looked at his sister standing in the doorway across the room. She had changed out of her jeans into her Hello Kitty pajamas and she really didn't look good. Her face was chalk white and covered with strange spots. Her arms had weird splotches too.

He blinked back at her, not sure what to do. He jerked up off the couch when Lily leaned over and vomited on the carpet.

His legs moved toward her without his even thinking about it, but before he could reach her, she slumped to the floor, jerking as if she'd stuck a finger in a light socket.

Panic flew through him as he reached her and pulled her away from the vomit.

"Lily! Shit!"

Her little heels pounded the floor as he tried to hold her still. His mind swirled in shock before it cleared enough for him to pull out his phone and hit the speed button for his mom's cell.

"Come on, come on!" he grumbled into the phone as he listened to it ring on the other end. Lily's tremors came to a stop as voice mail picked up.

"Mom! It's Ethan. You've gotta come home right now! Lily is really sick, Mom. I don't know what's going on with her. She puked and, well….I don't know what to do! Call me, call me right away." He hit the end button and stared at the phone trying to think. His dad was probably too far away to do anything. Should he call 911? Then he remembered their neighbor Ann was a nurse.

He stood up and looked down at his sister. She lay completely still, out cold, but she was breathing. He took off like a shot down the hallway, front door crashing behind him as he sprinted out and down the sidewalk.

Finger jammed into the doorbell non-stop, knuckles wrapping on the door frame, Ethan hit Ann's front porch like a tornado dropped down out of the sky.

"Come on, come on, Ann…please, God, let her be home." He stood considering whether to run around to the back of the house when the front door swung open and Steve stared out at him.

"Hi Ethan."

He looked at the little boy, mind completely blank for a second, trying to process Steve being the one to open the door instead of Ann.

"Is your mom home? It's an emergency."

"What happened?"

"Is she home or not?" Ethan snapped without meaning to.

"She's here." Steve looked back at him, his body blocking the space between the entrance and the heavy oak door.

"Steve, who is it Honey?" Ann called out, her voice growing nearer.

He hollered over Steve's head, "Ann, it's me, Ethan. Lily is really sick! Can you please come over and take a look at her?"

She appeared, dishtowel in hand. "Ethan, what did you say? I didn't quite hear you?"

"Ann, please, you gotta hurry, Lily is really sick. I don't know what's wrong with her. She puked, started shaking all over and then she passed out, all in less than a minute. Will you come and take a look at her?"

"Of course, let's go. Tell me everything you can while we head back over there. Come on Steve—"

The boy was already crowding past Ann's hip to get through the door before she could finish the sentence.

"Hurry, Mom!" Steve shot across the lawns and through the Noble's front door.

Ethan and Ann ran behind while he told her the details of what happened.

"My mom didn't answer her cell and she hasn't called me back yet."

They reached the end of the hallway and he saw Lily still lay where he'd left her. Her face looked so pale, even more than when she'd first come into the family room.

"Oh Ethan, this is not good, Honey. Call 911. Right now. They can get here faster than we can get her across town at this time of day."

Ethan punched in the numbers then handed her his cell phone and listened as she called in his sister's condition, word for word from what he'd told her but with more jargon. His brow furrowed as he listened to her conversation while he stared down at his sister. Ann told the dispatcher Lily's symptoms in a calm tone and a fast clip as she knelt and examined the little girl.

"The patient is presenting a severe rash across all visible skin surfaces; face, neck, arms, hands and legs. Spots are approximately a quarter-inch to half-inch wide in an odd spiral pattern, color of the rash is a bright florescent orange base with tiny yellow dots. I've never seen anything like it. The rash sites appear to have a slightly raised surface with no pustules visible. Eyes are dilated. Patient's breathing is shallow, pulse is thready. She is unresponsive to touch and sound. Convulsions have ceased for the moment."

He watched as Ann reached out and felt his sister's forehead. "She doesn't have much of a fever. That's strange."

She looked at him and asked, "Have your parents ever said anything about her having epilepsy? Has she ever had seizures before?"

Ethan blinked back at her, "No, never. Is she going to be okay?"

"I'm sure she's going to be fine. I don't know what's wrong with her, it looks serious but it could turn out to be not a big deal. Just have faith, it's the most important thing we can do for her in the next minute or two. She's breathing on her own and that's a good sign. Now, try to call your mom again while we wait for the ambulance."

They listened to the cell ringing then it went to voice mail again. Ethan looked a question at Ann, who nodded and held her hand out for the phone.

"Hi Chelsea, it's Ann. Listen, Lily is really sick—she's got a rash and is unconscious. We've called an ambulance and will be heading to the hospital most likely. I'll call you when we get there. Ethan and Steve will go with me in my car. We'll follow the ambulance in, okay? Call me as soon as you can."

Just as she disconnected the call they heard the ambulance coming down the street.

"Go out in the yard and wave at them, Ethan, then just step back out of their way because they'll be coming inside in a hurry, okay? Thanks."

He took off down the hall and shot out the door, barely glancing at Steve who stood silently in the corner, staring at his best friend, tears running down his face as he watched his mom's every move.

"Is she going to be okay?" Steve's small voice pleaded with her.

"I'm sure she'll be fine, don't worry." Ann repeated her nurse's mantra, her last two words were completely drowned out by the sound of the emergency crew bringing in the gurney as they hustled down the hall toward the family room.

Ethan came in behind them and felt Ann put her arm around him with a gentle squeeze. They stayed out of the crew's way and watched the men load Lily on the gurney.

CHAPTER 30

"**M**yelin." Chelsea said aloud as she stared at the computer screen in front of her.

"What about it?" Brad slid his chair across the tiled floor and stared over her shoulder.

She straightened up from the computer screen, chagrined at speaking aloud without realizing it. "Oh, nothing. Just pondering."

"Come on. I know you. You've got something." His eyes sparked with hope and bright white teeth glinted in the overhead lights as he smiled at her.

She took a sip from the bottle of water at her elbow and watched him wiggle on the wheeled chair while she considered how to answer. In spite of her resolve to contribute nothing worthwhile before she flew the coop at BioGen, she was a scientist at heart and needed to do something to occupy her eight-to-five time. Excitement had grown as she read about the possible link between autism and Alzheimer's. The plan to shut her brain off flew out the window as she finished reading the article on the screen.

But as the statement about the possible myelin link slipped out, she realized she needed to stop and think practically for a moment. If she was seriously going to get another job, it would be far better to take the new-found idea and run with it at another company.

She logged off the computer screen as she answered him, "Really, it's no big deal. I was just reading about the myelin membrane." She slid the keyboard tray back under the monitor then stood up, forcing Brad to scoot out of the way. "My eyes are done for today, no more screen time for me."

"Come on Chelsea. What's up? We've been lab partners for two years now. I know you. Something has rung that pretty bell of yours. I can see your neurons firing. Tell me what you're thinking about the myelin angle." He stood up and stuffed his hands in the lab coat pockets.

She looked silently back at him a moment. Helping Orlon Millard look good was the last thing she wanted to do on her way out the door. Not to mention, as soon as she performed any work or typed up a single report related to her thoughts on the myelin connection, it would become proprietary information and she would not be able to work on the potential project at the new job without legal jeopardy. She decided right that minute, although Brad was a great guy and fun to work with, she needed to tread carefully if she was going to make a smart move.

Instead of answering him, she snagged the insulated go-bottle, glancing at her watch as she walked over to the water cooler for a refill. It was just past four o'clock. The kids should be home and she'd give them a quick check-in call. It would get Brad off her tail for a few minutes.

She gave his insistent needling a response from the water cooler in the corner, "I wish I had something concrete to discuss but I don't."

They'd spent the majority of the day surfing the internet and reading volumes of information about autism. The more she read, the more her heart went out to Ann and Steve. It really was a terrible thing for a child and his family to deal with. Modern science understanding so little about the cause behind autism made it even worse. With no glimmer of a cure and no method of prevention it was heartbreaking to know the rate of autism was rapidly increasing.

The article she'd just finished reading discussed the theory of the protective myelin sheath not being completely formed until age two, thereby making the brain susceptible to toxins that could impact the brain as the child grew, leading to a diagnosis of autism. Conversely, she knew from her Alzheimer's research that after age fifty, the myelin sheath began to shrink, once again exposing the brain to toxins like the body's own beta-amyloid protein. She needed to think it through and make some notes but wasn't about to do so at BioGen.

"Excuse me a minute, I need to check in with the kids." She could feel his eyes on her back. She ignored him and pulled her cell phone. BioGen was history and she wasn't going to weaken just because he looked good, smelled good and seemed to be a good friend. As long as he was a loyal employee of BioGen, she'd keep him at arm's length.

The voice mail icon flashed at her. She hit the button to listen to the messages as Brad drifted over to her again. Annoyed, she turned and walked toward the back of the room, wanting space. Brad didn't seem to be in the mood to give it to her but that was his problem.

She looked up when Orlon walked through the door, stepping in just as her son's voice reached her ear. Concern flew through her while she listened to the message and the men spoke across the room. Her fingers began trembling when the second message played.

"Chelsea, would you mind? I'd like to discuss your idea about the myelin sheath for a moment." Orlon glared at the phone in her hand.

"...*We'll follow the ambulance in, okay? Call me as soon as possible.*" Chelsea's heart dropped to the floor at hearing Ann's words. She had hoped from Ethan's message she was just dealing with a stomach bug and a spooked teenager. Ann's message completely eliminated that possibility. Her hand shook so bad she missed hitting the voice mail button twice. She slipped the phone in a pocket while Orlon continued speaking.

"Chelsea, really. You know we'd prefer you refrain from unnecessary personal calls while at work. Now, tell me about the myelin possibility Brad mentioned you'd found this afternoon."

It took a moment for her brain to come out of its panicked fog enough for his words to register. She glanced from his pig's snout to Brad's sheepish shrug, panic soaring. She needed to get the hell out of there and go see about her daughter.

"What did you just say to me?" The words were shaky and she drew a steadying breath.

Orlon's lips smacked in exasperation, "I want to discuss the myelin sheath research."

"I can't, I've got to go. My daughter is sick. I just got a message from my neighbor. It sounds serious—they've taken Lily to the hospital. I'm leaving. You'll have to wait or talk about it with him." She gave Brad a look that would split a redwood tree then brushed past Orlon to get to her purse and the door.

He snagged her arm as she passed, "Wait just a minute young lady. Where do you think you're going? We have serious business to discuss. The board meeting is next week. Let your husband see about your daughter for a few minutes. This is the twenty-first century."

It took every ounce of self-discipline she had to keep from punching him. The last thing she needed was an assault charge or a lawsuit. But she damn sure didn't need her job that bad.

"Go to hell, Orlon. Go to hell in a basket on fire." The words ground out like broken glass and she whipped her arm out of his grasp.

The cabinet door banged against the wall. Purse in hand, she flew out of the lab without looking back.

CHAPTER 31

The emergency room doors crashed open and Ethan watched the ambulance crew push the gurney inside. Ann had managed to keep up all the way through town and they'd climbed out of the car just in time to watch the men unload Lily from the back of the bright red truck. From the brief glimpse before the doors swung shut again, his sister had not yet regained consciousness. He looked over his shoulder at Ann, worry flowing between them.

They hustled inside, Ann leading the way over to the check-in station as Ethan watched the emergency crew take his sister behind another set of doors.

"Hi Grace. The little girl that was just brought in, her name is Lily Noble, and her mother should be here any minute."

The woman behind the desk began typing on the computer keys. "Do you have her insurance information or do I need to wait for the mother to get here?"

Ethan pulled his eyes away from the doors his sister had disappeared through. "I think I've got our insurance info. Hang on a second." He reached back and fished his wallet out of his pocket. He'd been carrying it ever since he got his driver's license. His mom had given him an insurance card in case he got hurt in an accident. He fumbled out the blue and white rectangle.

"Thanks." The woman plugged in the data as Ethan thought about what she was typing.

"Her real name isn't Lily."

"Oh, what's her name then?" The woman glanced at Ann then back to him.

"It's Catherine Elizabeth Noble."

"Okay, thanks."

He watched her type another second then glanced back at the door.

"Do you know if she has any allergies or other information the medical team might need to know?" The woman was looking at him again.

"Not that I know of," Ethan replied.

"Okay. That's enough info until her mom gets here to sign all the forms," the nurse said.

"Come on Ethan, let's take a seat over there while we wait."

He followed Ann to a large grouping of chairs with a T.V. mounted in the corner. They sat down and she pulled her phone out to try Chelsea again.

It rang twice then they heard traffic noise and a horn blaring.

"Chelsea?"

"Ann! Thank God. I've been trying to reach you for the past ten minutes, but all I got was a busy signal. Is Lily okay?"

Ethan could hear every word his mom said even though Ann didn't have the speaker on.

"Are you on your way here?"

"Yes, I should be there in five minutes. How's Lily?"

Ethan heard another horn blaring from the phone. His mom must be running lights.

Ann hesitated, "They just brought her in. We gave the check-in desk the insurance info Ethan has with him. They have forms you'll need to fill out when you get here. We're in the emergency waiting room." She paused then said, "We don't know what's wrong yet, Chelsea. They're checking her over to find out, drawing blood and that sort of thing. I'm guessing it will be a little while before we hear anything from the doctor."

"Oh, God! I can't believe this is happening. She seemed perfectly fine last night and this morning. I can't imagine what it could be that it came on so fast, can you?" A symphony of horns blasted through the phone as Chelsea spoke.

"I haven't got a clue. But listen, we'll talk when you get here, I don't want you to have a wreck. I'll see you in a minute."

He looked over at Steve. The boy sat on the floor next to Ann's chair, forearms stacked on top of his pulled-up knees, head down. He watched as tears trickled off the boy's arms and ran toward his jeans. Like an instant reflex, tears sprang to Ethan's eyes as his own emotions welled out. He abruptly stood up and started pacing the waiting room floor.

Pulling out his phone, he looked at the time as he paced—four-fifteen. His dad might be close to home. He hit the speed dial, waited for it to ring but it went straight to voice mail. He left his dad a message to come to the hospital, trying to stay calm while he spoke. Knowing his mom would be there any minute helped.

Ethan sat again and looked around the waiting room. It was jammed with people. Maybe whatever was wrong with Lily was contagious. He scanned faces and arms—no one had any orange spots. There were only two empty seats left.

A minute later the glass entrance doors slid open and he watched his mom's long legs cover the distance across the room. He stood up and she reached out, enveloping him in a hug. It felt good. His nerves were shot.

"Are you okay?" she asked.

"Yeah, I'm okay. I'm not sick. Just Lily."

She turned and hugged Ann, "Thank you for your help. The doctor hasn't come out yet?"

"No, but Lily's only been back there about ten minutes, so it's probably going to be a little bit yet, unless they have questions for you."

Just as Ann finished speaking Ethan saw a tall man dressed in green hospital scrubs come out the same doors the ambulance crew had taken Lily through. The doctor spoke to the check-in nurse and she pointed at them.

The doctor hurried over. "Mrs. Noble?" He had an intense expression on his face.

"Yes. I'm Lily's mother. How is she? Can I go see her now?"

Instead of answering, he hurriedly asked, "Has your daughter recently been exposed to any unusual foods or plants? Is she taking any medications or vitamins?"

"No, not that I'm aware of. How is she doing? Can I go back and see her?" His mom's voice strengthened as she asked the question a second time.

"I'm afraid your daughter is in bad shape. She's unconscious and is unresponsive at this time. I gather from what the emergency crew said she's been unconscious for the past thirty minutes. Is that right?"

"Did Lily pass out right before you called me?"

"Yeah, Mom. She came in the family room and puked then her eyes rolled back in her head and she hit the floor before I could catch her." His palms felt hot and he rubbed them on his knees as he spoke.

"Did you see her eat anything unusual after she got home from school?" Chelsea asked.

"No, she went straight up to her room because she didn't feel good."

The doctor seemed frustrated. "With nothing to go on, all we can do is run tests, treat her symptoms and hope we can get her stabilized. Her spots have got me really puzzled."

"What spots? She has a rash?" Chelsea asked.

"She has these really weird spots, Mom—bright orange with little yellow dots."

"I've never seen anything like it before in my life." The doctor shook his head. "You're absolutely sure she hasn't been exposed to any chemicals or plants recently?"

"To the best of my knowledge, she hasn't been around anything new at all." His mom looked back at the doctor, worry swimming in her eyes.

Ethan watched the man frown and lift his glasses off his face. The doctor rubbed his eyes, put the glasses in his pocket. Then he said, "I hate to do it, but I have to call the Centers for Disease Control and report this, Mrs. Noble. Your daughter is seriously ill and we have no idea why. I would hold off making the call, but the fact that Lily remains unconscious combined with those strange spots has me really worried."

He rubbed a hand over his eyes a last time then said, "Lily could be contagious and the CDC is the best source for some kind of record of the spots. They may be able to help us with the diagnosis. In the meantime, we're going to run more tests and hope for the best. I'll speak with you again after we've got some of the blood work back. For now we can't allow any visitors."

They watched as the man rushed back through the door and into the patient care area.

She turned to Ann, "I can't believe this. Do you think Lily's going to be okay?"

Ethan had never seen his mom so upset and he could hear tears in her voice although she wasn't crying yet.

"I think so Chelsea. Her rash is so unusual, it's really hard to say what the problem might be. I'm sure they're going to get things under control, but it might take awhile." Ann's voice remained calm. "Dr. Gammond is one of the best doctors I've ever worked with. He's an internist and a surgeon. We've got to give him time to dig into what's causing the problem. Once he figures that out, I'm sure she'll begin improving right away."

His mom stood up and paced the length of the lobby. It was hard to watch as she walked and swiped at tears every few seconds. He wanted to comfort her but he could tell she was too agitated to stand still long enough for him to try and he sure didn't know what to say. He really wished his dad was there.

His phone was in his hand and his finger hit speed dial before he completed the thought. He got dad's voicemail again. A ragged breath escaped him when his mom took a seat beside him.

The rocking motion of Steve's small huddled figure came to a stop. Steve raised his head, cocked an elbow and used a forearm to wipe tears from his face and give his nose a quick scrub. Ethan thought he looked miserable. Then the kid opened his mouth and shocked them all.

"Mrs. Noble, can I go see Lily now? Please? She's probably scared back there by herself with all the doctors. I need to help her." Steve gave his eyes a last swipe and stood up, ready for action.

* * *

Craig opened the door and the smell of vomit hit him in the face. He reeled back a moment, then stepped into the kitchen, looking around as he set the briefcase on the table. The house was completely quiet. He walked into the family room and the smell grew overpowering. A puddle of bright yellow-green vomit sat on top of the carpet like a pile of stinking alien road kill. Alarmed at the sight of someone being too sick to clean up, he took off down the hallway.

"Ethan? Lily? Anybody home?" he hollered, trotting up the stairs.

He zipped through all the rooms. When he didn't see anybody he went back through one more time, looking for signs of who had made it home, trying to figure out who was ill. Lily's little jeans and t-shirt lay on the floor beside her bed. The covers were mussed and he knew she must be the one that was sick because Chelsea was tough on making beds in the morning.

He pulled out his cell to call his wife. It was four-thirty and she wasn't due home for an hour. The battery was dead. Damn. He walked back into Ethan's room. The boy's backpack was on his bed so he'd made it home as well. But where were they? If Lily had thrown up, maybe Ethan panicked and called his mom to come home early. Maybe Lily was running a fever and Chelsea had taken her to the doctor.

Maybe Ethan had gone next door to get Ann's help since Chelsea was at work and Lily had been vomiting. He flew back downstairs, out the door and over the grass to Ann's. The bell rang loudly inside the house but no one answered the door. Her car wasn't in the drive, maybe she was at work.

His teeth ground as he walked slowly back across the lawn and inside the house, straight back to his den. He snatched the house phone off its cradle and stared at the buttons, realizing he didn't know his wife's or his son's cell numbers by memory—they'd been on his speed dial for years. He shook his head at himself and rummaged through his briefcase for the phone's charger. After a fruitless search he realized he must have left it at the hotel. It was the third time this year he'd forgotten it and would have to buy another one tomorrow.

"Damn it!" He stood staring out at the back yard a moment, wondering what to do next, trying to remember the kids' pediatrician's name. For the life of him he couldn't think of it. Chelsea was always the one to take the kids to the doctor. She probably had their pediatrician's info written down somewhere but he didn't know where to look. The kids were rarely sick.

Knowing he was out of options right then, he decided to clean the vomit up while he waited. Maybe Chelsea would call on the house phone while he cleaned. Stepping to the sink, he turned the hot water on, grabbed cleaning supplies from the laundry room and got to work.

Ten minutes later the family room floor was reasonably clean again and he went in search of the Lysol spray. He found it under the sink in the hall bathroom and used a liberal dose on the floor then sprayed the air. Cleaning supplies put away, he washed his hands and looked at the time. It was almost five o'clock. He pulled a bottle of water out of the fridge then sat down at the kitchen table and stared blankly out at the yard. His mind swirled and the feeling of doom that had been riding his shoulders all the way home grew stronger.

"Think, Craig, think. Okay, Lily's sick, home alone with Ethan. What would he do?"

He looked across the lawn at Ann's, knowing that option was out, and realized Ethan had to have called Chelsea by now. He shook his head at how dependent he'd become on cell phones and rushed back to the den.

His fingers flew across the computer keys as he looked up the phone number for BioGen. Another sweep of anxiety hit while he listened to the phone ring. He could only hope the receptionist would still answer since it was a minute past five on a Friday night.

"Good afternoon, BioGen Technologies, how may I help you?" the receptionist asked.

The breath he'd been holding came out in a whoosh of relief, "This is Craig Noble. May I please speak with Chelsea Noble?"

"One moment please." A beat of quiet then a blast of Muzak as he waited.

"This is Brad."

He paused at hearing her lab partner answer. "Hi Brad. This is Craig Noble. Sorry to bother you, but my cell phone is down and I'm trying to get in touch with my wife."

"She's not here."

"Oh, did she leave early today?"

"She got a call a little while ago. I guess your daughter is pretty sick. Chelsea said they took Lily to the hospital."

He rubbed his stomach as he asked, "Did she say which one?"

"No. Chelsea grabbed her purse and left. I didn't get a chance to talk to her, so I have no idea beyond that. I assume they took her to Hawkins Memorial here in Hollister but I don't know for sure. Sorry I can't be any more help."

"Okay, thanks." Craig set the phone back in its cradle and stood up. The hospital was only fifteen minutes from the house. He headed out the door, heart in his throat.

CHAPTER 32

"I'm sorry Honey, the doctors said we can't go back to see Lily right now. They're busy working to make her feel better and we need to stay out of their way for a little bit."

"But Mom, Lily needs my help. I know she does." Steve's eyes pleaded with her.

"No, we can't go back to see her yet. We'd get in trouble with the doctors. We have to wait a little while longer."

He stood staring at her, his little eight-year old hands fisted. It was a strange feeling because she'd hoped for years her son would learn to look her in the eye and now that he was, she hoped he'd give her a break and look away. She broke the eye contact, glanced at Chelsea .

Her friend sat, staring from Steve to her and back, worry and frustration edged aside momentarily. It was obvious Chelsea wanted to ask how Steve had managed to leap out of his autistic bubble but Ann had no answer for that question. Besides, how could she sit there, talking about the miraculous progress her son had suddenly made while Chelsea's daughter lay in a coma? That was a conversation better saved for later.

She looked back at Steve, "Why don't you and I go down the hall and get something to drink? You can have whatever you like."

"Can I have a Pepsi?"

"Sure, you bet. I think I'll have one too. Can we get either of you anything?"

"No thanks," Chelsea replied. Ethan shook his head.

She took Steve's hand and they headed down the hall to the nearest soda machine.

"Can I put the money in?"

"Sure." It was another first to watch him feed dollar bills into the machine.

Steve pulled the bottle of soda out, gave it to her, repeated the process. The caps twisted open with a loud hiss and he took a couple sips standing silently beside her.

After a minute he quietly asked, "Is it still Joy Day, Mom?"

An emotional cocktail swirled through her as she looked back at her son. His blue eyes were as confused as she felt. She took a swallow of the fizzy drink then answered, "Yes. It's still Joy Day, Steve." A smile came back to her face for a moment. "I really enjoyed going to the park with you today."

"Me too. But it would've been better with Lily there." He rubbed at the sweat forming on the side of the bottle. "Do you think the doctor will let me go see her now?"

"No, Honey. She's really sick. Lily's mom and dad will be the first people allowed to see her. We might have to wait until tomorrow, but we'll see her just as soon as they say we can, I promise."

Ann's heart ached for Lily and her family, as well as her son. She would give anything to help the sunny little girl and her mother whose friendships were such a gift. It was doubly sad that Lily became so ill today. The day Ann had hoped for the last eight years had finally come to pass. She prayed it was the first one in a better life for Steve.

"Oh, God, please help Lily get well," she whispered out as they started back down the hall. They rounded the corner to the lobby and relief swept through her at seeing Craig had arrived. She watched as he gave his son a hug and Chelsea stood off to the side, scowling at her husband. Ann slowed her steps, trying to give them a minute but the lobby was small and Ethan had already spotted her. They rejoined the group and Steve sat back down, this time with legs pretzeled under him, quiet as a mouse in between sips of Pepsi.

"Hey Ann. Thank you for helping Ethan get Lily to the hospital." He stepped over and gave her a hug.

"I'm so sorry you had to come home to an emergency like this. Hopefully the doctors will figure out what's going on soon." Her words dwindled off at reading her friend's face over Craig's shoulder. She mentally kicked herself for mentioning he'd been away.

"You mean they don't know what's wrong with her? What are the doctors saying?" The concern on his face increased as he looked at Chelsea.

"Our daughter is really sick and the doctors can't seem to figure out why. She has a weird rash and is comatose right now, Craig." Her voice broke and tears started again. "They're running blood tests. The doctor will come back out and give us an update as soon as he can."

"You've got to be kidding me? With modern science and all the data available on the internet? They can't find any other cases like hers? How can that be?"

Ann looked at his stunned expression and tried to explain, "Lily's rash is very unusual. I've never seen anything like it after ten years of nursing. The doctor said he's going to contact the CDC to find out if they have anything similar on record. Hollister is not a big city, so there's a chance another physician has seen this ailment although Dr Gammond hasn't."

A few minutes later the doctor walked into the waiting room. His face grave, more so than the last time he'd spoken with them. Ann knew that face and her heart stuttered a moment at what it might mean for the Noble family. She held her breath as he stopped in front of them.

"I take it you're Lily's father?" the doctor asked.

"Yes, I'm Craig Noble." He shook the doctor's hand. "Have you found anything out?"

"We have the preliminary blood work in, but unfortunately the test results have come back confusing rather than helpful. And I'm afraid Lily is getting worse. When she came in her blood pressure was low, we gave her some medicine to try to bring it up, but so far we aren't making much progress. If it doesn't improve soon, there could be complications."

The doctor pulled his glasses off and tucked them in a pocket as he continued, "In addition to the blood pressure issue, Lily has not responded to the stimulants we've given her in an attempt to bring her out of the coma. Back to the blood tests we've run—the results are surprising because we fully expected to see a high white blood cell count, anticipating it would indicate an infection of some kind. However, that is not the case. In fact, her red blood cell count is a little high, but that's acceptable. To make matters more confusing, we just got the results back of the urinalysis." Dr Gammond paused a moment as another family passed by close enough to overhear.

"Although there is no fever present, and her white blood cell count is normal, it appears Lily is approaching renal failure in addition to the other issues we are dealing with. We can find no cause for the symptoms she's presenting. I have to ask once again— has your daughter been exposed to any sick children, new foods, or other substances recently? Could she have gotten into a jar of vitamins without your knowing it?"

Ann watched as Craig glanced from the doctor's face to Ethan's then Chelsea's. The three of them shook their heads.

Dr Gammond pressed them, "Lily is in serious jeopardy. If we cannot quickly determine the underlying cause for her symptoms, she could go into total renal failure or cardiac arrest. She could die. I implore you to think more carefully about what she has eaten, any medications she's taken, the places she's been, the people she's been exposed to. Anything out of the ordinary. No matter how small, it may very well be the reason behind her illness."

He waited a moment but no one spoke up. "If you think of anything, please let me know. For now, we're doing what we can. I'll give you another update once we get the skin analyses back but that will likely be tomorrow. If her condition changes for the worse or the better, I will let you know immediately." The man turned to head back to the patient area.

"Doctor, wait just a second, please. We'd like to see our daughter, if only for a minute or two. When will we be allowed in with her?" Craig asked.

"As I told your wife, because of the strange rash, combined with the severity of her other symptoms, we have had to place Lily in isolation. We cannot risk contaminating other patients or medical staff. This is a small hospital and we have limited resources to work with in a situation like this. I've contacted the Centers for Disease Control and advised them of the symptoms. Until we get clearance from them, we cannot allow any visitors."

"What are you saying, doctor? I'm not allowed to see my own child? Surely there is some kind of mask I can wear or some other type of protective gear and cleansing routine available so that I won't risk contaminating others?" Chelsea's voice escalated as she spoke and Ann grasped her hand.

"Chelsea, until someone from the CDC gives the okay, the hospital is legally required to follow specific procedures. I'm sure you'll be allowed in to see her soon." Ann worked to calm her friend but she understood the heart of a mother and knew Chelsea wasn't going to be held off for long.

"Okay, I'll wait a little while. But whether there are any hazmat suits available or not, I'm going to see my daughter today so she knows we're here for her. Nothing is going to stop me from doing that, do you understand?"

The doctor studied Chelsea's face, his mouth forming a firm line. Ann knew Gammond must be completely exhausted on the tail end of his twelve hour shift. He was a great doctor but had never been known for his bedside manner and when he got tired he got cranky. She held her breath as the doctor's eyebrows lowered.

Gammond's voice rumbled out like distant thunder, "Mrs. Noble, do you understand how serious this situation is? Not only could your daughter die, if others are exposed to the disease, we may have an instant epidemic on our hands. Do you want to be held responsible for that?"

Chelsea blanched as his words rolled over her, but she was clearly ready to fight with everything she had to be with her daughter. Her fists bunched, "Look—"

"If we're able to get Lily stabilized and confirm she's not contagious, you will be allowed to spend as much time as you want with her. If her condition worsens, I'll let you have a hazmat suit so you can say goodbye."

Ann couldn't help wincing. The doctor turned and hurried into the restricted area without another word. She watched Chelsea fight to get her breath back and tears streamed down her cheeks. Ann's heart ached even more for their family when she watched her friend jerk away from Craig's arms.

"I'm going to the restroom," Chelsea choked out. Silence fell on their small group while her heels clicked down the tiled hallway.

CHAPTER 33

The cloak of doom tightened around him and his wife's slim figure disappeared down the hall. It took him a long moment to pull out of the stun from her rejection on the back of the doctor's bad news. His eyes zipped around the lobby and he forced himself to focus. Ethan sat, elbows on his knees, forehead resting on steepled fingers while he stared down at the floor.

Emotions hit every surface as he sat down beside his son, thinking about the doctor's words. How could a child become so deathly ill out of the blue in this day and age and no one have a clue why? It made the whole situation much worse, seemingly beyond control. Nausea rolled at the thought of losing Lily. He was desperate to help her but had no idea what to do. He was way too keyed up to just sit.

"Do you want to get a bottle of water or something?"

"I guess." Ethan stood up and shuffled toward the doorway. "I think the soda machine's this way." They headed down the hall, hands in their pockets, not talking until drinks were purchased.

Craig leaned up against the wall next to the machine and cracked the lid on his water. "Thanks for helping get Lily to the hospital, Ethan. It's a good thing Ann lives next door, I'm sure glad she was home. You must have been pretty scared when your sister passed out."

"Yeah, it was pretty freaky. She's really sick, huh?"

"Yes, very sick." He turned and paced off a few steps, came back, let out a long breath and asked, "Did you ever find that sphere?"

"What do you mean?"

"You know what I mean. I think it's time you were honest with me—don't you?"

"Dad, I don't have it, I swear."

He studied his son, trying to keep a lid on his emotions. "Look, Mr. Connor told me they have a security video from the day we were at the mine. They've got you on camera putting the sphere in your pocket."

He watched the color leave Ethan's face. Fear joined the worry in his son's eyes. He waited in silence for a minute, needing Ethan to get it together and give him a straight answer.

"I.....I'm really sorry, Dad." His son's eyes filmed up around the strangled words. "I did take it. But I don't have it now. It's missing."

Craig pushed off the wall and turned to fully face his son. His daughter's life was on the line— it was no time for a disciplinary scene but he had to cover the basics. Right now. Teenagers had a way of looking at the world in a vacuum.

"Do you have any idea how much jeopardy you've put our family in? Not only could we be facing legal charges—taking that sphere could get back to my boss—I could lose my job over it. I used my company's name as a foot in the door with Connor, otherwise we'd never have had the opportunity to examine those spheres. Did you think about any of that when you slipped it in your pocket?" It was impossible to keep the angry scorn from his voice. Besides, the kid damn well deserved it.

Ethan hung his head. "I'm really sorry. I'll try to make it up to you somehow." He squeaked the toe of his shoe on the tiles. "I wish I was the one about to die instead of Lily."

"Ethan James, you look at me right now." His son's head whipped up. "This is no time for quitting. And it's sure as hell no time for lying. You know how I feel about that. Now tell me the truth—where is the sphere? Connor said if we give it back to him he'll drop the issue. So where is it?"

A speck of relief washed over his son's face but it was quickly replaced by panic.

"Dad, seriously. I don't have it. I mean—I did have it. When we got home I put it in the toe of one of my basketball shoes. I know I put it back after I finished working on my paper. But now it's gone…just gone…I don't know…it's like it puffed into thin air."

Craig batted the water bottle against his thigh. He was already beyond upset about his daughter, sick over Ethan taking the sphere and lying to him on top of it. Now the boy was going to stand there and refuse to give it back. The urge to hit his son was overwhelming. It took everything he had to keep from hitting him right then. Everything.

He turned his back on Ethan, trying to get it together. He forced a deep breath into his lungs. *Ten count….focus on the family….we have to be able to go on from here….I love my son. Work from love, work from logic, not anger…*

"Ethan, did you hear me say Connor will drop the issue if we give him the sphere back?"

"Yes, Dad, I heard you. I don't have it. I wish I did. I've looked all over my room. I even looked in Lily's room, but I can't see her messing with my shoes, you know how bad they stink." Ethan's eyes pleaded with him to believe the sphere was missing.

"Seems pretty strange that sphere would just up and disappear. Are you sure you didn't put it somewhere else?"

"I'm sure. I looked in every inch of my room, my book bag, Lily's room. It's not there. It's gone…just gone. I can't explain it."

"Well, since you can't explain the missing sphere, let's move on to more important things—like what Lily might have been exposed to. We just got back from Africa five days ago. Did you bring anything home with you, other than the sphere, that Lily might have got a hold of? You collected rocks and brought those back, right? Are any of the rocks missing?"

"I don't think so. They're still in the plastic bag in my suitcase."

"You never unpacked?"

Ethan shrugged, "I usually do my laundry on the weekend so I figured there was no rush. I had other stuff to wear. What does it matter?"

"I'm just trying to nail down what your sister might have touched or been exposed to. Has she been in your room at all this week?"

"Not that I know of. I've yelled at her enough about it she pretty much stays out."

Craig rubbed his neck, trying to relieve some of the tension. "Okay, process of elimination—I know I didn't bring anything back from Africa except what I took with me. Are you sure the only things you brought back were the rocks and the sphere? You didn't accidentally bring grasses stuck on your shoe or anything like that?"

"No. Some dust probably stuck to my shoes but that's it."

"Do you feel sick in any kind of way?"

"No, Dad. I'm fine. No spots, see?" He stuck his arms out. "What about you, how do you feel?"

"Me?" Craig thought a moment. "Well, my stomach's been kind of acting up, but that started before we went to Africa. Other than that, I'm fine." He looked down at his arms—no spots.

"It seems to me the only new thing your sister might have been exposed to is that damn sphere. I realize she probably didn't take it, but maybe she did— it's missing, right?" His mind wheeled over where Lily might have hidden the sphere if she'd sneaked it from her brother's room. "Did you look inside her dollhouse?"

"That's the first place I looked." Wistful glances exchanged, they stood in silence, both brains spinning.

"But Dad, even if she took the sphere, how could it make her sick? You and I handled it. We touched more than one sphere, so have lots of other people, and nobody's gotten sick."

"I don't know, Ethan. But logically, what else could it be? If another child at her school had come down with what Lily has, we'd have heard about it from one of the neighbors or the school. You know your mom, she talks to the teachers every day. She'd definitely know if another child was in the hospital or really sick."

"Yeah, I guess you're right. I tried to think about all the stuff we've eaten this week, but it's pretty much been the same things we always have. Mom's been kinda stressed out about work, so we didn't go anywhere in the evenings. Lily and I came home from school, Mom came home from work and we hung out. You know, the usual routine."

Craig stood listening to his son's words and realized he had no idea what his family's usual routine was during the week. He had no way of knowing what Lily had been exposed to. He hadn't been home since Tuesday morning. He didn't know what his family had eaten, or what activities they'd shared. Other than his thoughts on the sphere, he had nothing to contribute.

"I guess we'd better get back out to the lobby. I give your mom another hour then all hell is going to break loose if they don't let her in to see your sister."

CHAPTER 34

Chelsea watched a man in a suit and tie step through the entrance doors. He carried a briefcase and seemed to be in a hurry. The woman accompanying him was also dressed for business and held a laptop case in her hand. They went straight to the check-in desk and spoke with the nurse. She listened a moment then picked up the phone and made a quick call then nodded toward the waiting area.

The strangers quick-stepped over to Chelsea. The man appeared to be in his late forties, the woman in her early thirties. Both wore stern expressions and got right down to business.

The man spoke first, "Are you Lily Noble's mother?"

"Yes, I am." She saw Ethan and Craig step back in the lobby and approach the group as the man continued speaking.

"I'm Bob Wilson and this is Karen Sanders. We're with the Centers for Disease Control and we need to speak with you about your daughter."

"Hi, I'm Craig Noble." The man looked at Craig's outstretched hand and ignored it.

Chelsea didn't bother participating in the social graces. She was too anxious to hear what these people had to say. Hopefully they'd heard of the rash Lily was suffering from. She scanned Wilson's face, trying to gauge what he knew. She didn't like what she saw. The man looked like he was about to fire someone.

"We need to ask several questions before we decide how to proceed." Bob pushed a stack of magazines aside and set his briefcase on the coffee table. He pulled out a clipboard, handed it to the woman who took a seat opposite Chelsea and Ann.

"You're aware that your daughter is suffering from a severe illness that is so far unidentified?" Bob asked.

What was with this guy? He was giving off vibes like he was in charge and she had just walked into the room and needed to be brought up to speed instead of the other way around. She forced herself to keep her tone civil, "Yes, we are aware of that. Dr. Gammond said he was going to contact you to find out if your database has any other cases of the same rash Lily's got. Did you come across anything yet?"

"No. That's why we're here. We've got to run through a list of questions to try to pinpoint the source." He nodded at Karen.

"We need to document every place your daughter has been in the past seventy-two hours. Let's start with that." The woman's voice was disconcerting. It was deep and rough, like she had a bad sore throat or she'd smoked three packs a day from the age of ten. She didn't smell like cigarettes, so maybe it was a medical condition. Chelsea forced her mind to focus on the woman's question.

"We've been doing the usual routine – school and work, home in the evenings. Lily went to school, rode the bus home the past three days and that's it. We haven't been anywhere else."

The woman looked at her, "Are you absolutely sure about that? Did you happen to take her with you to the grocery store or a fast food restaurant, anything along those lines?"

"No." Chelsea gritted her teeth. It had been a bad week all the way around, her daughter was gravely ill, she didn't have the patience for repetitive questions.

"Okay. Have you had any company in the past three days? Anyone who spent time at your home that isn't normally there?"

Chelsea started to say they had had Ann and Steve over but they spent so much time with them she knew there wasn't any reason to think her neighbors were the source of Lily's illness.

"No, we haven't had any company this week."

"Have you heard of any other children being ill at Lily's school?"

"No."

"Is anyone else in your family presenting the same symptoms Lily is suffering from?"

She looked from Ethan to Craig. "No."

"Have you introduced any new foods to her diet this week?"

"You know, we've been asked all of these questions by the doctor already. I don't see how this is going to help my daughter. It's a waste of time."

Bob gave her one of those executive-in-charge unhappy with the underlings looks, "Mrs. Noble, we are required to go through these questions with you and your family. Please allow us to do our job." He nodded at Karen and she scanned down to the next one, pen at the ready.

"Has she taken new medications or vitamins of any kind?"

"No."

"Have you used any new cleaning products: laundry soap, bath soap, dish soap?"

"No." Her temples began to pound. Her little girl was critically ill and all she wanted to do was be with her. Instead she was being forced to play twenty-questions again.

"Where do you work Mrs. Noble?"

Chelsea glanced up at the woman. What in the hell did that matter? She drew in a breath and forced herself to remain cordial. "BioGen Technologies."

The woman looked up at her, "What does your company do?"

"We are a research and development firm. Our focus is on finding cures that can be derived from plants. We also work on genetic engineering of plants to increase crop production, reduce the need for insecticides, that sort of thing."

Karen looked at Bob then made a long notation on the clipboard in front of her. "Have you recently worked with any new plants or processes that you hadn't previously been studying?"

"No."

The woman looked at Craig, "And you Mr. Noble, what do you do for a living?"

"I'm a geologist. I work with rocks and dirt."

"Have you come across anything unusual at work this week your daughter might have been exposed to?"

"No—I've been out of town all week."

"Is this your son?" Craig nodded in answer.

"Hi, I'm Ethan."

"What school do you attend?"

"I go to San Benito High."

"Are you working on anything out of the ordinary or is anyone seriously ill at school?"

"Not that I know of."

"Have you been anywhere unusual lately? Played in a field somewhere you don't normally, that kind of thing?"

"Well, I was in Africa a few days ago with my dad."

"What area of Africa were you in Mr. Noble?" She looked at Craig. Her expression changed, now intense instead of just business-like.

"We were in South Africa. We spent a day at the Wonderstone mine outside of Ottosdal, then we spent a couple days at the Impodimo Lodge on the Madikwe Game Reserve."

The woman wrote on her clipboard a long moment then looked over at Bob and stood up.

Bob opened his briefcase and pulled out a digital camera. "I'm going to speak with your daughter's doctor for a few minutes. Don't go anywhere. I'll be right back." Bob gave them all a stern look and walked back over to the check-in desk.

Chelsea watched the nurse pick up the phone again and point to the door they'd seen the doctor coming and going through.

"So you guys don't have any similar cases on file that might relate to what's going on with our daughter?" Chelsea asked the woman.

Karen cleared her throat and rumbled out, "No, unfortunately, we have nothing on record that comes close to the type of rash the doctor described over the phone. It sounds very unusual. Typical rashes aren't multi colored and the bright orange has really got us stumped."

She fell silent, shifted around in her seat and reached down to open the case leaning against her chair. She pulled the computer onto her lap and booted it up then began typing away.

Several minutes went by then Wilson reappeared with the doctor at his side. He stepped back over to their group and addressed Craig.

"Mr. Noble, we have to ask your family to voluntarily quarantine yourselves to your home for the next forty-eight hours. You need to leave immediately and drive straight home. Do not stop anywhere. Once you're home, do not leave. We have to take precautions to ensure your daughter's disease doesn't spread among the public."

Chelsea looked at Craig's shocked expression and spoke before he could summon a response. "We aren't going anywhere. Our daughter is critically ill. She needs us here, not sitting at home. I'm not leaving."

The doctor addressed her, "Mrs. Noble, as we discussed earlier, do you want to be held responsible for potentially causing an epidemic?"

She jumped up, letting her anger fly out of her eyes, pinning all three of the idiots in front of her. "I don't care about what happens to the rest of the world. All I care about right now is my daughter. I'm not going anywhere. And I'm going in to see my daughter. Now." Her body trembled with emotions. Her daughter needed her—she wasn't going to back down or go home.

"Mrs. Noble, don't make this difficult. We are bound by federal procedures to require your family to quarantine themselves for a short period of time until we can be sure your daughter's illness is not communicable. We have the legal ability to force you into quarantine. It would be better for everyone if you voluntarily submit to isolating yourselves from the public."

"My daughter might be dying and I'm not leaving here." She bit the words out at the man, her temper completely blown at being forced to abandon her sick child.

Wilson turned to Dr. Gammond, "Call security."

The doctor nodded and hustled over to the nurse's desk. Chelsea watched as the woman's eyes grew wide and she snatched up the phone.

"I don't give a shit if you call security—I'm not leaving my daughter alone to die!" She shouted at the top of her lungs, desperation racing with fear at the thought of Lily dying without ever seeing her again. No way was she leaving. Every eye in the waiting room focused on her. One family got up and hurried outside. She flinched as someone grasped her hand and jerked away then realized it was Ann.

"Chelsea, I understand how you feel but unfortunately, you really don't have a choice. They can charge you with a criminal misdemeanor and put you in jail for not cooperating."

Chelsea watched Wilson nod at hearing Ann's whispered words.

"Jesus Christ, help me, please. I can't believe this. My daughter needs me. I'm not leaving." Her words came out in a choking sob as the security guard hurried through the front door and stepped over, hand on the gun at his hip.

"Is there a problem here?" the man asked.

The doctor spoke to the man in a navy blue uniform. Chelsea's heartbeat took off when she saw he wasn't just a security officer—he was a policeman from the badge on his chest.

"Officer, this gentleman is with the Centers for Disease Control. He has determined that these people need to be quarantined due to a strange illness in their family. They've been asked to voluntarily leave and stay in their home. However, Mrs. Noble is refusing to cooperate—"

"Officer, my daughter is here in the hospital, possibly dying, and they are trying to force me to leave. I haven't even been allowed to see her since they brought her in." Tears tracked down her cheeks. She let them drip off her face as she spoke.

Craig spoke up, "Look, Officer Sanchez, surely we have the right to see our daughter, if only for a few minutes. I can understand they want us to avoid possibly contaminating the public, but how can they refuse to let us be with our little girl? She's only seven."

"I'm really sorry about your daughter and I completely understand why you don't want to leave." Chelsea watched as the man gave the doctor and Wilson a questioning look. "Is it really necessary that they be forced under quarantine? Are you sure the girl's illness is contagious?"

"Officer, we don't know for certain the child's contagious but we can't take any chances. From everything the family has told us, her illness came on suddenly and is getting worse by the minute. She's suffering multiple symptoms, including a strange rash. Until we can find out what the problem is, there is a huge risk of the disease being spread. We are obligated to protect the public." Wilson spoke with authority, drawing himself up as he looked at the policeman, clearly expecting the law to be on his side.

"Now assist us with getting the family out of the building and into their car. I would appreciate it if you or someone else on the police force would follow them to make sure they go directly home.

They cannot leave their house for forty-eight hours or until we determine whether the illness is contagious. If you aren't willing to assist us, I'll call Homeland Security and ask them to send a team over."

Officer Sanchez scowled back at the man, "That won't be necessary, sir. I'm sorry, I didn't get your name?" Chelsea felt hope blossom as she watched the officer grill the jerk.

"It's Robert Wilson. I'm director of the California division of the CDC and have full knowledge of the legal rights our office has in a situation like this. I expect your assistance."

"And you will have it. Give me a minute, I need to speak with my supervisor about this situation before I do anything." Sanchez gave the man a curt look as he pulled his phone off his belt and stepped away from their group.

After several minutes the police officer came over and addressed Gammond. "Our Chief is saying that the parents have a legal right to see their daughter, doctor. I'm waiting for a call back to confirm our authority to force these folks into quarantine. In the meantime, you need to make arrangements for them to see their little girl for a few minutes."

Relief swept through her as she thanked the officer.

The doctor gave the cop a cold look then turned to Chelsea. "As I advised you earlier, you will need to wear protective gear and you can only stay for five minutes. Lily's in very bad shape and we're trying our best to turn things around for her. We don't need distractions. Both of you follow me."

Chelsea almost walked on the doctor's heels while they headed into the restricted area and onto an elevator. He led them down a short hall and through a door with a biohazard symbol. The doctor pointed to the white one-piece suits hanging on a rack. Plastic face masks hung on a hook beside the suits.

"Put the suits on first." He pointed at a large cardboard box, "Take boots out of there and put those over your shoes. Make sure you tie everything shut securely. After the boots, put the plastic masks on then the gloves." He nodded at another box. "I'll be outside the door."

Chelsea rushed to put the suit on. It was made of a tightly woven fabric that felt like parachute material and had Velcro closures at the wrists and ankles. She struggled into it as Craig worked to get into his beside her. They got the booties on over their shoes then helped each other with the plastic face masks.

The masks were awkward—large clear plastic squares with a slight curve were bolted to a heavy plastic band which appeared to fit around the head. A large cloth made of the suit fabric was attached all around the plastic face shield, forming a small tent that had to be lifted over their heads. The bands fit like a crown, the cloth tents had to be spread out over their shoulders and the plastic shields adjusted in front of their faces. Finally they got the rubber gloves snapped on and stepped back out into the hallway.

The doctor raked them with his eyes and pointed at a door next to the room where they'd donned the suits.

"That is the decontamination room. When you're finished visiting your daughter, go in there and remove the suits, booties and masks and put them in the bin. Throw the gloves in the trash. You will see a sign with instructions for the decontamination shower. After that you can leave. I'll tell the CDC man to expect you back in the lobby in fifteen minutes. If you aren't back out there I'll send security for you."

He sounded pissed off and she resented the hell out of it. All she wanted to do was be with her daughter and he was acting as if she was staging Armageddon.

The doctor headed off down the short hall with a frown on his face, stopped at a clear glass door with another biohazard sign and knocked sharply. A nurse clothed in similar biohazard gear rose from the chair beside Lily's bed and stepped over to the door. Gammond pressed a button beneath a small speaker mounted on the wall.

"Rhonda, these are Lily's parents. Give them five minutes then they need to leave. Call me if they give you any trouble about leaving, okay?" He turned and stalked off down the hall.

Chelsea fought back tears as she approached her daughter's bed. Her little girl lay still, eyes closed. Her face was very pale, making the strange orange and yellow spots stand out that much more. An I.V. was attached to the needle taped to her small hand, a pulse oximeter sat on the end of her index finger, a clear oxygen tube was strapped below her little nose.

She glanced at the monitors above the bed and felt another wave of dread wash over her. The blood pressure gauge read eighty-five over fifty-nine. The oximeter read eighty-seven. Her little girl was in serious jeopardy. Dark shadows smudged below Lily's eyes and her chest seemed to barely lift with air as she breathed. Chelsea reached out and gently held the hand without medical equipment on it.

"Hi Baby, Mommy's here, Sweetheart. I love you so much, Lily." Emotions choked her throat and she bowed her head praying through tears for her daughter. Craig stroked a hand over her shoulder and she ignored it as she studied her little girl's face, fighting to get herself under control. They only had five minutes and she needed to make the most of them.

"Lily, I love you with all my heart. I hope you can hear me. We're here for you, Honey. Your dad and I love you very much and we're praying for you to get better. If you can hear me, please try to open your eyes Sweetheart. You've been asleep a long time and we're worried about you."

Her words strangled off as more tears rolled down her face. She couldn't reach up and wipe them away because of the plastic shield and the drops ran down her neck into her blouse as she held her little girl's hand.

Craig spoke beside her, "Lily's it's Dad. I love you, Princess. We're here for you, Lilybit. We're right here and we love you very much." Chelsea looked up at her husband and saw tears running down his cheeks under the plastic shield. The suits were stifling but she ignored her discomfort as the nurse stepped over to the bed and placed a thermometer on Lily's forehead. She watched as the red digital numbers flashed – 99.5. Only a slight fever.

"Has the doctor prescribed an antibiotic for her?" Chelsea asked the dark-haired woman, words muffled behind the plastic.

"Not yet. The doctor said the test results aren't showing any sign of infection and we're not able to give antibiotics without justification."

"So what is the doctor doing to help her? What's in the I.V.?"

"The I.V. has a stimulant in it to help increase her blood pressure and hopefully revive her from the coma. It's also a mixture of glucose and water to help keep her hydrated. That's all we've given her so far. Until the doctor figures out what's wrong with her, there isn't much more we can do without possibly causing harm."

Chelsea sat holding Lily's hand. Craig stepped to the other side of the bed and stroked her hair as the nurse glanced at the clock on the wall.

"I'm sorry but you have to leave. Doctor's orders. But please know I'll be here with your daughter for the rest of my shift. We'll take good care of her and won't leave her alone for a minute, I promise."

Panic swept over her again. She gripped her daughter's hand tighter, "Lily, I love you so much. Try to wake up Honey. If you wake up I'll give you a big hug and a kiss." She waited, watching Lily's eyelids. Her eyes twitched beneath bluish skin but didn't open. She'd give anything to be able to hold Lily in her arms and kiss her little cheek but she couldn't.

"Mrs. Noble, I'm sorry, you have to leave now," the nurse repeated.

Craig tried to help her up and she jerked her arm out of his gloved hand.

"Don't touch me," she whispered then stood up on her own. She looked at the nurse, "What's your name?"

"Rhonda."

"Please take good care of my daughter, Rhonda. She means the world to me."

Chelsea slowly walked to the door. She took a last look at Lily over her shoulder as it shut behind them.

They went through the decontamination routine then headed back out to the lobby. The CDC director and the woman sat a few chairs away from Ann and Steve. The police officer stood close to the front door, his back to the wall, eyes roaming over the waiting area and lobby.

Chelsea didn't waste time, she walked straight over to the cop.

"Have you had a chance to verify whether they can legally force us into quarantine Officer Sanchez?"

He gave her an apologetic look and slightly relaxed his stance. "I'm afraid so, ma'am. I'm being told that per the Public Health Service Act, the Centers for Disease Control and Prevention is empowered with the ability to detain, medically examine or conditionally release individuals believed to be carrying a communicable disease. That would be Title 24 of the United States Code, section 264 if you want to look it up yourself."

"You bet your ass I'm going to look it up," she spit out then forced herself to calm down. The man was obviously trying to protect her family's rights but was obligated to do his job. "I'm sorry, I know you're trying to help us."

"Ma'am, I'm sorry your family's in this situation. But I strongly recommend you do what the man from the CDC said and go home with your husband and son for now. The Chief said if you don't go voluntarily the CDC will call in the guys from Homeland Security to force you into quarantine. Believe me, ma'am, you don't want to mess with the Feds."

She studied the man's face then looked at her husband beside her, "I can't believe this. We're supposed to go sit in our house while our daughter is dying."

Craig reached out for her hand but she turned and stalked across the lobby to where the CDC people sat. She stopped in front of Wilson. He looked up at her, unable to rise because she was too close to his legs.

"We're going to leave because you aren't giving us any choice." She took a half-step, placed the toes of her shoes against his and leaned over him close enough to see his grey nasal hairs. "You better damn well hope my daughter doesn't die while I'm stuck in my house, Robert Wilson. Because if she does, I will hunt you down and I will kill you. I swear to God, I will kill you." The words hissed out as her green eyes lashed him.

"Chelsea, come on. That's not going to help." Craig spoke quietly. "These people are just doing their jobs. Give the guy a break."

She rounded on him, "Shut up!"

Wilson took the opportunity to stand before she could pin him again.

"Mrs. Noble, do you realize you just threatened the life of a government employee? That is a felony offense. I could have you put in jail for it. I strongly suggest you think about what you are saying." He ground the words out as Officer Sanchez stepped over to them.

"I meant every word you overzealous asshole. It's not your daughter lying in an isolation room! It may be your job, but I think you're taking it way too far. No one's proven Lily's contagious and yet your exercising police state laws to force us into quarantine."

Officer Sanchez stepped over before Wilson could respond. "Ma'am, your family needs to leave now. Here's my card. Please call me if you have any problems or questions."

She took the card, knowing she had no choice but to go home. "I'm not leaving until I get a direct phone number for Lily's intensive care nurse. Once I get that, I'll go."

"I can give you the number, Chelsea. Who's the nurse on shift right now?" Ann asked.

"She said her name's Rhonda."

"Oh, good. Rhonda's a really great nurse. Lily's in excellent hands, I promise you. Do you have your cell phone? You can plug it into your speed dial."

Ethan handed Chelsea's purse to her and she whipped the phone out, tapped in the number for the isolation room.

"Thanks again, Ann. I guess we'll see you later." Her voice wobbled, "Bye Steve."

The little boy didn't say a word, his face wet and miserable as he looked back at her.

A river ran down her cheeks as she walked out with Craig and Ethan at her side.

CHAPTER 35

Ethan sat beside his dad, wondering if he was going to throw up before they could get back to the house. The world had been turned completely upside down and it was mostly his fault. His stomach squeezed as he thought about his little sister, sick and alone in a hospital bed, maybe dying without her family around her.

Not only did his dad know he was a thief, he'd jeopardized his reputation, maybe his dad's job and lied to him twice on top of it. He wasn't sure if they'd ever be as close as they used to be. If it turned out the missing sphere was the reason Lily got sick he didn't know what he'd do. His dad would probably disown him.

Watching his parents go through hell over his sister was hard, but seeing his mom refuse to allow his dad to comfort her rattled Ethan to the core. His parents had always been close and now suddenly they weren't. His mom seemed so angry, plus she was upset about Lily. Not good, really not good. He couldn't believe how fast everything was falling apart.

His dad pulled in the driveway behind his mom's Escalade and they all climbed out. He looked over his shoulder as a police car came to a stop alongside their curb. "Whoa."

"That is just unbelievable." His mom jerked the door open and stomped inside the house.

He waited on the porch with his dad to see if the cop was going to get out of the car but after a minute they realized he was just going to sit there to enforce the quarantine. They went inside and shut the door.

"Let's get started Ethan."

"On what?"

"Looking for that damn sphere. What else are we gonna do while we're stuck in the house? Let's start in your room and go from there."

"Okay." A sigh escaped him. Maybe his dad didn't believe him about the sphere disappearing.

He followed his dad up the stairs. They searched the entire house for over an hour, trying to not let on to Chelsea what they were doing. She cooperated by staying in the kitchen. They worked their way to the garage and had started on the last two storage bins when they heard the house phone ring. His dad rushed inside, a worried look on his face.

Ethan put the bins back on the shelf and stepped inside just in time to watch his mom slam the phone back on its cradle.

"I can't believe people. That is too much."

"Is Lily okay?" he asked. His dad had already left the room.

"That wasn't the hospital." She shook her head as she sat back down at the round wooden table and resumed her position. She'd been staring at a glass of red wine the entire time they'd been searching the house and, as far as he could tell, she had yet to drink any of it.

"Who was it?"

"What?" She looked up at his question.

"Who was on the phone?"

"Just some idiot from the newspaper, asking a bunch of questions, trying to get the scoop for a story about Lily."

"What did you tell him?"

"I told him it was none of his damn business."

Ethan scowled at hearing the press was involved. That couldn't be good. Not in any way.

They sat for a minute then he said, "I'm really sorry about Lily. I hope she's going to be okay. I said a prayer for her." It had been a long time since he'd prayed—hopefully God wouldn't hold that against him.

His mom looked up from the glass in front of her, "Thanks Ethan."

Silence stretched until it became uncomfortable.

He stood up, "I guess I'm gonna go clean my room or something. Do you want any help with dinner?"

Her eyelids closed as she absorbed his words. "Dinner. Right. I'm not even hungry and I sure don't feel like cooking. Would you mind making yourself a sandwich or something?"

"Nah, it's okay. I'm not hungry either, my stomach's been bothering me all day."

She looked up, alarmed, "You're not getting sick too?"

"No, I don't think so. I'm pretty sure it'll pass. Well, I'm gonna go up to my room." He snagged a water from the fridge and headed up the stairs. It was going to be a long night.

CHAPTER 36

"What do you want for dinner?" Ann looked at her son across the kitchen table. They had followed Chelsea's family home. The doctors weren't going to let anyone in to see Lily so there was no point waiting at the hospital.

She watched as Steve shook his head in answer. He'd slipped back into silence at the hospital and hadn't said a word since buying sodas from the machine. She prayed he wouldn't fall back in his autistic bubble but he seemed to be headed that way. At least he wasn't rocking in his chair.

"It's getting late. I think we should eat something, Honey. Can you at least eat some cheese, maybe a little fruit?"

He shook his head again and continued to stare at the place mat.

Ann couldn't help the sigh that escaped her lips as she stood up to get a glass of iced tea. She needed the caffeine. In spite of a rare solid night of sleep last evening, she was completely worn out from the emotional highs and lows of the day. It was only seven-thirty— it felt like midnight. She was exhausted and longed for her pillow but scared to death she might wake up to find Steve back in his bubble and Lily even worse.

Ice clinked into the glass and she opened the fridge for the pitcher of tea. A bowl of oranges stood next to it. She snagged one and walked back over to the table.

She sat staring out the sliders at their back yard, thinking about Lily and Chelsea and her son. The sunset lit up the sky in a kaleidoscope of colors. Beams of golden light burst through the puffy clouds like spotlights. Joy Day was almost over.

Another sigh escaped as she looked at the orange. Maybe if she sliced it up Steve would eat some of it. She set it on the table and pushed back her chair to get a knife but before she could stand he looked at the orange and rocked the night with his words.

"It's got yellow spots, kind of like those berries."

She glanced down at the fruit. It looked like most oranges, with a few less than perfectly orange areas that appeared yellow, nothing unusual about it but the hairs on the back of her neck stood up as her son's words sank in and she thought of Lily's rash.

"What berries, Steve?"

He shook his head. "Lily told me not to tell 'cause she might get in trouble."

Her heart raced as she leaned forward and said, "Steve, Lily is really sick and the doctors can't figure out why. If the berries are the reason, we need to know about them so we can help her. Where did Lily get the berries, Honey?"

He hung his head and mumbled, "From her plant."

"Her plant? From their garden?"

"No."

"Well, where then?"

"From her secret plant."

Ann worked at keeping her voice calm, "What secret plant?"

"The one behind the swings."

A buzz of adrenaline ran through her, completely erasing the weariness she'd felt just a moment ago.

"Come on Steve, let's go ask Chelsea to look for the plant before it gets dark."

* * *

Craig looked up from the computer as he heard the doorbell. He stepped into the hall and saw Ann through the entry window.

"Hey Ann, Steve, come on in."

Ann's voice shook and her words came out almost faster than her lips could handle, "Craig, Steve and I were just talking. I got an orange out of the fridge a few minutes ago and he said it looked just like 'those berries' from Lily's secret plant behind the swings. Do you know what he's talking about?"

His pulse picked up at hearing her words. "No, we don't have plants next to the swings. But I haven't been out there for awhile. Let's go check."

Chelsea looked up as they walked in the kitchen. "Oh, hi Ann."

"Have you seen any plants out by the swings?" Craig asked.

"No, why?"

"Well let's go take a look."

He headed toward the back yard without answering and heard Ann repeating what Steve had said as they hurried across the lawn to the swing set.

"It's over there." Steve rounded the slide ahead of them and pointed along the fence.

Craig followed Steve's finger and stopped in his tracks as he looked down at the small plant. He'd almost stumbled over it. Shadows cast from the fence and trees overhead hid the dark leaves. He didn't spot any berries but it sure looked different than any plant he'd ever seen.

"What in the world?" Chelsea bent down and examined the small bush.

He reached out and fingered a leaf. It had a short fuzz of growth on top and felt like velvet. He picked the leaf, held it to his nose and sniffed. It had a very medicinal smell, like Vicks vapor rub.

"Have you ever seen anything like this before, Chelsea?"

'No." Urgency rang in her voice as she pushed clusters of leaves back, one after the next. She moved to the other side, frantically combing through the dark plant. Her hands swept aside branches at the back then her eyes lit up. She plucked off a stem.

"Look!" Four bright orange berries rested on her palm, florescent yellow dots swirling around their equators. The bright dots seemed to glow in the shadowed darkness.

"They look just like Lily's rash." Craig stared at the strange little balls as Ann stepped forward to get a better look.

From behind him Steve said, "They taste like ice cream."

The adults turned in unison and stared at him.

Ann rushed to his side as she asked, "Steve, did you eat any of these berries?" With shaking hands Ann turned her son toward her.

"I ate some when we came over for dinner. Lily must have eaten the rest 'cause they're all gone. There was a bunch of them." Craig watched as Ann's face turned white.

Chelsea stepped over to her. "Ann, I'm so sorry. I know how you must be feeling right now, but let's look at this from a scientific stand point. If Steve was going to get sick from the berries, he would have already. It's been two days since you were here for dinner. If he only had a few, maybe it wasn't enough to poison him. Lily must have eaten a lot more than he did." His wife's voice trailed off in despair as she studied the little orange orbs in her palm.

A loud bark made them all jump and they turned to look at Bell. Their old Irish Setter stood next to the slide, a bright green tennis ball in her mouth. Her tail wagged as she dropped it at her feet and let out a quick yip then nudged the ball with her nose.

It took Craig's mind a moment to pull out of the intense thoughts about his little girl and the berries. He looked down at their dog as she nudged the ball again with her nose.

"She hasn't wanted to play fetch for the past year because of her hip. I wonder what's gotten in to her?" He stepped over and picked up the ball, drew back and tossed it to the other side of the yard. Bell took off in a streak, chased the ball down and bounded back to them in a flash, tail wagging as she dropped the ball at Craig's feet. She yipped at him to throw it again. He obliged and the dog did a repeat, running after the green orb like a puppy.

"That's amazing. She acts like her arthritis is completely gone." Chelsea said in a whisper then she turned and stared down at Steve. "We have to get these berries analyzed. Right now." She set off across the lawn at a clip then stopped short. "Damn it! I can't leave."

Craig looked at his frustrated wife, "We can call the hospital, talk to the doctor. They've got labs there, right?"

Chelsea glared at him. "We only have four berries, Craig. I'm not about to hand them over to Gammond. Who knows how long it will take the hospital to get the results back? They might not have the right equipment to properly analyze these. Lily's life is in jeopardy, we don't have time to wait. We need to know what the berries consist of, right now."

She stood thinking for a moment. "I'll call Brad."

CHAPTER 37

"**H**ow's Lily?"

"Not good, Brad. She's in critical condition and headed toward renal failure. And to top it off, our family's been quarantined to the house."

"Why?" Alarm rang in his voice. "Do they know what's wrong with her?"

"No, they don't. She has a strange rash along with a lot of other serious symptoms but they can't find any indication of infection or poison. But listen, I called you for a reason. I really need your help."

"You've got it. What do you need?"

Chelsea explained about the berries. "They need to be analyzed as fast as possible. The problem is I only have four, the rest are gone. I don't know if the hospital has the right equipment to run the tests or if they can work fast enough. We need to figure this out before it's too late for Lily. I'm hoping you can run a full spectrum on the berries tonight."

"Of course, Chelsea. It might save Lily's life. Do you want me to come to your house?"

"There's a cop out front enforcing the quarantine. I seriously doubt he'll let any visitors ring our doorbell." She looked at the berries in her palm. "Go to my next door neighbor's house. Ann's got a gate to our backyard. She lives on the west side of our house. How soon can you get here?"

"I'll head your way right now."

Ten minutes later they were standing on the patio in her backyard. She handed him a small plastic bag containing the four berries.

"That's all we have."

"These will have to do, then. I'll make the most of them, I promise. I'm going to head straight to the lab. Hopefully it won't take long to analyze them."

"Lily might not have more than a few hours." Tears welled up and she swiped at them. "I don't know what I'll do if I lose my little girl, Brad." Her voice cracked as a sob escaped her.

He reached out and pulled her into his arms, wrapping her close. He held her for a long moment and she breathed in his clean scent. It felt so good to be comforted and she let him hold her longer than she should have. She slipped out of his arms and wiped at her eyes again.

"I can't thank you enough for your help. You've always been wonderful to me and I really appreciate it. Please call as soon as you know anything, okay?"

"Of course—I'll call you every hour if you want me to." He gave her a small smile and rubbed her arm. "Keep the faith and try not to worry too much, okay? I'm sure Lily's going to be fine. She's just like her mother, tougher than she looks."

He gave her another hug then headed back through the gate toward Ann's house, his silhouette disappearing in the growing darkness.

She turned to go inside and caught Craig frowning out the window in the den. She stared back at his wiry brown curls backlit from the desk lamp, eyes hidden in shadow. A coldness she'd never felt before toward her husband welled up and fogged the air between them. Dread pricked at her heart and she hurried back to the kitchen to check on her daughter.

CHAPTER 38

Ethan caught the sound of voices arguing and lifted his head from the pillow, listening hard. People were definitely going at it but it didn't sound like his mom and dad. The noise seemed too far away to be in the house. He sat up on the bed, untangled the Ipod gear from around his body and headed for the door.

The voices grew louder as he reached the top of the stairs. He skipped treads and pulled the front door open as his dad came down the hallway behind him. Ethan stopped short, eyes popping at seeing a gaggle of reporters standing beside the police cruiser. They were arguing with the cop who had climbed out of his car. A bunch of them grouped around the cop, all with mikes and cameras at the ready. Two news vans were parked across the street and cameramen stood holding serious equipment filming the scene.

"What in the hell?" his dad said over his shoulder as they looked out at the melee. The cop refused to allow anyone on their property as the group of reporters bounced from arguing about access to throwing questions at him.

"Officer, can you tell us if this family has been quarantined by the Centers for Disease Control today?" a reporter shouted out.

"No comment. Ladies and gentlemen, this is private property. I have to ask you to stay in the street or on the sidewalk. Do not block traffic or attempt to access the property."

"Officer! Is it true the family's little girl is in ICU with a strange rash and in a coma?"

"That is private information, no comment." The cop glared at the reporters and used his outstretched arms to shovel the small crowd back from the property.

"Can you confirm the wife works at BioGen Technologies?" the reporters continued. "What project is she working on? Is it for the government?" a man shouted.

Ethan shook his head, "Dad, I can't believe this. What's going on?"

Just as he finished speaking one of the reporters turned and saw them standing on the porch. "There they are!" The group surged toward the house and the cop whipped out his baton.

"Stay back!" He snatched the handset off his shoulder and called for back up.

"Come inside, shut the door Ethan."

His mom stepped out from the kitchen, "What's going on?"

His dad grimaced then said, "It looks like the news about Lily has gotten out in a big way. There are a bunch of reporters out there. So far, the cop's keeping them off our property. We should unplug the house phone." It had been ringing the entire time he spoke.

"Oh God, that's the last thing we need." His mom looked like she was going to cry again as she headed back to the kitchen. They followed her and sat down at the table. The cacophony dulled to a faint mumble as the kitchen door closed.

"I talked to Rhonda a little while ago. There's been no change in the past thirty minutes."

"I guess that's good." His dad fell silent as he stared back at her, a weird look in his eyes. He seemed pissed off at his mom now.

Ethan's stomach squirmed. He got up and opened the fridge as silence descended over the room. "Do you guys want anything?" he asked, trying to break the tension.

"No thanks," his mom answered.

"No." His dad sounded pissed. "Ethan, grab what you want and head to your room."

He stopped breathing a moment at the tone in his dad's voice. His fingers shook as he wrapped them around a water bottle and shut the fridge. Hairs prickled up his neck as the kitchen door swung shut behind him. He stood outside the door, considering listening in, but knew he was in so deep with his dad he didn't dare not follow the request for privacy. Feet like cement blocks, he climbed the stairs, wondering if his dad was going to tell Mom about the sphere.

* * *

"Chelsea, we need to talk."

"Not right now, Craig. I'm too upset. Unless you want to talk about what might be wrong with Lily, it can wait."

Her tone added fuel to his fire. "Yeah, I think it has something to do with our daughter," he spit the words at her, tired of her treating him like he was nothing but a problem when he was trying his best to be a good father and husband.

They had agreed eighteen years ago that marriage needed to be a two way street. That it had to be a partnership or it was meaningless to be married. They would decide things as a unit, talk things out and always speak respectfully to one another, no matter how angry they might get. He was trying his best to keep those vows in mind but after seeing his wife snuggle up with her movie star lab partner his temper had reached a line.

"Okay. What's on your mind?"

"What have you been working on at BioGen, Chelsea?"

"I already told you that the other day—a tomato vaccine for Alzheimer's."

"What are you doing in the course of the project? Did you develop a new plant or what?"

"Where are you going with this Craig?"

"You know where I'm going—a plant has made our daughter really sick. Something no one has seen before. You work at a company that genetically alters plants, Chelsea." He couldn't keep his tone from escalating into accusation, "You wouldn't let anyone but your lab partner have the berries. Why?"

Her words came out clipped as she pushed the glass to the side of the table to clear the space between them. "The hospital here is a small one. They don't have the funding or much need for the kind of equipment BioGen has. What if we'd given the berries to them only to find out they had to ship them somewhere else for the tests?

We need to know as soon as possible what those berries contain. Brad's help is the fastest way to do that."

He stared back at her, trying to control his breathing, trying to deny what his eyes had told him a few minutes ago as his wife embraced her lab partner like a lover on the patio. He hadn't been able to see her face but he had sure as hell seen Brad's.

"You know what? I don't think you're being honest with me, Chelsea. Where else would that weird-ass plant have come from? Tell me?" His volume had approached a shout and he forced himself to calm down. "You and I both know that the chances of a plant like that existing anywhere around here are zero. It looks like something created in a lab or some science fiction book. I think it's time you told me what's going on."

She shoved out of her chair, stood up and slapped a hand down on the table in front of him. The wine glass wobbled, threatening to tip over but came to a stop as his wife fumed, her face six inches from his. Her voice was a tightly controlled whisper as her eyes scraped him.

"Are you really that blind Craig? Do you really think if I'd any idea what's wrong with Lily I wouldn't have said so from the start of this insanity?" A bottomless pool of pain welled up in her eyes as she spoke and he knew right then he'd made a terrible mistake. The moment she finished speaking he realized how stupid he'd been for entertaining the thought and an even bigger jackass to say it out loud.

She snapped up her cell phone and headed toward the door.

"Chelsea, wait. I'm sorry. I shouldn't have said that. I'm just worried about Lily and grasping at straws." His words tumbled over each other as he moved to grab her before she walked out.

"Keep your hands off me." Her words strafed like bullets, "According to my attorney you and I have a lot to talk about, but now is not the time. Lily is all that matters. Our problems can wait."

The door swung shut behind her as the boulder in his stomach smashed up against his heart.

CHAPTER 39

She felt like a black hole had opened up and sucked her through to an alien planet. She suddenly seemed to be living in a dark place where nothing good existed and never would again. Her daughter might be dying and the man she'd loved for eighteen years thought she was capable of knowingly letting it happen. That he would think such a thing for even a second shredded her last hope of working things out with him. Every corner of her heart ached and she slumped onto the edge of the bed completely drained.

Escaping into sleep was not an option. The hospital could call at any minute, she needed to stay alert.

She forced herself up and into the large master bathroom. In a zombie-like haze she stared at the glass and tumbled marble shower. Her hand reached out and turned the hot water on almost by itself. Her brain was on overload and she desperately needed a clear head.

As she stripped off her work clothes she flashed on the hope Brad would call soon with information about the berries. She wanted to be sharp in case he needed her input. He was good in the lab but she was better. He didn't always think things through to the next level or make the possible connections as fast as she did, although he usually got there if she left him to it. She'd give anything to be at the lab right then instead of trapped in her damn house.

She let the water hit her face then turned and cranked the temperature as hot as she could stand, felt it pound on her neck. As the glass walls steamed up around her she thought about her husband staring at Brad and her on the patio. Pain lashed again at knowing even if it had been jealousy talking, Craig accusing her of being callous enough to let Lily die was the last straw.

Shock had struck like a lightening bolt in the kitchen, forcing her to realize the man she'd thought loved her and understood her so well had been faking it all along. It was that or he'd completely changed along the way without her noticing.

Her mind flashed back to the conversation she'd had yesterday with her attorney. Carol seemed to really know what she was talking about. The self-employed attorney was in her early forties and a single mother, twice divorced. She'd made a lot of sense when she'd advised her to talk with Craig over the weekend before preparing any formal paperwork for a divorce.

Carol had said lots of men ran around looking at the world through a whole different lens than their wives without even realizing it. The words attorney and divorce had a way of waking them up. Chelsea had been hoping she'd be able to finally get through to him over the weekend and he would agree to change things before it was too late. But it was past that point now. He had crossed a line she never thought he would. Her husband seemed to have his head so far up his ass there was no point in her continuing to try to pull it out. As soon as her daughter recovered she was going to move forward with the divorce.

Chelsea shut the water off and climbed out. The towel had just hit her shoulders when she heard her cell phone ringing. Water dripped off her arms onto the floor as she lunged.

"Mrs. Noble? This is Dr. Gammond. I'm calling because Lily is getting worse. Her lungs are filling with fluid and her temperature has shot up to over a hundred-one degrees. We've started her on antibiotic and are hoping we can get this under control quickly. We need to intubate her and I'm calling for your permission."

"Oh God, please help my little girl." She gulped back tears, "You have my permission. Do whatever you need to do to help her. Please, Dr. Gammond, don't let my little girl die without me. Let me come to the hospital now, just in case."

He said nothing for a beat, then in a subdued voice he continued to toe the line, "Mrs. Noble, give us a little bit to try to get Lily stabilized again. I'll give you a call with an update in the next thirty minutes. If things get any worse I'll let you come back to the hospital to be with your daughter. We'll need to make special arrangements for getting you up to the floor so the rest of the patients and staff aren't exposed, but we'll get you up here, I promise. Now let me get back to helping Lily."

The dial tone buzzed in her ear before she could get any words out. She stood dripping onto the carpet as despair rolled through her. Tears started up again and she realized she was standing there, naked and wet, and might need to leave at any minute for the hospital. Shoving the despair aside, she rushed over to the closet. A pair of old jeans and a worn t-shirt would have to do. She couldn't concentrate on anything except the vision of her little girl, alone in that big hospital bed, barely able to breath.

The phone rang again, startling her out of the trance she'd been standing in. She swept it off the dresser and saw it was Brad.

"What did you find out?" Her words tumbled out as blood pounded at her temples.

"Chelsea, you aren't going to believe me, but I double and triple- checked the results, so I know they're right." She heard him draw in a breath then he continued in a rush, "Just one of those little berries contains more vitamins and minerals than twenty of the typical over-the-counter multi vitamin pills we all take. I'm still running some other tests, but as far as I can tell, the berries aren't poisonous in moderation. I'm a little concerned about some strange enzymes and what looks like a couple new proteins. But I don't think those are poisonous. I think Lily's suffering from an acute vitamin and mineral overdose."

Her mind absorbed his words, started running over what little she knew about vitamin overdose symptoms.

"Really, Brad? You think that's all her problem might be?" Her heart galloped with hope of Lily's cure being something as simple as a treating a vitamin overdose instead of figuring out a remedy for some bizarre disease.

"Yes. I definitely think so. I took a few minutes to refresh myself on the symptoms of overdose. Some vitamins overlap each other but there are two that are probably causing the biggest problem—calcium and iron."

She held her breath as she listened to him explain.

"Too much of either of those can cause a person to go into coma, iron can cause the low blood pressure, both can cause renal failure and fluid in the lungs. Vitamin overdose can also cause a rash. From what I've read, the biggest part of the treatment will be to draw those main two culprits out of her system as quickly as possible."

"Oh I hope that's all it is. Did you read whether there are any long term complications from an overdose of those?"

"There seems to be a strong chance that she'll recover just fine, Chelsea, but they've got to get on the detox right away. I just emailed you the results to give to her doctor. Let me know if you need anything else to get them going on detoxing her. I'll call you later if I find out anything else that's important to what's going on with her, okay?"

"Okay. Thank you Brad. Thank you so much."

She hit the speed dial for the intensive care unit.

"Hi Rhonda. I need to speak with Dr. Gammond right away. I think we've just figured out what the problem is with Lily."

CHAPTER 40

"This is Dr. Gammond."

Chelsea's words flew at him as she explained about the berries and the test results. She made herself stop for a breath.

The doctor's voice rumbled through the phone, "Mrs. Noble, I certainly hope you and your lab partner are right but I'll need to run tests of my own before I proceed with treating Lily based on that theory. I'm going to send someone over to pick up some berries right now."

"I'm afraid that's not possible doctor. I could only find four berries on the plant and I gave them all to Brad Peterson at BioGen. He emailed me the reports from the test results a few minutes ago. Can I send them to you now?"

"Yes, send them to me right away, but I don't understand why you didn't keep some of the berries for me to run tests with. Your daughter is dying, we need those berries to be sure of what we're dealing with here."

"Doctor, I'm sure you're aware of what BioGen does. The test results I'll be sending you will be far more detailed than anything you could have done at the hospital, believe me. There isn't enough time or berries to shuffle around. Take a look at the reports then call me back."

"All right." He let out a harrumph of air then gave her his email address.

Ten minutes later the doctor called back and his tone had completely changed, he sounded excited.

"Mrs. Noble, from reviewing the reports it looks like you're right about the vitamin overdose. I don't know why I didn't think of it before, other than you assured me she wasn't taking any vitamins so we didn't run a blood work up for that. But she's presenting the most severe symptoms of iron and calcium overdose as well as other vitamins."

"So does that mean you'll be putting her on a detoxification treatment?"

"Yes, exactly. I'm going to start her on a chelation treatment as well as activated charcoal and a few other things to detoxify her system. Hopefully we've caught it in time to reverse any damage to her kidneys and lungs. Expect a positive call from me later."

Tears of relief ran down her cheeks as she disconnected the call and stood up to go give Craig and Ethan the news.

* * *

"Jimmy, I'm afraid I have bad news about Lily. Give me a call when you get this message." Things had been moving so fast he hadn't thought to call his brother until his wife left him alone in the kitchen.

He'd sat there feeling like a giant ass for several minutes. But as he thought back over the conversation with his brother earlier that day and his mind replayed the hugging scene on the patio, the phrase 'blind spot' began to take on a whole new meaning.

When Jimmy had refused to tell him exactly what he'd meant about the comment, he'd assumed his brother was implying he was not being a good husband in some way. Jimmy had said he needed to look at things through Chelsea's eyes and he'd figured that meant he was at fault. But after witnessing the lovers' hug and hearing his wife had met with an attorney, he'd suddenly realized his brother might have meant something else entirely.

Maybe Jimmy had seen them together somewhere or heard rumors from a client or friend? He didn't blame Jimmy a bit for not wanting to break that kind of news to him.

No man wanted to hear his wife was having an affair. It was emasculating. The thought of another man being with Chelsea made him sick. She'd been a virgin the first time they'd made love. He'd lived the past eighteen years believing he was the only man to have been inside her. It was a big part of the reason he'd never given in to screwing around on her. He didn't want to be the one to rupture that trust and the rare bond between them.

He scraped a hand over his face as he waited for his brother to call back and wondered what the future held for his family.

CHAPTER 41

"**Y**ou guys! It's just a vitamin overdose!" She shouted the good news as her feet hit the stairs. Craig was rising from the table as she swung through the door. Ethan came rushing in behind her as she babbled out what she'd learned.

"So she's going to be okay?" Craig asked.

"It looks like it. They've started her on a detox regimen and the doctor said we should see steady improvement from here on." Her good cheer dimmed a little as she said, "Brad claims most people make a complete recovery, but it's contingent on how quickly the detox is started. Hopefully she won't have any long-term damage from it."

Although her husband seemed relieved to hear their daughter wasn't suffering from a disease, he still seemed upset. The word attorney must have pulled his lids open after all.

"So can we go see her now that they know it's not contagious?" Ethan asked.

She let out a sigh, "Not yet. Dr. Gammond said we need to hold off while they get her stabilized and he gets the okay from Bob Wilson." Her teeth ground over the man's name.

"Gammond said he'd give me a call with a positive update."

* * *

Ann hurried into the hospital, anxious to get clocked in and check on Lily. She had called to find out who was scheduled to take the night shift on the intensive care floor. With the list in hand and two hours to go before the shift began, she'd phoned every nurse and offered to take it for her. She'd quickly found someone willing to take Friday night off.

It would mean working a double shift herself but she was way too keyed up to sleep and knew Chelsea was worried sick about her daughter. The least Ann could do was be there on her behalf because the only way to have access to Lily was on duty. She'd called her mom who had quickly agreed to spend the night with Steve. Her mother had already been planning to take care of him during her regular Saturday morning shift.

She punched in a few minutes early and took the elevator up to intensive care, crossing her fingers that she'd find Lily had improved since they'd left the hospital four hours earlier. The floor was buzzing with the usual crises and she headed down the hall toward the isolation room to relieve the nurse on duty.

Dr. Gammond swung out the door as she approached Lily's room and she stopped short at seeing him. She'd hoped he had given in to fatigue and gone home by now. He must be running close to twenty hours on duty. He surprised her with the smile on his face and she felt her lips grin back at him involuntarily. Lily must be doing much better.

"Good evening Ann. Have you heard the good news?"

"Did they get the test results back?"

"Yes. Her mother phoned me up a few minutes ago. Her lab partner figured out Lily's been suffering from a massive vitamin and mineral overdose from the berries. We've just started chelation therapy and are intubating her with activated charcoal. Hopefully she'll come around for us by morning."

"That's wonderful Dr. Gammond. I'm so happy to hear it." Relief made her fingers go numb. "I haven't had a chance to talk to Chelsea yet but I'm sure she'll be calling soon. Thanks for letting me know."

"So you're on duty tonight?" he asked.

"Yes, I just came on. Is there something you need?"

"No. But I want to make you aware the press got a hold of the story and we've been turning them away on an hourly basis at the front desk. Keep your guard up. We don't need a law suit. We're keeping Lily in isolation until we get the okay from the CDC to release her. I'm running some more lab work on her and then I'll be writing up a report for Mr. Wilson in the morning. For now, I'm heading home to get some sleep."

"All right, Dr. Gammond. I'll make sure to keep the press out of here. You go home and get some rest. The dark circles are beginning to meet in the middle of your forehead."

He gave her an exhausted smile, "Good night, Ann. Keep a close eye on Lily for me."

She watched as the doctor headed for the elevator. Most of the nurses couldn't stand Gammond but she'd always admired him. He was tough when he had to be, abrupt more often than not because he was always pressed for time but underneath the surface he seemed to be a really caring person. He was a doctor after all. He was also single but he worked so much it was probably necessary.

She turned back and tapped on the glass door of Lily's room then pushed the button to talk to Rhonda. "Hi, I'm taking over for Melissa tonight. I'm going to get suited up and relieve you. Give me five minutes."

Rhonda gave her a thumbs-up through the glass. Ann zipped into the room next door and wiggled into a biohazard suit as fast as she could. She was back in Lily's room in a flash.

"How's she doing?" Ann asked.

"Dr. Gammond has started her on chelation therapy. He said he's going to try a niacin flush in the morning if she hasn't regained consciousness by then. He thinks it might help wake her brain up as well as aid with flushing the toxins out of her. The poor little thing. I feel so bad for her and her family."

"I hate to think about that. The itching alone will probably wake her right up." Ann shook her head as she thought about what the little girl would be facing over the next couple of days while the medical team worked to cleanse her system of the overdose. God willing, after a couple days of suffering she'd be back to normal.

"Yes, you're probably right about that. I've seen patients undergoing the niacin treatment, it looks really uncomfortable."

"It beats being in a coma."

"That's for sure. I hope you have an easy night on the floor, Ann. See you tomorrow."

She turned back to the little girl as the door sucked shut behind Rhonda and studied the monitors above the bed. Her oxygen count and blood pressure readings were better but still low. Hopefully the detoxification regimen would begin to turn things around by morning.

Her cell phone buzzed in her pocket but she couldn't get to it through the hazmat suit. Maybe it was Chelsea calling to tell her the good news about Lily. She couldn't leave the room until a nurse came to relieve her. The buzzing finally stopped as she sat down in the chair next to the bed.

"Hi Lily, it's Ann. I hope you can hear me, Honey. We're giving you some medicine to make you feel better. I know you're probably really tired but if you want to open your eyes, it's okay." She watched Lily's lids flicker but they didn't open.

A sigh escaped her as she settled back on the chair and picked up the magazine Rhonda had left behind. The moment she laid it in her lap the cover flew open on its own and pages started flipping. It fell open on an advertisement for Tropicana orange juice. She told herself the ventilation system must be playing games with the magazine as she stared down at the small oranges in the tree. They looked like the berries Lily had eaten, minus the glowing yellow dots. She shrugged off the coincidence and turned to an article about the latest Hollywood drama.

* * *

It was close to midnight when Gammond called back but he had good news and her mood instantly brightened. Lily had been on detox for only two hours and already showed signs of improvement. Her oxygen level and blood pressure had increased and her fever had dropped.

"Can we come to the hospital now?" she asked.

"No, I'm afraid not. Right now your family is still in quarantine mode and I don't have the authority to override it. Give me a call in the morning—hopefully I'll have heard back from Director Wilson by then and can give you the green light for a visit."

"Okay, I'll wait until morning. But regardless of what Bob Wilson says, I'll be heading to the hospital before ten. Mark my words. I'm going to see my daughter and I'm not staying in this damn house while she wakes up alone in a strange bed surrounded by medical equipment and people she doesn't know." The words pushed out with the angst she'd been feeling for the past eight hours. She tried to rein it in, needing the doctor's cooperation in more ways than one.

"Look, I understand completely. But we are dealing with the government here. They have processes that have to be adhered to. Give me a call before you come. In the meantime, I suggest you get some sleep and I'm going to try to do the same. It's going to be a short night."

CHAPTER 42

An image of her daughter's pale face haunted her from the moment Chelsea opened her eyes. Gammond was right—it had been a short night.

"I'm going to the hospital. Do you want to ride with me?" she asked Craig as she walked into the kitchen and straight over to the coffee pot.

He gave her a strange look from his seat at the table. "I'll follow you. Ethan, do you want to ride with me?" A wisp of tension that didn't seem to fit the moment floated between father and son.

"Um, sure Dad."

She watched her son's eyes. Something was going on between the two of them but she didn't have time to figure it out right then. "Okay, I'll see you guys there."

Coffee and keys in hand, she went out the kitchen door and hit the garage's auto button. The heavy door was only halfway up when a herd of feet came running toward her across the driveway. Unseen voices began shouting out questions and she reacted on instinct, slapping the garage door button and sending it slamming back down. She let out a groan and stepped back inside. Craig and Ethan stood staring at her as she shut the kitchen door behind her.

"I forgot all about the press," Craig said. Chelsea's eyes flew to the clock as he spoke. It was only seven-thirty in the morning.

"Me too. They must have taken a break during the night and come back at sunrise." She went down the hall and looked out the entry windows. "I forgot all about the cop." A patrol car sat at the curb and a different police officer stood barking at the reporters to get off the property.

"What a mess. I guess the fact that it's only a vitamin overdose hasn't made it out yet. Surely that isn't newsworthy," she said.

"I take it the doctor has lifted the quarantine off us?"

She avoided his eyes. "The doctor said only the CDC can lift the quarantine."

"So did they?"

She paused and hitched her bag higher on her shoulder. "I don't know and I don't care. The doctor now agrees there is no need for quarantine. He's waiting to hear from the guy at the CDC for the official okay to let Lily out of isolation. I assume that will also mean we're no longer in quarantine."

She'd flung from beneath the covers, needing to know the status on her daughter and get to the hospital as fast as possible. She'd fallen asleep sometime after three and had startled awake just past seven. A fast brush of her teeth, a rake with the hairbrush, the same jeans and t-shirt and she was ready to go. The thought of calling for permission to go to the hospital hadn't even entered her mind until the flock of reporters had descended.

"I'm calling Ann. Maybe she can give me a ride to the hospital." She had her phone out when she remembered Ann was at the hospital and would be until two that afternoon. "Damn!"

"What?" Craig asked.

"Ann's at work." Her temper shot up at being trapped in her own home for no reason other than government stupidity. It was Saturday. Wilson was probably out golfing somewhere.

"I'll call Jimmy."

"That's a great idea." She felt the hope of freedom as she watched her husband dial. "Tell him to pull into Ann's driveway and wait. We'll go out through her garage."

Fifteen minutes later they were slipping through the backyard and into Ann's house. She had taken her car to work so Jimmy was able to pull his Lincoln Navigator in the garage and they climbed in unseen by the press and the police. They stayed low on the seats until they were a couple blocks away then sat up for the ride to the hospital.

As they rounded the corner and the medical facility came into view Chelsea's heart sank at the sight of the news trucks and reporters gathered outside the front entrance.

"Oh no. What are we going to do?"

Jimmy grinned and pointed to the ambulance entrance. "We'll take the fast lane."

He pulled up in front of the emergency entrance and told them to climb out.

"I'll go around and park."

Chelsea's eyes swept from side to side as they stepped through the emergency room doors. She'd caused a scene in here yesterday. Eyes flicking to the check-in desk, relief swam at seeing a different nurse. No security personnel, and the lobby held only a handful of people.

"Come on, let's just keep moving and hopefully no one will say anything."

She hit the elevator button and they stood with their backs to the room.

They stepped off on the ICU floor and headed straight for the isolation area. It was a short hallway and no one was in it. Chelsea rushed up to Lily's door and looked in as she hit the buzzer to talk to the nurse. Relief swept through her when she saw Ann turn from the chair and step over.

"Good morning. We're here to see Lily. How's she doing?"

Ann smiled behind the plastic shield as her voice tin-canned through the intercom, "She's doing much better, thank God."

"Let us in, okay?" Chelsea asked.

Ann frowned, "I can only let one of you in at a time and you have to suit up first. You can only stay five minutes each. You're still under quarantine so we have to keep this off the radar or I'll lose my job."

Chelsea struggled into her suit, getting her legs in the wrong hole and the mask on backwards in her haste to get in to see Lily before the doctor showed up. Craig and Ethan agreed to wait in the changing room while she went in first.

"Thank you Ann." Chelsea reached out and squeezed her hand through their rubber gloves then turned to her daughter. Her coloring was much better. The spots were starting to fade and her blood pressure was up to ninety over sixty-eight, her blood oxygen at ninety-two.

"Good morning, Lily, it's Mommy. Can you hear me, Honey?" She watched Lily's eyes flicker and her lips parted as if she would speak but no sound came out. Her lids remained closed. "I love you very much, Lily. You've been sick from eating the berries. The doctors are giving you medicine to make you better." She paused and glanced at Ann who stood by her side.

"Did she wake during the night?" Chelsea was sure Ann would have called her if that had been the case.

"No, she hasn't opened her eyes yet. We're supposed to start her on a Niacin flush at noon. The doctor thinks that might jolt her out of the coma in addition to helping cleanse her system. The poor little thing. It might be best if she stays asleep until we're through with that procedure, it's really uncomfortable."

Alarm ran through her as she asked, "What is it?"

"We'll put a strong dose of niacin in her I.V. and it will dilate all her capillaries very quickly. The capillaries feed blood to the finite cells of our bodies and run right beneath the surface of our skin. That's partly why they call it a 'flush'—it makes the body flush red as the blood flows faster and stronger through all of the capillaries."

Chelsea forced herself to remain calm as Ann continued explaining the process.

"The other reason for the term is the capillaries expanding so quickly forces a fast flushing of the blood's circulatory system, drawing toxins from throughout the body. The process is uncomfortable. Most people experience an extreme itching sensation during the flushing, sometimes temporary but painful nerve reactions. But Lily will be fine within thirty minutes of the process with absolutely no side effects from it."

She slowly let the breath out that she'd been holding as Ann described the details of the procedure. Her heart squeezed at the thought of her little girl going through something like that without being there to hold her hand. What if she wakes up for the first time, in extreme discomfort with her parents nowhere around? That possibility was not acceptable.

"Ann, I don't want to get you in any trouble, but you must know how I feel about Lily going through that without me here."

"Hopefully the quarantine will be lifted by then and you can be here."

"I'll be here, Ann. Either way."

Silence sat between them as Chelsea turned back and stroked Lily's hand then reluctantly stood up. "I'll go so Craig can come in."

CHAPTER 43

Saturday dawned bright and sunny on Villa Pacheo. Orlon took time for a few slices of toast and a cup of coffee before he headed to BioGen. With the investors meeting only six days away all key employees would be working through the weekend.

As he pulled in his reserved spot at the front of the parking lot he saw a small crowd gathered near the main entrance. It seemed odd, especially on a Saturday.

"There he is!" A cry rose from the group and they mobbed him as he stepped onto the sidewalk. He cringed as reporters hurled questions at him, squawking over each other while jockeying for a better position with their mikes. He could hardly make out a word anyone said.

A big man shoved his way to the front of the pack and shouted, "Mr. Millard—are you aware that one of your employees has been quarantined to her home?"

Orlon's head whipped around at the question. He picked up his pace as he neared the door, knowing it would not do well for him to seem unaware of a situation that might impact the company. Before he could get the door open someone grabbed hold of his arm and jerked him roughly back through the crowd of reporters. He was now headed toward the parking lot again.

Orlon didn't recognize the tall man who had a tight hold on him. The stranger wore scraggly brown hair pulled into a ponytail, faded blue jeans, a wooden cross hanging from a long chain around his neck and a pissed off expression. He was clearly on a mission.

Orlon's heart beat faster as he struggled to loose his arm from the man's vice-like grip and stop their forward motion.

"Get your hands off me! What are you doing?!"

The reporters turned en masse and raced behind, snapping pictures and shouting questions as they followed them toward the lot.

Orlon's blood froze as they reached a white van parked next to the sidewalk. Protestors marched with large signs in front of the van. His eyes quickly scanned the messages:

"Stop Growing Devil Plants!"; "The Girl is Now an Alien!"; "BioGen Grows Diseases!"; "BioGen Brings Hell to Earth!"

As he and the ponytailed man reached the van, a short chubby man slid the door open, and his assailant attempted to drag Orlon inside. Out of desperation he dug his heels in harder and leaned back, using the benefit of weighing significantly more than the other man as he tugged to free his arm.

"You people are crazy! Get your hands off me! Someone call security or I'll hold you all responsible for letting this happen!" Orlon screamed out as he looked back over his shoulder at the frenzied reporters.

The crazy man had managed to pull him almost all the way in the van when Orlon's words and dire situation finally sank past one woman's zeal for the story and she whipped out a cell phone.

A bullhorn sounded from the front of the building. Orlon managed to yank his arm loose as his assailant froze in response to the amplified message.

"Everyone! This is security! Step back off the sidewalk immediately! This is private property! The police have been called."

Orlon gasped with relief as he spotted George coming toward him through the throng of reporters. He looked back to make sure the crazy man wasn't following him just as the nut climbed the rest of the way into the van and slammed the door shut. The van peeled out of the parking lot, catching its right rearview mirror on a camera, sending it crashing to the pavement as the reporter jumped back.

"Mr. Millard, are you all right?" George asked.

He couldn't answer as he stood panting, trying to get his heart to calm down. He raked the security guard with his eyes as white-hot rage took hold of him. Just as he opened his mouth to unload on the incompetent he remembered the reporters were listening, recording devices and cameras rolling. He switched gears fast.

"Thank you, George. I wish you'd come a little sooner. That man almost had me in his van. Did you get the license plate?"

"No, I'm sorry sir, it all happened too fast. We've had a busy morning. I was on the other side of the building, trying to run a crowd off over there, when the front desk called me and said I needed to get over here. There's not enough of me to go around today."

Orlon stared at the man, "What do you mean? Another crowd on the other side?"

"At the employee entrance, sir. All these reporters are trying to get the scoop. They've been shouting questions at people as they come in to work."

His pulse shot higher. He needed to get an understanding of what was going on. Immediately. No doubt he already had messages waiting from shareholders. He glanced at his watch as George accompanied him back toward the entrance. It wasn't even nine o'clock yet and he was seriously behind the eight ball already. Damn.

"George, what is going on? Why are all these people here?"

"Sir, didn't you watch the news this morning?"

Orlon sent the security guard a cold look. "George, I don't waste the morning on local news." He smoothed his suit jacket as he spoke. "I read scientific and medical reports with my coffee. I don't have time for nonsense. Now what is going on?"

"Mrs. Noble's daughter got real sick yesterday. She's got a weird rash and is in a coma. The CDC got called in because of the rash, and last I knew the whole family was quarantined to their house. Their little girl's in critical condition at the hospital."

Orlon stopped in his tracks as he absorbed the man's words.

"What does that have to do with BioGen other than the fact Chelsea works here?"

His cage had been completely rattled over nothing. He was royally pissed but quickly made to remember they had an audience as reporters started shouting questions again.

"Mr. Millard! Where did the plant come from?

"How did the little girl get hold of the berries?"

"Do you have any more of the plants and if so, where are they?"

The reporters were off to the races again and George went into action. He flung his arms out and shouted, "Everyone get off the sidewalk or you'll be arrested for trespassing!"

The press doggedly ignored him, knowing it was a publicly traded company, and continued shouting questions as they pushed their way toward the entrance.

"Get inside and I'll lock the doors behind us." George held the door open for him.

Orlon shot past him, knees shaking as he bypassed the security equipment and headed to his office. He plowed down the hallway and stepped through the doorway to his office. Ice dripped from his words as he addressed his secretary.

"Janice, are you aware there is a crowd of reporters and protestors outside the building?" He focused hard on keeping his voice at a professional volume. The woman had been hired as a temporary three weeks ago and things had seemed to be working out well until that morning.

"Yes, sir," she squeaked out.

"What is the reason you didn't alert me of the situation?"

He glared at her then backed off. She was only a temp, not worth his time. He would give the agency a call and ask them to send a replacement over on Monday. An executive secretary needed to have more on the ball than this woman.

"I'm sorry, sir. I'll make sure to give you a call next time."

He winced at her words. "Never mind. Call the police and ask them to send someone over to take a statement. Some nut with a bunch of sign-waving lunatics tried to drag me in a van against my will. I want to file a complaint."

He heard the woman gasp as he stalked toward his office and resisted the urge to snap as he instructed her.

"Please get me a cup of coffee and a bottle of water."

The briefcase landed on his desk with a slap and he pulled out the leather chair with impatience. The keyboard tray slid smoothly from beneath the cherrywood console. He forced himself to calm down as he opened the contact list and scanned down to the N's.

CHAPTER 44

Chelsea stood in the decontamination room, waiting for Craig and Ethan to return from visiting Lily. She jumped as her phone rang. The caller I.D. showed BioGen. Maybe it was Brad with an update on the berries.

"Hello?

"Chelsea?" a man's voice barked out.

"Yes, who's this?"

"This is Orlon Millard. I don't know what kind of trouble your family is in Ms. Noble, but when it starts causing a problem for the company, I can't sit back and allow it to happen. You are fired—effective immediately."

A red haze descended over her at hearing his words. All the stress and anger she'd been through festered into her voice as she responded to the ludicrous statement.

"What part of go to hell did you not understand yesterday, Orlon?"

She fought the urge to throw the phone against the wall and slapped it in her purse as her husband stepped back in.

"I swear that man does not have a humane cell in his body!"

"What now?" Craig unzipped the biohazard suit and threw it in the bin. Neither one of them had bothered with the decontamination shower.

"That was my former boss—he just fired me because the press and protestors showed up outside BioGen this morning."

She watched as incredulity flashed across his face, quickly replaced by anger.

"Now that is my definition of a true asshole." Craig shook his head as she watched him thinking it through. "Who the hell is violating Lily's right to privacy by informing the press of her medical condition? And how in the hell does that give your boss the right to fire you?"

"I'll tell you who violated Lily's rights—it was that other asshole—Robert Wilson. He should never have discussed the quarantine while we were standing in that crowded lobby. There were at least twenty people sitting there. Most of them heard every word, I'm sure."

Claustrophobia set in as she paced the small dimensions of the room and waited for Ethan to come back in.

"You're right, that guy was out of line, but once the cops got involved it went out over the police radio." Craig tossed his rubber gloves in the trash as he said, "The press was aware of it from then on. Lots of places for a leak."

She stopped pacing and closed her eyes, fighting off the need to lash out at him. They had vowed to each other they'd always keep a civil tone, no matter how tough a situation got, but she'd been repeatedly pushed beyond the limits of what any woman should have to endure. She was pressed to the breaking point in every corner and the pressure was still coming.

Forcing herself to take a couple deep breaths, she tried to focus on the actions they needed to take instead of the emotions slicing at her. They had to figure out how to proceed after they left the decontamination room. They could sit in Jimmy's car in the parking lot and make calls but that wasn't going to help ensure she'd be allowed in with Lily during the Niacin treatment. She needed to figure something out quick.

* * *

Ethan looked at his little sister through the plastic mask. Ann stood quietly beside him as he glanced from Lily's face to the equipment attached to her. He didn't think it was possible to feel any worse about the situation but he did after taking one look at her. The sight of his little sister lying there, looking so helpless and small, pale as a pearl—all those tubes and wires made him feel terrible. The thought that he might be the reason for it bottomed his stomach out but he couldn't leave without talking to her, letting her know he cared and that he was sorry.

"Hey Lil, it's Ethan. I don't know if you can here me but I'm really sorry this happened to you. The doctor says you're getting better. I really hope you get to come home soon. I mean it. I'll never fight with you over the TV again, I promise." His voice broke as his eyes threatened to water up. He would never forget watching his sister pass out in the family room.

His hand reached out and gave hers a gentle squeeze. He remembered her little fists pounding on him, begging him not to change the channel. He'd deserved every one of those fists and a whole lot more. Emotions choked his throat as Ann rubbed his shoulder.

"We all love you very much." Tears pricked and he knew he couldn't take any more. He was going to puke for sure if he didn't get out of there. There was no way he was going to let Ann see him crying like a baby and he turned abruptly toward the door.

"Bye Lil. See you later Ann," he called over his shoulder and stepped out.

His parents waited for him in the decontamination room and he quickly got out of the white suit, keeping his eyes on the floor until he had himself under control. His mom reached out and gave him a quick hug then they headed out the door.

They made it half way down the short hall when three men in suits rounded the corner, walking toward them. Ethan's pulse jumped when he saw it was the guy from the CDC.

"Mrs. Noble—what are you doing here? Your family is supposed to be in quarantine."

The guy looked seriously pissed off. The men standing beside Wilson moved their hands toward the opening of their jackets as they came to a stop in front of his family.

Ethan looked at his mom, not blaming her for whatever her reaction might be, but he sure didn't want to get arrested. How were they going to help Lily from jail? He gulped and braced for impact but his mom surprised him. She answered the CDC guy with a calm voice.

"Mr. Wilson, I think there's been a misunderstanding. Didn't you speak with Dr. Gammond?" His mom's green eyes looked genuinely confused.

"I spoke with Gammond early this morning and told him specifically that you and your family are still under quarantine." The guy looked really pissed off now and turned to one of the men beside him, but before he could tell the guy to arrest them his mom blew more smoke out.

"Wait—I spoke with Gammond late last night. He agreed there was no longer any need for the quarantine. Didn't he tell you that Lily's illness was caused by a vitamin overdose?"

"Yes, he did. However, he sent me the lab reports and they clearly show foreign enzymes and unidentified proteins. We have no way of knowing whether Lily's illness is being caused solely by the vitamin overdose at this point. The foreign proteins could very well be morphing in her body, feeding off the strange enzymes and growing into some new disease even as we speak. The quarantine remains in place. In fact, I may be requesting a judge to order it be lengthened."

"What?" His mom's voice rose at hearing the quarantine might be carried past Sunday.

"I'm waiting on additional lab work results before I make that decision." Wilson gave his mom an ugly look then said, "For the sake of keeping this civil, I'm going to give you one break and won't have you arrested for violating the quarantine this morning. But—if you leave your house again without my express written permission I will have you arrested. I cannot stress enough that you are jeopardizing the public's safety. No more, do you hear me?"

"We'll leave now and go back home. But when I get there, I'm calling my attorney. No way am I going to let you carry this farce past the initial forty-eight hour mandate. My family has rights and you and the government aren't going to keep stepping on them. I'll go to the press or whatever else I have to do to get our daughter released to our custody." She stepped toward the men, her eyes slicing at their dark suits and muted ties as she went around them.

His dad hit the elevator button and they climbed on. Ethan jammed at the close-door button, wanting to get out of there before that guy changed his mind and came back after them. They got down to the lobby and headed out the door before they remembered the press was out there. Shouting and shoving, the reporters lunged as they headed down the walkway.

"Mrs. Noble! Do you work for BioGen?"

"Mrs. Noble—is it true your company developed a plant that made your daughter sick?"

More questions were shouted and the din got so bad the voices all ran together. Ethan couldn't wait to get out of there. His dad stepped in front of them, lowered his head and his shoulders and went at the press like the lineman he'd been in high school. The reporters quickly realized he wasn't holding anything back and stepped out of his way. Ethan stayed close behind so they wouldn't get separated by the hyenas and wolves holding cameras and microphones.

They reached the end of the sidewalk and tires screeched to a stop in front of them.

Jimmy flung the door open. "Get in!" They ran the last few feet and jumped in, slamming the doors shut. Jimmy hit the gas and whipped the truck toward the exit.

As they reached the end of the hospital's driveway a group of sign-waving protestors stepped off the sidewalk and into their path, forcing Jimmy to slam on the brakes. The group of fanatics immediately surrounded the truck, shouting at them through the glass.

Ethan read the signs: "Aliens Go Home!"; "BioGen brings Hell to earth!"; "The girl is an Alien!"; "Death to Aliens!" It was shocking to see the angry messages and tense faces.

"Why do they think this has anything to do with aliens, Dad?" he shouted to be heard over the protestors as Jimmy slowly inched the truck forward and the press came running.

"I don't have a clue, Son."

His mom looked out at the protestors with disgust, "These are the same yahoos who are always outside BioGen every time we announce a new breakthrough. They think science shouldn't mess with nature. Somehow they heard a plant is what made Lily sick and they're automatically assuming it came from BioGen."

She shook her head at their stupidity. "They'd rather see people starve or suffer crippling diseases than have us make advances that can save millions of lives. Their philosophy is if God didn't make it we shouldn't have it. But keep in mind these same people take antibiotics when they get sick. Go figure."

Just as she finished speaking a man with hair in a ponytail ran up to his mom's window and smashed at the glass with a wooden sign. Chelsea screamed but the glass held.

"That guy is nuts!" Her voice shook as she looked out the window.

Ethan heard the man shouting, "You're daughter needs to die! She's now an alien bitch—she's going to infect us all!" He hauled back to strike the window again and Jimmy hit the gas, managing to shoot past the other protestors without running anyone over.

The Lincoln shot out into traffic and Jimmy jerked the wheel to avoid colliding with another car coming down the road. The car's horn blared and the driver flipped them off as he righted his vehicle in the lane and continued down the road.

Ethan turned in his seat and looked back, "You better hurry Uncle Jimmy, I see that weird guy climbing into a white van—he might be coming after us."

Jimmy's eyes flew to the rearview mirror as a stream of protestors and reporters made it to the street behind them. He floored it and they shot down the road, doing fifty in a thirty zone.

CHAPTER 45

Chelsea was relieved to see only the police car and two reporters remained in front of the house. Evidently the rest of the press gaggle had gone to the hospital when they'd heard the family was there.

Jimmy pulled up in Ann's driveway and waited for Betty to open the garage door. He pulled the Lincoln in and they waited until the door met the pavement before they lifted their heads from the seats and climbed out.

Back in her own kitchen again, Chelsea's purse hit the counter with an angry thump and she decided it was more than okay to throw convention out the window under the circumstances.

"I'm having a bloody mary, anybody else want one?" A glass was in her hand before she finished the sentence.

"No thanks, Chelsea. I had one more Manhattan than I should have last night. I'm sticking to water today." Jimmy said.

Craig brushed past her and grabbed two bottles of water from the fridge, motioned for Jimmy to follow him. That was fine with her. She sure didn't feel like sitting around making conversation with anyone.

"Thanks for your help this morning, Jimmy," she said.

"No problem, that's what family's for." He gave her a smile as he reached the doorway.

Ethan tagged behind, "I'm going to my room."

The door swung shut behind them and she poured a generous shot of vodka into the crystal glass, topped it with V8 and stirred. She'd drained a third of it when her phone rang. The cell was in the outside pocket of her purse and she fumbled it out, trying to get it answered before the call went to voice mail, worried it was the hospital.

It was Brad calling for an update on Lily. She felt the beginning of a smile as she sat down at the table and swirled her drink then sipped.

"It looks like you were right Brad. I just came from the hospital and Lily's doing better now that she's had twelve hours of the detox regimen. She's still unconscious though." Her words trailed off at the thought of her little girl still in a coma.

"I'm glad to hear she's improving. I bet she'll be out of the coma before long. It sounds like her blood pressure is still a little low. Once that's up she'll snap back to us, I'm sure."

She took another pull of her drink then told him about the niacin treatment that Lily was scheduled for in two hours. "I hate to think of her going through that alone Brad, but there's not much I can do. If I show back up at the hospital the CDC guy is going to have me arrested. I think he and Orlon must be related, their faces are very similar—both are shaped like assholes."

Brad's chuckle made her smile flicker back until he asked, "Did you check that plant to see if any berries grew overnight? I'd like to run some more tests but I don't have enough material to work with."

Chelsea froze as his words sank in. "I hadn't thought to check this morning. I'm going to take a look now. I'll call you right back."

She dropped the phone and rushed out. The ominously dark leaves bore no new fruit.

* * *

"So Lily got sick from eating berries off the plant?" Jimmy asked.

"It looks like it. We have no reason to think otherwise. And her rash looks just like those damn berries. It's scary as hell to think it was out there growing in the backyard without our knowing it."

Craig leaned back in his desk chair and flipped the drawer pull up and down as another thought formed. "You know, I wonder if the neighbors behind us have a plant growing on their side of the fence that rooted underneath and sprouted on our side or vice versa?"

"That's a good point. We should get a ladder and look over the fence. And now that you mention it, I'm surprised the lawn guys didn't mow it down before it could cause a problem. From what you said, it's growing where it shouldn't be and hard to see. I'd think they'd have mown it down without even noticing." Jimmy said.

"I hadn't thought about that, but you're right. Our lawn crew comes every Monday morning. Let's get a ladder and go look over the fence real quick."

Craig led the way down the hall and out to the garage. A minute later they were in the backyard and Jimmy held the ladder as he hiked up two rungs and looked over.

"I don't see anything. They've got a few decorative bushes but that's it. The leaves are so dark on that damn thing it's like a shadow, but I don't see anything right on the other side of our plant. I think they're okay." He clambered back down and folded the ladder. The men stood staring at the plant a moment.

"Damn. Now that's a vicious bush."

"What do you mean?" Craig asked.

"Well, it's kinda Gothic looking. The leaves are almost black and they've got all that weird fuzz. The jagged spikes on the ends are just plain wicked." Jimmy plucked one off and inspected it. "Let's take this bad boy inside and look at it under a magnifying glass."

"Yeah, let's do that. Let me put this ladder away and I'll meet you back in the den. Then we'll take a closer look at that leaf."

* * *

Chelsea headed back to the kitchen and called Brad back.

"No more berries," she said in place of a greeting.

"Damn it! I was really hoping it would have at least a few more." Brad sounded frustrated. She instantly got a mental image of him scraping a hand through his black hair as he spoke.

"Chelsea, these berries are incredible. I've got to do some more tests, but right now it looks like they contain at least four unidentified enzymes and two new proteins. You'd have to eat a case of oranges to equal the vitamin C in just one of these little berries."

"That's incredible. No wonder Lily got so sick. We're lucky she's not dead. I wonder how many of those berries she ate…"

Chelsea cringed at the thought of her daughter being outside in the backyard, snacking up fruit from an unidentified plant without her mother having a clue what was going on. What kind of mother did that make her? A bad one. She silently resolved to be more aware of everything in their home and yard.

"That's a good question. Can you tell from looking at the stems where the berries were growing?" Brad asked.

"Not really. I tried to do that when I was out back a minute ago. I can see the little stems they were hanging off but it's hard to gauge how many were there without cutting the plant down and being able to examine it under good light. Plus our neighbor's son ate some of the berries too, so who knows for sure how many Lily had?"

"What? Your neighbor's boy—is he sick too?"

"No. In fact, he seems better than ever."

"What do you mean?"

"Steve's suffered from a pretty severe case of autism his whole life but this week he made a miraculous recovery. He seems normal now." She let the sentence hang in the air.

"Are you kidding me?"

"No. This is no time for kidding, you know that."

"But Chelsea, do you realize what this might mean?"

She let out a sigh, "No, I don't know what it means. Do you?"

"I think the berries may have amazing healing powers, provided they are eaten in moderate amounts. At least, I assume the boy ate a lot less than Lily since he's not sick, right?"

Chelsea's heart beat picked up. Her mind had been so wrapped around what was going on with Lily, the scientist in her had been temporarily shelved. Her words came out in an excited rush, "Brad, you might be right. Can you imagine what this could mean for the world?"

Her breathing quickened as she set the drink down on the table with an absent click. Her mind raced over the images and facts that she'd been almost unconsciously gathering over the past two days.

In addition to Steve's miraculous recovery from his autism, Bell now seemed like a puppy again. The Irish Setter had suffered from a severe case of arthritis for the past two years and it had gotten so bad Bell couldn't even handle going for walks with the family.

"Chelsea, I know Lily is your first priority right now, but as soon as she's better I need you to get in here and help me with this. These berries could be the answer to what we've been trying to achieve for the past year."

She drained her drink before she responded. "That's not going to happen, Brad."

"What? Why not? Are they saying Lily's going to be ill long-term?"

"No. From what you and the doctor had to say about the vitamin overdose, she should be almost back to normal within a few days, maybe less if we're lucky."

"Then what's the problem? I can wait for you if I freeze the little bit of sample I have left and work with you on it when you can come in." Brad's voice had a pleading note in it.

"Ask your boss."

"Orlon?"

"Yep. O-hole fired me this morning."

Brad let out a riptide of curses that almost made her feel better about getting fired. At least somebody cared about her.

"Look Brad, I appreciate your support but you know I planned to leave anyway. Do what you can with what you've got. I wish you the best of luck on it. Listen, I've gotta go. I need to make some calls. They're doing the niacin procedure on Lily at noon and I want to be there for it. Call me if you learn anything else about the berries. Lily's not out of the woods yet."

* * *

Craig hustled into the den and found Jimmy examining the leaf under a magnifying glass he'd pulled from the desk drawer.

"This is crazy. I don't know my plants very well, but I damn sure haven't ever seen anything like it before." His brother looked up with a puzzled expression.

"Let me take a look."

Craig reached out for the leaf and glass then moved so he could hold both under the desk lamp. He examined it a moment then set the magnifier down and motioned for Jimmy to move a bit so he could get out his digital microscope. "Time for a little field work," he said as he pulled a small black device out of a pouch. A USB cord was attached to its end and Craig plugged it into the laptop on his desk.

"What's that? It looks like a car lighter or something." Jimmy asked.

Craig booted up the computer then clicked a small button on the side of the device and its end lit up. "It's a portable microscope. I'm going to hold it over the leaf and it'll put the magnified picture up on the computer screen so we can get a good look at this hairy beast."

A minute later the men sat staring at the image on the computer screen.

"Will you look at that?" Craig mumbled as he moved the eye of the hand-held microscope down to get a better look at the section of the leaf where it met its stem. He clicked the magnification up a notch and they let out a low whistle at the same time.

The greatly enlarged image showed tiny clear hairs on the leaf, each hair contained a sack of dark liquid. It looked like the fuzzy hairs were miniscule storage units of some kind. The fluid ran from the swaying tubes into veins that met in the center of the leaf.

"Is that normal?" Jimmy asked.

"Hell if I know. I'm not the botanist in the family. Do me a favor, go out in and pluck a big branch off that damn thing. I'm going to set up the big microscope while you're out there. Tell Chelsea to come take a look. She'll want to see this, whether she's pissed off at me or not."

Jimmy paused in his stride to the doorway. "You mean she's holding on to her mad through all this stuff with Lily? Brother, you are in some serious sheee-it with your wife. I guess you haven't had a chance to talk with her since you got home, huh?"

"Oh we talked all right. For all of about thirty seconds when we got home from the hospital last night. Long enough for her to tell me she met with an attorney while I was gone this week." Craig's throat clogged with emotions and he got busy opening the deep desk drawer on his right He bent over and pulled out the heavy microscope.

"Come on, no way. A divorce attorney? I never in a million years would've thought Chelsea'd go there."

"Well, that makes two of us."

Craig set the heavy microscope down with a solid thud, bent over the side of the desk to plug it in. He straightened back up, kept his eyes on the equipment.

"I think I finally saw that blind spot you were telling me to look for."

Jimmy waited in silence for him to go on.

The words squeezed past the chalk in his throat, "My wife is having an affair."

"No! Hell no, Craig. I don't believe that for a minute." Jimmy seemed pissed off. Craig wasn't sure if it was on his behalf or Chelsea's, either way he was surprised.

"I thought that's what you were trying to tell me without having to come out and actually say it when we were on the phone yesterday. You know, before your big date at the Brasserie." Craig couldn't keep a note of resentment out of his voice.

"What? You thought I meant Chelsea was screwing around on you? Where the hell did you get that idea?"

"From you, like I said."

"Now I'm really confused. What did I say that made you think some stupid-assed shit like that?" Jimmy was definitely getting pissed.

"You told me I should look at things from Chelsea's viewpoint. That sometimes a person needs to see things for himself instead of someone else telling him what to look at."

"Right. So how's that equal an affair to you? I sure can't follow your logic on it."

Craig paused a minute, trying to get his head around the fact that Jimmy was telling him the opposite of what's he'd assumed ever since last night. A feeling of relief mixed with total confusion engulfed him until he recalled the lovers' hug in his own backyard.

"If you'd seen what I did last night you'd realize why I'm saying the 'A' word. I didn't start thinking that until Chelsea's lab partner came over to get the berries so he could test them. It was just the two of them in the backyard." Craig turned and pointed out the window. "He couldn't come to the front door because of the quarantine, so Chelsea met him out back. They talked for a couple minutes then she gave him a real-close, real-long hug goodbye. I had an air-conditioned front row seat." He pointed at the desk chair.

"So? She's upset, he's helping your family. I think you read too much into it."

"Well, I can tell you this much 'cause I saw the man's face when he finally let go of my wife—they're either sleeping together and his lust bell is on full ring—or he's deeply in love with Chelsea. Hell, maybe both. That's how I've always felt about her." His voice thickened and he turned around to snap the light on beneath the microscope, slid the leaf under it but didn't bend down to examine it.

"Come on Craig, seriously. I think you should give Chelsea the benefit of the doubt here. Don't make things worse than they are already."

"Okay. Let's just say for a minute that I choose to believe she's not having an affair. Even though her lab partner looks like a damned movie star and I'm just an average Joe. Trust me, I'd like to believe she loves me enough not to fall for a guy's looks over mine. So if that's the case, what the hell is she so pissed off at me for that she's gone and talked to an attorney?"

Jimmy stared at the floor as he rubbed his thumb over his bottom lip. It was obvious he was having a hard time saying what was on his mind.

"Just say it, Jimmy. Don't worry about my feelings, okay? I need to figure this out. The last thing I want is a divorce. But I'll be damned if I can figure out how too much traveling equals a wife wanting a divorce." He shoved a pencil jar back on the desk and looked at his brother. "I guess I've still got my blind spot if she's not having an affair."

"Okay. You're right. You're in deep shit, this is no time for being subtle. I'm gonna give it to you with both barrels and you damn well better not let this come between us."

Jimmy walked over to the windows and stood looking out with his back to him. He shoved his hands in his pockets as he spoke, "This is gonna sound like jealous older brother bullshit but it's not. I think you're blind spot where Chelsea's concerned goes all the way back to high school. Maybe a little further back than that."

"What? You mean she's been mad at me for more than eighteen years? We got married right after she graduated. I don't think she was pissed when she said 'I do'." Craig felt a glimmer of hope as he told himself Jimmy was way off base to take things that far back.

"Hold on, hear me out. You're not gonna like it, but I guess you need to hear it, and you damn sure need to understand what I'm saying if you want to save your marriage." Jimmy glared at him over his shoulder then turned back to the window.

"Craig, you've had everything way too easy your whole life. From what I've seen, absolutely everything has gone your way. You made excellent grades without much effort, you wanted to play on the basketball team and made first-string center as a freshman. That's unheard of most of the time, but not for you. You were the star player for four years. You wanted to date Chelsea, even though the whole school thought she and Mike Thompson would never break up. Next thing you know, she's madly in love with you."

"Aw now, come on, this is starting to sound like a jealous tirade. I know you warned me, but how the hell is the past supposed to make a difference about my traveling now?"

Jimmy didn't bother to respond to the question. "You wanted to be a geologist since junior high, got a full-ride scholarship to Berkley and never looked back. You've always gotten exactly what you wanted without any obstacles to overcome or compromises on your part."

"Get to the point here or let's change the subject."

"You want to fix your marriage or not?"

"If you've got a point, get to it."

"All right. Here it is. How many days a week are you home, on average. Full days. You can't count Fridays if you don't get home until dinner."

"Three, well sometimes only two if I can't count Fridays. Sometimes I'm home by Thursday. So let's call it an average of home ten days a month."

"Okay. So let's do the math—that puts you at work twenty days and at home ten, right?"

"I knew that already. Get to the point"

Jimmy turned and looked at him like he'd just wrecked his brother's new truck.

After a beat of silence he said, "Your wife is a very beautiful woman. Inside and out. Just about every man I know would love to have her for his own. You agree with me on that much?"

"Yes. That's why we're having this conversation."

"Chelsea's in her prime, Craig, and so are you. She's thirty-six, you're thirty-seven. But she only gets to sleep with her husband two nights a week. And she's been living that schedule for years.

"In addition to sleeping alone, she's had to deal with the kids' illnesses plus all the chores and other stuff that comes with having kids. All while you've been out of town. And on top of it, she's always worked full time. That's my definition of Super Woman. I don't know how she's done it this long." Jimmy shook his head and turned from the window to face him. Craig couldn't look him in the eye. He stared at the carpet as his brother continued.

"I think what you're dealing with is a lonely woman who's feeling like she and her husband need to make the most of their prime years. Together. So you tell me, Craig. How's Chelsea supposed to make the most of her life if she loves you with all her heart and you're only with her a third of the time?" Jimmy stopped speaking and headed to the door. With one foot in the hall he said, "I'm gonna go get those leaves. And your wife."

Craig stopped him, "Wait. Get the branch but let's take a look at it first. I need a little bit to process what you just hit me with before I face my wife."

Jimmy nodded once then went out the door with a look on his face that Craig had never seen before.

He sat in the desk chair, absolutely stunned. His brother had been wrong. It wasn't just a blind spot he'd been suffering from—it was the Grand Canyon of blind spots. How could a man with two college degrees be so stupid?

The boulder in his gut scraped at him and he jerked sideways to lessen the sudden pain. He drained the water bottle on the desk, hoping to dilute the acid pouring into his stomach. The doorbell rang as he reached in the drawer for a Tumms.

CHAPTER 46

Craig reached for the door knob, wondering why the cop had allowed someone to ring the bell while they were under quarantine.

"Hello. Are you Mr. Noble?"

His brow lifted at seeing two men standing on the porch. The one in front wore a dark suit and an even darker expression. Like someone had died. His red tie seemed symbolic and Craig had to fight the urge to slam the oak slab shut and turn his back on the man without asking the visitor's name. He focused on maintaining a calm front while he mind spun over the possibilities of why these men were here and why the cop let them knock on the door.

"Yes. And you are?"

"My name is Thomas Blackstone," he motioned to the man standing behind him, "and this is my partner, Gordon Smith." The partner gave a nod and said nothing. "We're with the FBI and would like to come in and speak with you and your son, if we may."

A long shadow stretched off the man, across the doorway and into the hall. The urge to slam the door became almost irresistible as the man's words rocketed through him. He forced himself to get a grip. Before he allowed the men inside he wanted to know why they were there.

"What's this about?"

"We'd prefer to discuss it with you inside."

"I need to know why you're here before I let you into our home. You may not be aware of it, but my family is under quarantine. Our daughter is extremely ill." He had had enough of the government pushing them around. No one was getting inside without a warrant or a good explanation of why they were there.

Blackstone looked back over his shoulder at the patrol car parked at the curb and the growing crowd of reporters who snapped their pictures from the sidewalk.

"Yes, we're aware of the situation. However, that is not why we're here."

"Why are you here then?" He shifted the Tumms to his other cheek.

"It has to do with your trip to Africa."

The man spoke quietly, unaware the words had caused Craig's heart to stop. Holding back a grimace as he stepped aside, he motioned the men in. A few steps across the foyer and he led them into the formal living room the family rarely used. He gave the room a swift glance over. Chelsea had decorated it in what she called upscale New York loft meets Zen. The furniture was streamlined, expensive neutral fabrics mixed with eclectic accessories. He and Ethan had already combed every inch of it on Friday evening.

"Please have a seat while I get my son."

He raced up the stairs, knocked on Ethan's door and opened it without waiting for a response. Ethan lay on the bed with his Ipod in his hand. The boy sat up, popped the earbuds out as Craig reached back and shut the door.

"We've got real trouble, Son."

"Is Lily okay?"

"Your sister's on status quo. There are two men from the FBI in our living room. They want to talk to you." His anger at Ethan for stealing the sphere came flooding back as he spoke.

"What? Are you serious, Dad?"

"Ethan, do I look like I'm joking? Now come on, get real a minute. I know you said you lost that damn sphere and we looked over the entire house together, but I want to ask you one more time—before we go down to face those guys—do you have the sphere?"

A hurt expression crossed his son's face.

"No, Dad. I really don't have it." His son's shaky voice matched how Craig felt.

He stared him down a moment. He'd believed him when they'd finished searching yesterday, and the look in his son's eyes told the truth. Damn.

A heave of air left his lungs. "All right. I guess we've got to talk to them. They haven't said anything about the sphere yet but they mentioned our trip to Africa, so I assume that's why they're here. Let's go."

They stepped into the living room together. Blackstone stood looking out the window, hands folded behind his back. Smith sat on the sofa wearing the look of someone used to waiting. Craig moved into the room and Ethan hung just inside the doorway, eyes flicking from the men then back to him. His son looked scared out of his mind. Good—so was he.

He tapped down on his anger and forced himself to take a seat at a right angle to Smith. Blackstone walked over and joined them. Ethan stayed on the edge of the doorway.

"Mr. Noble, we're here because our supervisor is concerned that you and your son may be involved in an international theft. Are you aware of that situation?" Blackstone's eyes were dark and unreadable, his voice an ominous rumble—like the sound of distant level five rapids reaching a drop that couldn't be avoided.

"I believe you're referring to a sphere that is missing from the Wonderstone mine."

"That's correct. I understand you spoke with Mr. Connor, told him you don't have the sphere." The man looked at him like a bug, something to be stepped on if he didn't cooperate.

"Yes. I spoke with Mr. Connor and told him we don't have the sphere."

"Mr. Noble, it appears that there is a miscommunication between you and your son. Whether it is deliberate or due to a lack of knowledge on your part remains to be seen. I suggest that you and your son return the sphere to Mr. Connor as he asked. We're authorized to convey it back to him on your behalf."

"My son has admitted that he took the sphere, Mr. Blackstone." He glanced at Ethan. His face had gone chalk white and he leaned heavily against the door jam.

Craig looked back at the FBI man. "Unfortunately, the sphere has been misplaced since Ethan brought it home—without my knowledge—and we've searched every inch of the house trying to find it. Believe me, I want to give the sphere back as much as Mr. Connor seems to want it back. If we knew where it was we would have returned it already."

"Are you willing to allow us to search your home?"

Craig didn't hesitate. These guys were with the government, it was no time to mess around demanding a search warrant. A federal search warrant. "Of course. Search all you like. We looked through every crevice in this house yesterday and couldn't find it."

His mind flashed on the conversation he'd had with Connor on Thursday. The manager had seemed understanding, almost sympathetic, but the man had expected Craig to call back after he'd talked with Ethan yesterday. He hadn't had time to call Connor, but even if he had, the man probably would have contacted the Feds anyway. The manager would likely no more have believed the sphere had gotten lost than Craig had when Ethan first told him he'd misplaced it.

To have the FBI here this quickly, on a Saturday, and over something relatively trivial must mean Connor had connections very high up or something more was going on here. Craig could understand the man wanting his property back but after all, it was just a sphere. It seemed really heavy-handed to pull in the U.S. government over a little brown ball. A letter from an attorney threatening legal action if the sphere wasn't returned would have made sense. A call to the FBI was a red flag. Something else was going on. Maybe he could learn about it from these men— preferably not from the inside of a jail cell.

Blackstone studied his face, evidently believing what he saw. Instead of jumping up to begin searching he asked another question.

"What did you plan to do with the sphere?"

Craig blinked back at him a moment. "Nothing. I had no idea Ethan had taken it. My son is working on an essay for college. He's planning to become a geologist. We took the trip to the mine so he could examine the specimens before writing his paper." He turned to his son, "Ethan, tell these men why you took the sphere."

His son visibly flinched at being told to address the men himself. He stood up from the doorframe, shoved his hands in his pockets.

With a white face and a small shrug he responded, "They had some kind of emergency at the mine while we were looking over the spheres. The secretary rushed in and told us we had to leave. I was holding one of the spheres when she came in and I stuck it in my pocket without thinking about it."

The three men studied Ethan's face. Craig could tell Ethan was holding back on why he'd taken the sphere. Chances were Blackstone could read his face just as well, if not better.

The man proved it by saying, "You stuck a one-inch sphere in your pocket without noticing you'd done so?" His brows lowered as he looked at the boy.

"Um, yeah."

Craig watched his son squirm under the heavy gaze of the FBI man.

Blackstone continued to push, "When you realized you had the sphere, why didn't you return it right then? Why did you smuggle it out of the country?"

Whoa, now there was a heavy punch. He watched his son's face tighten with fear. He was on the verge of feeling sorry for him, after all he was still a teenager, but Ethan finally admitted the reason he'd jeopardized his father's reputation and sympathy flew out the window.

"I guess once I realized I had it, I figured they had a bunch of them and probably didn't need it back. I mean, they keep most of them stored in a big box anyway."

Ethan fumbled on, "Then I thought about writing my paper and decided to bring the sphere back so I could run some tests on its center. My paper's about a controversial issue, and these spheres are supposedly unexplainable. I hoped testing the centers would clear the issue up for good."

"Ethan—if you had wanted to do extensive testing on the center of a sphere why didn't you say so? Do you realize Mr. Connor probably would have given us one that was already cleaved for you to test? He mentioned he'd allowed the spheres to leave the facility for scientific testing in the past. You heard him say that right?"

"I'm sorry Dad. I guess I just didn't think it through. I was gonna ask Mr. Connor if he'd let me take one to run tests on but he took off before I could."

Craig nailed him with a dirty look, "You didn't want to risk hearing 'no'. That's why you took it. Now you sit and you think about that."

Blackstone let Craig finish then shot the boy with his laser eyes. "What were the results of the tests?"

Ethan's mouth took on the look of a fish on dry land. No sound came out for a moment. He gulped then answered, "I never got a chance to have it tested. I had the sphere on Sunday night but it was gone when I looked for it on Wednesday."

Craig turned to the men, getting really tired of feeling the pinball in this game he hadn't started. He needed to concentrate on Lily and Chelsea.

"Gentlemen, I realize international theft is a serious charge, and my son broke the law under my watch. What I don't understand is why the FBI is involved. Can you explain it?"

Blackstone glanced at Smith then looked back at him.

"Mr. Noble, you said it yourself. The FBI is involved because it's an international theft."

Craig looked steadily back at him, trying to read his eyes. It was impossible. They were like mud puddles, totally without expression.

"I realize that. I think you know what I'm asking here."

Blackstone nodded and stood up. "Mr. Noble, we're just here to do a job. You know how these things go. Wonderstone wants their sphere back and evidently the owner of the mine has some significant connections. That's all I know about the situation."

He studied Blackstone's face but it was a waste of time. Whether the man was speaking the truth or not, he clearly wasn't prepared to shed any light beyond what he'd just said.

Craig had to ask the question, even though he dreaded the answer, "Is the owner of the mine pressing charges against us?" He couldn't help the gulp—his stomach was on fire.

"Not if he gets the sphere back. Soon." Blackstone stood up. "Since you've offered to allow us to search the premises, we're going to do that now. Where can we start?"

"You can start right here and go through the house as you please. We have nothing to hide. But you're aware my family is supposed to be under a CDC quarantine right now. I see that you aren't wearing biohazard gear." Craig scrambled to get a glimmer of information out of the man and didn't know how else to do it.

Blackstone paused. "It's my understanding that the quarantine is going to be lifted tomorrow morning and was only a precaution. No one else is ill in your family, correct?"

"The CDC director told us this morning he may be extending it." Let them sweat a little.

Blackstone scanned his face again then nodded. "Okay, that's fair warning. We're going to search for the sphere. We won't break anything, at least not intentionally. The house might get a little messy though. Consider that our fair warning."

Craig glanced at Ethan. If his son's face was anything to judge by, no doubt a second family member was not feeling well right then but Craig knew it was from nerves not berries. He didn't wish ill will on Ethan, no father would, but he hoped he had learned a damn good lesson. As soon as Chelsea found out what was going on they would both have hell to pay. Round two would soon be coming— the moment she spotted the FBI searching their home.

He nodded back at Blackstone then said as calmly as he could manage, "I'm going to do some work in my den. It's down the hall at the back of the house. If you have any more questions, I'll be there. Ethan, why don't you join me?"

Craig could feel their federal eyes boring holes in his back while he walked out of the room. As he and Ethan neared the end of the hall intense pain lanced through him. He stopped and rubbed at his middle.

"Dad, are you okay?"

Craig didn't answer. The pain was too sharp right then. He gulped saliva, waited a moment until the stabbing sensation began to pass.

"I think so. My stomach has been cramping up on me, but right now I have bigger things to worry about."

CHAPTER 47

Chelsea felt bad for calling her attorney on a Saturday, but the woman had told her to call if she had any problems, day or night. She needed help, now, although it had nothing to do with a divorce. Maybe Carol didn't handle things like the government infringing on their rights as parents, but hopefully, she'd know someone who did. There were no other options for her right then. She didn't know any other attorneys and sure didn't have their cell phone numbers. Her fingers crossed as she listened to the phone ring, then a sweep of relief as it was answered.

"Hi Carol, this is Chelsea Noble. I hope I didn't catch you at a bad time?"

"No, this is perfect. What can I help you with Chelsea?"

"Well, the problems I'm having right this minute don't have anything to do with divorce, but I'm hoping if you can't help me you can recommend someone."

"Okay. Tell me what's going on."

Chelsea laid it all out for her and just as she finished explaining about the niacin flush that was scheduled in less than an hour, the doorbell rang. She paused as the sound of the bell peeled. Craig or Ethan could get it. This call was more important.

"So you can understand why I'm calling. I need someone to put pressure on the doctor and the CDC guy to allow me in with my daughter. I don't want to ask the procedure be postponed because she's critically ill—the flush is to help detoxify her, she needs it right away."

"Chelsea, I can't believe the Centers for Disease Control has the right to keep you away from your daughter. Especially during medical procedures. But to be honest, I've never worked any civil rights cases before so I don't know the answer. Let me make a couple calls and I'll get back to you as quick as I can."

"Okay Carol. Thanks for your help. I'll be here." Her words deadpanned on the last sentence. The phone went next to the empty bloody mary glass. She pushed out of the chair and began pacing the kitchen. Her nerves were so tightly strung it was affecting her breathing. It felt like an elephant was sitting on her chest as the walls closed in around her.

Out of desperation to maintain her sanity, she snatched the phone back up, stuffed it in her pocket and snagged the vegetable basket off the counter. In the yard under the sunshine and fresh air, her nerves began to calm a smidge. She knelt alongside the tomatoes. Basket at her side she pulled weeds then harvested two ripe red orbs. Her ears remained pricked for the phone as the smell of the rich soil made it to her brain.

She thought through the possible scenarios available to her between now and noon. Ann was the nurse on duty until two o'clock, a huge benefit for them, but she didn't want to compromise Ann's job. Risking arrest, she could show up at the hospital, sneak into Lily's room and stay during the niacin flush, refusing to leave until someone forced her out.

Preferably, Carol would call to say someone had given her clearance to be there for her daughter. Those were the only two options she was willing to accept.

She stood and stretched her back then moved over to the corn, unable to take her mind off her daughter for a moment. Her teeth ground as she acknowledged her third option. Much less palatable but enough to keep her sanity, would be staying at home and concentrating on knowing Ann was there with Lily. Her daughter loved Ann, and at least she'd have a familiar face beside her. If she couldn't sneak into the hospital or go in with permission she'd have to settle for option three. Tears choked her as she snatched weeds faster from between the corn stalks.

The phone rang at her hip and she jumped up to fish it out. It was Carol calling back. Her pulse shot up as she listened to the tone in her attorney's voice. The first word out of her mouth told her she wasn't going to like the rest.

"I'm sorry Chelsea, but a friend of mine who specializes in civil rights cases is telling me the CDC has the authority to isolate your daughter for forty-eight hours without a warrant or court order. They changed the law to increase the CDC's power during that avian flu scare a few years ago. Provided certain indicators are present at the time of quarantine, and from what you tell me that is the case, their office has police power to a limited extent."

Chelsea kicked at the base of a corn plant as she listened to Carol explain her rights, or lack of them. The stalk's roots gave way as she continued to kick at it.

"The good news is, once the forty-eight hour window passes, assuming no one in your family is presenting similar symptoms, they have to allow you to be with your daughter. But, until tomorrow afternoon, they're in charge."

She let out a grunt as she gave the cornstalk one last vicious kick, then stood panting as her desperation increased and her eyes flashed over the yard. She saw Jimmy coming out from behind the play fort and knew he must have been checking out the plant. If she weren't so desperate for it to grow more berries she would set the damn thing on fire.

"Chelsea, are you okay?" Carol asked.

"As okay as a mother can be in a situation like this. It sounds like I don't have any choice but to go along with them. Thank you for getting me a fast answer on it."

She blew out a breath then said, "Listen, I have another issue that is less pressing but also may not be in your arsenal of experience."

"What else is going on?"

Chelsea explained about Orlon's phone call earlier that morning and being fired. She could care less about her job. Lord knew it was like living in hell working there, but she wasn't going to let the asshole get away with firing her.

"Chelsea, I can't believe your boss did that! My god, what kind of a jerk is that guy?"

"Exactly. The world's biggest and he deserves to be taken down. For a lot of reasons, but this is the best one I've got to shoot him with."

"Well, believe me, he broke several laws when he fired you today. You could potentially get a lot of money out of this. We probably won't get anywhere near court with it. I'm sure the board will vote for a quick settlement to make it go away."

"I'm not looking for money—I want justice—maybe even a little revenge. That guy has made my life absolutely miserable for the past three years. The stories I could tell you."

"Maybe you should."

"I should what?"

"Tell me the other things he's done over the years. If he's that big a jerk, we probably have several charges against him. Guys like him need to be taken down and the companies that let them get away with it need to pay for the suffering caused by bad managers." Carol sounded deeply offended on her behalf.

A wave of something almost like comfort washed over Chelsea as her attorney spoke. It was so good to feel like she had someone in her corner. She wasn't all alone, facing everything life was throwing at her.

"Carol, I'd like to hire you as my attorney on the wrongful discharge case, as well as my divorce. But right now, I need to get off the phone and talk to the hospital to check on my daughter. I'll give you a call in a couple days, okay?"

She disconnected the call and hurried back inside, frantically trying to decide if she should risk going to hospital and getting arrested. Wilson or one of the guys with him might be sitting outside Lily's room for all she knew.

The kitchen faucet flipped on with a squeak and she washed her hands, debating what to do. She tore off a wad of paper towels just as the doorbell rang. Who in the world kept ringing the bell? Wasn't the cop out there keeping people off their property? She stepped into the hallway, expecting to see Craig or Ethan answering the door but neither one of them appeared.

She pulled the front door open and her heart did a flip flop. Bob Wilson stood on the porch with the two men from the hospital earlier. Her temper instantly shot to the ceiling.

"What do you want?" She noticed they weren't wearing protective gear.

"We're here for the plant."

"The plant?"

"Mrs. Noble, please don't be obtuse. We need the plant the berries came from. I've been asked to collect it for testing and identification. It could be a risk to the community. We're here to confiscate it. I've got a court order if you want to see it. His hand reached toward his jacket pocket as she considered how to answer.

"Look, the only problem I have with you taking the plant is there were only four berries left on it when Lily got sick. I just checked it again this morning—there's no new growth. I would have dug the damn thing up myself but we need more of the berries to do additional tests. It might be critical to Lily's health. If you dig it up, there certainly won't be any new growth." Her anger escalated with each word. She'd never felt so railroaded in her life. And to have it happen over something as critical as her daughter's health was unacceptable.

"Let me see the paperwork." She stuck her hand out and left the men standing there as she read through every word. It wasn't a long document as far as a legal pleading went. Only three pages, but she made sure to read slowly. When her eyes hit the bottom of the last page she knew she had absolutely no choice except to let them dig up the plant. But she didn't have to let them in her home.

"I'll let you in through the gate at the side of the house. Give me a minute to go around. I'll meet you on the east side."

She started to swing the door shut and Wilson shot out a hand, stopping the door from closing. "Mrs. Noble, I strongly recommend that you not try anything funny. We need the plant. Now. You've already pushed yourself to the breaking point with me."

It took every ounce of self-discipline she owned to keep from kicking the man. To hell with his backup. This guy was every bit as big an asshole as Orlon Millard. Maybe they really were related. She lowered her head and glared at him from beneath her lashes.

With an ugly look she hissed out, "There's nothing funny about this situation. Go to the east side of the house."

She leaned back and slammed the door as hard as she could and shot the dead bolt into the lock. It was amazing the glass panes managed to hold up as the door frame vibrated around them. Turning around to head down the hall, her eyes landed on the living room. Everything seemed to be a bit out of place, like someone had been searching for something. She dismissed the rumpled room and stomped down the hall to the garage.

* * *

"Sit down and don't talk to me for a little while." His dad said the words calmly but with a bite to every consonant. Ethan knew enough to take a seat on the small sofa and shut up.

Uncle Jimmy looked up from the bunch of leaves. "What's going on? Who was at the door?"

His uncle had clearly picked up on their FBI-vibe. He hadn't thought to ask his dad if Jimmy or his mom knew about the missing sphere until right that moment. Shit. He'd been running on the wrong side of the snowball for the past four days and it didn't look like he was going to get a break any time soon.

"That was the FBI." His dad shot Jimmy a 'don't ask' look.

Of course, Uncle Jimmy asked anyway, "What's the FBI here for? Is it about Lily?"

"No. Something happened while we were in Africa. They had an emergency at the mine while we were examining the spheres and one of them got misplaced. They're trying to find it." His dad's tone was deadpan, change-the-subject. He moved over to the desk and picked up the small branch of leaves Jimmy had laid down next to the microscope.

Just as Jimmy opened his mouth to ask another question the door bell rang again. His dad rolled his eyes, looked at the closed door of the den then at him.

"Go see who's here."

Ethan stood up, wondering what the next round of trouble would be. He stepped into the hallway and saw his mom speaking to the guy from the CDC and the two goons that had been at the hospital. What did those idiots want now? They'd come straight home from the hospital like they were told.

His mom shifted her body and the man's voice became clearer. When Ethan heard they were going to pull out the plant in the back yard he zipped back into the den.

"Dad, that's the CDC guy and he's got an order to rip out that plant in the back yard."

He watched his dad's eyes fly to Jimmy's then down to the branch in his hand.

Craig handed the branch to Jimmy and said, "Here, you take this and go home. Put it in a plastic bag in your fridge. I know it will be important for Chelsea to examine it while it's as fresh as possible. We might not get another chance at it."

"You got it. I'm outta here. I'll head back over to Ann's and take off."

Ethan watched as his uncle went out the door and hoped he could make it past the FBI, the CDC and the cop outside at the curb without anyone stopping him.

* * *

The side door sucked open with a squeak and she stepped over to the wooden gate in the privacy fence. The latch flicked up with a heavy clunk and she swung the gate inward to allow the men inside. One of them carried a trash bag, the other held a shovel in his hand and both wore rubber gloves and surgeons' masks. They must have pulled them from their car before coming around to the gate. But rubber gloves and paper masks were nowhere near biohazard gear. It seriously pissed her off.

"It's over this way." She bit the words out then took deliberately large strides across the lawn. She stopped beside the yellow slide and pointed along the fence. "It's over there."

"Where? I don't see anything?" Wilson asked.

"Right there. Just follow the fence. The plant is very dark, you'll see it when you get a little closer."

It dawned on her as she watched Wilson moving toward the plant that if he was here, he wasn't at the hospital, and neither were his two cronies.

She abruptly turned and zipped around the slipper slide then sprinted back into the house and locked the door.

Her purse was in her hand and she headed out the side door in the garage a second time, across the yard to Ann's. The cop might see her, but hopefully the reporters had him so busy he wouldn't notice her second escape. She was going to be with her daughter and to hell with the law.

CHAPTER 48

"What the hell were you thinking?" Orlon looked up as Brad stormed into his office without knocking, a sneer of disgust on his face that was close to insubordination. The lab man's tone pushed it across the line.

"Excuse me?" Orlon asked coldly.

"You know exactly what I'm talking about. We have six days until the board meeting and you fire my lab partner? I ought to walk out of here right now." Brad's rage jangled him more than the lunatic protestor's attempt to kidnap him.

The police had come and gone after taking Orlon's statement but had left him with little hope the assailant would be found, much less detained. But Brad could hit him where it hurt—in the wallet. Orlon attempted to play politics while subtly back peddling.

"Brad, I understand you may feel the need for Chelsea's help due to the tight deadline we're facing, but really, she's more of a liability than a plus at this point." He watched Brad's face go from rage to incredulity.

"Wait a minute. You don't have a clue what you've done, do you?" Brad's movie star mouth smirked at him as he advanced toward the desk.

He broke eye contact and looked down as he pulled open a desk drawer and fumbled about until his hand landed on the thick silver letter opener his mother had given him. His fingers wrapped around the metal and pulled it out. He slid the drawer shut with a quick jut of his hip.

"I've had an incredibly bad morning already. I need to make several calls. Get to the point." Orlon slid the opener through his fingers as Brad stopped at the edge of the desk and glared at him.

"You're aware Chelsea's daughter has been quarantined due to a strange illness caused by an unknown plant?"

"Yes, that's why the press is outside."

"Are you aware that she gave me four of the berries to test last night? She needed to know as soon as possible what the berries contained because they were the only new thing her daughter had been exposed to recently."

A protestor's sign flashed in Orlon's mind: "Stop Growing Devil Plants!"

A shudder of dread ran down his back. He forced himself to keep a civil tone—he still needed those reports.

"Get to the point, Brad."

"The point is, I ran extensive tests on those berries and they are like nothing anyone has ever seen before." Brad sketched out the berries' extreme vitamin content, their unidentified enzymes and proteins.

"So we've discovered a new super vitamin—so what?" Orlon's patience had come to an end. "How is that a reason not to fire Chelsea? She put the company in a bad light by allowing BioGen to be blamed for a plant that had nothing to do with our firm."

"God, you really are thick-headed."

Orlon blanched at the words and the tone. He'd missed something, obviously. Brad liked his money and wouldn't be insulting his boss just to defend his lady love.

"I think you left something out along the way of making your point, Brad. There's no need to be insulting. Clarify yourself." Orlon sniffed and wiped a finger at his nose.

"Those berries are more than just vitamins, Orlon. They've got some kind of super-healing properties that seem to affect the two things you're asking us to cure."

Brad's grin turned into a smug insult as Orlon fought to keep the shock from his face.

"But we've got the berries, right? What do we need Chelsea for?"

"Because Lily ate all of the berries except the four Chelsea gave me to run tests on. I've only got one berry left, Orlon. What can we accomplish with one little berry?"

"I don't know, you tell me. You're the lead man in the lab. Can you develop a vaccine that can be synthetically reproduced from what we've got?"

"No. Absolutely not. There's not enough to run the additional tests it will take to isolate the strange enzymes and proteins well enough to determine how they work, much less replicate them synthetically."

"So get more berries."

"Open your ass and listen! There aren't any more berries. That's the whole point—

we need Chelsea's cooperation if we're to have a chance at getting our hands on more. The only other option is to get blood from Lily—and you just fired her mother—so what do you think our chances are there?"

Another disgusted look flew at him. Orlon ignored it and concentrated on what was important. The timing of the situation could not be more critical.

"What about the plant itself? Do we have any of that?" Orlon asked.

"No, only a small stem the four berries were attached to."

"Damn!" Orlon turned and stared out the window at the cluster of reporters still grouped around the front entrance. He had messages from two board members and countless shareholders that needed to be returned. A plan born of desperation began to form and he turned to Brad, knowing he had to be careful how he approached it or Brad would probably quit on him.

"Let's talk about the best way to move forward, given the overall situation. I want to hear your recommendations and we'll decide the next step together." He fought to keep the perfect tone in his voice and a careful expression on his face. He let out a stale breath and said, "Give me ten minutes and then we'll try to think this through a little more."

"Don't screw anything else up while you take ten minutes to finish pulling your head out of your ass."

Orlon ground his teeth as the door closed with a thump behind the candyface he'd jumped into bed with. He sat thinking the situation through then decided it was time to spread his eggs amongst more baskets and picked up his cell phone. He had to force himself to stop clenching his jaw as he waited for his brother to answer. Oswald picked up on the fourth ring.

"How's Ma? Is she okay?"

"Our mother is fine." He resisted the urge to snarl the words and forced himself to get on with the reason for his call. "I have a situation that I might need your help with."

"What makes you think I give a shit about helping you Oddball? I got more than enough money to take care of Ma. I care about her, not you."

"I'll make sure it's in your best interest. Come by the house tonight and I'll explain. I don't want to get into it on the phone."

Seconds ticked by before Ozzie replied, "Okay. I'll stop by. I wanna check on Ma anyway. But that don't mean I'm gonna help your fat ass. I'll see you around seven."

The dial tone buzzed before Orlon could get another word out.

CHAPTER 49

"**I**'m sorry to keep bothering you, Betty." Chelsea felt bad they were constantly dragging Ann's mother to the door but she didn't have a choice.

"Oh, nonsense. You're not bothering me. I feel so bad for you and your daughter. Ann and I want to help your family anyway we can. It's a miracle what those berries of yours have done for our Stevie." Chelsea watched as the woman looked over at the boy. Steve was sitting at the kitchen table and looked up at hearing his name then his eyes fell back on the board game in front of him. He looked as worried as she felt.

"Thank you for your help. I need to leave again, but can I use the restroom first?"

"Sure, of course. You know where it is."

A minute later she stepped into the garage and stopped short when she saw Jimmy climbing into his truck.

"Jimmy—I didn't know you were leaving. I almost took off in your truck without you. I need to go back to the hospital. Can you give me a ride?"

He gave her a strangely muddled look then said, "Of course, get in. Hopefully I can get you past those crazy protestors and reporters. They know what my truck looks like now."

"Just get me to the emergency room door and I'll take it from there. I don't care if you have to drive on the sidewalk. They're going to start a treatment on Lily in ten minutes and Ann tells me it can be extremely painful. It might even jolt her out of her coma, it's so uncomfortable. I can't let her go through that without me."

Jimmy looked over his shoulder at her, his eyes full of emotions. "I'll get you there Chelsea, don't worry."

After a minute of riding along she thought to ask him where he'd been planning to go. It surprised her that he would take off with everything that was going on. Jimmy was the guy that always stuck around to help.

"Where were you headed?" she asked.

His face broke into a Cheshire grin as he unzipped his jacket and flashed her. The scent of BenGay drifted out. She stared a moment as the dark leaves grudgingly revealed themselves, then looked a question at him.

"Craig sent me to get a branch off the plant so you could test it, right before the FBI guys rang the bell. He told me to take the sample back to my house and put it in the fridge in a plastic bag…is that the right thing to do with it?"

"FBI guys? You mean the CDC?" Her mind shot right past the idea of being able to test the plant. "Why is the FBI involved?" she asked.

He gave her an odd look then shrugged, "FBI, CDC—it's all the same isn't it? Who knows how many letters of the alphabet will be involved before this thing comes to an end?" Derision flared as he ranted out, "CIA, NSA, EPA…we've got such a smorgasbord to choose from these days."

His irreverent tone almost brought a smile to her face. Classic Jimmy-mode. She'd needed a note of normal, if only for a moment.

She shrugged it off as well then said, "I'm really glad Craig thought to ask you to do that. The CDC guy took the whole plant, so that would have been that if you'd been five minutes slower. Thanks for helping us Jimmy." She gave him a small smile then turned and looked out the window, watching houses fly past as they made their way toward the other side of town.

Ten minutes later they were on the street in front of the hospital's driveway, looking toward the main entrance. There were at least ten reporters and more of the protestors than she'd seen earlier. They couldn't get to the emergency room entrance either without being seen. If the news cameras caught her, Wilson might have her arrested after the fact.

"Oh, God. How are we going to get past all of them?"

Chelsea's heart squeezed as she looked at her watch. She needed to get inside.

"Hang on a minute, let's go around the block. There's got to be a loading dock area for supplies." She watched as a look of determination grew on his face. She had always liked Jimmy and felt grateful to have him beside her.

They drove along the side street and Jimmy hit the brakes when she called out, "There! See that little sign—it's got delivery hours on it."

Jimmy whipped the truck into the entrance almost hidden by trees and shrubs. They could barely see the hospital through all the greenery and the driveway seemed to stretch to eternity as she looked at her watch again. At last they pulled up to the back of the building. Two supply trucks were parked in the loading area and people swarmed around, stacking boxes on dollies, coming in and out through the wide doorway.

She looked at her brother-in-law, "Wish me and Lily luck. I'm praying she'll wake up from the niacin treatment."

"Good luck, Chelsea." He paused a beat then said, "For what it's worth, I think you're the best mother a kid could have. I'll be waiting here for you. Take as long as you need."

Chelsea felt tears prick as Jimmy's words settled over her like a balm. Her voice came out a croak, "Thank you Jimmy." She slid out of the truck then took off at a sprint toward the doorway, not bothering to notice any of the workers as she hurried through the entrance.

She made it into the hallway and realized she was completely disoriented. She'd never been in this section of the hospital. It had to be connected to the rest of the building, it was just a matter of figuring out which hallways would lead to the main elevators so she could get up to the intensive care floor. The frantic urge to get to her daughter drove her down the hall. After several turns she let out a breath of relief at the sight of the elevators.

"Come on, come on," she urged the elevator to sweep her up. The doors were barely open as she bolted out of the metal box and down the hall to the isolation area.

She didn't bother going into the decontamination room. Her finger hit the buzzer as her other hand knocked on the glass. She could see Ann sitting beside Lily, a worried expression on her face as her head jerked up at the sound of a voice coming through the speaker.

"Ann, let me in."

A mixture of relief and concern swam on Ann's face as she pressed the speaker, "Chelsea, you need to get suited up before you come in."

"To hell with that Ann. You and I both know she's not contagious. Let me in, right now." She gave her friend a determined look through the glass.

Ann hesitated then pushed the door release and Chelsea let out a sigh of relief as she stepped into her daughter's room. "Thank you."

"Have you started the niacin yet?" She strode to the bed, eyes locked on her daughter.

"Yes, a couple minutes ago. Dr. Gammond left instructions to put it in her I.V. at noon and that's what I did. Her skin will likely start flushing red any moment. The niacin works quickly on an empty stomach." Ann followed her over to the bed.

She took Lily's hand in hers and greeted her still form, "Hi Baby, it's Mommy. The doctor's have given you a new medicine to help cleanse your system and they said it might make you itchy. I love you very much, Sweetheart, I'll be right here beside you. Try to open your eyes if you can."

Chelsea watched her daughter's eyelids—they twitched but stayed closed. She leaned over and kissed Lily's forehead then sat down and waited for the medicine to kick in.

* * *

"Mr. Noble, we didn't find the sphere. I'm sure that's no surprise." Blackstone deadpanned as he stood in the doorway of the den. Smith stood behind him, silent.

Craig looked away from the computer screen and stood up. "Okay. What's the next step?" He hated asking the question but needed to know what they were facing.

"That depends on what Mr. Connor decides to do. We've done what we were asked to and will report back on the situation." Blackstone stared at Ethan a long moment then the man's eyes shifted back to him. "I recommend you contact an attorney." A tick of silence. "I hope your daughter gets well soon." Blackstone turned and headed down the hallway.

He tagged the man's heels to the front door. The FBI left without another word and Craig quickly shut the oak slab behind them. He heard the reporters come to life as he stood in the foyer thinking. Thank God Chelsea hadn't caught the men searching their home. He rubbed a hand over his eyes, trying to function past the strain the FBI men had put on his already overtaxed brain.

"What a mess."

He glanced at the living room and realized they had a lot of work to do before Chelsea came in from the backyard. He hurried back to the den and told his son to head upstairs and put things right while he worked on the lower level.

CHAPTER 50

Chelsea watched as her daughter's skin quickly turned the shade of a sunburn after a long day at the beach.

"I can see it," she said to Ann. "Does that mean the discomfort should be happening right now also?"

"Yes, the itching and nerve-tingling sensations follow right on the back of the flush."

Her daughter's eyelids trembled and the corners of her mouth moved slightly. She held her breath as Lily's fingers and toes twitched against the sheets. Chelsea's lungs told her to breathe but her head wasn't sure how as she watched her daughter's obvious but silent discomfort.

"Ann, isn't there anything we can give her to help reduce the itching reaction?"

"A person can take aspirin and antihistamines to help fend off the affects of the flushing but in Lily's case, the doctor doesn't want anything put into her system that will lessen the flush or tax her organs. Her liver and kidneys are completely maxed out from the vitamin overdose."

Ann's calm voice and sound explanation helped but it was all she could do to keep from ranting with agony over her daughter's silent suffering. She gripped Lily's hand a little tighter.

"I love you Sweetheart. I know you must be feeling very itchy right now, and I'm sorry. The medicine is causing that but it will pass in a few minutes." She tried her best to keep her voice steady and reassuring but it was hard to do with tears so close to the surface.

Lily's small heels thrashed up and down against the mattress as her head jerked from side to side and she began mumbling, "Stop it, stop it, stop it!" Her heels beat harder against the bed.

Chelsea looked at Ann with alarm but her friend had a huge smile on her face.

"She's coming around, Chelsea!"

A scream broke through Lily's lips and her eyes flew open as she shouted, "I want my Mommy! I want my Mommy!"

Chelsea leaped off her seat, still holding Lily's hand as she leaned over her little girl.

"I'm here, Honey, I'm here."

A sob followed her words and tears spilled down her face at seeing her little girl awake again. "You're going to be okay Sweetheart. You're going to be okay. The itchies will go away soon, I promise. You've been really sick, Honey."

Lily turned toward her voice, eyes struggling to focus. "Mommy?"

"Yes, Honey, I'm right here."

"Mommy, I don't feel good."

"I know Honey, that's why you're in the hospital. But you're going to be okay, sweetie, you're going to be okay." An enormous smile broke through her tears as the dam of relief burst. She leaned closer and kissed her daughter's forehead, fighting to keep pent up emotions in check so she wouldn't scare her little girl.

* * *

Craig straightened a cushion on the sofa then adjusted the lamp shade. His mind was like a rabid squirrel in a cage, hitting too many points at once, none of them making much sense.

He was still trying to figure out how Chelsea had managed to not notice the FBI men. The kitchen had been really torn up. There were lots of little hiding spots in there and it had taken him several minutes to get it back in order. She hadn't made an appearance the entire time. Maybe she was upstairs lying down. He wasn't about to go searching for her. Not until he had a chance to sort through what Jimmy had said.

As he righted the lampshade the doorbell rang again. "What now?" he growled out to the empty room. He'd never felt so overwhelmed in his life as he headed to the door.

The porch appeared to be empty then he looked down and saw Steve standing there. The boy shot past his hip and into the foyer then turned back to him with a frantic look on his face.

"Mr. Noble! Lily's awake! We have to go help her – bugs are crawling all over her and she's screaming for help!" Steve's words came out in a jumbled choke of panic and he stood there clearly expecting him to take action. Immediately.

It took Craig a moment to process the words spoken with such intensity—then his blood ran cold as he looked back at the boy.

"How do you know what's happening to Lily right now?"

Steve's eyes clouded with confusion for a second then he gave an impatient shrug and said, "We have to go to the hospital—right now! Can we Mr. Noble?"

The boy's grandmother stepped on the porch behind them. Craig hadn't even realized he'd failed to shut the door until he heard footsteps. He saw the cop out on the street, holding reporters back and frowning over his shoulder at the front porch. The reporters had their cameras out and trained at the entrance.

"Hi Craig. I'm really sorry. Steve was just so upset all of a sudden. He jumped up out of his chair and headed out the door shouting something about Lily. He's too fast for me. I'm just now catching up."

Skin still prickling he said, "Actually, Steve was just telling me Lily's going through the affects of a treatment they were supposed to start her on at noon. He's wanting to go to the hospital to see her, but she's in isolation right now." He stopped and shrugged, "I guess you know all that since Ann's working a double shift to be with her on our behalf."

"Yes, I think I'm up to speed on everything. I hope you don't mind."

"Of course not. Thanks for your help today. Come inside, while I get Chelsea."

Betty's expression shifted to surprise. "Chelsea left with your brother. I think she was going back to the hospital. I'm so sorry to bother you." She paused awkwardly for a moment then said, "Steve and I are heading back to Ann's house. Let me know if I can help in any way."

"Oh. Okay," he responded woodenly as his mind struggled with learning Chelsea had taken off without telling him. He knew she'd wanted to be there for the niacin treatment. His heartbeat stuttered as he thought about Chelsea getting arrested. Shit.

He rushed upstairs and found Ethan. "I'm heading to the hospital. Do you want to go?"

His son popped out the earbuds, "What?"

"Your mom took off with Jimmy. Steve's grandma says she went back to the hospital. Let's go get her before she gets in trouble."

The doorbell peeled over their heads as they hustled down the stairs.

"I'm going to cut the wire on that damn thing." His stress level was off the charts and it went up another notch every time the bell rang.

A muscle in his jaw twitched as he jerked the door open.

"Mr. Noble, I need to speak with your wife for a minute before we leave."

Craig blinked back at the man. He'd forgotten Ethan had said the CDC people had come to take away the plant. He caught himself just in time.

"She's upstairs taking a nap." With an accusatory tone he said, "She took a pill since we can't leave the house until tomorrow."

Shoulders wide, he lifted an arm to the doorframe, deliberately blocking the man's view.

"I need to speak with Mrs. Noble about the berries she removed from the plant we confiscated."

The man handed a business card to him.

"Have her call me when she wakes up. I need to collect whatever BioGen has left of the berries and they're not answering the phones. I understand BioGen only operates until noon on Saturday. I need a cell number for the person she gave the berries to. You wouldn't happen to have it, would you?"

Craig took the card, glanced down at it. "No. I don't have any of Chelsea's work contacts. You'll have to wait until she wakes up."

He studied the portly man as he asked, "The quarantine's off at four o'clock tomorrow, right?"

"Make sure your wife calls me with that cell number. I'm not lifting the quarantine until I get it."

The man turned and walked off the porch. Craig watched from the doorway as reporters descended on him, circling tight. Wilson's body was hard to make out from the rest of them. There was too much noise for him to tell whether the man responded with any comments. Wilson climbed into the passenger seat of a waiting sedan and drove off as the reporters chased behind, snapping pictures.

CHAPTER 51

It took thirty minutes for Lily's body to recover from the affects of the niacin flush. Her little girl thrashed the covers in agony for several minutes after waking but quickly grew too worn out to keep fighting the sensations. She finally lay still, mutely suffering, eyes closed.

"Ann, you don't think she's gone back into a coma, do you?" Fear flew through her as she watched her daughter.

"No, Chelsea. She's just tired. Her body has been through so much and she hasn't had any solid food since early yesterday. Let's give her a little bit then I'll wake her and give her some juice."

Ann reached over and hugged her through the bio suit's bulk. "She's going to be okay, Chelsea. Things are going to improve very quickly from here on. She'll probably be home in a couple days, maybe less."

"Really?" She felt a smile shifting her cheeks into her eye sockets as she hugged her friend back. "Thank you so much Ann, for being here for us, for caring." Tears of relief popped and she fought them back. Her head was killing her from all the stress and the crying.

She forced her thoughts to the future and gave a small laugh as the vision of having Lily home swept over her. "I can't wait to see the kids flying on the swings together!"

She laughed and hugged her friend as Lily opened her eyes. Chelsea turned back to the bed and took her daughter's hand again.

"I'm here Sweetie. Are you feeling better now?"

"Hi Mommy." Lily looked back at her, blue eyes slowly focusing on her face.

"Would you like some juice?"

A mini fridge hidden behind a cabinet door revealed a small selection of juice and bottled water. She gave Ann a smile and took the apple juice from her. They watched as Lily sipped weakly at it.

"That tastes good." She rested her head a moment then asked for more.

"I love you so much Lily. I'm really glad you woke up." Chelsea couldn't help herself, she needed to speak her emotions or she'd burst.

"I love you too, Mommy." Lily whispered the words out as her face crumpled. Chelsea watched in confusion as tears swam into her daughter's eyes.

"I'm really sorry." Her little sob at the end of the words tore at Chelsea's heart.

"Oh, Sweetheart, you don't need to be sorry. I should have realized that plant had grown by the fence. I'm just glad you're going to be okay."

"No, it's my fault Mommy." Tears ran down Lily's face as she sputtered, "Tell Ethan I'm sorry, okay?"

"I'll tell your brother you're sorry, but why? He's not sick, only you got sick."

A tear trickled around the corner of her daughter's lips as she said, "I took that ball from him, and now he's in trouble for it—and we can't get it back."

A cold shot of fear ran up her back as she looked at her daughter. "Lily, what do you mean? Ethan's fine, Sweetheart."

"No, he's not Mommy. And it's my fault...." Lily's voice took off on a low wail as more tears cascaded down.

Chelsea stared down at her daughter, completely at a loss for words. She decided no matter whether Lily's angst about Ethan had merit it could wait. She wanted her daughter to feel safe and comforted before she had to leave or risk getting arrested in front of her. She opened her mouth to reassure Lily just as her daughter's panicked eyes flew to hers.

"Mommy! Quick, go in the closet!"

The hair on Chelsea's neck rose as she looked at Ann with alarm then down at her daughter. She forced herself to speak calmly, "You're right, I need to leave. I love you very much. You rest and I'll be back. Ann will be here with—"

"Hurry Mommy!"

Fear scraped as she leaped up from the chair. Somehow she knew her daughter was right. With no time to question the warning, she followed Lily's directions and sprinted out the glass door into the decontamination room.

CHAPTER 52

They were in Betty's car and three blocks away from the house before his scattered brain thought to call Jimmy. He listened to the phone ring twice before his brother picked up.

"Hey Jimmy. Where are you? Is Chelsea with you?"

"I'm at the hospital, outside the vendor entrance. Your wife is upstairs with Lily."

He pulled the phone away from his ear and stared at it a moment. The tone in his brother's voice told him whose side he was on. Resentment boiled until he reminded himself that Jimmy cared about all of them. A deep breath helped.

"Thanks for getting her to the hospital. We're heading that way now. I'm going upstairs to get Chelsea before she gets arrested."

"Craig, she wants to be with Lily. Your little girl is going through hell right now, based on what Ann told her."

"If they started the treatment at noon it's over already. Ann told Chelsea the affects would end after thirty minutes. I'm going to get off here and text her. I'll call you back."

He typed a message asking Chelsea where she was and how Lily was doing. The phone rested on his leg as he thought for a minute then looked over at Ethan.

"Jimmy says your mom is upstairs with Lily right now. How much do you want to bet those CDC guys are at the hospital now? I saw the look in that guy's eyes when I told him your mom was asleep. He didn't believe me for a minute."

He tapped out another text message: "Get out now! Wilson's at the hospital."

* * *

She felt the phone vibrating against her hip as the door closed behind her. The caller I.D. told her it was Craig. He had finally noticed she was gone and sent her a text. She hit the button and adrenaline blasted through her as she read his message. Shit!

The room was only nine feet wide by ten feet long. A shower stall comprised of floor-to-ceiling stainless steel walls and a clear glass door stood in the corner. She could see multiple jet heads inside the shower. The sign mounted on the wall beside it showed a picture of a person in full bio gear, standing inside the shower. A short bench waited at a right angle to the shower, a large plastic bin on wheels sat parked next to the bench. A tall metal rack holding towels stood against the remaining wall. No place to hide.

She forced herself to calm as she took a seat on the bench. She needed to focus on getting out of the hospital and into Jimmy's truck without being spotted. Maybe the best thing to do was sit tight for now.

Her cell buzzed again and she read Craig's third message; "I'm outside at the delivery entrance. Come out as soon as you can. I'll be here."

Her heart did a small flip at knowing he'd come to help but then she got her back up and reminded herself Jimmy was already out there. Someone else had helped her first. Again.

Slim fingers flew as she texted him back, "Jimmy's already here, I'll ride with him. Go home so we don't both end up in jail."

* * *

Craig read the message with a coating of ice slipping over him. He stared down at the screen a long moment trying to think with his head instead of his heart. Maybe he was just taking the message too harshly. Chelsea was right—it would be a catastrophe if they both ended up in jail.

He looked across the parking lot at his brother sitting in his brand-new Lincoln. He could go to talk to him but if someone from the press noticed they'd be screwed. The phone would work, it was probably best anyway.

"Hey Jimmy. Chelsea just texted me and said she wants me to go home so we aren't both arrested. I guess I'm out of here if you can stick around. She's going to come out any minute. I texted her to let her know the CDC guy is here."

"Shit! How do you know he's here?"

"Wilson left the house just a couple minutes ahead of us. He came to the door and asked to see Chelsea. I told him she was asleep, but you know how well that went over. Dollars to donuts the guy is here as we speak."

He let out a tense breath then said, "Call me if you need me."

* * *

She sat on the small bench, mind racing as the walls closed in around her. There wasn't any reason to hold out hope that Craig would somehow see the light through all this insanity with almost losing Lily. The look on his face last night as she'd given Brad a hug told her the man was a lot more dense then she'd ever let herself believe. The blinders were off. She needed to get on with trying to have the life she'd always planned for herself.

As hard as it was to see Lily suffering, it had opened her eyes in many ways. She now realized there were several people in the world who genuinely cared about her and would stand by her. They were present at her side when she needed them. She'd be just fine on her own. A husband, especially one who put his work first, didn't solve life's problems. A woman needed to be able to count on herself and as many good friends as she could get. That was the surest bet, no doubt about it.

A sudden thump outside the door smacked her right back to the present moment. Her pulse quickened as her eyes zipped around the miniscule room once more. She scanned the dimensions of the laundry basket. No way was she going to squeeze five-feet nine inches in there without it being obvious.

She jumped up from the bench and scooted the basket away from the wall then sat down behind it, hoping the shelves would help block her from view. The basket rolled easily and she pressed herself into the corner, trying to get it as close to the wall as she could.

The door sucked open. She thought she heard breathing but no footsteps sounded. Her breath held as she waited for the door to close again. It was cramped behind the laundry bin but she didn't dare come out too soon. It seemed like two or three minutes had ticked off when she finally heard the faint hiss of the door's hydraulic arm.

Breath slowly trickling out of her, afraid to make a sound, she continued to wait. Her left calf began to cramp so hard she wouldn't be able to walk if she didn't stand up soon. She forced herself to wait a thirty-count against the pain then her cell buzzed against her hip. With no choice but to stand up, she pushed the basket away and took a look at the room. It was empty.

Her phone buzzed again—it was a text from an unknown caller. Every hair on her body stood on end as she read: "Go now!"

She didn't hesitate. It was no time to question her instincts, much less a mystery helper. The door sucked open with a faint hiss that seemed loud to her. She glanced down both directions of the short hallway. Clear. She sprinted twenty feet to the corner and paused, trying to glance into the adjoining hall and down to the elevators. There was no way to see if anyone was standing out there without exposing her head.

The floor plan of the intensive care unit flashed through her mind. If a nurse was sitting at the front desk she'd be spotted. Someone standing at the elevators would instantly see her and she'd have to wait for it to come up to the fourth floor and hope no one was on it, or got on it on the way down. Not good. She couldn't recall passing a sign for the stairs.

It was time to go. She stepped into the main hallway, headed toward the elevator. Ten feet down the hall she spotted a stairwell decal on a door to her left. In a flash she shot through it, hustling down three flights to the ground floor. She popped out into the hall, glancing around trying to orient herself. She needed to get back to the convoluted hallway that led to the delivery entrance.

CHAPTER 53

Heart racing at the close call, Ann pressed the release button to allow the man from the CDC to enter the room. He wore a biohazard suit and a stern expression behind the plastic mask. She stepped back over to the bed and sat down in the only chair.

Wilson joined her at Lily's side and stood staring down at the sleeping girl.

"Has she come out of the coma yet?"

Ann hesitated, her instincts were to tell him Lily had remained unconscious but she'd already updated the medical log on the nightstand. He could easily pick it up and read her notations about Lily waking a few minutes ago.

"She came around briefly right after the niacin flush but she's still in really bad shape and worn out. I think she's just sleeping right now."

"I want to speak with her before I head back to Los Angeles. Can we wake her up?"

She couldn't believe the man. The little girl had been fighting for her life and he didn't want to let her rest. She firmed her lips and responded, "No. She needs to get as much rest as possible while her system fights to clear out the toxins. The niacin treatment was very taxing on her. She may still have some discomfort from it and I don't want to wake her. Surely you can come back later?"

"I need to get back to my office. We have to run tests on the plant the berries came from before it deteriorates from being uprooted." He paused and looked at Ann, "Did she say anything about the berries when she woke up?"

Ann shook her head.

"Have the doctor give me a call when he comes in to make his rounds. I'd like to speak with him. I'll be sending someone from my office tomorrow to confiscate all of Lily's lab work and get copies of her medical records. We need to draw blood samples from her to determine if she's presenting any lasting affects from the berries before I lift the quarantine. Have Gammond call me as soon as possible." He handed her a business card.

She watched the man head out the glass door. A small shudder ran at the thought of him continuing to pursue Lily's case. Wondering briefly if it was legal for him to take blood from the little girl without her parents' consent, she shook her head at herself. Since 9/11 the government seemed to have the right to do whatever it pleased. Drawing a couple vials of blood wouldn't hurt Lily, other than the small poke of the needle. Perhaps they could learn something useful from it. Hopefully it wouldn't bring more trouble for the Noble family.

The clock on the wall told her she had an hour and fifteen minutes left on her shift. She was exhausted and needed some sleep before she reported for duty again tomorrow morning. She settled back down with another magazine but before she could get her mind on the story Lily opened her eyes and turned toward her.

"Hi Ann. Is my mommy still here?"

"No Honey, she had to leave. But she'll be back later. They won't let her stay in your room for long because of your being so sick." She didn't know how to explain isolation and quarantine to a seven-year old so left it at that.

"I know," the little girl whispered in a sad voice. "Can I have some more juice?"

"Sure Honey." Ann jumped up and opened a fresh juice box for her, held it while she drank almost all of it. Just as she started to ask Lily how she was feeling tears welled up in the little girl's eyes.

"I wish I'd never taken that stupid brown ball from Ethan."

"What ball Honey?" Ann wasn't sure what the little girl was referring to, but she was obviously upset and needed to talk about it, even if it had only been a bad dream or a petty sibling fight.

"The one he brought back from Africa."

Goosebumps galloped along Ann's arms. Instinct told her where this was headed but they needed to know for sure. "What happened to the ball, Lily?"

"I planted it in our yard. It looked like a big seed." More tears trickled out. "Plus I wanted to hide it from Ethan."

"Oh, well you can dig it up for him when you get home, can't you?"

"No." Blond curls hid her face as she hung her head. "It grew into that plant the berries came from. Now it's gone."

* * *

Chelsea made it back to Jimmy's truck and climbed in with relief.

"Thanks for waiting."

"No problem. How's Lily?"

She grinned at her brother-in-law, "She woke up!" Then her grin dimmed as she recalled the agony her little girl had just gone through. "The niacin flush was tough on her but I guess it was a good thing since it brought her out of the coma."

"So she's going to be okay now?"

"That's what the doctor is saying. I'm going to give Gammond a call when I get back to the house. Unless Wilson gets a court order over the weekend, the quarantine is off at four tomorrow afternoon. I want to know how soon we can take Lily home after that. Ann said it might be another day or two."

"I hope you can bring her home tomorrow. Now that her system's detoxified, what else does she need to be there for if she's out of the coma?"

"That's why I want to talk to Gammond. I'm damn sure not going to leave her in the hospital a minute longer than absolutely necessary for her health."

Jimmy nodded as he drove back down the delivery entrance to the street. He seemed very quiet for Jimmy. She glanced at him from the corner of her eye. Maybe Craig had said something to him about her seeing an attorney. Her mind went back to Lily as they rode and her heart did a little flop at recalling her daughter's misplaced angst.

"When Lily woke up she told me she was sorry. It was so sad—she's blaming herself for getting sick, the poor little thing. She even told me to tell Ethan she's sorry. When I asked her why, she said he's in trouble because of her."

She watched Jimmy's eyes as he absorbed her words. His neurons seemed to be kicking into high gear as he drove then he turned and looked at her.

"Did she say why?"

"No. I needed to get out of there and she's feeling really rough so I didn't try to get into it with her. She just insisted his trouble is her fault."

"That's strange isn't it?"

"I wonder if she was having a bad dream or something and woke thinking it really happened? Those two are always arguing over the TV remote or who gets the last cookie and so on. She must have been dreaming about getting him in trouble." She gave a light laugh and shook her head as Jimmy drove toward home.

Trying to connect the dots she said, "I still can't figure out where that damn plant came from. Not only is it a very unusual species, having it turn up in our backyard out of the blue is really weird."

"Craig and I were saying the same thing earlier. We got to thinking maybe it was growing on the other side of the neighbor's fence so we got a ladder and checked but there isn't anything on their side."

"That was good thinking. I'd hate for this to happen to anyone else's child."

She fell quiet as she speculated on where the plant could have come from. There was no way it had sprung up through a natural occurrence or accidentally. It was beyond unusual—there was nothing remotely similar, not even under exotic plants on the internet—there was no chance it had just blown in on the wind.

"I guess it's safe to take that plant sample you have back to my house now but let's split it, just in case the CDC comes knocking on my door with a search warrant. I really want to look at it under Craig's microscope and run some tests at a lab once the quarantine is off."

"Craig said you would. He had the big microscope and the held-held set up on the desk, all ready to have me go get you, but then the doorbell rang and things got derailed real quick."

She nodded, "It's been a crazy day already, that's for sure."

"That reminds me—Craig said the guy from the CDC wants to talk to you."

Her heart skipped a beat. "What does he want now?"

"He wants a number for BioGen so he can confiscate the berries from your lab partner."

She frowned for a moment then popped a grin at realizing the best way to handle the request would be a small bit of double justice. She'd take every ounce of payback she could get.

"I wouldn't do that to Brad—I'll give him Orlon's cell number and let those assholes deal with each other." A wicked chuckle escaped her. "The world's largest asshole deserves to dance on hot coals a little bit after firing me this morning."

She watched shock hit Jimmy's face as he turned to her, "What the hell did he do that for? Your family's having a medical emergency. There are laws to protect people from having to go to work during a situation like Lily's."

"Yeah I know. But I wasn't scheduled to work today. He fired me because he's pissed off that the press and the protestors got wind about the plant and Lily being sick. He somehow thinks it's my fault that BioGen has been accused of growing the plant."

She frowned and shook her head. "BioGen has had to fight negative media for years because of the public's fear of genetically engineered plants. The situation with Lily is impacting the company only because I worked there, so he figured if he fired me it would make it all go away, I guess. He's a complete idiot." She stopped herself just in time from letting it slip about her attorney's reaction to the situation. Jimmy would wonder why she had an attorney's number at hand on a Saturday.

She changed the subject back to the plant, "I can't do much in the way of tests at the house but I can do some research on it over the internet once I've examined it under the microscope. It's hard to believe there isn't another one like it somewhere in the world. It couldn't grow out of thin air."

They were only four blocks from the house when her phone buzzed and she fished it from her pocket. It was Ann calling.

Worry squeezed her chest. Maybe Lily was awake again and crying for her. She fought back tears as she answered the phone.

"Chelsea!" Ann sounded excited.

She released the clogged breath she'd been holding as Ann hurried on.

"Lily just told me where the plant came from. She's saying she took a little brown ball from Ethan that he brought back from Africa. She buried it in the backyard and says it grew into the plant the berries came from."

Jaw hanging open against her will, she turned and looked at Jimmy. "Drive faster."

CHAPTER 54

He had been home only twenty minutes when his cell phone rang. If his secretary had given the number out to the press he would never use Kelly Services again. He forced his fingers to stop drumming against the desktop.

"This is Orlon Millard."

"Mr. Millard, this is Robert Wilson. I'm the director of the Centers for Disease Control."

Orlon's head snapped back at hearing the man was with the CDC. Anger coursed deeper at the onslaught he was continuing to suffer because of Chelsea Noble's mess. Quickly shutting the door of his home office, he sat back down at the desk.

The split bedroom floor plan had played a large part in his decision to purchase the property. He'd conceded the master suite to his mother because it was located on the ground floor. Her eye sight had become so poor over the past two years she was now legally blind and stairs were difficult for her. He consoled himself over the loss of the sumptuous master bathroom by making the spare bedroom into a home office that he kept locked whenever he left the house.

"What can I do for you Mr. Wilson?"

"I need you to hand over all of the materials and reports that BioGen has related to the berries Chelsea Noble gave her lab partner yesterday."

A thick panic hit him. They had to have those samples in order to proceed with tests needed to achieve a vaccine or cure for autism, possibly Alzheimer's as well. No way would he voluntarily give those samples and proprietary reports to a government agent. He cleared his throat, pressed his heels against the floor.

"Do you have a court order requiring my company to comply with your request?"

Silence dribbled through the receiver for a moment. "Not yet. But it would be much better for BioGen if you'd voluntarily hand over the materials."

"That sounds like a threat, Mr. Wilson."

"It's not a threat. It's a fact. We have reason to believe, based on a report generated by your company yesterday, that the berries contain unidentified enzymes and proteins. Your employee's daughter is in critical condition at the hospital from eating those berries. I have no doubt I can get numerous court orders within twenty-four hours, Mr. Millard. And I certainly have the capability of speaking with the press at any moment."

"That sounds like another threat, Mr. Wilson." Orlon managed to keep his voice at an even keel. "Until you have a court order or search warrant, my company will not voluntarily turn anything over to you. I will be notifying our attorneys immediately of your verbal request. Now, who do you want them to contact? You—or the CDC's attorneys?"

"I'll get back to you on that. Shortly."

Orlon slapped the phone on the desk and leaned back in his chair, forcing his breathing to calm. His eyes drifted to the credenza behind him and its small private bar. He snagged a crystal snifter and the cognac from the cabinet, poured a generous measure. He deserved a shot of courage after being nearly kidnapped, accosted by the press and threatened by the government all in one morning. All due to Chelsea Noble.

He grimaced as he thought of the woman who had been the burr under his saddle for the past three years. Letting her go was the best decision he'd made all week. She'd been nothing but trouble since he'd hired her. The pile of yellow message slips from board members and shareholders sat on his desk like a ticking bomb.

Shooting a cuff back, he looked at his gold Rolex. The man from Gourmet on the Go would be there in ten minutes. The calls could wait until after lunch and a chilled bottle of Puligny Montrachet.

CHAPTER 55

Chelsea swept into the den with the force of a category five hurricane, pinning them to their chairs with her eyes.

"I think there's something the two of you forgot to tell me." She kept her voice quiet—like the eye of the storm.

She watched her husband flinch and Ethan's face go chalk white.

"First tell us how Lily's doing?" Craig's concern demanded a response.

"Lily went through hell, but she's okay now. The good news is she's out of the coma."

She plunked her purse on the desk.

"Sit down with us and let's talk."

She ignored his request to sit on the sofa and pulled the dark branch out of her purse, turned it in her fingers as she spoke.

"So, Lily woke up. Guess what the first thing was she had to say? That is, after she got through screaming from the pain she was in."

The men in her life did not respond.

"Go ahead, guess what she said?" Anger bubbled through her softly repeated words. She felt like a volcano, rage threatening to erupt beyond her control. She wanted to scream at them for withholding information from her—the very thing her husband had accused her of last night.

Her son hung his head a moment then looked at her, tears rimming his eyes. "Mom, I'm really sorry. Lily must have said something about the sphere I brought home from Africa." He looked a question at her and she nodded her response.

"What's going on Ethan? I thought you said the mine wouldn't let anyone purchase the spheres? How did you end up with one?"

Trouble seemed to be brewing from a depth she never thought she'd have to face. Her son's voice came out huskier than she'd ever heard it.

"Mom...I took the sphere. Without permission. I'm really sorry." Ethan kept his eyes on the floor as he spoke.

"You've known about this for how long, Craig?" Artic wind blew through her words.

"I'm sorry. I should have told you sooner." Her husband looked at her with an array of emotions swirling across his face. "I found out about the sphere on Wednesday when I got a call from the manager of the mine. Jeff Connor said they're missing a sphere and asked me to check with Ethan about it." He blew out a hard breath. "Ethan denied taking it until yesterday. The problem is, we can't find it. I gather from what Lily said, she took it. Did she say where she put it? We need to get it back to Connor or he might press charges."

She blinked at her husband a moment, absorbing the impact of learning her son was a thief and potentially facing charges for it. She couldn't stop her eyes from squinting tighter as she looked back at him. "And you were going to tell me this when?"

"Chelsea, look, this is all coming at me almost as fast as it is you. And Lily's been fighting for her life. I figured it could wait until our daughter was out of the woods."

She stared at him as it dawned on her neither of them knew what had happened.

"Well, Ethan is in deep shit then because we can't give the sphere back."

Her son's jaw dropped. "Why not? What did Lily do with it?"

"She planted it— right where that damn bush grew—the one with the berries. It must have been a seed of some kind. The CDC dug the plant up along with a foot of dirt all around it. That sphere is long gone."

Craig and Ethan stared back at her, their worried eyes asking a hundred questions.

"All I know is what Lily told me." She looked at Ethan, "Lily said to tell you she's sorry you're in trouble because of her." Her fists squeezed at her side as she told them about the call from Ann on the way home. "Lily's sure the plant grew from the sphere—and I sure as hell don't know where else it would have come from."

Her son's face was a shifting cascade of emotions—shame, panic and confusion swam along with natural curiosity. He looked like he was going to cry as he said, "Mom, I'm really sorry. It's my fault Lily got sick."

She studied him, a mix of love and anger combined as she realized he still needed her every bit as much as Lily.

"I can't believe you stole that sphere, Ethan. Do you realize how much jeopardy you've put yourself and your dad in? I thought we raised you better than that. Do you know how it makes a parent feel to find out their child has broken the law? It's like getting my final exam back with a great big 'F' on it—only worse because I'm worried about you on top of the shame."

She watched as Ethan's shoulders sagged lower, he kept his eyes on the carpet. A drop hit the toe of his shoe, then another.

After the stiff poke he deserved, she gave him the succor he needed. "Even though you're now an international thief, at the end of the day, it's not your fault your sister got sick. She stole the sphere from you and she ate the berries on the sly. She might only be seven years-old, but she knew better."

Her son's head whipped up and he looked at her with a sweep of relief.

"The sphere was the catalyst to Lily's problems because she made bad choices herself. Try to remember that."

"Your mom's right, Ethan."

The room was dead quiet for a long moment as they all attempted to absorb what they were dealing with. It was almost impossible to comprehend. It scared her to death—her daughter had ingested who-knew-how-many berries, grown from a strange seed pod, and her son might be arrested for it any minute. Double jeopardy had fallen and they had no control over it. She looked down at the plant in her hand. It seemed to grow darker by the minute. Pushing away the leaping anxiety, she pointed at the microscope in front of Craig.

"Do you mind moving? I want to take a look at this thing before more deterioration sets in. It's been over an hour since Jimmy pulled it off the plant."

She slid a portion of the branch under the lens and adjusted the settings as she stared into the microscope. Equal shots of fear and wonder raced through her as she studied a leaf. It was like nothing she'd ever seen before. There was no doubt in her mind the plant had not previously existed on earth. If the public got wind of Lily's illness coming from a completely foreign plant, not just a normal one they assumed BioGen had altered, the crazies would really come out in full force. Hands shaking, she leaned back from the scope.

"Tell me more about where those spheres came from."

"Do you want to read the articles Ethan printed out?"

"Later. Right now just give it to me in summary."

Craig looked at Ethan, "It's your project. Go ahead."

"Okay." He palmed his eyes dry as he spoke, "The spheres were found embedded in pyrophyllite that is three billion years old. You know the location and all that. What else can I tell you about them?"

A blast of shock hit her as the words sank in. She must have missed that part when her son had explained why he'd picked the spheres for his essay. She recalled having the impression the little brown orbs were old, controversial and in Africa but that was it.

If word of the plant blooming from a three billion year-old African sphere got out every government agency and nutcase in the world would be climbing their walls. The media would be relentless. A shudder went through her as she looked down at the six-inch branch lying on the desk. It suddenly felt like their trouble had just started.

Her voice came out a strangled whisper, "Does anyone else know about the sphere other than the manager at the mine?"

She watched Craig's expression grow darker at the question. He glanced at Ethan then back at her. His words had the same affect as pointing a gun at her.

"The FBI was here a little while ago, while you were at the hospital. The mine owner called them to report the missing sphere and they came to search the house."

The blood drained from her face as she thought about Ethan being in trouble with the FBI. She flashed back on Jimmy's words in the truck. He had been right about the FBI—but they had ridden to the hospital together. That meant the FBI had been in the house while she was still there. Her husband was lying to her. In front of their son.

"You and I need to sit down and have a serious talk." She kept her voice quiet for Ethan's sake. "But now is not the time, Craig. Every minute could be crucial to our daughter's health. Lily may be out of her coma, but that doesn't mean she's out of trouble on this. I need to get to work on identifying everything I can from this plant.

"Brad tells me it's got strange enzymes and proteins. They could be impacting Lily's system in ways we might not be able to do anything about. Who knows what side affects she may end up with from such an extreme exposure to those berries?"

She jumped up from the chair and grabbed her purse. "I've got to call Brad and ask him to run tests on this branch." Her hands shook as she pulled the phone out.

"Chelsea, wait a second."

"Why?"

"Your boss just fired you a few hours ago. That guy Wilson was here earlier. He wants to confiscate the berries and all lab reports. Stop and think about it— if the CDC wants the berries, they'll want that branch, too."

"Damn it. You're right. It would be completely asinine for me to give that branch to Brad right now."

Her mind raced, trying to figure out a way she could access the sophisticated lab equipment needed to fully test the branch. She was quarantined until four o'clock tomorrow and felt like a watch dog on a short leash with a burglar in sight.

The media onslaught over the past twelve hours had surely caught the eye of all of her previous employers in the area. She had left the last three companies on excellent terms and all of her supervisors had said she was welcome back if she ever changed her mind. But they likely wouldn't want to get involved with the situation at this point. No company wanted the CDC on their backs. Access to one of those companies' labs was out.

She forced herself to calm down and think harder. Even if one of her previous employers consented to her performing the tests she wanted to do, it would increase the risk of the source of the plant leaking out to the media. They would also have grounds for claiming proprietary rights to any information she might glean or scientific discoveries made through the tests. Both of those risks were unacceptable.

If it turned out the plant was capable of curing the things it appeared to so far, there was no way she'd let the formula be chained to a big pharmaceutical conglomerate. The money men would demand the cures be patented and priced beyond the means of the tens of millions of people who needed them. She could not let that happen.

The only other place she'd had access to a lab was at the college she'd attended. She and her professor had stayed in touch through the years. He would probably let her use the school's equipment, and she knew she could trust him, but Berkley was two hours away.

She looked at Craig and said, "As soon as we get Lily home from the hospital I'm going to San Francisco."

CHAPTER 56

Ann woke to the sound of her son singing beside her bed.

"…and all the little horses said wake-up sleepy head!"

She grinned at hearing the song she'd sung to Steve when he was a baby and had slept through the night. Memories of standing by his crib, wishing he would wake up so she could hold him again flooded through her sleepy brain as she sat up and tossed the covers back.

Soreness from working sixteen hours straight the day before seeped from her muscles and hit her brain. Within a nanosecond of the pain hitting, the fact that Steve had been less than a year old when she'd last sung that song to him zapped her mind wide awake.

Her eyes met his and the smile on his face dimmed as he looked back at her.

"What's wrong, Mom?"

It was almost scary how fast he'd become at picking up her every emotion.

"Um…nothing. I guess I don't feel like going to work again already."

"Oh." He blinked back at her then moved toward the bedroom door as he asked, "Can we have pancakes again today?"

"Of course we can have pancakes again."

She'd been forced to save serving the standard breakfast item only on special occasions before Steve snapped out of his bubble. The gluten content was off the charts and the doctors had told her it was a major no-no for kids with autism. She personally had never noticed a difference in Steve's demeanor or alertness from one day to the next the few times she'd served flapjacks in their house. But as a nurse and a mother, she'd tried to follow the doctors' advice to the letter.

Since Joy Day had dawned in their lives, Steve seemed to be a completely normal and healthy young boy. She'd decided the only way to be sure he'd really come all the way out of his autism was to treat him as she would any child. It was like a scientific experiment to her. If she followed none of the autism precautions for his diet and stopped all his medicines, she figured they'd know for sure after a week's time that he really was living a whole new life.

She shrugged off the brief worry about his super-memory moment and hurried into a robe as she glanced at the clock beside her bed. Six-thirty. Her Sunday shift began at eight so she'd have to hurry through making breakfast. She couldn't be late—not only was her job on the line, she wanted to check on Lily. If the CDC planned to do more lab work on the girl, she wanted to be there to keep an eye on things for Chelsea and Lily.

An hour later she backed the Prius off the drive and stopped in shock as she looked over at the Noble's house. There were news vans lined up along the curb on both sides of the patrol car. Reporters were clustered in several groups – all forced to stay off the property line but they had their cameras and microphones ready. She shook her head as she drove away. Hopefully the press would let go of the story once they learned Lily was going to be fine. She hoped the CDC guy and the doctor would both allow Lily to go home today. Steve missed his friend and Chelsea was suffering every minute her daughter was in the hospital.

She pulled into the employees' entrance at the side of the building and almost ran the car off the drive as the protestors' signs and reporters' cameras caught her eye. They were clustered around the door, waiting for victims. Dread seeped through her at having to make it through the pack and into the building. Chelsea had told her about the lunatic smashing a sign on her window yesterday. She consoled herself with the thought that the biohazard suits mostly concealed her identity from anyone who might have looked in through the glass door in Lily's room. These people didn't know she'd been the one to provide the majority of the nursing care for Lily over the past twenty-four hours.

With breath held tight, she hurried to the entrance, saying nothing in response to the reporters shouted questions. The protestors restrained themselves to waving their signs and chanting their messages. She let out a gusty sigh of relief as the door shut and locked behind her.

Upstairs and glad to be headed for a secured room, she suited up and was at Lily's door buzzing to be let in with two minutes to spare. Lily lay on the bed, enraptured by a cartoon.

"How's she doing Marge?" Ann asked.

"Oh, she's much better. She ate every bite on her breakfast plate and has gone through three boxes of juice since she woke at six. I'm so happy she's on the mend."

"Me too. Thanks for the update. Get some sleep." Ann smiled at the woman and watched her head out the door.

She stepped toward Lily's bed as the girl sang out, "Good morning, Miss Ann!"

"How are you feeling, Lily?"

"Much better. But I'm still hungry. Do you think I can have some more breakfast?"

"I'll call downstairs and see what we can get for you. What would you like?"

"Toast with peanut butter and cereal and a donut and a banana! Is that okay?" Lily's smile was irresistible.

"I'm sure that can be arranged." She grinned back at her tiny charge then asked, "Lily, when did your front teeth come in? I don't remember you having them a couple days ago."

"Aren't they pretty!"

* * *

Craig offered to cook a big breakfast but no one seemed to be hungry. When he realized they'd started on a second pot of coffee with nothing in their stomachs he insisted they at least eat some toast.

Ethan and Chelsea sat across from him at the round oak table, taking small nibbles of the whole-wheat triangles on the plates in front of them. He studied his wife's face as she stared out the window. Never had he seen her look so tired, not even when the kids were first born.

He'd finally convinced her to stop calling the hospital every hour and get some sleep shortly after midnight. She hadn't given in to bed until he'd said he needed to go over some reports in the den before he called it a night. It had hurt to realize she'd been avoiding sleeping with him. A flare of worry had surged when he'd walked in their bedroom, expecting to see her asleep only to have the empty king-size bed greet him. He'd looked in the bathroom, thinking she might be soaking in the tub but it had been empty too. His heart squeezed even tighter when he finally found her asleep in Lily's bed, clutching their daughter's pillow to her chest.

Chelsea had awakened at five o'clock, and her first call of the day to the hospital had roused him from the deep sleep he'd finally fallen into sometime after three. Guilt and regret mixed with fear for both their kids had rushed around his mind all night.

He took a sip of his fourth cup of coffee and asked, "Have you talked to Gammond yet?" The toast tasted like sawdust and he dropped the slice on the plate, gulped more coffee.

"Not yet. It's only a minute past eight. I don't want to talk to him until Ann calls me with an update on Lily's condition. I'm hoping to convince him to let her come home with us this afternoon, but I'm not even going to ask him if Ann thinks she's not ready."

"That makes sense. So from what the nurse told you, Lily hasn't awakened again since the niacin treatment?"

"No, she slept through the night. I'm waiting for Ann's call. She went on duty at eight." Just as she finished saying the words, his wife's cell rang at her elbow and a gamut of emotions played across her face as she listened to the caller.

"Hold on a second, Ann. I want to put you on speaker phone."

Chelsea's grin was a mile wide as she pulled the phone away from her ear and set the phone down in the middle of the table. "Okay Ann—go ahead, put her on."

"Hi Mommy! Hi Daddy!" Lily's voice rang out in the kitchen, instantly lighting up the room like the sun at high noon on a blue sky day.

"Well, good morning Princess!"

"Hey Lily." Ethan spoke quietly toward the phone. Craig could hear guilt in every syllable and it was written all over the boy's face.

Lily's exuberance audibly dimmed. "Hi Ethan...I'm really sorry I took that ball from you." Tears sounded in her voice and swam in Ethan's eyes.

Craig glanced at Chelsea, reading a mother's double-sided worry in her eyes. He wanted to reach across the table and take her hand in his but the rift between them was too wide.

He focused on his son as Ethan said, "No, Lily—I'm sorry. I really am. You wouldn't have taken the sphere from me if I hadn't given you such a hard time about the TV. I'd be mad too if someone called me names and changed the channel during my favorite show. So don't worry about it."

A frown shaped his son's lips as silence drifted out of the phone. The three of them glanced around the table at each other and Chelsea leaned forward to check the phone's display to make sure the call hadn't dropped. Then Lily came back, her voice soft and incredibly sincere.

"I love you Ethan. I'm glad you're my brother."

Tears sprang to his own eyes as he watched his son swiping away.

"I love you too, Lil." Choked emotions came out as Ethan responded, "I hope you get to come home soon. We'll make up that T.V. chart we talked about."

"Okay." Then she changed the subject, "Guess what I had for breakfast?" Before they could respond she squealed, "Tell them Annie! They won't believe me."

Craig's heart lifted higher than he thought possible as he listened to Ann reciting breakfast item after item and his daughter said, "I ate every bite, too!"

They chatted with the little girl another minute then Lily said with a yawn, "I'm getting sleepy. I think I'll watch T.V. for a little while. Call me back later, okay?"

Craig watched his wife's face as she promised to call Lily after her nap. His heart did a little trip at seeing the profoundness of her love for their daughter in her eyes. She was a fantastic mom. And a good wife. Now that they knew Lily was on the mend, he and Chelsea needed to clear the air between them. Hopefully he wouldn't screw it up.

Chelsea smiled from ear to ear as she punched the speed button for Dr. Gammond. He listened as she spoke with the doctor then got off the phone.

"Gammond says he's heading to the hospital now. He said if the blood work looks good and she checks out okay, we can bring Lily home this afternoon."

"That's great, Chelsea. I can't wait to get our daughter home."

"Me either." She jumped up from the table and took her plate to the sink. "I'm going to clean her room then get on the internet and research that plant." Chelsea hustled out the kitchen door as he looked over at Ethan.

"What a weekend." Craig said.

"No shit."

He looked closer at his son. He was pissed as hell at the boy for stealing the sphere but just about every kid he knew, including himself, had stolen something at some time in their lives. His anger slipped away as his empathy and love for his son washed in, mingling with the upbeat mood from knowing Lily might be coming home that day.

He smiled and said, "I don't think anyone could deny those spheres are ancient artifacts now."

Ethan raised his eyes from his coffee cup. "Concretions wouldn't have plant cells in them, would they?" Curiosity flickered in his eyes.

"I don't see how. The concretions were supposedly formed in volcanic ash, which eventually changed into the pyrophyllite they were found in. I don't see how loose plant cells could have survived long enough to have been trapped inside as concretions formed."

"So we're saying those spheres really are ancient artifacts?"

"I guess so," Craig said.

He watched Ethan's face come to life with excitement, washing away the anxiety he'd been suffering from the past four days. Craig was ready to move on, too. Hopefully, the FBI would feel the same way. He would have to give Jeff Connor a call on Monday.

"Dad, I was wondering...if we're dealing with ancient artifacts purposely generated as seeds...why were the spheres found where they were?"

"What do you mean?" Craig's curiosity continued to peak as they discussed the idea. It was fun seeing his son's mind in action.

Ethan reminded him so much of himself at the same age it was almost spooky. Curiosity was never stronger than in one's youth. It was a kid's winning edge over all the jaded adults in his life.

"Well…did those spheres just fall off an alien space ship as it flew by or what? They had to come from somewhere, right? And based on what you've told me, and from what I've read, it seems kinda crazy the spheres would just happen to be embedded in that pyrophillite."

He studied his son's face as his mind absorbed the boy's words. The boy was definitely on to something with that train of thought.

"You are absolutely right to ask that question. So, let's assume for a moment that not only were the spheres created by ancient beings, they were purposely placed there by those same beings."
The legs on his chair squeaked as he scooted back, energy coursing through him as his geologist's mind began working through the facts they had to work with.

"You know, pyrophyllite has a lot of really interesting and very unusual properties. Did you study up on any of that stuff while researching the spheres?"

Ethan hesitated. "Not really. I was focused more on the spheres and then everything I could find about the concretion process. What about the pyrophillite? Does it make a difference?"

"The first thing a person should do when they're trying to understand something that happened millions, or in this case billions, of years ago, is get all the facts surrounding the situation down on a piece of paper. Kind of like spreading the puzzle pieces out. Every little fact is important because you never know which ones are going to fit together and start to make the picture come clear." He paced the kitchen as he considered the facts they did have.

"Okay, first, pyrophyllite has excellent thermal stability. Second – it has a negative electromagnetic charge. Third fact, and maybe most important, it has a potent absorbing capability for drawing positively charged toxins like radiation and heavy metals from the human body and the earth."

Ethan stood up, took his plate and cup to the sink as he said, "Okay—pyrophyllite has all these interesting properties and it's formed from lava and the spheres were found embedded in it—so what?"

"Now we start asking ourselves questions based on various assumptions. For instance, let's assume ancient beings purposely put the spheres there, knowing the metal orbs would survive through the intense conditions and become embedded in pyrophyllite."

"All right...then the next question would be...why? Right?" Ethan asked.

"Exactly. Why would ancient beings purposely do that? They would have known they weren't going to get them back out, at least not during their lifetime. That tells me they put them there for the long run." Excitement trilled in his blood as he thought about the incredible possibility of ancient beings planning ways to help man survive billions of years down the road. The idea boggled the mind while it lightened the heart with hope.

A smidge of a theory began to form at the back of his brain but Craig wanted to lay out the facts before he started conjuring a picture of the puzzle they contemplated.

"What do you mean—the long run? How would ancient beings have had any clue that there would be catastrophic events they needed to prepare for?"

"Listen, if those ancient guys were smart enough to create an artificial seed pod that can withstand a cataclysmic event and bloom three billion years later, they knew a hell of a lot, right? My guess is they knew exactly what they were doing and had a solid plan behind their actions."

"So...the next question is...what was their game plan?" Ethan grinned as he asked it.

"Exactly. Let's go in the den, I want to look up all the known locations of pyrophyllite."

He headed toward the kitchen door with Ethan following right behind. A minute later they were looking at a map of the world with red dots highlighted on the computer screen.

"Interesting. I thought pyrophyllite was spread pretty well around the globe and this website confirms it. See here—it's on both coasts of the United States, a couple places in Canada, Japan, Brazil, Switzerland, Africa and a few others." He looked over his shoulder. "You know what I'm thinking?"

"This stuff's located pretty much all over the world. So what? We already knew there are volcanoes all over, right?"

"Exactly my point." He raised a teacher's eyebrow at his son. "Do you know what would happen to our world if two of the major volcanic calderas were to blow within a short time of each other?"

"From what I've read, it would cause an extreme catastrophic change in the earth's atmosphere. The ash cloud would filter out the sun's light for years. Just about all the plants and animals would die. Millions of people would die from the toxic air, and anyone who survived would basically starve to death."

"Yep, that's right. But what would happen if the pyrophyllite deposits were blown open?" Craig was enjoying every minute of their discussion. He couldn't wait to see his son's face when he told him the basis of the theory that had formed in the kitchen.

"Ummm…I guess the pyrophyllite would help the earth recover from the toxins and the spheres would be exposed."

"Right." He grinned at the look on his son's face. "Back to the role the pyrophillite plays in this theory. Did you know that pyrophillite clay was used to cover the burning Chernobyl reactor in Russia to help prevent the radiation from escaping? It really is amazing stuff. It's got a donut shaped combination of tetrahedral molecules that mimic the shape of a red blood cell. The geometric shape of a red blood cell constitutes the most efficient shape known for the absorption of nutrients."

"So, once the spheres are exposed to toxic conditions, soil and water, they sprout and people have food to eat while the pyro cleans up. Is that what you're thinking?" Ethan asked.

"That's exactly what I'm thinking. We already know the spheres survived the volcanic activity, so we have to assume they'd come out just as they went in. And remember where that plant was growing? There was hardly any sunlight in that spot. Between the branches overhead, being on the north side of the fence and shadowed by the play fort, I doubt much sunlight ever hit that plant. Plus those dark leaves are perfect for absorbing whatever light they might get."

"You know what else?" Ethan's face glowed with excitement as he said, "That plant grew from a seed to producing berries in only two days. I had the sphere Sunday night. The earliest Lily could have planted it was Monday. Steve said he was eating berries over here on Wednesday night."

Craig looked at his son as chill bumps slipped down his neck.

"That's gotta be it, Ethan. Think about it—if just one berry has the nutrients of twenty vitamins, a little would go a long way to helping people survive. So now for the next two questions..."

Ethan grinned back at him but had no ready answer on his tongue. Craig waited a beat, drawing out his son's anticipation. This was almost getting fun.

"...Are those spheres located anywhere else besides South Africa? And what do the other spheres produce if you plant them?"

He watched his son's eyes widen as he said, "Now that I think about it, maybe those lines on the spheres are like identification tags—so the ancients could tell what they were planting?"

CHAPTER 57

Lily's eyes drooped shut within minutes of speaking with her family. Ann smiled again at the memory of watching Lily's face when Ethan said he couldn't wait for her to come home. An almost visible veil of worry had lifted from the little girl's shoulders and her eyelids had quickly grown heavy afterward.

Ann glanced at the clock as she shifted on the chair. Lily had been sleeping soundly for the past four hours and that was good. The little girl had opened her eyes at six o'clock and stayed wide awake for several hours that morning. It was a lot of waking time for someone who'd gone through what Lily had.

The doctor had been in earlier and asked Ann to draw a vial of blood which he'd rushed through the lab. She'd been thrilled when he told her Lily could go home after four o'clock, provided the man from the CDC did not obtain a court order to keep her in the hospital. She doubted the man could do that since the doctor was going to release Lily. The little girl would need to remain on bed rest at home for a couple days but there was no valid reason to keep her in the hospital according to Dr. Gammond. The detox regimen had been completed and the child seemed to be almost back to her normal self.

No one from the CDC had shown up yet to collect Lily's lab work or take new blood samples as Wilson had threatened yesterday. Maybe someone had finally talked sense into the man and convinced him to let the matter drop. She certainly hoped so.

Catching herself watching the clock again, she knew she had to stop. Her sore muscles reminded her how many hours she'd been sitting. She stood up and paced the room a minute. Maybe Steve would want to go for a walk with her when she got off work? That would be another first for them. The thought of getting some good exercise and spending time with her son appealed after sitting at Lily's side for the majority of the past two days. Her shift ended at four and she planned to stay until Chelsea picked her little girl up. No matter how tired she was, that was a sight she didn't want to miss.

Now that she thought about it, she probably wouldn't get Steve out for a walk if Lily was home. He'd want to sit by Lily's side no matter whether she was sleeping or not, and she planned to let him as long as Chelsea was okay with it. It had been hard to tell him he couldn't see his friend over the past two days.

With a small sigh, she sat back down beside the bed and smiled at the thought of her son and Lily on the swings together again.

* * *

Chelsea felt like a lion in a cage as she clicked off the internet and pushed back from her laptop. As she'd expected, the world-wide web had not given her a clue as to the mystery plant's origins. Who had ever heard of a plant growing from a metal pod? But she'd needed to occupy her mind and her time while the hours ticked off toward four o'clock.

She stepped over to the fridge and pulled out a pitcher of iced tea. Massive amounts of caffeine were the featured item on the menu for the day. The emotional highs and lows were taking as much a toll as the loss of sleep over the past two nights. One minute she felt like a live wire, strung out with tension, worrying that Wilson would call and tell her she couldn't bring her little girl home, and the next she was forcing herself to stop yawning.

A squeak of disbelief escaped at the thought of taking a vitamin to help increase her energy. She was throwing out the bottle of vitamins she kept on hand for herself. There was no question in her mind whether Lily had taken any of them – the pills were huge and tasted like dirt going down. No way would they appeal to a small child. She'd double-checked the jar after they learned of the vitamin overdose. The bottle hadn't moved from the corner spot of her medicine cabinet.

Her cell phone buzzed against the table and she snatched it up.

"Mrs. Noble?"

"Yes, this is Chelsea."

"This is Dr. Gammond. I'm calling with good news."

"I'm ready for some. Hit me."

"You can take Lily home this afternoon."

"Thank you Dr. Gammond. I appreciate all the hours you've spent helping Lily over the past two days."

"You are more than welcome." A beat of silence then he said, "Listen, I want to apologize for calling in the CDC people. I know this has been a nightmare for your family and the quarantine only made it worse."

"I appreciate you saying that, but I know you were trying to do the right thing by everyone when you made that call. No hard feelings. My daughter's going to be okay, and she's coming home today. That's all that matters to me."

She forced herself to ask, "Have you heard anything from Wilson? He told us he might get an order extending the quarantine."

"I talked to him earlier. He told me he's sending someone to the hospital to pull all of Lily's lab work from us as well as a couple fresh samples from the girl. He also wants copies of all her medical records, but he didn't say anything to me about extending the quarantine."

Fear lifted her hair and blew on her neck.

"Why does he want Lily's lab work and medical records?"

"He wants to do research on the impact of the berries. He's concerned about the unidentified enzymes and proteins. In my professional opinion, that doesn't give him any reason to extend the quarantine. Lily's clearly not contagious or you and your family would have become ill by now. At the very least your son would have presented symptoms by now since he was by her side when the ambulance was called. Don't worry—if I get word the CDC is extending the quarantine I'll do my best to fight them on your behalf."

"Thank you. I really appreciate that. So, can I go to the hospital and get Lily now?" She looked at the time—it was just past one-thirty.

She heard his silent hesitation before he said, "Look, I'm legally required to tell you to wait until four, since that's the official end of the quarantine. That way I'm not on the hook, just in case the CDC shows up. I seriously doubt they will, but I need to officially go on record that I told you to wait. You know how it is. I've already signed her dismissal paperwork."

"I understand. Well, thanks again. Take care."

She laid the phone down and sat thinking. It had almost sounded like the doctor was condoning her picking Lily up early but didn't want to be the one to give her the okay to break the forty-eight hour quarantine mandate. Her fingers drummed against the wood a moment then she said aloud to the empty room, "To hell with it. I'm getting my daughter. What difference could two hours make anyway?"

She grinned as she hurried through the kitchen door to tell Craig she wanted to go to the hospital and get their little girl. Four o'clock be damned.

As her feet stepped onto the hardwood floor of the hallway she realized she'd better check and see if the cop was still out there. She held her breath as she peeked out the entryway window. A sweep of relief flowed at seeing the cop car was no longer at the curb. Her joy ebbed only slightly at the sight of the press, but at least the number of reporters had dwindled down.

CHAPTER 58

The straggle of reporters rushed their vehicle, shouting questions as they backed out.

Ethan thought his mom buzzed the window down to give the press an update but instead she stuck her hand out and flipped them the bird.

"Good one, Mom." He laughed as she turned around and grinned back at him.

"Let's go get Lily."

It was good to see his mom smiling again. Then his stomach squeezed as he thought about how fast her smile would vanish if the FBI came knocking on their door again, this time with an arrest warrant. He shook the thought off and tried to concentrate on getting his sister back home.

Fifteen minutes later his dad pulled in the vendor's entrance at the back of the hospital. They'd seen a handful of reporters standing at the front doors again and a few of the sign-waving protestors. Ethan found himself wondering if the reporters and protest people ever slept or ate. They seemed to have taken up permanent positions over the weekend. It looked like they had a couple new signs, too. After his conversation with his dad that morning, the messages about alien plants didn't seem so off base. But the protestors still seemed kinda crazy to him. It was probably a good thing his sister was in isolation so they couldn't get to her.

* * *

The speaker buzzed behind her and Ann turned to see who it was. Her heart fell as she saw two men in biohazard suits standing outside the glass, waiting to be let in. She slid off the chair and stepped with reluctant feet toward the door.

She pressed the speaker button as she scanned their faces. It was hard to see them beneath the glare on the plastic face masks. The taller man wore thick eye glasses and had a dark mustache. The other man was short and appeared to be overweight. She didn't recognize either of them.

Instead of pressing the door release button she asked, "How can I help you?"

The shorter man leaned toward the speaker, "We're with the Centers for Disease Control, please open the door." The man lifted an official looking badge pinned to the front of his bio suit so that she could have a clear view of it through the glass.

Knowing she didn't have any choice, her finger pressed the buzzer and a feeling of dread rode in the door with the two men.

She quickly stepped back to Lily's sleeping form then turned to the men and asked, "Are you here for the blood samples?"

Before the taller man could answer, the squat one said, "No. We're here for the girl. We've been authorized to move her to a more secure facility."

"What do you mean? You're moving her? I thought she was being released to her parents this afternoon?" Alarm rang through her. She took a closer look at their badges. The plastic rectangles had the words Centers for Disease Control printed in large type across the top, an official-looking seal and other info typed too small to read without holding the badge in her hand. The pictures of the men were too small for useful identification purposes and she couldn't ask them to remove their masks.

The shorter man spoke again, "That's why we're here— to relocate her someplace safe until additional tests can be completed."

It was hard to see the man's eyes behind the glare on the plastic shield. She gave herself a mental shake as thoughts of refusing to allow them to take Lily ran through her mind. Her job could be on the line and that was the last thing she needed but she owed it to Chelsea and Lily to try to stop this from happening.

Forcing her mind to function past the panic and act professionally, she asked, "Do you have a court order for this? I can't let you take this child without seeing written proof that you've been given legal permission to do so. You're not taking this little girl anywhere until I see some documentation. I'll call security." Her voice strengthened as she spoke the words, knowing she was absolutely doing the right thing by Lily and her job. What if these men weren't really authorized to take Lily and she let them? She could lose her job for that too, as well as putting Lily in serious jeopardy.

The short man told the taller one, "Go get the paperwork out of my jacket next door. I'll wait here."

A minute later she was buzzing the taller man back in the door and taking a multi-page document from his hand. Her heart sank as she saw the heading at the top of the first page. It was clearly a legal document. She glanced down the first page, which had the words 'Court Order' in bold type beneath the upper section which showed the Centers for Disease Control as the claimant on behalf of the State of California, Chelsea and Craig's names appeared below that along with the words, 'As the legal guardians of said minor child'.

Anger galloped along with fear as she scanned down to the second page and read:

"Patient shall be removed to a secure facility under the direction of the Centers for Disease Control. Patient shall be returned to her family once medical testing has been completed to the satisfaction of the Director."

Tears swam in her eyes as she flipped to the last page to check for the judge's signature.

Panic continued to strike her as the taller man went back out to the hall and wheeled in a gurney. Lily had been asleep the entire time they'd been speaking.

She watched as the men tried to be gentle while they lifted the sleeping girl onto the gurney beside the hospital bed. Lily didn't weigh much so it was a quick motion and the poor little thing mercifully stayed asleep as they placed the safety straps around her still form. They moved toward the door as Ann's brain kicked back in.

"Wait! Where are you taking her?" she asked.

"We're not allowed to disclose the location." The short man continued to be the speaker for the two. "Are you aware there are a group of protestors outside the building who are calling for the girl's death?"

"Yes, I've seen them."

"It's in the child's best interest that the location of the facility we're taking her to be kept to as few people as possible. Her parents will be told but no one else. Now we need to be on our way. Please hold the door open for us." Impatience rang in the short man's tone.

A blast of anxiety hit her as she watched them move Lily's gurney through the door. The men wheeled Lily down the hall and she rushed to pull out her phone to call Chelsea. She'd call Dr. Gammond next to make sure he was aware of the situation also. It seemed odd that he hadn't said anything to her earlier about the CDC's decision to move Lily. Maybe he didn't know about the change in plans either.

Chelsea's phone rang and rang then went to voice mail.

"That's odd," she said aloud to the empty room then left an urgent message to call. She stood holding the phone in her hand, staring at the spot where the men had disappeared around the corner with Lily. She looked back at the empty bed and shook herself. No reason to stay in the room, her patient was gone.

She hurried into the decontamination room and went through the cleansing routine then stepped back into the hallway and pulled her phone out again as she headed toward the nurses' station. Chelsea's phone was still going to voice mail. Damn. She didn't have Craig's cell number but she did have their home number. She hit the button and listened to it ring until the house phone's voice mail picked up. "Double damn."

She called Dr. Gammond and got his voice mail as well. It wasn't a surprise. The doctor had worked the entire weekend on Lily's behalf and had signed her dismissal paperwork an hour ago. He was probably out on the golf course or getting some much-needed sleep. A growl of frustration escaped her lips as she stepped up to the desk and told the clerk that Lily had been removed by the CDC and therefore she needed to be reassigned for the remainder of the two hours left on her shift.

* * *

Ethan and his parents hurried inside the elevator. He would be glad to never see the inside of a hospital again. The place was creepy; the smell of medicines and strong cleaning fluids permeated the air, sounds of equipment beeping and squeaky nurses' shoes were surrounded by an endless sea of white walls, metal fixtures and cold air.

He looked over at his mom's beaming face as they walked down the hall and tried to stay focused on their mission. As much as he'd always thought his sister was a giant pain, he was really looking forward to her coming home with them and their lives getting back to normal.

At the glass door of the isolation room they all stopped and stared in disbelief. Lily's bed was empty and so was the room.

"Where is she?" his mom asked as she looked from the empty room to his dad.

"I don't know—we're here two hours early, Chelsea. Maybe they took her down for some tests or something now that they've decided she's not contagious."

He watched his mom's face as she absorbed his dad's words then she shook her head and reached in her purse for her cell phone.

"Damn! I must have left my phone on the kitchen table." She looked from his dad to him and asked, "I don't suppose either one of you would have Ann's cell number on your phones would you?" Her eyes pleaded with them to tell her yes.

"Sorry Mom, I don't even have my phone with me. I didn't think I'd need it since we wouldn't be here that long."

"I don't have Ann's number either. But I've got my phone if you want to use it." His dad held it out to her but she shook her head.

"Let's go check with the front desk, maybe they know what's going on."

His mom's legs covered the short hallway in six strides as they hurried behind her. No one was at the desk. They stopped beside the counter and looked around.

"I guess we'll have to wait until we see a nurse," his dad said.

"I'm not going to stand here and wait."

His mom hustled down the hall, peeking into each room, looking for a nurse. He stayed at the front desk with his dad. He didn't want to see a bunch of sick people. They stood with an elbow on the counter behind them and waited. His mom made it down to the fourth room before she went inside. A moment later she stepped out and headed back to the desk.

"One of the nurses told me the woman in charge of the floor took a quick break and should be right back. We have to wait for her."

It was hard to watch his mom fidgeting, her expression growing more upset as the clock ticked. After five minutes the elevator doors opened and a woman in a nurse's uniform walked over to the desk.

"Can I help you?"

"I'm Chelsea Noble. Our daughter Lily has been in isolation here all weekend and we've come to take her home, but she's not in her room. Do you know where she is?"

Ethan saw a flash of worry in the woman's eyes as she answered, "I'm sorry Mrs. Noble, we thought you were aware of the situation. The men from the CDC took your daughter out of here about fifteen minutes ago. Didn't Ann call you?"

He watched his mom's face contorting with emotions.

"What did you just say to me?" she asked in a choked whisper.

The nurse gulped and picked up the clip board in front of her, hugged it to her chest like armor. "Mrs. Noble, Ann told me the men from the CDC took Lily to a secure facility for additional tests. She asked me to reassign her so she could finish her shift." Her words trickled off as his mom turned and looked at his dad.

"Craig – did anyone call you? Check your phone."

He looked and shook his head, "No new calls since yesterday."

His mom turned back to the woman. "Where is Ann right now?"

"She's up on the maternity ward. We had enough people here, so I sent her upstairs to help because they're short-handed today."

His mom turned and headed for the elevator without looking back. They rode up to the next floor in silence. She shoved through the doors before they'd finished opening and shot down the hall toward the nurses' desk.

"Can you tell me where Ann Mathers is?" He could see his mom trying to hold in her panic long enough to talk but he was starting to worry what would happen once they found Ann.

"She's with a patient right now. You'll have to wait a few minutes. I can't let you go in there—the mom's in labor."

"Will she be out soon?"

"Yes, she just went in to check on the woman's progress. It shouldn't be long."

His mom turned and stepped over to the small seating area in the corner and began pacing a square. "Craig, do you happen to have Dr. Gammond's number on your phone?"

"I'm sorry Chelsea, I don't have that one either. He's been calling you direct, not me."

"Ethan, go back to the desk and ask that lady to give you Dr. Gammond's cell number. Tell her it's an emergency. If she gives you any grief, come back and get me."

The woman must have known serious trouble was brewing because she jumped right on her computer and handed him the doctor's phone number without hesitating. He handed the slip of paper to his mom and she punched in the numbers with a trembling finger. From his mom's expression It must have gone to voice mail.

"Damn it!"

Two people in the hall turned around and gave his mom a dirty look. Ethan glared at them. They needed to mind their own business. They'd be swearing too if someone had taken their kid without permission.

He was getting really worried about his sister. Lily didn't like being around people she didn't know. Their mom had drilled it into her head that she shouldn't talk to strangers and she'd taken it seriously.

His mom paced another square as Ann came out of a room down the hall and spotted them. A strained look came over her face as she stepped up to them.

"Chelsea, I'm really sorry. I guess you heard about the CDC taking Lily?"

For a second Ethan thought his mom would hit Ann but she kept her fists at her side and used her words instead.

"What in the hell were you thinking Ann? How could you let someone take Lily without even letting me know?" Her voice escalated to a shout and his dad tried to calm her down.

"Chelsea, come on, it's not Ann's fault. She's done everything she can for us. Back off."

She ignored him as she continued to pound, "Why did you let them take her? What if it had been Steve? Would you have let them take him?" She'd lowered her voice to a tolerable level but the anger and pain spewing through her words were just as bad as if she'd been shouting. Ethan flinched as he watched tears come to Ann's eyes.

"Chelsea, I'm so sorry, but they had a court order with them. What else could I do? I read it over—everything seemed to be in order. I tried to call you several times, but you didn't answer the phone. I also tried to call Dr. Gammond and he didn't answer either. There were two of them, they had CDC badges and a court order, and well, I didn't know what else to do." Ann's voice quavered as tears rolled down her cheeks.

He could see his mom forcing herself to back down as she listened to Ann. She took a deep breath then spoke in a slightly calmer voice.

"Did you recognize them? Was one of them Bob Wilson?"

"No, it definitely wasn't Wilson. I didn't recognize either one of them. The taller guy had thick glasses and a mustache but you know how hard it is to clearly see faces through those plastic masks."

"What did the other guy look like?" his dad asked.

"He was short and chubby, or at least he appeared to be through the suit. He looked like he was in his forties. It all happened so fast. I was shocked to see them, especially so late in the day. I mean, they showed up at one-forty and Lily's quarantine ends at four. I was sitting there hoping the CDC had decided to back off when they showed up."

"Did they say where they were taking her?" his dad was thinking better than anyone else right that minute.

"I asked, but they wouldn't tell me. They said the location is being kept confidential for Lily's safety. They told me you were the only ones who would be informed of it. So nobody from the CDC has contacted you?"

He watched his mom shake her head and tears start down her face. A sob made it past her lips and the sound ripped at his heart. Ethan reached out and pulled her close for a moment.

"Don't worry, Mom. We'll find Lily. Right, Dad?"

"You bet your ass we're gonna find her. Today."

His mom lifted her head and looked over his shoulder as his dad called Jimmy.

"Thanks for the hug Ethan, I needed it." She took a step back and wiped at her eyes as his dad explained what was going on. He could hear Uncle Jimmy swearing through the phone.

They talked another minute then his dad said, "We'll meet you at the house. I'm going to talk to security and alert the hospital director of what's happened. We'll see you in a bit."

He stuffed the phone in his back pocket as he said to Ann, "Do you have a security office on site? We need to talk to them and see if they have any video footage from this afternoon. Hopefully we'll see something that will help us."

Ann hesitated, "So you don't think those guys were really with the CDC?"

"I could be wrong, but my gut and Jimmy are telling me something's not right here. At the very least the court order should have been served on us at the house. Can you tell us where the security office is?"

His mom and dad met with the security officer and explained what had happened while Ethan waited outside the doorway. The security office was not much bigger than a cubicle and there wasn't room for all of them to stand inside. He could hear every word discussed and that was good enough. The man sounded alarmed that a child had been removed from the hospital without her parent's permission but when the security guy learned the men who'd removed her were supposedly with the CDC he changed gears.

"What makes you think it wasn't an official CDC intervention Mr. Noble?"

His dad explained about their not being notified by the agency of the intended action, never receiving any court documentation and that Lily's doctor had not been notified.

The man seemed like he wanted to help them but less than enthusiastic about it. "Well, sometimes the government works in mysterious ways when they plan to make a move that will be protested by the parents. Let me make a couple calls and see what I can find out for you."

"Go ahead and make the calls, but first, the main reason we're here is to find out if the hospital has security camera footage we can view." His dad had a mission and he stuck to it, "We're hoping to get a look at the men who took our daughter. The nurse, Ann Mathers, said they came in wearing biohazard suits and it prevented her from getting a good look at their faces. The men didn't leave the supposed court order with her, they only let her read it through then took it with them."

"Let's take a look and see what we can see. You wouldn't happen to know what entrance they came through would you?"

"No, but there's a crowd of reporters and protestors at the main entrance and the employee entrance, so I doubt they went through either of those. Since they took Lily out on a gurney, I assume they went through the emergency entrance. Check that one first, okay?"

The man motioned them down a short hall and into a room that wasn't much bigger than a long closet. It was lined on both sides with shelves of electronic equipment. Three monitors with a single keyboard sat in the middle of the shelves on the left. The man did some clicking on the keyboard then an image of the emergency room entrance popped up on the middle screen.

"What time was your daughter removed from her room?"

The video scrolled back to one-thirty, he hit the play button and they stood watching. An older-looking red and white ambulance pulled up to the side of the entrance and two men climbed out of the truck, dressed in biohazard suits.

"Shit!" his dad said at seeing they weren't going to get any better visuals on the men.

Ethan looked at the security guy and asked, "Do you have a camera that could give us a different angle on that ambulance?"

"No. We've only got the one camera mounted at the top of the emergency entrance. This is a small hospital in a small town. We're pretty low tech, which until today, is more than we've ever needed. This is a medical facility, people come here when they're sick, not to rob the place. We do keep cameras on the drug cabinets and that sort of thing. But otherwise, they really aren't necessary. The one outside the entrance is mostly for insurance purposes."

His dad backed away from the screen as he said, "Okay, I understand. Thanks for letting us take a look. Let me give you my cell number." He handed the man one of his business cards. "We're going to call the police to report Lily's abduction—whether you or they agree, I think that's what we're dealing with here. Sooner or later, the cops are probably going to want a copy of that tape you let us watch, for whatever it's worth."

Ethan worked to keep up with his mom whose long legs were eating up the tiled hallway as they headed toward the exit. His mind wanted to deny someone had kidnapped his sister but he knew his dad was right. He'd give anything to get his sister back, better yet— be able to turn the clock back—to never have seen that stupid article on the spheres in the first place. What if they never got Lily back?

CHAPTER 59

They climbed back in his dad's Lexus and headed home, making the drive in silence. His mom rushed to the kitchen table, snagged her phone and played back the voice mail from Ann. Her eyes welled up as she listened, shaking her head at what had happened.

"Ann left me messages, like she said. I feel bad I spoke to her that way, but I'm so upset. I still can't believe someone just took Lily and we have no idea who!" She scrubbed both palms over her face then walked over to her purse and pulled out the card Wilson had given her. She dialed the number, got his office voice mail and left a detailed message, demanding that he call her back as soon as possible.

His parents looked at each other a moment then his dad said, "Time to call the cops."

A few minutes later a patrol car pulled up and two police officers stood at the front door. His dad told them every detail he could about the situation but his mom didn't say a word—she just stood there with an angry face, drumming her fingertips on her forearm.

"Can you put out an amber alert on Lily right away?" his dad asked.

"Sir, I'll have to call this in to my supervisor." Ethan listened in disbelief as the cop looked his dad in the eye and told him the law wouldn't do anything to help find Lily. "With the CDC being involved all weekend, and Mr. Wilson telling the doctor he might get a court order, I don't think we can consider this a kidnapping yet. Give me a few minutes to go out to my car and make the call to my boss."

The female officer remained standing just inside the doorway while the other cop went out to the patrol car. She wouldn't meet any of their eyes as they waited. A few minutes later the other cop was back and shaking his head.

"Until we can get confirmation from the CDC that they definitely did not remove your daughter from the hospital, we have to hold off on the amber alert and pursuing this as a kidnapping. I'm really sorry."

"Mike, can't we do something for these people? What if their daughter really was kidnapped? It's been over an hour now..." The female officer's words trailed off as her partner gave her a curt look.

The male cop turned to his dad, "There is no way we can put an APB out to stop all ambulances. Without a clear description of the men or a license plate number there isn't much we can do. Once it's determined the CDC did not take her, then we can issue the amber alert. I hate to say it, but without more to go on, we're going to be running uphill on this."

His dad thanked the police officers and closed the door behind them. They all stood in the foyer, staring back at one another.

"Damn it!" His mom came out of her shocked trance at hearing the cops couldn't help. "I'm calling my attorney. Maybe she can give us some advice on getting in touch with someone at the CDC on a Sunday."

Ethan's eyebrows popped at hearing his mom say she had an attorney. Since when? He gave a mental shrug and told himself she must have contacted someone about the quarantine.

She headed back to the kitchen and her phone. They followed her down the hall and saw her open the patio door to let Uncle Jimmy in. He must have seen the cop car and thought they were still enforcing the quarantine so he'd gone through Ann's back yard again.

"Hey Jimmy." His mom sat down at the table and dialed her phone.

"Let's go back to the den." His dad led the way down the hall.

"So I take it you just finished speaking to the cops. What did they have to say?"

"Nothing useful. It looks like we're on our own for now."

"Well damn it all to hell and back!"

Uncle Jimmy looked really upset. He had always treated Lily and him like they were his own kids. He never forgot their birthdays, went all out at Christmas and never missed his basketball games or Lily's dance recitals.

"How's Chelsea holding up?"

"Right this minute she's on the phone with her attorney."

He saw his dad grimace at saying the word attorney and the glance the men exchanged. Something was going on and Ethan wasn't sure he wanted to know about it. Another stick of fear landed on the pile his mind seemed to be made of these days. If things didn't let up soon his brain was going to combust.

His dad looked at his watch then said, "I need to call my boss and let him know I'm probably not going to be in to work tomorrow, maybe not for several days the way things are shaping up." He placed the call and it sounded like it was going to be a long conversation.

Ethan looked at his uncle. "You want something to drink Uncle Jimmy?"

"Sure. A bottle of water would be fine, if you've got it."

They headed back down the hall and joined his mom at the kitchen table. She was still on the phone, and Ethan assumed she was talking to the attorney she'd mentioned. A minute later his dad walked in and sat down with them as his mom ended the call.

Jaw clenched tight and eyes twin scimitars slicing at them, his mom said, "I just want to remind the two of you this would never have happened if you hadn't gone to Africa."

She shoved out of the chair. "I'm going over to Ann's to apologize."

Silence slapped at them as she went through the glass door without looking back.

CHAPTER 60

Chelsea rang the doorbell, wondering if Ann would even answer the door after the way she'd spoken to her at the hospital. She stood chewing on her bottom lip a minute until Steve opened the door.

"Hi Steve. Is your mom home from work yet?" she asked.

The boy stood silently appraising her then nodded his head and stepped aside so she could enter the house. He took off down the hallway and she followed him into the kitchen.

Ann stood at the counter putting dishes away and didn't look at her as she stepped into the room. Chelsea drew in a breath, not sure what to say to make up for accusing Ann of allowing Lily to be taken away. Craig had been right. Ann had gone out of her way to help them over the past few days and once she'd had a chance to calm down a little from the agony of learning Lily was missing, she knew she must have hurt her friend terribly with the accusation.

"Ann, I'm really sorry—"

"Chelsea, I'm so sorry—"

They stopped and looked at each other then quickly stepped forward and hugged.

"I'm the one that owes you an apology, Ann. I know you were caught up in a situation that came out of the blue. And on top of it, you were already worried about your job. Really, I should never have talked to you that way. I hope you'll forgive me." Emotions choked her and she had to stop speaking.

Ann put a gentle hand under her arm and led her toward the table. "Chelsea, I appreciate your apology but in reality, I'll never forgive myself for letting those men take Lily. I should have called security—the police—somebody. What would it have harmed the CDC guys if I'd slowed them down? I'll never forgive myself if something happens to Lily over this."

Chelsea didn't like the tone in Ann's voice. She'd heard her friend sound tired, maybe even depressed, but never like this. She glanced at Steve who had taken a seat at the table with them. He looked every bit as upset as his mother.

"Did the security tapes show anything?" Ann asked.

"No. The men had biohazard suits on when they got out of the ambulance, so we weren't able to see any more of their faces than you did. They parked the ambulance far enough back from the camera's range we weren't able to get any information from it either."

"Hmm…seems kind of odd, don't you think?"

"What?"

"Well, both things. I've never heard of ambulance drivers wearing biohazard suits into the hospital. Of course, now that I think about it, we've probably never had a patient transferred from Hawkins before that required the use of protective gear, so maybe it's normal procedure. But I find it odd they parked the ambulance so far away from the door the camera didn't pick up much of it. Did you see another ambulance parked in their way at the time?"

Chelsea thought back on the video she'd seen an hour ago. "No, the driveway was clear."

She stopped her nervous fingers drumming on the table by placing her hands in her lap. Her knee began to jig and she forced it to stop. She needed her energy to think, not fidget.

"What about the man from the CDC, were you able to reach him?"

"Not yet. I had to leave a message on his office phone. It's the only number he gave me, and with it being Sunday, that's a dead end until tomorrow most likely."

Ann reached out and squeezed her hand.

"I talked to Carol. She's going to call her friend that works for the CDC. I'm hoping they'll have a cell number for Wilson. She's also checking on the legal authority of the CDC to take a child from the hospital to another facility without the parents' permission."

Ann hesitated then said, "Well, they had a court order. Maybe that's all they needed to make it legal?"

"God, I hope not. I sure as hell don't want to live in a world like that." Chelsea caught herself after the fact and apologized for swearing. "Sorry Steve."

The boy didn't respond. He sat staring at his place mat, almost imperceptibly rocking himself on the edge of the chair. Chelsea held back a wince at seeing him slipping into autistic habits again.

"I hate to say it, but I think we should be looking at this from a worst-case scenario." Her temples pounded and her chest felt like it was caving in from the weight of worry.

"What do you mean?"

"At this point, I'm hoping it was the CDC that took Lily. Because otherwise I have no idea who took my daughter today."

Silence fell like a brick onto the table as shock hit Ann's face.

"Chelsea—no. Who would take Lily, if it wasn't the CDC?"

She forced herself to keep tears from starting again. She needed to think instead of feel right now. The lump in her throat made the words come out in a croak, "Maybe it was the crazy fanatics that have been waving signs for the past two days? That man with the ponytail tried to smash the car window yesterday. That's pretty extreme, don't you think?"

Ann didn't answer, obviously not wanting to go there.

Chelsea ran a finger along the pattern of the wood grain of the table. "Did you read the messages on their signs? They're saying Lily's now an alien. One even sounded like a death threat." Another jolt of fear lanced at the thought of the lunatics having her daughter. They might kill her—or maybe worse—do things that would damage the girl the rest of her life. Chelsea shuddered violently then shifted her thoughts to something she could take action on.

"Okay—let's not dig all the way to the bottom of the pit yet. If it wasn't the CDC and it wasn't any of those protestors, then who would have taken Lily? Did you notice anyone loitering outside her room the past two days?"

Ann shook her head, "Security had to run a couple protestors and several reporters out of the lobby but they never made it up to the intensive care floor."

Chelsea jerked in the seat as her cell buzzed in her pocket. She whipped it out and listened as her attorney gave her an update on the CDC situation. The lump in her throat grew as Carol spoke. It was a short conversation and not one word of it was good news. She resisted the urge to throw the phone across the room as she disconnected the call. Ann and Steve looked back at her, worried expressions on their faces.

She forced herself to breathe, closing her eyes until she could speak again. "Lily's in big trouble. Carol's friend talked to Wilson and he's insisting the CDC had nothing to do with Lily being removed from the hospital. He's calling the cops right now on our behalf."

"Chelsea—no, I can't believe it." Ann's face had gone chalk white.

Choking back a sob, Chelsea stood up. "I need to get back to the house and let Craig know." Her legs could barely support her as she ran across the backyard, her mind twisting around who might have taken Lily and why.

CHAPTER 61

Craig resisted punching a wall as he listened to Chelsea recount what the attorney said. He settled for pounding his fist on the table.

"God damn it! Who in the hell has our daughter Chelsea?"

Fear for his little girl racked through him as he shot up out of his chair. He took two steps from the table then doubled over as the pain hit him. The boulder he'd been fighting for the past month crashed inside his stomach and the sudden agony was beyond anything he'd ever felt before. His guts squeezed into his throat and he barely made it to the sink in time as vomit spewed out of him.

"Craig – oh my god! What's the matter?" Chelsea jumped up and rushed to his side as he leaned over, vomiting with each spasm.

When he realized the sink was full of blood he knew he was in serious trouble. After the fourth spasm his stomach backed off and he leaned heavily on the counter, afraid to stand back up. The jolting pain ebbed slowly away only to be replaced by a searing coat of acid hitting his stomach. He wretched again, but his stomach had nothing left in it.

"We've got to get you to the hospital—right now! You could be hemorrhaging. Jimmy, can we take your truck? I don't think I can drive." Chelsea's voice and hands shook as she gently rubbed a hand on his back. "Do you think you can make it out to the truck?"

He took a few breaths, waiting to see if the spasms would start up again in reaction to the pool of acid stripping his guts. He slowly straightened from the sink, relieved when the pain didn't increase. "I think so. Can you get me a bottle of water for the ride?"

"I'll get it." Ethan popped the fridge open.

"My truck's in the driveway, let's go." Jimmy sounded as shaken as Chelsea did.

The fear he'd been feeling for his daughter doubled at seeing the blood in the sink. This was no time to be getting sick. What in the hell could be causing the pain and now the blood? A cold sweat broke out on his forehead as he walked beside his wife out to Jimmy's truck. He climbed in the back with Ethan and sat down on the seat with relief. His knees were shaking so bad he wasn't sure he could have made it farther than the driveway.

"Dad—are you okay?"

Craig didn't answer, instead he reached for the bottle of water and drained a third of it then leaned his head against the seat, concentrating on his stomach. It seemed to be easing up with the water diluting the acid. He glanced at Ethan's worried face.

"I think I'll be okay, I guess we'll find out at the hospital."

Jimmy backed out of the drive as reporters rushed them again and he shot down the road. Craig was glad his brother was driving fast as another twinge of fear struck knowing he might indeed be hemorrhaging. If that was the case, every minute would count.

They made it to the hospital in under ten minutes with Jimmy blowing every speed zone by twenty miles an hour or more. He pulled the truck to a quick stop under the emergency entrance and everybody climbed out. Chelsea took his arm as they made their way inside. She walked with him over to the waiting area.

"Sit here while I go talk to the nurse. Hopefully they can get you in to see the doctor right away."

Craig watched as the woman's eyes grew at the sight of his wife. It was the same nurse who'd been working on Friday when they'd rushed Lily into emergency. It was hard to believe only two days had passed since then. They spoke for a minute then Chelsea walked quickly back to him with a clipboard in her hand.

"She said they'll get you in to an exam room in just a minute. Dr. Gammond's not working today, so you'll be seeing someone else. I don't know who."

"It doesn't matter which doctor I see. I just hope they can get me in and out of here quick and can tell me it's nothing serious."

"Dad, you threw up blood, that's gotta be serious." Ethan's voice was strained.

Craig looked at his son and didn't try to come up with a reply. He drained the last of the water as he thought back to when the pain in his stomach had started. A scraping sensation had hit his gut a few weeks ago on the ride home from San Francisco but he'd put it down to stress. He'd been popping Tumms on a regular basis over the past couple months to fight off the stomach acid that seemed to be a constant companion.

A nurse came out and led him back to an exam room. Chelsea went with them and stood quietly by his side as they waited for the doctor to come in. Ethan and Jimmy waited for them in the lobby.

The doctor asked numerous questions and after performing a cursory physical exam the man gave him a stern look and said, "I believe you're suffering from a bleeding ulcer, possibly a perforated one. There are tests we can run to confirm it. I think we should check you in and get you scheduled for X-rays and an upper gastrointestinal series immediately."

Craig looked back at the doctor and shook his head. "I don't have time to sit in the hospital. Our daughter was kidnapped from this place earlier today. Didn't you hear about it?"

The man blanched at his words. "My god! I did hear about that. I'm so sorry. No wonder you're under so much stress." The doctor pulled at the stethoscope that hung around his neck. "Look, I understand you want to get out of here but you aren't going to be able to do a damn thing for your daughter if your guts are bleeding out."

Chelsea pressed her lips together as her worried eyes roamed over his face, then she looked at the doctor and asked, "Is there a quick test you can do now to find out if Craig's bleeding internally? And if he's not, is there something you can give him to help alleviate the ulcer and let us go home? We can come back for the G.I. test you want to do once we find our daughter." Wetness tracked down her cheeks and she swiped at them with impatience.

The doctor hesitated then said, "I can run an occult blood test and take an x-ray of your upper stomach before you leave. We can get both tests accomplished in less than an hour. Those will tell us whether you have internal bleeding or a perforation. If the x-ray shows you've got air in your upper cavity it means the ulcer has eaten all the way through the stomach lining and you're leaking gut juice as well as blood. If that's the case, you're headed for emergency surgery tonight."

Craig stared back at the doctor—stunned at hearing he might need surgery. He shook his head and tried to stay calm.

"Okay, take the blood and my picture and get me out of here."

"Give me a minute and I'll send the nurse in."

Blood was drawn and Chelsea wheeled him down the hall for an x-ray then back to the exam room. The doctor came back in.

"Assuming the tests comes back negative for internal bleeding, I'm going to give you a couple prescriptions and let you go home." He pulled a pad out and wrote as he explained, "I'm giving you a proton pump inhibitor to cut down the acid hitting your stomach and an antibiotic to get rid of the H. pylori bacteria. It's likely the reason the ulcer formed."

The doctor ripped two pieces of paper off the pad, handed them to Chelsea then turned back to Craig, "Stay away from alcohol, caffeine and anything that contains acid. Also avoid rough things like nuts and popcorn for the next thirty days."

"Okay, I can handle that." Craig said as he shrugged back into his shirt while the nurse came in and handed a file to the doctor.

He read the lab report, looked at the x-ray then said, "All right. The good news is you're not leaking—yet. But make sure you fill those prescriptions and get started on them right away. I can't emphasize enough how important it is to stick to the bland diet. The bloody vomit tells me your stomach lining is close to being perforated—blood vessels are already compromised. Your stomach lining can rupture at any minute in the state it's in. If you have any more episodes of vomiting blood you need to come back in immediately."

The doctor stood up and placed a hand on Craig's shoulder, "I wish you the best of luck in finding your daughter. I'll be thinking of your family." He glanced at Chelsea and said, "Make sure he sticks to the diet." She nodded her agreement.

Craig looked at his wife as she silently picked up her purse. She looked just as scared as he felt. He took a chance and pulled her into his arms, holding her tight a long moment as relief and a sweep of deep love hit him hard.

He made himself let her go and said, "Let's get the hell out of here and go find Lily."

CHAPTER 62

Reporters swarmed as they stepped out of the emergency room. Chelsea thought Jimmy was going to start punching them as the press continued to shout.

"Is it true your daughter has been kidnapped?"

"Mrs. Noble—is it true the government has taken your daughter away?"

They ignored the questions and rushed to Jimmy's truck, slamming the doors shut in unison. He whipped the vehicle out of the lot, punching the gas with no regard for the reporters who surrounded the truck as they shouted more questions out. Luckily the idiots had enough sense to get out of the way and no one got hurt.

She looked back over her shoulder, scanning the front entrance as they pulled out.

"The protestors are gone." The words whispered out as icy terror climbed over her head and plastered the ceiling above them.

"That's good, right?" Ethan asked.

"What are you thinking Chelsea?" Jimmy glanced over, studying her face.

"Ann and I were talking about who took Lily. We know it wasn't the CDC. My second guess was the protestors."

She swallowed back panic, a hard rain of cold fear falling on all of them as she spoke, "If the protestors have left, it's for one of two reasons; either they heard Lily's no longer in the hospital or they know she's not there because they've got her."

A black and ominous silence floated as her words sank in.

"Who else could it be?" she croaked out, praying the men would think of something she hadn't. Her little girl had been missing over three hours already. What were they doing to her?

Jimmy drove for a couple more blocks then said, "Let's stop at the pharmacy then go back to your house and think this through a little more."

Twenty minutes later they were at the kitchen table again. Craig sat with another bottle of water in his hand, Jimmy and Ethan with Cokes. Chelsea had a stiff vodka and sprite in front of her. The strain of all that had happened snapped at every nerve fiber. She was hoping the alcohol would calm her mind enough to be able to think clearly.

"I don't think the protestors have our daughter, Chelsea." Craig spoke quietly, sliding the plastic water bottle in a small circle. "We know it wasn't the CDC, and whoever took her today showed up with what we now know were falsified name badges and a dummy court order. The protestors probably aren't that well connected or organized, at least I wouldn't think so. They've been too busy waving their damn signs around and shouting about aliens."

A tense quiet wound around the room until the icemaker chugged out a fresh round inside the freezer, making them all jump. Craig looked at her, his eyes squinting slightly—she didn't like the look on his face. She could tell he was going to say something she didn't want to hear.

He glanced at Jimmy then back at her, "So, if it wasn't the CDC and it wasn't the protestors, who would it be? Who would want to kidnap a sick little girl from the hospital?"

She winced as he leaned back in his chair, rubbing at his stomach.

"The question we need to ask ourselves is who would benefit from taking our daughter?"

Jimmy spoke, "You guys are doing pretty well for yourselves but you aren't rich, so I don't see anyone taking her for ransom. I seriously doubt it was any of the usual suspects like a pedophile or a childless woman. A pedophile wouldn't want a sick kid and people who are desperate for a child usually go for babies, right?"

The room fell silent again as they considered the facts. Then Craig let loose with what she'd read in his eyes.

"Chelsea, maybe you should give Brad a call, ask him about it."

She jerked back as if he'd struck her. "What are you saying Craig?"

"Your lab partner already has the berries in his possession, but not very many of them. Your boss has been on a tear, demanding you generate positive reports for the shareholders. Maybe they took Lily to do research on her."

She couldn't keep the shock and hurt from her face. Every time she turned around he was trying to put Brad in a bad light. The man had done nothing but help her from Day One and her husband was bound and determined to take him down. She pushed back from the table and got up for more ice, afraid to open her mouth while the anger seethed through her.

"Let's not jump to conclusions." Jimmy hesitated then said, "But, I think the idea has merit. Whoever took Lily had a strong motivation to do it. Kidnapping is a heavy charge. Who in the hell would risk something like that unless they had a huge stake in doing it?" Jimmy fell silent and looked from her to Craig and back.

"Okay—so it has to be someone with a strong motivation. BioGen is not the only company in town, you know. There are lots of people who would love to get their hands on Lily to run tests on her."

"Chelsea, I understand where you're coming from, but let's look at this logically. How much have the other companies learned about the situation at this point? Only what the press has reported, right? Brad and Orlon certainly didn't pick up the phone and spread the word about the berries to their competitors." Craig shook his head then nailed her with the truth. "Only BioGen, the CDC and Lily's doctor know about the berries and what they contain. The hospital has the lab reports, but what are the chances the information leaked out in enough detail to whet the appetites of pharmaceutical companies or whoever else to make it worth kidnapping our daughter?"

She flashed back on the description of the two men Ann had given; one tall guy wearing glasses and a short chubby man. From a generic viewpoint it would describe Brad and Orlon. Brad could easily add the glasses and mustache. Orlon was so fat she hesitated to think Ann would have described him only as short and chubby. The man was beyond obese. But Ann was such a nice person, she may not have emphasized how huge he was. On the other hand, those hazmat suits made everyone look chubby.

She ran it all through her head twice before letting herself buy in to the idea. With ice-cold fingers she picked up the phone and hit Brad's speed dial button. It rang four times and went to voice mail.

Her words came out in a sad monotone as she left him a message, "Brad, it's Chelsea. Give me a call. I really need to talk to you. Right away. Call me."

CHAPTER 63

Craig looked at his wife as she set the phone back on the table. He didn't blame her a bit for having a stiff drink. Hell it was after six o'clock anyway. He glanced at Jimmy's Coke, knowing his brother was probably wishing it was a beer but had likely abstained in solidarity with him. Learning he had a bleeding ulcer had thrown him a huge curve. The news made him feel weak as a man and physically vulnerable. Ulcers were for pansies not tough guys.

But having his daughter missing trumped everything else. To hell with his stomach. It was driving him out of his mind wondering what was happening to Lily. He couldn't keep just sitting there. It was time to take action.

He looked back at Chelsea, "Until we find another avenue to follow, let's assume Brad or your former boss snagged Lily. The most likely place they would have taken her would be BioGen, right?"

"I guess so." More of the vodka and sprite tipped down her throat. The glass met the table with a small click as she pushed it away from her. "But I don't see how they could keep Lily on the premises for long. I mean, it's Sunday, so chances are no one is at the building for the remainder of the day, but that place will be like a bee hive by seven tomorrow morning. The investors' meeting is in five days."

"BioGen's building is huge, Mom. Have you been in every room there yourself?"

"You're right, it's a big building. There's a chance they could keep her hidden for a day or two, but that's it. The janitorial staff goes through the entire building twice a week, Tuesdays and Fridays."

Craig looked around the table then stood up. "Let's take a drive by there right now while it's still light."

"What good is that going to do Dad? Are we going to try to get inside?"

"Chelsea, do you still have your access card for the building?" Craig asked.

"Yes, but I doubt it's still working. I'm sure O-hole told security to deactivate it."

"Maybe so, but it's worth a try, right? At least we can see if there are any vehicles in the parking lot. Do you know what kind of cars Brad and Orlon drive?"

"Yes. Brad drives a black Porsche and Orlon drives a powder blue BMW." She picked up her purse as she spoke and moved to the door. "Come on, let's go."

They piled in Jimmy's Lincoln again. Craig noticed most of the reporters had gone home for the day. Hopefully they wouldn't be back. He had had enough of their presence for one lifetime. The intrusive questions and constant cameras would be hard to handle under normal circumstances but dealing with the media while facing the pressure they'd been under the past two days was worse than having impacted wisdom teeth.

BioGen's building was located on the far outskirts of town. Jimmy turned off the main road and headed down the long drive toward the front of the building. When they got within fifty yards it became clear where all the protestors had gone. Twenty or more of them marched along the sidewalk in front of the building.

"There goes any chance of slipping in the building unnoticed. What the hell are they doing marching outside a business on a Sunday evening? Hardly anyone's around to notice their damn signs anyway." His brother had a good point.

"Don't stop, just drive around to the back so we can look for Brad and Orlon's cars. If either of them are here, it might mean they've got Lily inside. If they did snatch her, they wouldn't leave her here alone. I'm sure they're in a hurry to get their damn tests done before they get arrested for kidnapping." Craig ground the words out as his eyes scanned the protestors.

The fanatic with the ponytail led the march. A breath of relief escaped his lips at seeing the man. The ponytail guy seemed the craziest and most violent of all the protestors. If the guy was here it likely meant the protestors didn't have their daughter.

Jimmy headed around the corner of the building as the mob spotted the truck. They recognized the Lincoln and it energized the group. Their vicious shouts made it through the glass from fifty yards away as the mass of sign wavers came sprinting toward them. Jimmy hit the gas and the SUV shot through the parking lot.

The facility was huge. It took a minute to get to the backside of the building. Once they rounded the corner of the structure, three parked vehicles came into view. Two of them matched the description Chelsea had given them.

"I don't see an ambulance," Ethan commented.

Craig studied his wife's face from the back seat. He could only see her profile but her eyes narrowed at seeing the cars here on a Sunday evening. He knew she had a soft spot for Brad but she hated Orlon with a passion. The guy was a walking dead man if Lily was in there. He would kill the asshole in cold blood without looking back if Chelsea didn't get to him first. To hell with the law. Nobody kidnapped his daughter and got away with it.

Jimmy made a circle in the back lot then looked at him in the rearview mirror. "What do you want to do now, bro?" The Lincoln slowed to a stop while he waited for Craig's answer.

"Chelsea, give Brad a call again. See if he answers this time."

She whipped the phone out and hit the speed dial. He heard it go to voice mail and she hung up without leaving a message.

"How familiar are you with the layout of the building Chelsea?"

"I could sketch it out for you, no problem. I don't know what every little closet is for but I definitely know the hallways and main rooms along with the executive office area. There's a big employee lounge at the back." She pointed at the section they sat in front of.

His eyes scanned the exterior. The long white building was built for service rather than aesthetics. It was a giant cement rectangle with dark green trim. The one-story structure had large reflective windows in front but few in back.

"What are those two doors for?" he asked.

"The one on the left side is the employee entrance and leads straight into a long hallway that feeds off toward the front of the building. The door on the right leads out of the employee's lounge. See the picnic bench?"

A sound of seagulls squawking made him look to the left as the group of protestors came running at them from around the corner of the building.

"Shit, let's get out of here," Jimmy muttered under his breath.

"Okay, I've seen enough, let's go."

"Uncle Jimmy, I don't see how we're going to make it past all of them without getting smacked by their signs again."

"Don't worry, this truck has four-wheel drive and I have no problem running one or more of those assholes over. What the hell is the matter with them anyway? A little girl gets sick and they start calling her an alien. That's just sick-headed." Jimmy floored it and shot across the lot. The Lincoln went from zero to forty in less than three seconds and they were almost on top of the protestors within seconds.

Jimmy let out a wicked chuckle and kept his foot on the pedal. The fanatics realized he wasn't going to slow down and jumped out of the way. Except for the ponytail guy. He stood his ground, heavy wood sign with its evil message held at the ready. Jimmy didn't flinch—he aimed straight for the man.

At the very last second the guy flung himself out of the path of the heavy Lincoln with its reinforced steel bars across the front grill. The nose of the truck missed hitting the man by an inch. Craig saw him rolling on the pavement as the truck crushed the sign into pieces. Chelsea buzzed the window down, stuck her bird finger out.

"Go to hell!" she shouted. She put the window back up and slumped against the seat.

"Let's come back in a couple hours, after it gets dark." Craig looked at Jimmy in the rearview mirror. "Hopefully the crazies will be gone by then."

CHAPTER 64

Lily opened her eyes to bright lights overhead. Squinting against the glare, she glimpsed around—the room was all white and bigger than she remembered. They must have moved her. She saw a fat doctor in a white coat, sitting with his back to her. Clanking noises came from the counter in front of him. A peek on the other side showed only a white wall and cabinets. There were no windows.

She sensed motion and turned her head back toward the doctor. The man approached her bed with a long strip of white cloth in his hand. A shiver ran through her when she saw his face. His looked like a pig with that big nose and round belly. He got closer and she could see warts growing in patches under his eyes. Gross.

"Who are you?" Where's Ann?" she asked the man.

Instead of answering the doctor frowned and wrapped the cloth over her eyes. He knotted it tightly at the side of her head and a zing of terror struck her at not being able to see anything.

"What are you doing? Why can't I see?" she wailed out.

"We're going to do a couple tests on you and the x-ray machine isn't good for your eyes. We'll take the cloth off later."

She gasped in pain as a needle pricked her arm. "Ouch! What are you doing to me?" Then she sucked in a breath and shouted, "I want my mommy! I want my mommy!"

The sound of her voice echoed off the cement walls as she thrashed her head and tried to kick her arms and legs. When she realized she was tied up she got really scared and let out a long piercing scream until the medicine from the shot made her sleepy and she had to close her eyes to rest.

CHAPTER 65

They huddled around the kitchen table, waiting for darkness to fall. Chelsea sketched a detailed layout of BioGen's interior, highlighting areas that were not currently in use. The company had planned ahead for growth when they'd built the structure four years ago and there were still a few unused spaces in the northwest corner.

"Once we're through the initial card swipe are there any others after that?" Craig asked.

"There's a second swipe access needed at each of the laboratory doors."

"What about an alarm system? Are the doors and windows wired?"

"Yes, but if Orlon's in there, the alarm will be off."

"What about the security guard?"

"They only have a guard there during the day to protect the employees. In the past, the crazies only came around during business hours. We've never had a problem with vandalism so they don't have anyone patrolling at night."

Craig stared off through the sliders a moment then looked at Jimmy. "Let's go out in the garage and load up some tools." The men headed to the door and Ethan followed them out.

Chelsea called Brad again while she waited, got voice mail and hung up. The kitchen was a large airy room but right that minute the walls seemed to be only two feet apart. She paced off the open distance from the door to the table several times then forced herself to stop. She made a pot of coffee and a third of it had brewed before she remembered the doctor's instructions to Craig about not drinking coffee.

Twenty minutes passed before the men came back in.

"That coffee sure smells great," Jimmy said then gave Craig a sheepish look.

"Listen, you guys enjoy the coffee, don't worry about me. My stomach is so sore I can't drink anything hot anyway. I'm good with water until I heal up."

She poured mugs of coffee, grabbed cream and a bottle of water from the fridge then looked at the clock as she sat back down. It was only seven. It wouldn't get dark for another thirty minutes.

"So what are you guys going to do if my access card doesn't work?"

"That's what the sledge hammer's for." Ethan flashed a sly grin.

Chelsea's eyes pop at hearing their plans for breaking and entering but she knew they didn't have a choice. The cops had told them they couldn't search BioGen without probable cause and a warrant and they had no grounds for obtaining one. She said a prayer for the card to work as she sipped at the coffee. It took a moment for her frantic mind to process Ethan's comment to the next logical step.

"Wait a minute. Ethan—are you planning on going with your dad?"

"Yeah, I'm going with them. They need me to be the lookout."

Alarmed, she asked Craig, "Are you sure you need him there? What if something goes wrong and you all get arrested—or worse—what if Orlon's got a gun?"

"Chelsea, Ethan's going with us. We really do need him to be our lookout. He's going to wait in the car in the parking lot and text us if he sees someone coming. But listen, I wanted to talk to you about something else." His expression made her brows wrinkle in concern.

"Jimmy and I have been talking about what we're going to do after we get Lily back."

"We're going to celebrate, what else would we do?"

"Well, that's what I want to talk with you about. Let's say we have Lily in the truck and we head back here. What's going to keep someone from breaking a window in the middle of the night and snatching Lily again?" Craig paused then went on. "Who knows how many more days the press is going to stay camped out here, especially when word gets out about BioGen's employees kidnapping our daughter. And the crazies will be right behind the reporters."

"Damn it! I hadn't thought that far."

"Chelsea, there's also a chance the government could jump back on the bandwagon. We're the only ones who know right now that plant came from the sphere, but how long do you think that's going to last?" Jimmy grimaced as he made his point. "This has all come to light over the weekend. Once all the government offices are open on Monday and this thing blows wide, how many people do you think will be banging on your door? Multiple agencies will want to know where the plant came from and asking for vials of Lily's blood."

"Stop you guys—you're freaking me out. Where in the hell are we supposed to take Lily then? You know she's going to want to come home." Tears started up again and she fought them back with a small growl.

Craig glanced at Jimmy then back at her, "I think we should leave the country for a few weeks until everything calms down here and we can get a better grip on our legal rights. We need to let some time go by so the press moves on to other stories and the fanatics have backed off before we can safely live here again."

She knew he was right but she didn't want him to be. "What about your job?"

"Our family's safety is more important than my job. I've already told my boss what's going on and that I won't be in for a few day, maybe longer." Craig reached out and squeezed her hand.

She studied her husband, realizing he was finally doing what she'd wanted for so long—making their family a priority. She wasn't sure what to think of the fact that it had taken almost losing their daughter for him to see the light but decided it didn't matter right then.

"So where are we going to hide out?" she asked.

"How does Paris sound to you?"

"Are you serious?" She looked at Craig in shock, "How can we afford to stay in Paris?"

"That's what credit cards are for—emergencies. Jimmy knows someone who's got a private plane he'll let us use to get out of town under the radar. He called the guy while we were in the garage. We'll have to drive to San Jose, but it's only an hour away and Jimmy can get us there in less than that. You can pack while we wait for it to get dark. We're heading straight for the airport once we have Lily."

"How awesome is that, Mom? Paris here I come!" Ethan grinned at her as she worked to absorb the idea.

Her head swam at the idea of packing in less than an hour for a trip out of the country but she'd figure it out. She didn't have much choice.

"Thank you, Jimmy." Hope grew as she said, "Let's get Lily and go to Paris."

"Okay, I'll call my friend and ask him to have the plane ready to leave in a couple hours."

"I'm going to call Ann and let her know what we're doing so she doesn't worry and I'll ask her to keep an eye on the house for us until we get back."

"Chelsea, that's the other thing I wanted to talk with you about. Do you think Ann would come with us? I'm worried about Steve. He ate those berries too. Did you tell Brad that?"

Fear leapt again as she thought back on her conversations with her lab partner and realized she'd told him about Steve's incredible improvement. If he was in on kidnapping Lily then Steve was at risk. Especially if they got Lily out of BioGen's reach.

"Oh no—I did tell Brad about Steve's recovery from the autism. I'll call Ann right now."

They spoke for a couple minutes then Chelsea hung up frowning. "Ann says she can't go with us. She can't afford to lose her job and has to give at least thirty days notice to take a block of vacation time."

"But Mom, what if someone snags Steve?"

"I know Honey, but I'm not in charge of Ann. I'm having a hard time with suddenly leaving the country myself and I don't have a job to worry about. Lily's been quarantined, hounded and kidnapped. None of that has happened to Steve yet. I know Ann. She meant it when she told me no." Another brick of sadness and worry hit her in the chest at the thought of not seeing her friend for weeks, knowing Ann and Steve might be in danger.

Jimmy sat with a strange look on his face while she told them Ann had refused to go and why. He stood up abruptly and said, "I'm going next door to talk to her."

She looked at Craig in surprise. He shrugged and shook his head.

CHAPTER 66

Ann hurried to answer the door, thinking it must be Chelsea. She couldn't keep the surprise off her face at seeing Craig's brother on her porch.

"Hi Jimmy." She paused, not sure what else to say.

After a brief hesitation he spoke up, "I need to talk to you for a minute. Can I come in?"

"Sure. Come on back to the kitchen."

She stepped into the softly lit room and motioned to where Steve sat at the table, staring at the place mat. A coloring book and crayons sat on the table, untouched.

"Hey, Steve." The boy glanced at him with worried eyes but said nothing.

"Have a seat. Would you like something to drink?"

"No, I'm good. Thanks anyway. Listen, I want to talk to you about going to Paris with Craig's family. I know you told Chelsea you can't, but I honestly don't think you can afford to stay here. Not if you care about Steve."

"What are you talking about?" Steve asked.

"You want to rescue Lily, right?" Steve nodded his reply. "Okay, so here's the plan..."

She listened as Jimmy told her son the plan.

Steve's eyes flew to hers, "I think that's a good idea, Mom. We should go with them. We gotta help Lily, she's my friend. I haven't even seen her for three days." His words escalated to a quiet whine.

Ann looked at her son's face, wishing she was able tell him they could go. She resented having to tell him no. He wouldn't have known Chelsea invited them if Jimmy hadn't rung the bell and opened his mouth.

She softened her expression and said, "Honey, we can't. I'll lose my job if I leave. Then what would we do? And I can't afford to stay in Paris. It just won't work."

"But—why not, Mom?"

"Ann, that's why I wanted to talk with you. I realize you're on a tight budget and need a job to support yourself and your son. I don't know you very well—we've only had dinner with Craig's family a couple times—but you seem like a great person and a great mom. I really want to help you and Steve."

Ann stood there, almost unable to speak at the incredible feeling of a man giving her encouragement and help when she needed it most. She couldn't afford the trip, it just wasn't an option, but he was making her see that saying no wasn't an option either. In the nicest way.

Jimmy shuffled his hands in response to her silence then said, "I'll pay for whatever expenses you need the entire time you're in Paris. I want you and Steve to be safe. It would mean a lot to all of us if you would accept my help.

"I know you're a hard worker from everything Chelsea's said. When you guys are able to come back from Europe, I'd be happy to have you come to work for me. I've got a lot of things you can help me with. And I can pay you whatever it is you get at the hospital, probably more, and I have no doubt you'll be worth every penny, plus insurance. Talk to Craig if you need a reference." He gave her an irresistible smile.

She was in the middle of grinning back at him when a tornado hit her side. She wobbled and looked down—Steve's arms were wrapped tight around her hips.

"Say yes Mom, please." Huge brown eyes stared up at her.

How could she tell him no without hurting a lot of people for pride's sake? The corners of her mouth moved up without her realizing it until she felt the air on her teeth.

"Yes—on one condition."

Jimmy's grin faded. "What's that?"

"You have to go with us."

"You talked me into it." He held out his hand to shake on it.

"Stop fooling around you guys and let's go get Lily!" Steve exclaimed as he headed toward the door.

"Wait Honey, we have to pack."

"No Mom, I can go like this." The boy looked down at his blue t-shirt and jeans.

Jimmy beat her to the punch, and with a much better come back, "You don't want to end up the rotten potato in the barrel, do you?"

Steve blinked back at him, "Huh?"

"I'll explain it to you while we pack your suitcase." Jimmy's grin and the look in his eyes as he spoke to her son was like a warm beam of sunshine on a cold day.

God willing Lily really was in that building and they'd have her back in less than two hours. Ann tried to stay focused on the visual of all of them on the plane, headed for Paris as she hurried toward the stairs.

CHAPTER 67

"What's going on Orlon?" Brad whirled around on the barstool at hearing the door.

Orlon had stepped into the lab to get an update from him. Lit only from the florescent lights above, the white and silver room had a strange spaceship quality to it. A hushed quiet permeated the air, disturbed only by the whooshing of the ventilation system.

"Can you be more specific with that question?" He would not allow himself to be put on the defensive. He knew this was the only way to get what the company needed. It was imperative that Brad cooperate.

"Where did you get this blood you've had me testing tonight? And don't bullshit me or I swear I'll punch that ugly nose of yours."

Orlon backed up a couple paces then forced himself to stand his ground and make this work. It took a sharp knife to stay on the cutting edge.

After a reluctant hesitation he said, "All right, I'll tell you. I have a connection at the hospital, a nurse. When I learned Lily was being released today I asked her to get two vials for me before the girl went home. That's what you're testing."

"This is business, Brad. Orlon continued on as the lab man stood with an unreadable look on his face, "A tough business. A cut-throat, cutting-edge business. It's not for pansies. If you want to make big money, you have to make big moves at the right time." Orlon looked back at the movie-star face as Brad continued to say nothing.

The growing silence made him feel a need to wiggle and he straightened his lab jacket as he said, "Get me something concrete that I can plug into a report for the stockholders meeting on Friday and I'll personally give you a five-thousand dollar bonus on top of what you're already getting."

Brad continued to study him and Orlon's skin began to crawl from the look that had formed on the man's gorgeous face. He felt the hatred coming off the man all the way to his toes and yet, he sensed Candyface would go along with it. At least for now. Money was king for Brad Peterson. Orlon had assessed him carefully and knew where the man's heart lay. It wasn't with Chelsea Noble.

Brad finally spoke, "You make me nervous Orlon. You take this stuff way too seriously. We could do things legitimately, you know, but you don't have the patience. You're in a hurry and willing to break all the rules to get across the money line as fast as you can."

Orlon pressed his teeth together but couldn't stop the shudder from running down his back. The handsome and greedy man in front of him could ruin everything. He could not let that happen. He reached into his pocket to handle the problem but before he could get his hand out, Brad continued speaking.

"In spite of what I think of you, I've never made so much money in my life. That's why I branched into this field—it really is cutting edge. Some people will do anything to get ahead. But I don't want to work for you any more—you're crazier than anyone I've ever met." Brad's grin had the joker's edge to it. "I'm going to take the money and run. Make it another ten thousand and I'll write the report—but after the board meeting, I'm turning in my resignation."

Orlon shrugged off the insult. He'd find another lab jack to play with if Candyface jumped ship. As long as Brad turned in the reports on time, the proposed plan would work. He had to get rid of the evidence quickly but first wanted to be sure they had what was needed. If the company missed making the goals set out in its business plan a second year in a row, there was no doubt he'd be out of a job in six months. His executive bonus would be a thing of his dreams, along with the milestone bank balance he was planning to achieve with the check. Getting caught was unacceptable—for many reasons. He shuddered as he considered which would be worse—

going to prison or facing Oswald—one would be a lifetime of misery, the other certain death.

He gave Brad a curt look as he said, "I'm glad that's settled. It's your decision to make. Do you have everything you need to complete a preliminary report?"

"I've got a couple more tests to run. I also want to call Chelsea and check on Lily. We need an update on her health and whether she's presenting any odd mental or physical changes. Even from a simple vitamin and mineral perspective, she set the record by a mile for dosages consumed. It will be important to learn what changes it might cause in her. It will also help validate the report."

Orlon's eyes flared at hearing Brad speak of contacting Chelsea. He had interrupted the man in the middle of watching the ball game on a Sunday evening with an urgent request for him come to the lab and test the blood samples. Orlon had dangled green carrots and paid significant cash at the door to get him there.

A dual stab of anger and panic hit Orlon. "That call can wait. You're on my dime right now." He played the psychology card, "If Lily went home today, I'm sure her family wants to spend time together, uninterrupted. Call her tomorrow. That would be the polite thing to do.

"Give the blood samples your focus for another hour and then come back in the morning. I'm sorry to have taken up the whole of your Sunday evening. I appreciate your help."

Brad's cold poker gaze pinned him. "I appreciate your money. You get one more hour then I'm out of here."

CHAPTER 68

Jimmy steered the Lincoln through the parking lot with its headlights off, moon and clouds cooperating just enough to navigate. He parked next to the sidewalk for the employee lounge entrance and they sat with the engine running. "Those are the same vehicles that were here earlier, right?"

"Yeah, Uncle Jimmy. Brad and Orlon's cars, plus the white van."

"The van look like a company vehicle, parked at the back like that. I think Orlon and Brad are the only people in there," Craig said. "Let's do this."

"Damn straight." Jimmy picked up the bag of tools from the floor. "We're gonna get our little girl back and then we're gonna teach somebody a lesson."

"That's for damn sure." Craig looked back at Ethan. "Text me if you see anything – a car that looks like it might be turning in up at the entrance or someone walking around. Text '911' and I'll know what it means. Sit tight until we get back—unless the person you've spotted turns out to be one of those protestors. If that's the case, get the hell out of here and come back for us when I call you."

His stomach pain had eased significantly after taking the acid inhibitor and he felt fairly confident he could get in there and snag Lily without the ulcer shutting him down. It didn't matter though because he was going in either way.

They had agreed not to dress in black. It would be too conspicuous at the airport and there would be no time to change clothes. Jeans and a regular-guy t-shirt were the way to go. The women were headed for San Jose in Chelsea's Escalade and would wait with Steve in long-term parking for them to bring Lily in Jimmy's truck. His friend had confirmed the Cessna Citation XLS would be waiting for them. It was fueled and ready for takeoff.

If it turned out Lily wasn't in the BioGen building he would call his wife and tell them to head back to Hollister. Jimmy would call his friend to notify the pilot the flight was off, and they would meet back at the house to regroup. That was not an acceptable plan but they needed to think through all the scenarios.

Craig slid out of the truck with a muscle in his jaw twitching and Chelsea's access card in his hand. Jimmy came around the truck and stepped up beside him with Ethan's backpack slung over his shoulder. It was packed with a small sledge hammer and crow bar, screw driver, plumbers tape, box knife and zip ties. They figured it covered the basics.

Sounds of the night seemed amplified by ten as Craig walked beside his brother to the door. He heard every cricket, the call of birds in the trees and a faint swish of traffic in the far off distance. The air smelled of growing foliage, damp earth and danger.

He held his breath as the access card passed through the swiper slot on the side of the door. Seconds passed then the light turned green and the door clicked open. Air rushed out of his lungs as he grinned at Jimmy. They slipped through the door and stopped for a moment to get their bearings.

They were in a large employee kitchen. Cabinets and counters ran the length of the far wall, interspersed with appliances and a sink. Moonlight shone through the large square window, glinting off the silver metal chairs waiting around grey tables. The door to the interior hallway stood to their left and they crossed the room silently, glancing at the ceiling for cameras. Chelsea had assured them there weren't any in the lounge but it was instinct to look.

A long white hallway stretched in front of them and another one ran horizontal to the door. They knew from Chelsea's drawing they needed to turn right, go to the end of the hall, then a left and to the end of the second hall. They should begin checking doors once they reached the third hallway.

It was dead quiet except for the occasional sound of the AC equipment. Craig's heart slammed against his ribs and his adrenaline had every hair standing on end as they headed down the corridor. Underneath it all a seething anger twisted. What kind of a monster kidnapped a child just to prosper financially? Make that two monsters. If it turned out Brad had taken Lily he would kill him with his bare hands.

They worked their way to the third hallway and saw light coming from a room near the end. Silent steps and breath held, they reached the lab door. Craig inched his eyes over the small glass window pane. A huge man in a white coat sat at a counter across the room with his back to the door. He turned his head, straining to see the other side of the room but the window was too small. They would have to go through the door to learn whether Lily was in there.

Craig slipped away from the window and nodded at Jimmy. They had agreed that until they saw Lily, Jimmy would keep the gun in his pocket. He would have his camera at the ready instead. If it turned out the man hadn't kidnapped Lily they could be facing very serious charges for brandishing a gun while coming through a door they had no business entering.

He swiped the card, the light turned green and he raised his hand, silently counting down with his fingers...one, two, three! Jimmy jerked the door open and Craig followed right behind. His heart clutched when he saw his daughter lying on a gurney in the far corner.

Lily appeared to be asleep or sedated and had a white blindfold over her eyes. Straps bound her wrists to the gurney. Demon anger shot through him as he turned to lunge at the fat man only to realize Orlon had pulled a gun on them. He pulled up short as Jimmy slowed beside him and slipped the phone back in his jacket pocket.

"Stop right there." The fat man shook the gun at them. "You made a big mistake coming here, Mr. Noble. I planned to take Lily back to the hospital once I had all the samples I need. Now you've made that pointless."

"I'm sure as hell not going to let you hurt my daughter." Craig bit the words out, hands fisted at his sides, body weight on the balls of his feet.

"Language, Mr. Noble, language. There's a child present." The walrus lowered his eyebrows and jerked the gun, motioning them away from the door. "Now get over there, next to the sink. Set the bag on the counter."

With grudging steps he moved toward the sink and turned to face the madman. Craig could see the gun shaking in Orlon's hand as he backed toward Lily, keeping as much distance as possible between them. What was the man doing? Was he going to shoot? Try to run?

"Who else knows you're here?"

"Nobody knows we're here." Craig glanced at Jimmy then back to Orlon. "The cops told us they couldn't demand a search of BioGen without probable cause. That's why we came ourselves. We just want Lily. If you let me take her and go, I swear we won't say a word to anyone. I just want my daughter. We want our lives back. That's all."

Orlon stared at him, almost in a daze as Craig's calm voice floated over the man. Then the walrus shook his head, snapping out of the temptation of the intentionally soothing words.

"Nice try. I'm just waiting for Brad to confirm the results of the last batch of tests then all three of you are leaving." Craig knew from the man's eyes he would kill them.

Orlon smirked as his cell buzzed in his pocket. "That's probably Brad now. Your time's almost up with your daughter, Mr. Noble." Craig watched in surprise as the ugly man's eyes grew wide at reading the message and he whirled around toward Lily. The sheet undulated like a wave above her still form then settled back down. Orlon stood transfixed at the sight.

Craig and Jimmy didn't waste a second as they rushed the fat man, but with only another step to go to reach him, Orlon swung around in fright, flung the pistol up and pulled the trigger.

BLAM!

The shot flew past Jimmy's shoulder, grazing his shirt, forcing him to stop mid stride as his body reacted to the heat of the bullet.

Orlon shifted the gun toward Craig as he swung the backpack toward the fat man's head. The second bullet struck the sledge hammer and ricocheted off, just grazing Orlon's temple as the bag continued its arc and crashed into his skull with a sickening thud. He went down like a giant sack of lard and bricks, catching his chin on a table leg with a resounding crack. The gun and phone fell out of his hands and skidded across the tile floor.

Craig dropped the bag, rushed over to Lily and removed the blindfold. His daughter's eyes were open beneath the cloth and she gave him a sleepy smile.

"Hi Daddy. I knew you were coming for me," she whispered through a croaky throat. "I'm so thirsty, Daddy. Please hurry."

"Hi Princess. I'm sorry you're thirsty, we'll get you a drink real quick, hang on." He smiled down at her as he removed the straps from her wrists.

He pulled the sheet back and straightened her hospital gown as best he could. She sat up while he removed the straps from her ankles. He picked her up and held her tight. She felt so good. He had to stop a moment and concentrate on how her small body felt in his arms. He'd almost lost his little girl twice in the last two days—she was more precious to him then ever.

Jimmy got busy with the zip ties and the camera on his phone as Craig freed Lily. His brother rushed over to the computer on the counter and tapped the keyboard. It was open and running so he was able to access the internet without a problem. Jimmy tapped a few keys on his cell phone then brought his e-mail account up on the computer screen. He accessed the email he'd just sent from his phone, opened the picture files and clicked the printer icon.

A whirring noise came from a small black machine sitting next to the keyboard and it spit out two color photos. Craig looked at them over Jimmy's shoulder when he laid them on the empty gurney. The first showed Lily blindfolded and restrained on the bed with Orlon sitting a few feet away, a shocked look on his face. Jimmy took that one coming in the door. The second picture showed Orlon on the floor next to the gurney, handcuffed to the table legs with the zip ties. His eyes were closed, a trickle of blood rolled down the side of his head and oozed down his chest from the gash on his chin. Lily sat on the gurney behind him. Only Craig's hand was in the photo, untying the restraints.

Jimmy dropped a kiss on her head. "You okay Sweetheart?" Lily nodded.

He walked back to the unconscious man, hauled his foot back and kicked him in the ribs. Bones snapped in the quiet room. "That's for kidnapping Lily, wartface."

Orlon let out a groan and it took everything Craig had not to grab the gun off the floor and shoot the man dead. Jimmy looked at him and shook his head.

"Let's get the hell out of here." His brother snatched up the bag and went to the door.

Craig continued to stare at Orlon as a black cloud of hatred swirled through him. The only thing that kept him from shooting the asshole was the little girl in his arms. He didn't want her to see him kill a man, whether he deserved it or not.

"Close your eyes Princess." He settled for giving the obese clown a vicious kick in the middle of his sofa-sized ass as Lily hung on tight. "That's for firing Chelsea, you sick bastard."

Orlon's body jerked from the impact and he groaned out again. His eyelids twitched but remained closed.

"Let's go, Jimmy. You can call the cops and report him from the truck." They went out the door and didn't look back.

"Daddy, where are we going?" Lily asked in a sleepy voice from over his shoulder.

"We're going someplace safe. Have you ever heard of Paris?" he asked her, breath coming fast from the exertion. His stomach had begun to cramp again but he ignored it.

"That's where Madeleine lives, Daddy!" She sounded wide awake now.

They were in the second hallway when Craig's cell buzzed against his hip. He struggled to shuffle Lily into his other arm and pulled his phone out. His heart clutched as he saw the '911' message. "We need to hurry. Hang on tight, Sweetheart."

They sprinted through the remainder of the hallway maze and shot into the lounge.

"Hold up a second," Jimmy stopped and yanked open the fridge. He loaded four water bottles in his pockets and they headed out the door to the parking lot.

"Dad!" Ethan jumped out and opened the back passenger door as he shouted, "I saw a guy's head move inside that white van over there."

Craig bolted into the back seat with Lily as Ethan hopped in the front. Jimmy threw the Lincoln into gear and floored it. He headed for the end of the parking lot at an angle as the van's lights flipped on and its engine started.

"That guy's following us Uncle Jimmy and he's coming fast!"

Jimmy kept his foot on the gas until they reached the front entrance. They shot out on the road, tires squealing as he cranked the truck around the corner then hit the gas again.

CHAPTER 69

Brad set the vial in the caddy and stopped to listen. Had he heard gun shots? He jumped up from the barstool and stood debating what to do. Maybe one of the protestors had made it inside and shot Orlon? Shit! He pulled out his phone and dialed. Orlon's cell went straight to voice mail. Damn. Trouble was not what he needed. If his boss was dealing with protestors, the man was on his own. He wanted to get the hell out before he got sucked any deeper into the asshole's insanity.

He walked to the end of the hall with a tingle of fear creeping down his back. The hour he'd promised his boss had almost ticked off and he was leaving whether he talked to Orlon again or not. As he neared the employee entrance at the back of the building he heard tires squealing but couldn't get to a window in time to see what all the noise was about.

Outside in the parking lot, keys in hand, he saw two sets of taillights speeding from the grounds up at the front entrance. Something stopped him from just climbing in his car and leaving when he saw Orlon's beamer still parked a few stalls from his Porsche. Why hadn't the man answered his phone? Maybe those had been gun shots after all? If the guy died there would be no bonus at the end of the week and his time here this evening would be wasted.

He turned and went back into the building.

"Orlon?" No answer. It was a big building. The man probably hadn't heard him. Maybe he'd been shot? Hairs prickled as he walked to the front and checked Orlon's office. The lights were off.

Odd. Where was the man? He picked up his pace and reversed his steps through the dark executive offices and headed back to the labs.

It took several minutes to work his way to the far corner of the building. He seriously doubted Orlon was back there but something compelled him to check. He reached the last corridor and saw a light at the end of the hall.

"Orlon!" No sound came from the lab, only the light.

He reached the door and his heart rate picked up at seeing someone had jammed it open to eliminate the need for the security swipe. He stepped into the room and stopped short at the sight of Orlon's feet sticking out from the far side of a long table. With a few steps, he rounded the long surface and got a full view of the corpulent man.

"Holy shit!" Brad looked down in shock at his boss.

Orlon's wrists were bound to the table legs with zip ties. Blood ran down the side of his face and dripped off his chin, soaking into his shirt and jacket. His eyes fluttered open and he groaned. It took the man a moment to come around enough to realize he was bound to the table.

"Cut these off me!" He jerked at the ties in panicked frustration.

'What the hell happened to you?" Brad stared down at the three hundred pound man struggling against the thick ties. The table legs were bolted to the floor. He wasn't going anywhere.

"I've been assaulted! Get over here and help me, damn it."

The force of the jerks caused the table to vibrate, making Brad look up across the room to the gurney placed against the wall. Two pictures lay on top of it. He walked over and studied them. Controlled anger curled as he turned from the gurney.

He took a step toward Orlon, teeth clenched tight when the wink of a cell phone caught his eye from under the edge of the table. He picked it up and a text message glowed back at him: "Look behind you." It was from an unknown caller.

He looked from the phone to the gurney then down at Orlon as the fat and frantic man shouted, "Help me! Don't just stand there!"

Brad let out a howl of laughter and ignored him. He wiped prints off the phone, set it on the table above Orlon's head. He stopped at the door and sneered at the fat slug. "Sayonara asshole."

CHAPTER 70

Jimmy had the Lincoln up to eighty within seconds of hitting the two-lane highway but the van was hot on their tail only fifty yards behind them. Craig doubted the van had the horsepower of the Lincoln. A couple minutes down the road and they'd probably get away from the van. Just as he assured himself they were going to get clear a huge BANG! split the night and bullets hit the back of the truck. It sounded like a shotgun.

"Shit!" Craig dove down, covering Lily, keeping his back between her and the seat.

"Hang on, we've got a curve up here and he's gonna be top heavy. He'll have to slow down or risk dumping the van on its side." Jimmy nodded his head down toward his right side. "Take the gun from my jacket."

Craig laid Lily down flat on the bench seat, wrapped the sheet tighter around her.

"Stay down Princess and hold on tight to the seat."

Leaning forward, he took the silver revolver from Jimmy's pocket, turned and buzzed his window down then crouched beside the door, facing back toward the van behind them.

"Dad—what are you doing?"

"This is the real deal son. The asshole shooting at us is that sign-waving ponytail guy. I saw him when he leaned out. The man's crazier than your mom's boss—he's not going to stop until they have Lily. That's not gonna happen."

"Damn straight!" Jimmy growled out.

Craig aimed for the windshield, trying to get himself far enough out to hit the van but still keep his head out of the man's line of sight.

As they rounded the curve, the angle put the van's windows at maximum exposure and Craig pulled the trigger. BLAM! His hand jumped up with the recoil and the shot missed.

A second shotgun blast rang out. BANG! Craig barely pulled his head back in time to avoid being killed as the tink of pellets ran down the side of the truck. As soon as they stopped he popped his gun back out, but before he could fire another shot rang out from the van.

BANG! He was too slow that time. Hot pain roared as a pellet nicked his ear lobe and the back window shattered.

Lily screamed at the sounds and the increased wind whipped the sheet from her legs.

With gritted teeth and torso braced this time, Craig stuck his head out again and fired off two quick shots as the last of the curve ended his advantage. BLAM! BLAM!

The glass on the windshield shattered and the van's driver lost control. The vehicle swayed back and forth from one lane to the next for several yards then the driver kicked out the shattered glass. He straightened the van, hit the gas and came gunning toward them again, narrowing the distance.

Craig stretched out the window one more time and went for the tires. BLAM! BLAM!

The right front tire blew and that was it—the driver instantly lost control. The van whipped toward the side of the road as the driver jerked the wheel, trying to gain control but making it worse. The tires went off the edge at an odd angle, tipping the van on its side at sixty miles an hour and he watched it slide across the rocky soil on the side of the road.

A huge BOOM! sounded behind them and Craig saw fire light up the night sky. Jimmy grimaced and pressed the pedal to the floor.

"That was awesome!" Ethan turned around in the seat, grinning at him.

Craig's heart hammered like it was trying to climb out of his chest and the pain in his ear reminded him he must be bleeding. "Got a napkin?"

Jimmy grinned at him in the rearview mirror as Ethan handed him a stack of McDonald's napkins from the glove box.

"Nice shooting, bro. Now give me my gun back."

"Don't tell Chelsea." Craig placed the gun in Jimmy's outstretched palm with a wink.

"Don't worry, Dad, I got it all on video." Ethan's teeth glowed in the moonlight.

"You're kidding?" Craig realized his mouth was hanging open as he stared at the iPhone in his son's hand.

Jimmy let out a stiff chuckle and nodded his head for Ethan to open the console, then stowed the gun in it. He let out a grunt of pain as he fished his own phone out of his other jacket pocket. Craig saw a circle of blood soaking through Jimmy's jacket. His brother grunted again as he raised his arm to hand the phone to Ethan.

"Call the cops. Tell them there's been a roll-over accident on Highway 25. Then tell them a kidnapper had Lily at BioGen. Tell 'em you'll send 'em proof and ask for an email address then send them the photos off my phone. The ones with your sister in it."

"You guys took a picture of me? Let me see it!" Lily demanded in a muffled voice from beneath his arms.

Craig smiled and pulled her tighter as he swiped at the blood trickling down his cheek.

CHAPTER 71

"**W**here are those guys? Why haven't they called yet?" Chelsea paced the parking lot as they waited. She hadn't been able to sit still in the SUV.

"I'm sure they'll call soon." Ann had been praying out loud and under her breath since they left Hollister.

"Don't worry, they found Lily." Steve spoke from the side of the SUV. "They just had to get rid of those sign guys. They'll be here soon."

She turned at the boy's words and studied his face. Steve seemed to have an invisible link to Lily now. Her mind was too full of worry to pursue it right then so she let it go.

"Thanks for staying positive Steve." Chelsea replied.

He pushed away from the truck. "I've never been on a plane before. Is it scary?"

"No Honey, it's not scary, just different than a car." Ann rubbed his arm, "You'll get to see all the lights down below us once we're up in the air."

"Cool." He shuffled his feet a moment then asked, "Where will we live in Paris, Mom?"

Chelsea watched Ann pause, considering how to answer. Right that minute none of them knew for sure where they would be staying. They'd figure it out once they got there.

"Well…at first we'll stay at a hotel. Then we might look for a house or an apartment to stay in until we decide to come home."

"Can we live with Lily's family?" His eyes grew huge as he asked the question.

Chelsea couldn't help herself, she reached out and gave the boy a quick hug and he hugged her back as she said, "Of course you're going to stay with us. That's why you came, right? To be with Lily?" She ruffled his hair as she let him loose.

"I can't wait to see her!" His smile competed with the moon for a moment then Chelsea's phone buzzed in her pocket.

"Did you get Lily?" Her words rushed out and her breathing stopped as she waited for Craig to answer.

"Hi Mommy!" Lily's voice sang into her ear.

"Oh, Sweetie! It's so good to hear your voice. I love you Honey. I can't wait to see you! Tears of relief started down her face. "Tell Uncle Jimmy to drive faster."

She heard Lily laughing then her little voice telling Jimmy what she'd said. Lily came back on, "Jimmy says we're almost there, Mommy. Ten minutes."

"Thank God, thank God, thank you God!" Chelsea's smile was too big for her face as she shouted out her joy. "I'm going to give you the biggest hug you've ever had in your life when you get here. Then I'm going to kiss your entire face and hug you again." Chelsea laughed and cried through her words.

"Me too, Mommy. I can't wait to see Paris!"

CHAPTER 72

"Craig! What happened?" Chelsea almost lost it when the Lincoln pulled in the airport parking lot and she saw the back window had been shot out. The tailgate and right side of the truck were riddled with bullet holes. She let out a piercing shriek when the men climbed out of Jimmy's truck in. Blood ran down the side of her husband's face as he set Lily on the pavement. More dark splotches marked the leg of his jeans and a long red smear striped his forehead.

"Don't worry—it looks worse than it is. We just need to get cleaned up. We'll be fine."

A dark rose sat on Jimmy's left shoulder and both women let out a squealed when they saw the pool of blood on the back of his shirt as he tugged his jacket off.

"Jim! Let me take a look at you guys." Ann urgently motioned them toward the back of the Escalade. "Chelsea, do you have a first aid kit?"

Chelsea nodded as she pulled the tailgate down. "Sit here while we clean you guys up. You can't go through the airport like that." Her hands shook as she pulled the kit out for Ann. "Get in the truck kids." Her voice came out gruffer than she'd meant it to. She snagged a box of baby wipes and a bottle of water from the console while all three kids climbed into the middle seat. They immediately turned to watch the action at the back of the truck.

A grunt of pain slipped past his lips as Jimmy tugged his shirt off. "Don't worry, it's just a flesh wound, nothing serious, but it sure hurts like hell."

"We've got to disinfect these wounds then I'll give you some Tylenol." Ann rushed to open the kit as she stood between the men. "Jimmy you're going to need an antibiotic when we get to Paris—this wound is pretty deep but I don't think you need stitches." The bloody wipes piled up as the women cleaned the men off.

"So what happened?" Chelsea asked as they worked. Her mind raced over how they'd ended up with bullet wounds as she fished in the suitcases for clean shirts for the men, clothes and shoes for Lily.

"You should have seen it, Mom! Dad shot those guys' tires out and the van flipped right off the road and burst into flames—just like on TV. It was awesome!" Ethan's grin began to fade as she pinned him with her eyes.

"What guys? What van?" She stopped fussing with the suitcases and looked at Craig.

"Ouch!" Craig let out a squeal as Ann applied liquid bandage to his torn earlobe.

"Sorry, Craig. Try not to touch it until it dries." Ann gave him a sheepish smile and began storing things back in the kit as Craig answered her question, wincing through the words.

"It turns out the van in the BioGen lot belonged to that crazy protestor—the one that smashed your window yesterday. He had a shot gun and came after us when we brought Lily out. That guy is certifiable—and hopefully, dead." He shook his head at the insanity they'd just been through.

"What?" Chelsea couldn't keep the panic out of her voice. That was the last thing they needed—more trouble.

"Don't worry, we called 911. The cops will find their crazy-ass signs and the shotgun in the van then put two and two together."

"Ethan filmed it all on his phone for you." Jimmy grinned as he danced away from Craig's elbow.

* * *

They boarded the plane a few minutes later. Craig did his best not to act impressed but it was impossible to pull off. He gave in and let out a low whistle as he grinned at Jimmy. The Cessna Citation was the height of luxury in small private jets. It had capacity for eleven passengers. The main cabin area was embellished with burled walnut and plush neutral fabrics on the walls. It sported buttery leather chairs and sofas, a small kitchen fully stocked along with a nicely appointed bathroom and a stewardess to assist them.

The pilot was a tall man in his fifties with a reassuring demeanor and a helpful attitude. He greeted them outside the plane and stayed in the cabin visiting for a minute while the flight attendant helped them get settled.

"I need to call the gate for clearance then we'll be taking off. It's a long flight, so make your selves comfortable." The pilot slid the cockpit door shut behind him with a quiet whoosh.

"Jimmy—who is this friend of yours?" Chelsea asked as the aide handed her a soft blanket for Lily and winked at her brother-in-law. He hesitated, big smile on his face.

"I promised I wouldn't say. He's a client of mine and we've become friends over the past couple years. I'm gonna owe him big for this one. It's a helluva ride, huh?" His grin widened as he looked over at Ethan. "Now this is glidin' boy!"

Everyone laughed at that then the pilot announced they should prepare for take off. Once they reached cruising altitude, the flight attendant opened a bottle of champagne for the grown ups, sparkling cider for the kids. Flutes of bubbly were handed all around and Craig lifted his glass in a toast.

"To freedom, health and happily ever after!" The ping of crystal rang in the air as they all grinned and sipped. As the bubbles hit her tongue, Chelsea looked askance at Craig, reached over and plucked the glass out of his hand.

"No booze for you buddy, whether you earned it or not." She gave him a smile and rubbed his shoulder in commiseration as the attendant swapped his bubbly with bottled water.

"Thanks for reminding me," he smiled back at Chelsea until his thoughts spun on to Paris. "Just my luck—I'm going to the ultimate land of wine and food and I'm on a diet."

Jimmy winked at him. "No worries, Craig-O, we can take a few cases home with us. Once that weak belly of yours heals, we'll get the corks popping. And I'll be sure and describe every bite of gourmet food I eat while we're in Paris, in great detail, so you can live vicariously through me, brother." Jimmy's grin widened the insult and he ducked the champagne cork Craig lobbed at him. His brother's hand flashed out and caught it midair as the group laughed and settled in for the long flight.

The rest of the adults had started on their second glass of champagne when Craig pulled out his phone and called the police station in Hollister. He asked to speak with the sergeant on duty and explained who he was, and that he'd rescued his daughter that evening, so they could stop looking for her.

"I'm aware of that Mr. Noble. We went out to BioGen right after we got the email. We found Orlon Millard bound to the table. The pictures you left for us were very enlightening. The DA says we should have no trouble making a case against the man for kidnapping and a slew of other charges related to endangerment of a minor. But we'll need written statements from you as well as the nurse who was on duty this morning."

Craig paused, not wanting to tell the man they were in the process of leaving the country.

"Sergeant, I'm sure you'll understand when I say my family and I are headed out of town for a few days until the press and the protestors back off of the story. Orlon's arrest is going to fan the flame higher for a little while and we don't want to deal with the media frenzy right now. We've all been through too much."

"I understand. If you have an email address or a fax number I'll send you our statement form and you can fill it out and send it back to us. That way the DA can get started and we can keep that asshole off the streets."

Craig gave the man his email and hung up. He looked over at Chelsea and realized she must be talking to her former lab partner.

"Don't give me that crap, Brad. Even if you have a solid alibi for the time period Lily was taken from the hospital, you must have known she was at BioGen. Your car was in the parking lot next to Orlon's. You two were the only people in the building tonight. I'm not stupid." Craig tried to keep the grin off his face as his wife growled into the phone.

He watched as she listened to Brad a moment then said, "You're never going to convince me you weren't involved in this. The only reason I'm not going to send the cops after you is my husband and Jimmy said you weren't in the room with Orlon and Lily so we don't have any proof against you. Consider yourself lucky." She slapped the phone on the small table.

Chelsea looked at Ann, "I always knew that guy was too good looking to be trusted."

Jimmy glanced at Craig and gave him a discreet thumbs-up along with a huge grin.

His own grin came loose as Ann told his wife, "I know just what you mean—so was my ex-husband."

The attendant poured another round of champagne and juice for them. They settled against the plush seats, letting quiet fall as the steady sound of the engines calmed their frazzled nerves and stars flew past the windows.

CHAPTER 73

Their time in Paris was magical, blighted only slightly by the tasks that had to be handled long-distance in between the fun. It had taken two days for Lily to fully recover her strength and they spent those at the Park Hyatt. Jimmy booked them into a residence suite which consisted of a living room, dining room, full kitchen and desk area in addition to three bedrooms and baths.

The hotel was located at 5 Rue de la Paix and located on the northwestern side of Paris with views of the harbor. The suite had a small private courtyard and Chelsea spent the early mornings with her coffee at the wrought iron table as she listened to the city come alive. She was starting to think she never wanted to go home. It was total bliss to not have any household chores or other responsibilities to conquer each day. She reveled in the luxury of spending unlimited time with her family and good friends.

They all slept most of the first twenty-four hours. Meals, snacks and beverages were consumed in between naps as they recovered from the insanity they'd gone through. The hotel staff was incredibly helpful, the food was fantastic and the beds were like clouds but they all became restless at the dawn of their third day in Paris. It was time to get out and explore.

The Louvre was an experience none of them would forget. The artwork had been incredible and they had seen only a small portion of what the enormous museum offered when they realized Steve had become separated from their group.

Just as Ann hit the panic button Lily took her hand and said, "Don't worry, I know where he is—he's in the bathroom."

Chelsea watched as Ann forced herself to calm down at hearing Lily's words. When she got her breath under control she said, "Lily, did he tell you which restroom he was going to? Did you see which way he went?"

"No, but I know where he is. Follow me." She took off at a jog across the immense hallway and the grownups followed quickly behind. As they rounded a second corner Chelsea spotted Steve coming out of a doorway, struggling with his zipper. He looked up at the group and stopped fidgeting with his pants as he stood up straight.

"Are you guys waiting for me?" he asked with an embarrassed grin.

"Yes!" Lily giggled then looked at Chelsea, "Mommy, my legs are tired, can we go?"

"Mine are too. Let's go have lunch somewhere." She grinned up at Craig as he reached over and put his arm around her.

"Can we eat at one of those sidewalk places, Mom? I want to have pommes frites again and watch the cars go by," Steve said as they headed to the museum's entrance.

"That's a great idea, let's go."

Steve, Ann and Jimmy led the group toward the nearest café. Chelsea and Craig brought up the rear as they walked hand in hand and watched Lily slip her hand into Ethan's.

She smiled brightly up at her brother. "Thank you."

"For what?" Ethan asked.

"For thinking I'm gonna be really pretty when I get older and all the boys are gonna ask me out." Giggles popped out of her, floating on the air like music notes.

Ethan looked down at his sister, completely unaware Chelsea and Craig were listening as he zeroed in on what she'd said to him. "How'd you know I was thinking that just now?"

Hairs went up on Chelsea's neck and she glanced at Craig then back at Lily as her daughter answered, "I've got ears ya know."

"Come on Lily. Stop kidding around. How'd you know I was thinking that just now?" Ethan really wanted an answer and so did Chelsea.

The four came to a stop on the sidewalk as Ann's group continued walking ahead.

Lily shrugged and said, "I don't know. I can hear you whenever you're thinking about me. But don't worry – I can't hear you unless it's about me."

Craig spoke up, "Maybe we should continue this discussion at the restaurant?" Everyone nodded and picked up the pace.

Steve looked back and hollered, "Hurry up you guys! I'm starving!"

* * *

Back at the hotel, and spread around the living room, the group sat with all eyes sparkling, ready for the show. They'd learned at the restaurant that in addition to hearing people's thoughts, Lily also had the ability to manipulate cell phones and other small electronics. They sat around the coffee table, mouths hanging open and chill bumps climbing as she demonstrated her skills on their phones.

"So you're the one that distracted Orlon for us?" Craig was fighting to think past the stunned feeling that hit him at learning Lily had developed such skills. It would make her an even bigger target for the scientists and greedy businessmen in the world. Not to mention the crazy fanatics. He shook off the macabre thoughts and concentrated on her response.

"That man was going to hurt us. I'm glad you hit him."

"He sure was." Craig nodded, fighting off a choke of emotions. "Nobody takes my little girl and gets away with it."

He pulled her into his arms and gave her a squeeze. "Text me something again." He grinned at her and waited for the message to show up.

A moment later his phone buzzed and he read the words: "Mommy's not mad at you anymore."

He looked from his phone to his daughter's smiling face then at his wife. She sat on the sofa, staring in awe at their daughter, a huge smile as she asked, "What did she text you?"

"That's between Lily and me. But if you're real sweet to me, I might tell you later."

"I can do sweet, Mr. Noble—just you wait." She gave him a smile that sent an instant buzz to his toes. "There's something about Paris that makes a girl feel sweet."

If she smiled at him like that much longer they were going to need a nap.

Chelsea's cell buzzed, interrupting the moment. She looked at the screen. "It's Carol calling me back. Hopefully she has good news."

Craig watched his wife's eyes squint in concentration as she leaned back against the sofa cushion. He waited it out while the women spoke. It was a short conversation and Chelsea hung up smiling like the Cheshire cat.

"Carol says she got an immediate response from Wadsworth on our settlement demand letter she sent to him along with the termination complaint and the photos. BioGen isn't even trying to negotiate it down. She's going to email me the agreement for our signatures."

"That's wonderful. It's the least your family deserves after everything that awful man put you through. You guys will never have to work again if you don't want to." Ann grinned from the other sofa.

Steve sat on the floor beside her legs, thumbing away at a game on Ann's phone. Jimmy sat next to her, nursing a beer.

Craig grinned at his wife as her eyes flew to his. "I've taken a leave of absence already. I guess I'll have to extend it." His expression sobered as he looked back at Chelsea. "I certainly don't like being a millionaire because of Lily's suffering but it will allow our family to spend more time together. So that's exactly what we're going to do."

Chelsea gave him that special smile again and rubbed her hand along his thigh as she relayed the second part of Carol's good news.

"She spoke with Wilson and the director of the NSA. They both assure her our family will not be harassed. She said the CDC's been working with the plant from our yard but nothing of a viral nature seems to be associated with it. She also told me the protestors have vanished ever since you got Lily out of BioGen. I guess their ring leader being arrested at the hospital for attempted murder took the wind out of the group's sails."

Ethan looked at him with a frown, "Does that mean we're going home now, Dad?"

Silence fell in the room as they all waited for his answer.

He paused and glanced at Jimmy. His brother winked back so he said, "What? Go home? We just got here. I say we need at least a couple more weeks in Paris. What do you guys think?"

Everyone chimed in with a resounding, "Yes!"

Craig noticed Jimmy take Ann's hand and give it a squeeze as he smiled at her.

He turned to Chelsea, "Honey, you look really tired. I think you need a nap. Come on, I'll tuck you in." Lily and Steve giggled as they walked out of the room.

* * *

On their fourth day in Paris, Craig decided to bite the bullet and called Jeff Connor to discuss the missing sphere. He did his best to explain what had happened with it. When he got to the part about it blooming into a plant, Connor cut him off with a question.

"Mr. Noble, are you saying the sphere was really a seed?" Excitement rang in the man's voice along with a note of relief.

"Yes. Not only did it turn out to be a seed, it grew the most unusual plant I've ever seen. It had little orange berries on it that my daughter ended up eating and got really sick from."

Silence spooled out of the phone a moment then Connor said in a much more subdued tone, "I'm really sorry to hear that. Is she okay now?"

"Yes, she's better than ever, in more ways than one." Craig chuckled then said, "It turns out the berries aren't poisonous. They contain an incredibly concentrated amount of vitamins. Lily ate so many of them she ended up with extreme vitamin overdose. That's what made her sick, but she's fine now."

He looked out the window at the kids playing in the courtyard. They had paints, paper, easels and brushes and were going to town. The Louvre had inspired them all.

Connor's voice pulled him back, "So the plant wasn't poisonous?" Another quiet beat then he asked, "Did you notice any gas being emitted from the plant by any chance?"

"No. Why?"

"Since we're being honest here, let me explain what happened the day you visited us. It's a large part of why I had the FBI go to your house to look for the sphere." Craig could hear paper shuffling for a second then the man said, "We've had a couple odd things happen here at the mine over the last month. The day you were here, one of our workers passed the wall that the spheres came from and he was overcome by what he described as a gas cloud that suddenly came at him from a fissure in the slab of pyrophyllite where the spheres were found."

Connor must have taken a sip of a drink because Craig heard ice tinkling in a glass next to the phone. "We had to rush him to the hospital. He was unconscious for two days and seemed to be suffering from exposure to an unidentified gas that the doctors couldn't pinpoint. He had to undergo a detox program and take some other medications. He seems to be okay now. We still aren't sure what caused it."

"Huh, that's interesting. Any chance pockets of gas built up within the pyrophyllite?"

"We've been checking and can't find anything. A second mystery cloud was seen by another worker last week in the same area, but luckily he was far enough away that it didn't compromise him. It hasn't happened since and I'm not sure what to make of it. Now that you've told me what happened to the sphere, I'm really perplexed."

"So are we. Ethan and I have a theory about what the spheres are for. I really don't think the odd gas occurrences have anything to do with them." Craig quickly explained his idea of the seeds being intended to help the earth and man recover from a cataclysmic event.

"That is a very interesting notion, Mr. Noble. I'll have to give it more thought. Would you be willing to send me a copy of the lab report on your daughter? I'd like to read it over."

"I'll email it to you in a few minutes," Craig replied.

"I'd appreciate it. Meanwhile, I'll ask the FBI to drop the matter as far as the missing sphere goes. I'll give my friend a call in the morning." He fell quiet again for a moment then asked, "Does anyone outside your family know about the sphere being the source of the plant?"

"Not officially. We're sticking with not knowing where the plant came from as far as the government is concerned. But of course, the FBI is aware of the missing sphere. I'm sure they won't see it as a coincidence that the sphere and plant were present at our house at the same time."

A long South African silence then Connor said, "Fair enough. Let's keep it to ourselves while we can, if you don't mind. I guess I'll take a couple of the spheres home and try planting them, see what happens. Enjoy Paris, Mr. Noble."

"We'll do that. Let me know how you make out with your sphere garden."

CHAPTER 74

They strolled under the Eiffel Tower together and Craig took her hand, stopped their progress across the wide expanse. His eyes filled with emotions and made her heart beat faster at the memory of their lovemaking that afternoon.

"Chelsea, I was thinking...."

"What?" She smiled at the shy look that had come over his face.

"How would you feel about renewing our vows? I know it's only our nineteenth anniversary in June, and we should probably wait for the twentieth or whatever, but I'd really like to—"

"Yes." The word flew past her smile.

"So you're saying you'll marry me again Chelsea Carrington?"

"Yes." She squeezed his hand, thrilled to hear him say the words. It was almost better than the first time at the beach under a full moon.

"Good." He gently squeezed back, his eyes growing serious, "Because I'd like to say them with you again—now that I know what they really mean."

They had had a long heart-to-heart over dinner. Jimmy and Ann had encouraged them to take some time for themselves as a couple while the rest of their group hung out at the hotel and played board games. The restaurant had been a small intimate place the concierge had recommended. It was only a three block walk from their hotel and the balmy night added to the romantic mood. Over candlelight and a bottle of wine, her husband had apologized to her from the bottom of his heart. He'd explained his blind spot and swore his eyes would remain open to her needs. He'd also learned the importance of maintaining balance in his life for all their sakes.

"I love you Craig," her voice came out a husky whisper.

"I love you more."

"Okay, I'll go with that." She let go of his hand and wrapped her arms around him. They shared a long kiss then she said, "I'm ready to go home now."

CHAPTER 75

It felt a little strange to be home after three weeks in Paris but they quickly settled into the familiar surroundings and within an hour Craig found himself saying how good it was to be back.

Jimmy's friend had made his plane available again for the return trip but this time they'd had the opportunity to fly with their avionic benefactor. Richard had been lit with all the vitality and charm he conveyed in television interviews. Lily was especially drawn to him and he gave her his cell number after she let him in on her special talent. With an enormous grin he'd told her to text him whenever she pleased.

Ann and Jimmy had gone home to get their own houses back in order after the long absence. The kids were watching a movie and Chelsea sat with him at the kitchen table with an open bottle of red wine. They were nibbling on a plate of cheese and a basket of grapes. Part of Paris had followed them home in their new food preferences and the four cases of wine Craig and Jimmy had loaded on the plane earlier that day.

"It's going to seem strange not getting up for work." He still couldn't get his head around not needing a paycheck.

"It might seem a little strange at first because it's been our habit for years, but we have so many natural interests plus two kids, a dog, a house, a yard and a garden—it won't be hard to fill our days. I won't miss being at BioGen one bit."

He grinned at her, "I'm sure you're right. It won't take long before we don't even think about work any more."

She shook her head and laughed at him. "We're both curious people and you know it. I doubt either one of us will be able to stay away from our chosen fields. Sooner or later we're going to be tempted to do our thing again—no matter how much money we have."

Lily zipped into the kitchen. "I'm gonna go ask Stevie if he wants to swing with me before it gets dark." She flashed past them and out the back door before they could respond.

Craig grinned at his daughter's bouncing stride and golden curls as she ran across the patio then he looked back at his wife and responded to the challenge she'd tossed out.

"Well, I can't deny I love rocks and dirt. Jimmy says I've always been weird like that, guess I always will be. But—when the bug hits me—I'm sure I can find some contract work that won't require traveling, or at least not more than a day or two." His smile grew as he said, "In a few years I may be going to job sites our son's in charge of. That'd be fun."

She smiled back at him, "I can see the two of you now—out solving the world's geological mysteries—one at a time." Then her grin faded a bit as she said, "It's too bad that plant sample Jimmy got for me didn't survive being in the refrigerator." A small sigh escaped her lips. "I'd give both my eye teeth and three toes to have a bunch of those berries to work with. I can only imagine what we might be able to do for the world with those."

"That reminds me. Jeff Connor called earlier and seemed a little upset because the spheres he planted never germinated. If it weren't for Lily's lab reports, I'm afraid the man might not believe what happened to that sphere Ethan took. Connor drilled me about the soil content in our yard and whether we used fertilizer." He rubbed a hand over his razor stubble as he considered the facts. "I told him I wasn't present when Lily planted the thing. She says all she did was water it.

"Something had to set the germination process off. I'm fairly certain the spheres were intended to be triggered by toxic conditions, but I can't imagine what caused it. I'm not sure what to think of Connor's spheres not germinating."

"Me either." Chelsea shrugged, took another sip of her wine. They watched Lily through the window. She stopped to check out the garden, probably looking for mud puddles. Then her little legs pumped across the lawn toward Ann's gate.

Chelsea turned and gave him a smile that made his heart skip a beat. "So when do you want to get married Mr. Noble?"

"The sooner the better. " He reached out and took her hand, raised it to his mouth. "I can't wait to make you my wife again."

"We're very blessed, aren't we?"

"You're just saying that because I'm cooking dinner tonight."

Chelsea's laugh made his grin widen. "Steaks sound great. That's one entree Paris hasn't mastered yet. I'll do the dishes."

He raised his goblet of water, "To our new future together."

They tapped glasses just as a flash of blond curls caught his eye. Lily came racing back across the patio, stopped in the doorway.

"Mommy! Daddy!" Huge blue eyes. "They're back!"

"Who's back, Sweetheart?" Goosebumps exploded on his arms.

"The plant and the berries! Come see!" Lily took off toward the fence and they flew out the door behind her.

Fact or Fiction?

I hope you enjoyed *Finding Round*. As a reader, I like it when authors provide a vetting of the details at the end of a book. I'm including the information below for your pleasure and perhaps a deeper understanding of the story's components.

The Spheres:

Fact -- The story is based on spheres that were actually found at the Wonderstone mine in South Africa. There are numerous articles available that provide details, as well as making a case for and against whether the spheres are naturally occurring concretions or out-of-place artifacts left behind by ancient beings. You decide. See below for links to some articles.

Fiction. -- The author's imagination was used to germinate the spheres into plants.

http://en.wikipedia.org/wiki/Klerksdorp_sphere
http://www.virtuescience.com/grooved-spheres.html
http://ooparts.us/klerksdorp-spheres.htm

Wonderstone Mine:

Fact -- The mine exists and is located approximately ten miles north of the town of Ottosdal. The numerous factoids about pyrophillite, including its uses, are true.

Fiction -- The author has somewhat embellished the description of the mine and its structures to allow for the telling of the story. The manager of the mine, Jeff Connor, is a fictitious character. The 'gas' that was emitted from the pyrophillite during the Nobles' visit was purely a figment of the author's imagination, used solely to increase the entertainment value of the story.

The Centers for Disease Control – Fact. The United States government greatly increased the CDC's authority to quarantine individuals following the outbreak of the SARS 2003 epidemic. See the link below to the government regulated site for the CDC for details.

http://www.cdc.gov/quarantine/qa-executive-order-pandemic-list-quarantinable-diseases.html

Ocean Beach – Fact. Ocean Beach is located in the City of San Francisco and is the responsibility of combined government agencies. The beach, Great Highway and the sewage pipeline it protects are continually threatened by rough surf, especially during El Nino conditions. Various government agencies have been working to remediate the damage and keep the beach open to the public.

Alzheimer's and Autism – Fact. The brief facts stated within the story are based on scientific information contained in various articles available on the internet, one of which suggests a possible link between the two diseases related to the myelin sheath exposure as portrayed in the story. God willing, we'll find a cure for these horrible and inexplicable diseases soon.

About the Author

Alex Sheridan is the author of numerous suspense novels,
and is currently hard at work on a new thriller series
based on a Colombian drug lord's goddaughter who has
a DEA operative chasing her through the jungle.

The author is fascinated with the unexplainable and
readers can count on some sort of supernatural nuance
or unexplainable artifact turning up in almost every book.
Many of Sheridan's novels are based around true-life touchstones.

Alex lives in South Florida with twin teen daughters and
two cats. When not writing, the author enjoys traveling,
walks in the surf during low tide, any kind of competitive sport,
exploring the internet, time spent with family and friends,
especially if it involves a game of chess or a glass of wine,
reading lots of great books and answering Email.

You can write to Alex at:
AlexSheridanWrites@hotmail.com

Or check out the author's blog site at:
AlexSheridanWrites.blogspot.com

www.ingramcontent.com/pod-product-compliance
Lightning Source LLC
Chambersburg PA
CBHW020330180626
46812CB00001B/126